PSYCHO ACADEMY

THE CRUEL SHIFTERVERSE SERIES: ARAN'S STORY
BOOK 1

JASMINE MAS

Ebook ASIN: B0BK7H3VNW

Editing and proofreading by Lyss Em Editing

Cover artists: Damonza Book Cover Designs

Go to blog.jasminemasbooks.com to receive news of releases and sneak peaks straight to your inbox.

936 SW 1st Ave, Unit #56, Miami Florida 33130

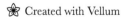 Created with Vellum

ALSO BY JASMINE MAS

The Cruel Shifterverse

Psycho Shifters

Psycho Fae

Psycho Beasts

Psycho Academy: Aran's Story Book 1

Psycho Devils: Aran's Story Book 2 (preorder now)

WARNING

They are true enemies. This is war. It is excessively violent.
This is a reverse harem. Everyone's a villain. This is a slow
burn romance. Don't panic.

"Hell is empty and all the devils are here."

—Shakespeare, *The Tempest*

INTO THE STARS

All myths are rooted in some truth.

This series is about different planets connected by black holes.

Aka, realms attached by portals with inhabitants you've heard of in myths and dismissed as fairy tales.

There are politics, deceptions, and secrets on the macro scale. And they vary from realm to realm.

In the human realm, the inhabitants learn they live in an anarchic system, that there is no supreme authority over different countries.

They're wrong.

The High Court secretly reigns sovereign over *all* the worlds. "Realm-Wide Peace" is their motto.

Monsters enforce this peace. A next-to-impossible task because wealth corrupts, but power destroys.

And among the hundreds of planets with sentient life, a few special individuals possess power on the nuclear level—more energy in their cells than an atomic bomb.

The truth: Most individuals go their entire lives without

knowing or caring about the other realms or the creatures within them. They live in bliss.

In this series, ignorance isn't an option for our main characters.

Through birthright or circumstances, they're players in the macrolevel game.

Now all they must do is survive.

MUST-READ RECAP:
ARAN'S STORY BOOKS 1-3
(SPOILERS)

I was born Arabella Alis Egan, Princess of the Fae Realm. Daughter of the mad fae queen who ruled on the seat of death.

Royalty in one of the largest, cruelest realms in the universe. Billions strong.

The fae manifested abilities at a young age over fire, earth, water, or air.

But I manifested nothing.

At sixteen years old, all elite youths took the fae standardized tests. I tested average on all sections except one.

I scored first out of thirty-three million in battle strategizing.

It wasn't a good thing.

With no fae abilities, and a mad queen as my mother, I was prime breeding stock. I had virginity, obedience, a propensity for strategy, piety to the sun god, and above all else, royalty. At least, that was what Mother said to the buyers.

But she set me aflame each night.

Mother hoped to awaken a single ounce of power in my

bones—but nothing ever came. She burned my body with her power that never left any marks.

It wasn't just to strengthen me, she had an unholy rage, especially when it came to controlling people.

I'd always aspired to run, hunt, and learn. Never to breed. But with no powers and an honorable test score, Mother made arrangements.

And she punished me for my insolence.

A few weeks after the tests, I disguised myself as a boy with an enchanted ring and fled from the sunny realm via a hidden portal into the frigid shifter realm.

In the new realm, a man in a cloak, with bright-blue eyes, had me tested and proclaimed me a beta shifter.

I didn't know why he lied.

Or who he was.

At a fortress in the shifter realm, posing as a beta male, I fought off arachnid monsters that infiltrated the shifter realm by portal. I lost myself in combat training and war.

I'd never been so happy.

At twenty-four, after making a life for myself in the desolate, wintery land, I met my best friend, Sadie. A scrawny alpha female who was covered in scars, with a terrifying tiger form.

We bonded over our mutual experiences with self-deprecating humor, war, and pain.

Mostly pain.

Sadie clashed with her three alpha warrior roommates: Ascher, Jax, and Cobra. But we read stories and hung out. She was my first true friend.

My first best friend.

The good times ended.

At a celebration of the new year, a kitten I'd found turned out to be an omega shifter—Xerxes, my mother's right-hand assassin. Working alongside Ascher, another spy, he kidnapped Sadie, Jax, and Cobra into the fae realm.

They didn't go alone.

Ascher grabbed me from the party because he recognized the bright blue of my eyes and short hair. So similar to the mad queen's coloring.

Mother was not happy to see me.

The enchanted ring was ripped off my finger, and Arabella, the pretty princess, was back.

Mother strapped a crystal collar around my neck, for reasons still unclear. And the queen wove a story that I was kidnapped and that it was a blessing to have me returned to the fae realm.

Each night, she set me on fire while her face blistered with rage.

Sadie, alongside Jax, Cobra, and Ascher, was forced to compete in the gladiator games. Forced to put on a show for a million bloodthirsty fae.

Mother tortured me in private.

I smiled in public.

The realm was grateful to have its pretty princess back. Relief was tangible, and breeding offers poured in.

But when I was alone with Sadie, a deep male voice took over her doctor's body and read a bloodthirsty poem to us in an ancient language only taught to fae royals. It sounded like a prophecy.

A nasty one.

We ignored it as best as we could. As one has a tendency to do with the unexplained.

Then one night, Sadie and I decided to lose our virginity at a fae sex clinic.

It was a rebellion.

A failed one.

The three half warriors, Demetre, Noah, and Shane, were some of the strongest men in the realm. Since a young age, I was forced to attend the gladiator games, and I'd befriended them. Helped heal them and begged my mother not to hurt them.

But her punishments became unbearable, and I stopped speaking up.

The half warriors' friendship turned to hatred.

It didn't help that over the years, I'd grown to look like my mother. Same unique turquoise hair and bright-blue eyes.

To the half warriors, I was just another spoiled fae royal who lived to torture those beneath them.

Mud beneath their boots.

Their hatred didn't lessen in the eight years I was away in the shifter realm.

It grew.

As a result, that night at the sex clinic, three half warriors followed me and brought me to my mother before I could lose my virginity.

Served me up to the queen.

Laughed in Mother's face and taunted her that her pious daughter was a common whore. What elite fae would want to breed with such scum?

That night, Mother didn't just light me on fire.

She beat me.

Then she took out an enchanted knife.

Inspired by the horrible scars on Sadie's flesh, she'd commissioned a blade that would never create a scar, just leave a gaping, festering wound.

A wound that would burn whenever a person became the slightest bit aroused, that would itch unbearably at all times. Torture.

Mother was creative.

She carved "WHORE" into my back.

And once again, Arabella Alis Egan was powerless at her mother's nonexistent mercy.

Unable to escape my fate, unable to be anything other than a pawn in a cruel, sunny realm.

I told no one.

A few days later, under the dual suns of the realm, Mother made a deal with the most ancient vampyre in all the realm—Lothaire. He was rumored to rule Elite Academy, one of the most terrifying and prestigious schools in the universe.

It was a plot.

Lothaire would taste gladiators' blood and decide if they were worthy, but he'd been paid off by the queen to kill Sadie and her three alphas. She knew from the half warriors that Sadie had gone to the sex clinic with me.

Mother had no tolerance for dissidence.

After all, she'd ruled from the seat of death for centuries.

She wasn't weak.

But on the sands of the gladiator ring, Sadie fell to her knees and flung her blood hundreds of yards into my mother.

Infected her with pure power and took over her will, hurtling through her defenses, until the queen was paralyzed and weak.

Sadie was a blood fae and a half-breed.

But history said that only males could be half-breeds, never a female.

Not only that, but Sadie was of a long-lost race of fae that had gone extinct, rumored to be distant relatives of vampyres. With her newfound power, Sadie ordered the queen to release the collar around my neck.

What happened next was fate.

Cruel, twisted, delicious prophecy.

I embraced my destiny.

The churning darkness in my soul blinded my vision and the slur burned on my back. Ice daggers, sharper than any blade in the universe, erupted from my fingers. I attacked.

I slammed my daggers through my mother's chest.

Broke her sternum, ripped out her beating heart, and consumed it. While an unknown man's voice praised me.

It was the only way to kill a fae monarch.

The only way to succeed to the seat of death.

Eat a royal beating heart.

But it was retribution, an act born of pure rage with no forethought. I didn't want to be queen, had no aspiration to rule over a land and people that I hated.

The other problem—no fae had ever manifested ice claws. I'd learned our histories three times over.

Arabella Alis Egan was now the rightful queen.

Of an awful realm.

I didn't want it. I found my old ring in my dead mother's room.

Disguised myself back into a boy.

Glamoured to appear as a man with short hair and a wide chest. It could only work with what was present, so the only thing the enchantment couldn't glamour was my vagina, but that was easily hidden.

And I fled.

We all ran.

That was how I found myself in the beast realm, with its glittering skyscrapers and terrifying Mafia. In a realm where shifters lived in packs. A land ruled by enchanted guns that were banned in the fae realm because they killed shifters and fae alike.

We'd escaped.

Cobra was revealed to be the son of the don who ruled the city. Cobra was a prince.

We all lived at Xerxes's mansion as Sadie and the men competed in the Mafia trials. I stayed at home disguised as a boy with her sister and Jax's three sisters. Four teenage girls, all varying degrees of annoying but still entertaining.

Not enough to make me forget.

That I was a fugitive.

That I had no future.

That my back burned unmercifully.

That I'd done the unthinkable to my mother.

With glittering technology, I acquired a long pipe full of numbing drugs that was enchanted to never run out. The drugs were the only thing that kept me sane. Ascher also got me a pinky-length pipe of the drugs. I smoked whenever I could.

I sank lower.

Then one day, I took off the enchanted toe ring I'd worn since birth. A gift from my mother.

My fae ears disappeared, and my pin-straight blue hair became a mass of wild curls.

She'd purposefully disguised me.

But I still had my mother's coloring and shared her dainty features. If I wasn't a fae, then how was the fae queen my mother?

The slur on my back burned unmercifully, and I showed it to Sadie.

Then flyers were sent out in the beast realm from the High Court.

A secret group that ruled over all the realms.

The papers read that someone had kidnapped the rightful fae queen, and they would kill anyone associated with my capture. It also described Sadie as a half-breed female with scars. She was a suspect in my disappearance.

The fae realm couldn't move forward with succession because they were in stasis until I was found.

Dead or alive.

The drawing on the flyer was of a beautiful woman, but I was disguised as a boy.

Another poem read itself to Sadie and me.

We ignored it.

Sadie left to complete her third Mafia trial.

Shifters looking for leverage against Sadie and her men sprayed the house with machine guns, shooting Walter—the butler—and myself over a hundred times with deadly enchanted bullets.

All so they could steal the girls.

Those men died.

The girls returned safely.

Walter lay dead in the foyer.

I lived.

Against all odds.

Covered in bullet wounds, yet somehow still alive, I attended the Equinox Ball with Sadie.

But the beast realm was a cruel place.

Two shifters sliced off Sadie's finger that wore the enchanted ring I'd gifted her that covered her scars. They called the High Court, expecting to be rewarded for turning over the scarred half-breed girl.

A man with wings, and the cloaked man with the bright-blue eyes who'd helped me escape the fae realm at sixteen, arrived in a flash of smoke. The winged man spoke to Sadie and handed her a small circle. She never said what they spoke of.

Then they left.

The shifters who'd removed her finger were still alive.

Swirling rage overwhelmed me, the same darkness that prompted me to act without thought.

To eliminate.

I threw two ice daggers at them, and the shifters shattered into a billion pieces and misted away.

Like they'd never existed.

But it wasn't a tragedy.

Sadie's men proclaimed their loyalty and asked her to be their packmate. They bonded in a public display, proclaimed her theirs, and unknowingly passed their third trial. It had been the test all along—a loyalty test.

The don initiated all five of them. Sadie got her men and the security of a prestigious job, and the girls went to school.

A happily ever after for everyone.

Except one.

A few weeks later, the doorbell rang at midnight, and I answered it.

Once again, everything changed.

And not for the better.

And So It Began

"I will take my father's place in battle."
—*The Ballad of Mulan*

.

CHAPTER 1
VAMPYRE VISITS

"I got it!" I yelled, not wanting to disturb Sadie and her men. The doorbell echoed.

My best friend deserved some peace, especially after everything. Her missing ring finger was a constant reminder that those fuckers had hurt her.

The darkness in my soul rattled against its cage.

Pausing with my forehead pressed to the wall, I breathed in smoke from my enchanted pipe.

You killed them. They're gone.

I willed myself to remain blasé and to calm the monster that lived within me.

Down the grand mahogany staircase, inhaling smoke with each step, I fingered my sweatshirt pocket.

Caressed the smaller, finger-length pipe Ascher had gotten for me.

Again, the doorbell rang.

What rude fucker was calling at midnight?

I gritted my teeth as my monster snarled louder, banging against its steel cage. Another pause, another long, deep drag.

Any stimuli threatened the carefully desensitized state I'd work so hard to create.

The space between my shoulder blades itched.

Breathe in smoke for five seconds. Hold five seconds. Breathe out for five seconds. Pause five seconds.

Repeat.

A storm howled outside, and rain slammed against the brick structure.

Thunder cracked.

With a falsely constructed sense of ennui, I opened the door, and the night storm echoed throughout the dark foyer.

"What do you want?" I asked calmly.

Silhouetted in the dark was a massive figure. Taller than the door with layers of muscles that could only be used for one thing: war.

Sucking in smoke, I pushed the door shut in its face.

Step one to being cold and callous: you don't engage in basic impulses like fear. You react to nothing.

Survival of the unfeeling.

Crack.

The massive *thing* slammed a hand against the door and stepped past me into the mansion.

"Are you Aran?" a baritone voice growled as he flung the door wide.

Wet shoes squeaked on polished marble. Pouring rain traveled on icy wind and slammed against the both of us.

I focused on my cage.

Fortified steel bars, until the slightest rattle of emotion was silenced by a prison. Assessed in a hazy inhale of smoke that if the creature was asking for me, it wasn't a threat to the others.

I relaxed my shoulders. "Who's asking?"

Lightning flashed.

Illuminated a towering male with a brutal scar slashed across his eye.

Long hair dragged in a wet braid against the marble floor, and a tailored suit stretched across an impossibly muscled figure.

Twin opal fangs protruded from red lips.

"I'm asking," Lothaire growled, voice dripping with anger.

He wasn't used to being questioned.

"Ah, Lothaire the vampyre. I've heard of you." I nodded and sucked in smoke, presenting a lazy, uncaring figure.

It was all a facade.

Because I'd done more than hear of him. Since I was a little girl, he was a regular visitor in the palace. Always standing beside Mother and letting her touch him with her claws as he sparked with power.

He was the only person besides Mother that the elite fae were afraid of.

Mother had even graced him with the title of prince consort, and he was the only man in her centuries of life to hold the title.

We'd seen each other constantly, but we'd never spoken. He'd never bothered to talk to me because he probably thought I was beneath him. Just like Mother did.

I knew who he was—the fucker that crawled into bed with a monster.

And then Lothaire had bowed to my mother under the dual suns of the fae realm, attacked Sadie on the hot sand of a gladiator stadium, proclaimed Sadie unworthy as he attempted to drain her blood.

He'd stood witness to my atrocities.

Lothaire had said nothing, just observed, as I ripped out

my mother's beating heart and consumed it. Somehow, I'd known he could've stopped me if he really wanted to.

But for some reason, he didn't.

Now my mental cage rattled.

My back burning, it took all my control not to scratch at the "WHORE" carved across my spine. It was an enchanted penance for a wrong I hadn't even gotten to commit.

The fucker in front of me had not only bowed to the mad queen but had spent years at her side, smiling and touching her as she committed atrocities.

I breathed in for five seconds. *Hold. Breathe out. Rest. Repeat.*

Now Lothaire stood inches away from me in the grand foyer, radiating power and hatred. He'd invaded the familiar space that was the manor.

The monster from my past stood in my home.

Lothaire's singular eye flashed like the storm that raged against us, and he spoke as if he read my mind, "A power anomaly was detected in this realm on the equinox, and rumors are that a man named Aran was responsible."

The ancient vampyre took another menacing step forward. "Are you Aran? I won't ask again." His voice dripped with warning.

Rain slammed against the mansion.

Thunder boomed.

The foyer shook.

I took a long drag of my pipe and focused on feeling nothing and expressing nothing. Being nothing. My body language was a blank canvas as I refused to give a reaction.

After all, Lothaire had planned this visit for that very purpose, to unnerve me.

But the one class I'd succeeded in above all else, beyond what I should have, was battle analysis.

Lothaire had come at midnight, in the height of a storm. Entered without invitation. Stepped into my personal space. Said nothing of why he was here, just cryptically demanded my name. Demanded I answer him.

I sighed heavily.

Somehow, everything was war: small skirmishes, allies, foes, all with changing allegiances, and every player possessed an agenda uniquely their own.

Game theory at its finest.

But how could I respond and best him when I didn't know his motive?

The facts I knew—he called me Aran, referred to me only as a man, was referencing the event three weeks ago when I killed Sadie's attackers, and came at night with the purpose of unsettling me.

Plausible deduction: he wasn't here for the fae queen, and he wanted something of me I wouldn't want to give.

I shrugged. "I'm not the person you seek. Don't know anything about a power anomaly. Why are you here?"

First rule of game theory: you don't give away information. *Only* rule of game theory: you don't give away information.

A threatening rumble filled the foyer.

He stalked forward.

Fuck.

I'd miscalculated because game theory assumed all actors were rational. Lothaire slammed his fangs into my neck.

The fucker bit me.

The enchanted wound on my back burned like I'd been set on fire, but there was no pain where he'd bitten me.

Which was strange.

Everyone knew that a vampyre's bite was extremely painful.

It was why they were largely feared even though they could technically reproduce with other species. Vampyres didn't like to procreate this way because only two pureblood vampyres could create a vampyre.

It was rumored that centuries ago, a fae king had forced a vampyre to have his offspring. However, when they'd grown up, the children only possessed part of the fae power of the king and had received no abilities from their mother.

As a result, they were half-fae and weak.

Rumor was that the king slaughtered them for not being strong enough to carry his legacy.

Ever since then, it was taboo in the fae realm to procreate with a vampyre. The punishment for such a transgression was death…of every mother, father, and child involved.

His fangs ripped through my flesh, but I barely felt it.

Lothaire stumbled away from me, wiping blood off his mouth, and his voice was raspy with surprise. "Who are you? What are you? Why are you so powerful?"

Shit. I'm a few wrong moves from him figuring out I'm not even Aran, that I'm Arabella.

I rolled out my shoulders slowly, like I was stretching, and pretended I wasn't seconds away from having a mental breakdown.

With no expression, I calmly said, "Water fae. I'm a cousin of the monarchy. Aran Egan."

In a battle, the best lies are those closest to the truth.

Lightning cracked and highlighted Lothaire's harsh features, and his lips pulled into a smile, the scar puckered tight across his missing eye.

Lothaire stared down at me with unnatural stillness as he

crowded my personal space. "Are you sure you're fae, Aran Egan? You have quite the power in your blood."

My face was a blank mask, eyes dead, muscles permanently relaxed with boredom.

With haughty male arrogance, I rolled my eyes. "Obviously I know who I am. I'm Aran, cousin of the royal family, and water fae."

My body language screamed that his question was preposterous.

Lothaire smiled like he'd won the war.

"Perfect. Congratulations, Aran Egan, water fae, you've officially been enrolled at Elite Academy."

My mask fell. "Excuse me?"

"This is a highly coveted institution, and you will be expected to perform rigorously." Lothaire didn't bother to hide his scorn.

Thunder boomed.

"Classes start tomorrow."

Before I could protest, reanalyze the situation, and decide the best path forward, Lothaire grabbed my arm. "We leave now."

Flames exploded.

We disappeared.

In the blinding red fire, the world shifted.

I went from standing in a foyer in the beast realm to kneeling on a massive island of black rocks.

An inky fortress, wide and stocky with four imposing turrets, sat atop black boulders.

A dark ocean surrounded the island.

Waves crashed across the rocks in an endless shriek. As far as the eye could see, water churned and slapped.

Wind whipped, and salt burned my eyes as cold rocks

dug into my bare feet. A salty, pungent, sulfurous odor overwhelmed my senses as I breathed in deeply.

Above us, in the dark night, a glowing ring of red surrounded a shadowy sphere, and it was an ominous outline.

A magnified lunar eclipse. Breathtaking and horrible because the solar phenomenon took up a quarter of the sky.

The moon was so large that the nape of my neck prickled.

Unknown instincts screamed at me to flee and to get away from this realm because a collision was surely imminent. The moon was so close to the planet that it defied physics.

The sky smoldered.

The fortress creaked.

The ocean screamed.

"Follow me," Lothaire ordered and stalked forward up steep stairs that were carved into the rocks.

Disoriented and eager to get away from the sky, I followed the deadly vampyre into the fortress.

Inside was empty of people and was just as shocking as the solar phenomena.

My jaw dropped as I followed Lothaire.

I'd expected dark and dreary, but it was anything but.

I walked into an architectural structure the likes of which were only painted in the pictures of ancient Renaissance books.

Gleaming gold trim lined the inky black walls. Endless black marble flooring was chilly beneath my toes.

The brilliant gold traveled along the ceiling and walls like a web of tree branches, or lightning strikes. Every single crack on the black ceiling, wall, and floors was filled with gold.

And as if that was not gorgeous enough, every couple of feet, the black and gold was interrupted by stunning stained-glass windows.

Thousands of flecks of warm-colored glass came together in mosaics that were more art than functional.

It was almost impossible to walk forward because the stained glass deserved to be stared at. I fought the urge to lie on the floor and stare up at each window.

The warm-hued mosaics threw flecks of colored light against grand crystal chandeliers.

Light danced across gold and black.

As I walked forward, it sparkled across my skin, and it was like traversing through an artist's mind.

Each stained-glass window depicted a different scene, but all were done in the same Renaissance style of soft lines and vibrant colors.

Men and women with wings falling from the sky.

Babies screaming in their mothers' arms.

Thousands of men tangled in battle.

Naked women kneeling in a garden paradise.

Beasts with strange horns dancing.

Monarchs ascending to their thrones.

Scholars writing in ancient languages.

There was nothing simple about the fortress's bones; it was crafted with a painstaking artisanship that was awe-inspiring and breathtaking.

SWOOSH. CRACKLE.

I blinked away white spots and tried to process white lightning had just streaked across the walls.

There was a storm *inside* the halls.

I stumbled backward.

Sadie had said Xerxes's room in the mansion was

enchanted to project different weather, but she'd described it as a mirage.

There was another loud crack, and I reached my hand out. My fingers traced across sharp stone.

Lightning flashed, but this time, there was a sizzle, and my teeth ached as the world trembled. My nerve endings screamed.

I jumped back and stared down in silence at the tips of my fingers blackened with scorch marks.

Lothaire said nothing, just stalked forward, while another crack sounded and lightning slammed down across the walls.

It was real.

There was lightning in the halls.

On shaky legs, I hurried to keep up with the long, trailing braid of my mother's consort. The beast from my past had no idea the boy he led down otherworldly halls was the princess he'd scorned.

Lothaire had said I was enrolled in Elite Academy, and here I was. This terrifying realm was the home of a glittering school, an academy, known realm-wide for its cruelty.

Everyone knew Elite Academy took the most powerful individuals in all the realms between the ages of nineteen and twenty-eight. Its harsh methods were rivaled only by its prestigious reputation.

It was impossible to be chosen.

There were rumored to be hundreds of realms with sentient life and quadrillions of people.

Those chosen for the academy were more godlike than human.

The school was a check on the most powerful. A way to collar monsters and make them obey the High Court before they brought genocide and war to all the realms.

It was also a way to amass power.

And for the strongest to find one another and form friendships, partnerships, and even marriages. To build alliances stronger than the militaries of multiple realms.

Elite Academy was the whispered tale of a bogeyman.

A dream for the powerful and depraved.

A warning for everyone else—a reminder that the realms were full of monsters and their might would eventually crush you.

Lothaire didn't bother to explain any of this to me as he stalked through the architectural paradise.

Even if the academy was more myth than reality, it was still common knowledge.

He didn't need to explain.

We both knew how powerless I was.

Lothaire turned around abruptly. "You'll sleep here. Academy starts tomorrow morning. Thunder will signal wake-up."

He shoved me into the room, then stalked away down the hall. Long braid dragging.

Bang.

A heavy door slammed shut behind me.

The room was small with the same black walls and gold trim, with no windows. A golden fireplace crackled warmly and threw shadows dancing across the four-poster bed. A small marble bathroom was stocked with toiletries.

There was a single black sweat suit hanging in the closet.

After trailing my hands along the soft emerald sheets, I lay back on the luxurious bed.

I gasped.

On the high ceiling, thousands of stars twinkled in constellations I didn't recognize.

But it wasn't pretty.

In the middle of the ceiling, a black vortex swirled around, swallowing the stars and destroying them in sparks of angry red.

It consumed.

The vortex burned orange in its center like a forge making the world anew as it lazily sucked the cosmos into oblivion.

A few years ago, I would have been amazed that I was at Elite Academy.

That it was a real place.

I would have been giddy with energy, studying the mosaic walls, trying to figure out where the lightning came from and if there really was a black hole on the ceiling.

I would have marveled at the stars, since naming constellations had been one of my favorite activities as a child.

Another hobby I'd lost with time.

I'd kept the dark ones.

For example, I'd always been enamored with being clean. Scrubbing myself, tidying my room, and basking in the euphoria of a polished and organized life.

Now permanent filth lived in a grimy cage that smudged my soul.

The urge to wash myself was still present.

But there was no aftermath of euphoria—no moment where I basked in anything that remotely resembled happiness.

No respite.

Your mother's consort just kidnapped you to a foreign realm. You may never see your best friend and the girls again.

Dragging myself into the room's small shower, I turned on the cold water and crumpled to the floor.

Puffed on my pipe and tried to forget who I was, where I was, and everything it entailed.

Academy starts tomorrow.

One rumor was always the same about Elite Academy: it was highly competitive, and anyone who attended had to give it their all if they were going to survive.

I had nothing left to give, and school hadn't even begun.

Breathe in. Hold. Release. Rest. Repeat.

It didn't work, and my monster bellowed to be released from its cage.

The cage in my mind was a constant reminder that— even though I was the technical ruler of the fae realm—my mother had lied to me about my birthright.

Now I knew why Mother had never spoken about my dad.

As a child, I'd just assumed it was because Mother had killed him in one of her fits of rage. But that wasn't it.

Mother must have kept my sire's identity a secret because he wasn't a fae; it wasn't possible.

Because I had power, but I wasn't a fae.

Still, with bright-turquoise eyes and shocking blue hair, I was the spitting image of Mother. As much as I wished it weren't so, the bitch had birthed me.

Only my mother could subject a child to such a tortuous existence.

My monster screamed louder in my head, emphasizing that I was twenty-four years old and still didn't know *what* the fuck I was.

Despair crushed me.

How dare the vampyre who dirtied himself with my mother try to dictate my life?

My vision bled black with rage.

I would stalk Lothaire down the hall, slice his throat with ice daggers, and rip off his head.

It would be satisfying to kill him and bask in the spray of his warm blood.

A worthy prey.

My fingernails broke as I crawled, desperate to get back to the hall where my kill had ordered me to follow him.

I cracked my face into the tile as hard as I could.

As everything faded to darkness, my beast screamed and rattled against its steel cage. Yet another hunt foiled.

I'd trapped it.

For now.

THE RECKONING

At Elite Academy we find the strong,
Those full of power and cruel desire,
And on the bark we spill their blood,
To reveal the few with souls on fire.

—The Sacred Tree

CHAPTER 2
HELL

Thunder cracked with such ferocity the warm bed vibrated beneath me.

Red lights flashed in the small room, and an enchantment made it sound like a male was shouting at me from all corners of the room.

The voice boomed, "You have five minutes to proceed to the great hall for the reckoning. Five minutes until the reckoning. Lateness will not be tolerated."

Glaring at the black hole swirling on the ceiling, I fantasized about banging my face again into the headboard until I lost consciousness.

Anything called a reckoning was not something I wanted to be a part of. Especially a reckoning at a mythical, supernatural academy known for its violence.

It made my homicidal impulses flare up. Since I was a little girl, fear always made me want to kill things.

I never pretended to be normal.

Instead of letting my monster loose, which was banging in my mental cage and screaming bloody murder, I focused on the peace of my everyday morning routine.

Stumbling into the bathroom, I splashed water on my face, slapped myself, scrubbed my teeth, spent a long minute smoking on my pipe with my eyes closed, then pulled on the black sweat suit and dragged my fingers through my short, curly hair.

It still shocked me, the harsh edge of my jaw and hardness in my face.

My natural features were disgustingly girly, but my enchanted disguise was badass.

As a girl, I was born to breed.

As a man, I was cold and hard. My features reflected how I felt on the inside—angry, depressed, dead. Most importantly, empty.

With a few more slaps to the face, I channeled toxic masculinity. The key to acting like you had a dick was being a dick.

I didn't make the rules.

The enchanted voice bellowed, "Two minutes until the reckoning. Proceed to the great hall NOW."

Swearing under my breath, I realized there were no shoes in the closet.

Dark marble was cold against the pads of my bare feet as I hurried out of my room, into the bustling hall. A crowd of people hurried forward in a silent, frantic rush through the black and gold.

The stained-glass windows and chandeliers refracted light across the colorful people in a way that made it seem like a dream.

Crack.

Lightning flashed and slammed down the walls in a fiery burst that made the hair on my arms stand up.

The hall reeked of ozone and old parchment, reminiscent of a library on fire.

For a long moment, I stood still and inhaled the caustic scents, letting them sink into my bones.

A lost soul in the glittering melee.

That was, if I even had a soul to lose.

Bodies rushed around me, and no one gave the lightning a second look. The two dozen men and women were rushing forward toward two gilded, arched doors at the end of the long hall.

All wore matching black sweat suits.

All were barefoot.

Hour one, and they had already stripped us of our individuality.

Wonderful.

With another deep drag of my pipe, I followed the stampede, but I refused to run like an imbecile.

After twenty-four years of surviving through what felt like Armageddon, the last thing I wanted to do was go back to school.

That was just *embarrassing.*

Growing up, I'd had the best fae tutors in the realm and had succeeded in the standardized tests at sixteen.

I scored first in battle strategy, an achievement that had made me more valuable to the fae elite who wanted to breed me.

Mother might have been the queen, but men led the military, and they'd told me my role was to birth the next great *male* general.

I might have been a royal, but above all, I was a birthing vessel.

But fae births were extremely rare, so once they were old enough to ovulate, women were expected to work hard to become fertile. Dangerous enchantments were injected into wombs, hordes of doctors studied cycles, while the men rutted constantly in an attempt to achieve the impossible.

I would have been a fertility experiment for my entire immortal life.

So I'd made the only rational choice I could. I'd run away.

I wished I could flee now because this academy had nothing to offer me.

Education had never taught me how not to be a monster. I'd never learned how to not let the rage overwhelm me. How to stop myself from doing the unthinkable.

It had taught me nothing useful.

I didn't need school. I needed training and answers; I needed something that no one could give me.

Walking down the glimmering hall of the Academy, I might as well have been walking backward.

Ripped away from my chosen family.

Alone and miserable.

Trapped.

A man bumped into me, and I grimaced as the enchanted wound on my back burned.

Lately, my back had been hurting more frequently. It didn't just burn when I was turned on, which was how Mother had said it would work. It ached every second of every day.

Maybe she'd fucked up?

It was a new enchantment after all.

Another gift of psychological torture from my dear mother. The letters carved into my skin were a constant reminder that an entire realm of sadistic fae were searching for me.

They were desperate to rip out my heart and take my throne.

I didn't have time to play student.

A booming voice echoed down the hall, "One minute until the reckoning."

People broke out into a run, and I rolled my eyes but refused to hurry. I would not debase myself by scurrying like a rat tethered to the whim of an enchanted voice.

The mass of flailing limbs shoved me through the gilded entrance.

"All newcomers, wait in the line" boomed louder as the enchanted voice echoed off the high, arched ceiling.

The jostling stopped as we filed into a short line. The doors slammed shut behind us.

Once again, I gaped.

The space was grand. A massive black brick room with high, arched ceilings; gold accents; massive, twinkling chandeliers; and long, stained-glass windows.

Just like in the hall, each window was an ornate mosaic; however, there were six windows and each portrayed a person. Three men on one side, three women on the other.

The three men each had a sun behind his head, and the three women each had a moon. Throughout all the glass, what appeared to be black ribbon sparkled and twined around them all.

The dark-red shadows from the eclipse shed a haunting light across the massive room.

There was no change in the sky's brightness to delineate night and day. Instead, the lunar eclipse was dark and insidious, eating up the cosmos with its glowing presence.

A massive grandfather clock on the wall showed it was 5:00 a.m.

However, even more disturbing than the early time was the massive tree that jutted from the marble floor like an insidious growth. Gnarled white branches reached toward students with an evil design.

The centerpiece of the hall, the tree coiled up to the four-story-tall, high ceiling.

There was nothing pretty about it.

Split down the center with a black scorch mark, the tree looked like lightning had struck it and was barren of leaves. It appeared dead.

Two long marble tables that spanned the length of the room flanked the centerpiece tree on both sides. One table had purple chairs and decoration, while the other was green.

I estimated about one hundred people were seated between the two tables.

Something divided them.

With matching black outfits, it was hard to distinguish differences, but you could sense a separation. Maybe it was the way they glared across the tables at each other, or maybe it was something else.

The people in the purple seats sat straighter, heads higher, and postures rigid.

The people in the green seats sat meaner, hunched lower, faces hardened.

Two sides split like the scorched tree between them.

But they weren't the only division.

To the far right, there was a small dais that had a much smaller table. The chairs were more intricate and shone gold underneath the dark eclipse.

Only seven men sat at it.

High above everyone else, they glared down with sneers across their faces like overlords.

Even a hundred yards away, I could smell the toxic masculinity wafting off them.

They reeked.

If the people in purple were prim and the people in green were hardened, then the men in the high gold seats were cruel.

They were different.

Seven massive men. The unnatural width of their shoulders and muscles strained their sweatshirts indecently.

My own clothes hung baggy and loose on my frame.

Even though my disguise made my shoulders appear wider and chest larger, I still had the narrow, lean build of my mother.

I might not have manifested any fae element, but I shared her blood in my unmistakable build and unique coloring.

Lithe and genteel.

Royal.

No matter how I pretended otherwise, I looked just like her. She also was a crazy bitch, and I was self-aware enough to know I, too, was fucked up in the head.

She'd bred me in her image.

A soft, feminine figure that was perfect for being shown off on the arm of an elite fae. Weak and lean, not too strong so my future husband wouldn't feel emasculated when he violently tried to breed me multiple times a day.

He'd be in charge.

A familiar prickle of heat crawled up my neck, and I focused on counting my breaths.

One. Two. Three.

I wasn't in the fae realm anymore. I was safe.

Kind of.

Sure, I was the reigning queen, but I was disguised, and no one knew who I was.

It will be okay, I lied to myself.

Sweat streaked across my palms, and I wiped them on my sweatpants. The perspiration reminded me of blood. It reminded me of the other time I'd wiped my palms across a torn dress, until it was covered in red streaks and gore.

Mother's heart in my mouth.

Steel rattled inside my mind, and my monster screamed. It always woke up when I thought about that awful act, like it was its pride and joy. The best thing it had ever done.

Five. Four. Three. Exhale.

Sun god, I was a mess.

Unfriendly faces filled the hall and stared at me.

Dragging my shaking hands through my short, curly hair, I glared back with indifference.

Forced my cheeks to relax and my eyes to look cold.

There were men and women of all sizes and races with unique coloring, but none had blue hair. From the way some people inspected me with something close to flippant curiosity on their faces, my vibrant turquoise curls were making me stand out.

The sneering students looked downright evil against the backdrop of the moon and with their eyes flickering as they sized one another up.

Everything glowed with a vitriolic haze, and the silence in the hall was sweltering.

There was no buzz of talking.

No excitement.

Just a massive gothic hall in a foreign realm with about a hundred people glaring at one another.

The marble floor was cold beneath my bare feet.

I inspected the students. Most people's attention was focused on the seven men at the dais.

More specifically, at the man who sat in the center.

He was larger than everyone else, and a tattoo of a

dagger wrapped around the darkly tanned skin of his neck. It was an intricate design that I'd never seen before.

But it wasn't what made people stare.

His features were severe.

Harsh and sharp, with an aristocratic edge so perfect it seemed like he'd been carved from a heavy element.

Not marble; that's too soft.

I narrowed my eyes as I tried to figure out what he reminded me of.

Red flames danced across his bronze fingers, and he glowed with heat. Literally. Fire trailed across his tanned skin in a fucked-up dance.

He's carved from lava.

He looked like he was born from a volcano, flames and fire carved into a deadly pyroclastic flow that formed a cruelly beautiful male.

Gold hardware curved across the top of his pointed fae ears; it was ear decoration I'd never seen before.

Even though he was fae, he wasn't from the fae realm; that was for sure.

Anyone who looked like him would have been a celebrity. The fae coveted beautiful things after all, and while his beauty was impossibly harsh, it was still enchanting.

Handsome.

Like a glowing machine gun.

Before the bullets ripped through skin and muscle and shattered bone. An experience with which I was intimately acquainted.

I'd heard there were fae who lived in other realms, dignitaries and colonizers from centuries past who had ventured through portals in search of new realms before the monarchy closed off travel.

He must be descended from one of those ancient fae travelers.

My breath caught.

Red flames danced across his buzzed dark hair like a crown.

Suddenly, the flames weren't red but a brilliant blue, masculine features were feminine, and dark, tanned skin was creamy white.

A soft voice tinkled in my head. Fingers snapped as they lit me aflame.

Mother laughed.

My monster shrieked.

I fought the overwhelming urge to bang my skull against the brick wall. Slam my fists in my face until the noises stopped rattling around my head and I gurgled softly into the darkness.

She's dead.

If death was the absence of life, then a person was not truly dead if they haunted your every waking moment.

And Mother stalked me. Every day. Every second. Every moment.

There was no peace.

Ten. Nine. Eight.

I gnawed harder on my inner cheek and tried to convince myself that I could look at flames without falling apart. Tried to pretend I wasn't closer to crossing the delicate line that separated the sane from the insane.

Seven. Six. Five.

Like usual, I lied to myself.

Four. Three. Two.

The problem was there was only so much counting you could do.

Only so much breathing and pretending.

I should have looked away from the stunning fae man's flames, but something about the way he leaned his face forward and whispered into the ears of the two men next to him mesmerized me.

He was a predator among predators.

Yet when he talked to the two other fae men with neck tattoos, who also had gold hardware decorating their pointed ears, he looked almost soft. Like he had a soul. Or maybe I was just projecting?

He grinned at them.

The three fae seemed close, like brothers.

The fae on his right was leaner with pale skin, short dark hair, and a massive eye tattooed on the side of his neck.

On his left, the fae seemed softer with a more delicate bone structure, gold skin, and wavy white-blond hair. His features were more feminine. He was almost pretty.

The massive flower tattoo on his neck was less insidious than the dagger and eye on his brothers' necks, but it still gave him a hardened edge.

Their ink was almost as cool as the "Loyalty" tattoo that Sadie had gotten across her back. My fingernails dug into my palms, and I tried not to keel over at the thought of my best friend.

Sadie was my rock.

I fucking missed her.

All alone.

Three. Two. One.

I was fine.

I was normal.

I was competent.

The lies scraped across my mind like claws digging into my psyche, and each one pushed me a step closer to madness.

You're being dramatic.

It wasn't like the entire hall was giving warm, cozy, loving vibes, and I wasn't the only person standing alone.

The four other men at the high dais constantly glanced over at the three fae like they were searching for their approval. Desperate for it.

But the fae didn't acknowledge anyone else because they were wrapped up in one another.

In fact, the more I studied the room, the more I realized these three were the epicenter.

Women looked at them with barely concealed longing, and men glared with different shades of envy and awe.

The three fae ran the show.

Suddenly, red flames flickered higher as the largest man whipped his head around, dagger pulling as his neck turned.

Harsh cheekbones glinted as he scanned the hall, then stared directly at me.

Silver eyes glittered.

My cheeks burned as he stabbed me with his gaze.

It was a classic intimidation tactic. He maintained eye contact to assert his dominance over me because for some reason, he'd decided I was an opponent.

Past events flashed around me like exploding grenades.

Fire.

Unrelenting pain.

I wrenched my head away and grabbed my small pipe.

Discreetly, I sucked in smoke and exhaled calm, the drugs flowing through me and blunting the screams in my head, the pain in my back, the heaviness in my chest.

My intuition screamed at me to run away from this place.

To escape.

The sky was collapsing above as the sun swallowed a

moon that was impossibly large. The room was full of predators who would do anything for power. I'd been taken from the only people I'd ever trusted and was all alone.

I was in danger.

But my intuition didn't control me.

My monster did.

The steel cage rattled as the monster screamed for blood. It never looked away first. It never ran away.

People ran from us.

We would kill them all.

No. Shut the fuck up.

I counted upward in squared numbers: *two, four, sixteen, 256, 65,536.*

Crash.

I jumped as the entrance doors slammed open, breaking the room's eerie silence with a loud bang.

Lothaire stalked down the path between the two tables, long braid trailing on the ground as his singular eye roamed.

Mother's consort wore a perfectly tailored business suit that stretched across his bulging muscles.

Lothaire stopped in front of the tree and cracked his neck, like he was preparing for battle.

Everyone sat up straighter. Shoulders pressed back as faces fell into stony masks of obedience.

Silence thickened with anticipation.

The ancient vampyre smirked as he looked around the room, opal fangs flashing against bloodred lips as he literally sparked with gold power.

"Welcome to the reckoning."

CHAPTER 3
THE BEGINNING OF
THE END

The reckoning: Day 1, hour 0

Lothaire addressed the room, and his voice was loud and harsh. "Elite Academy is where the strongest in the universe come to build themselves into something greater."

He spread his arms wide as he spoke.

"Everyone here has power running through their veins. This academy was created for a singular purpose—find the strongest, brightest, and most powerful in all the realms and bring them to new heights. Help them embrace their greatness. Seize their destinies."

Lothaire paused, and his voice echoed through the rafters.

Goose bumps crawled down my spine.

"Between twenty and thirty years old, you're all old enough to understand consequences but young enough to still learn control. Many of you understand the honor that's been bestowed on you. The chance to better yourself and serve the High Court. The rulers of the realms."

Bull. Shit.

It was classic political rhetoric.

He was twisting the situation to be something different from what it was. Whenever someone preached of serving something greater, they were always talking out their ass.

There was no glory in dying for a crown.

No pride in breaking for a monarch.

No honor in suffering for a realm.

Nothing to be gained but everything to be lost.

After twenty-four years of screaming on palace floors and fighting monsters in unknown wars, I refused to be someone else's pawn.

Lothaire paused and arched his eyebrow, an expression eerily similar to the one I loved to make that drove Sadie mad.

He stared at the line of new students with murder in his singular eye.

We were the fresh meat.

Lothaire's face scrunched as he spat, "But some of you've been taken against your will. Some of you are defiant. You believe you don't belong here. That this academy is a chore you don't wish to engage in."

His eye lingered on me.

My fingernails pinched my palms as I clenched my fist, and my head ached from the strain of not rolling my eyes and flipping him off.

Lothaire's features hardened, his fangs flashing as his voice dripped with malice. "But I don't give a fuck what you think about yourself. What you believe. If you're powerful enough to be here, you're a liability that the High Court would sooner exterminate than deal with."

He smirked and paused, letting it sink in.

Exterminate.

"But that's why they send me to every corner of the realms to find you. This academy is built on three tenets."

He paused as if he was about to impart some great wisdom, but when he spoke, his voice dripped with an edge of sarcasm. "First, we break you.

"Second, we break you.

"Third, we break you."

Lothaire smiled, and the horrible, jagged scar pulled tight across his missing eye. This was the beast who'd smiled at Mother. Gone willingly into her bed. Watched her torture and kill without flinching once.

I shivered as he continued to speak.

"But don't worry. Only those who're broken can be rebuilt. Only those who're shattered can rise to new heights. So far, you've lived cushy lives, more powerful than those around you. Unchecked lives where you've committed unimaginable atrocities because no one could stop you." He chuckled darkly.

Silence stretched.

No one in the room fidgeted, and no one breathed.

The weird thing was that he wasn't wrong; sure, I'd lived through horrors, but the real tragedy of my life was what *I'd* done.

I'd committed worse deeds than the ones done upon me. A reality I wasn't supposed to admit to myself.

But I knew what I was.

Pipe to my lips, I discreetly inhaled the enchanted drug and held the burning smoke within my lungs.

Lothaire's expression darkened as he spoke. "Now you're here to learn control. But don't worry, once I've decided you've discovered the depths of your abilities and learned how to harness them, you're free to leave. Everything you've learned at this academy will guide you."

He spread his hands wide, voice bellowing. "You will be given positions of leadership in the High Court. Given exclusive positions that only graduates of this academy are offered."

Lothaire's voice deepened with conviction. "You'll remake the realms and will be on the front lines of maintaining peace. There are unimaginable threats that only the people in this hall are strong enough to face. I will ensure that you'll be prepared not only to face them, but to conquer them."

Lothaire raised his fist, and everyone at the tables mimicked the motion.

Clenched knuckles held high in the moon's dim red haze.

No one spoke.

My nails dug harder into my palm at my side as warm blood trickled down my fingers and dripped onto the slate ground.

I didn't want to break.

Didn't want to rebuild.

Didn't want to lead anyone.

The wound on my back itched, a constant reminder that I didn't need anyone to break me, because I was already broken.

I'd already fallen as far as a person could fall and had fucked up my life so completely that there was no future waiting for me.

All it would take was one person recognizing me and my life would be over.

My fate was already sealed.

All this drama and pomp was just that, a facade that meant nothing in the grand scheme of things.

Lothaire lowered his fist and yelled, his voice shaking the rafters, "Academy tradition demands we start each school year with a reckoning!"

"Hurrah!" Everyone stomped their feet in synchrony.

The floor trembled beneath my bare feet.

Lothaire turned toward us with a massive smile, and it wasn't a pleasant expression. "All of you are here because your blood is filled with power. But every few years, a student arrives with unimaginable potential in their veins."

Opal fangs flashed.

Lothaire said reverently, "Lightning in flesh."

He gestured toward where we stood in line.

"You'll each be tested, and if you reveal yourself as one of these unique few, you'll be trained by me personally. The greatest honor in the universe."

Lothaire turned his head and pointed to the seven massive men who sat apart at the high dais. "You'll join the recruits and train in our assassin division. You'll suffer in the most prestigious program in all the realms."

Cold sweat broke out across my forehead.

Back in the fae realm, Mother's assassins were always the most depraved men. The ones with no morals who committed unthinkable evils.

I shivered, focused on cold analytics, and let the facts calm me.

Each man on that dais was impossibly large and strong compared to everyone else in the hall. They averaged about seven feet tall and had wide shoulders that took up the space of two men.

There were no women.

Beneath my enchantment, I was still a female and while decently tall at five eleven (six feet in shoes, thank you very much), my muscles were nothing compared to theirs. I was built lithe and agile, not wide and brutish.

I wouldn't be chosen.

There was no need to worry.

"Lyla," Lothaire said as he gestured toward a small table that I hadn't noticed was tucked into the far corner of the room.

Suddenly, a beautiful woman in a long black dress, with lime-green hair, sauntered forward. Pentagrams and runes were tattooed in white ink across every inch of her dark skin.

Holy sun god.

Immediately, I knew what she was. If it wasn't the darkness in her eyes, then the pure power that shimmered around her in a sparkly aura gave it away.

She glided smoothly, like gravity couldn't touch her, and everything about her was ethereal.

The pentagram on her forehead glowed. Dark-red rays from the lunar eclipse clashed with her green hair.

When she walked up to Lothaire, he bowed deeply, and his imposing frame bent low with respect before her.

There was only one creature that an ancient vampyre would bow to. Only one race was so powerful that even a monster would respect them.

Lyla was a witch.

She said nothing, just stared at Lothaire with her stunning features completely devoid of all emotion.

After a long moment, Lothaire uncurled back to his full height and stood beside her next to the tree. He gestured toward the scorched trunk, at the small object I hadn't noticed.

A dagger stuck out from the base of the tree.

Hilt buried in the bark.

Sharp edge pointing outward.

Lothaire smiled at us.

"You'll each press your hand to the sacred tree. It's been blessed by the sun god himself and can detect the most minute essence of power in your blood."

My face remained impassive, but I knew what he was going to say.

"You'll impale yourself on the dagger."

The people in the line shifted and gasped with horror. Men and women recoiled, and my shoulder was jostled, the contact slamming me into the wall.

The wound on my back burned.

My monster screamed with aggression, and I fought the urge to snap at the idiot who'd bumped me. Fought the urge not to beat his face until he was a bloody mess.

Instead, I took a long drag from my pipe.

The enchanted drug calmed me.

I wished I could say I was surprised and horrified like the people around me.

But I'd come to expect blood.

Endless pain.

Existential dread did that. Or was it insanity? I'd stopped telling the difference a long time ago.

"Lyla will heal you after. Come forward," Lothaire ordered with iron in his voice that left no room for argument.

Suddenly, I was very glad that I was at the back of the line.

The first man in line stepped forward hesitantly and walked up to stand before the tree. He was a large man covered in muscles and was probably in his midtwenties.

He bowed to Lothaire, then moved in front of the tree.

I couldn't contain my scoff.

He hadn't even acknowledged the witch. That was who he should have been bowing to.

Ignorant fuck.

He stared at the dagger protruding from the tree.

Time ticked by painfully.

He held his shaking palm forward, but stopped inches from the blade.

Five minutes passed.

Finally, Lothaire snarled down at him with disgust.

"This is Elite Academy. No one's going to do it for you. That's why it's called a reckoning. We'll stay here all day if we need to. This is your introduction to growing the fuck up and doing what needs to be done."

The man grimaced, his face falling as he stared down at the dagger.

He swung his arm back and forth like he was gaining courage.

Suddenly, a loud scream shattered the silence.

Tears streamed down the man's face as he pressed his palm against the bark of the tree. Red blood streaked down the white trunk.

Red.

Blood.

Beating heart in my mouth.

Gore gushing down my chin.

Draining across my throat.

Crusting on my skin.

I took another drag of my pipe and inhaled deeply.

Hold. Exhale. Pause. Repeat.

My vision blurred, but I focused on my breathing, barely aware of the man pulling his hand off the dagger with a sickening squelch. Of his turning to the witch with frantic eyes and shoving his bloody hand toward her.

She turned her nose up at him and looked away, refusing to heal him.

He whimpered like a dog.

Lothaire rolled his eyes. "You disrespected her by not bowing. A witch must always be shown reverence, especially if you want something from her. This is your second lesson at the academy. Respect those more powerful than yourself or suffer the consequences."

Tears streaked down his face as he clutched his bleeding hand to his chest.

If the blood weren't dragging me back into my memories and threatening to drown me, I might have chuckled at how pathetic he looked.

What had he thought would happen? He'd turned his back to a witch. They were more gods than women.

They were called the eyes of the universe for a reason.

"What's your name?" Lothaire demanded coolly as he looked down at the sniveling man with disgust.

"Uclydes Aerogopolys."

"And what is your station?"

Uclydes scrunched his eyebrows with confusion as he stared up at Lothaire. "I'm a water siren from the Olympus realm. My family are traders."

Lothaire rolled his eyes with a sass that reminded me of Jinx, the twelve-year-old who lived to torment my best friend, Sadie.

My gut told me she would get along with Lothaire.

They had the same energy: death, doom, and gloom. I could practically hear them gossiping over how inept people were.

Lothaire asked impatiently, "Commoner or royalty? The academy is divided based on your station, and your curriculum is tailored based on what skills you need to learn."

"Commoner," Uclydes said on a watery choke as he clutched his hand tighter and sobbed.

Lothaire pointed to the green table, and Uclydes hurried over.

I analyzed the two tables with renewed curiosity.

So that was the distinction I'd sensed. The purple table was royalty, and the green was commoners.

Instantly, my curiosity turned to nails in my stomach.

Lothaire knew I was a cousin of the monarchy. Did that mean he'd put me with the royals? I didn't want to be stuck with a bunch of self-righteous brats who thought they were better than everybody.

The red air in the hall shimmered with malice and otherworldly things I couldn't identify.

Panicking, I barely heard the screams of pain as people impaled themselves on the tree.

The tree never changed.

Slowly but surely, everyone was sorted between the commoner and royalty tables.

During the ordeal, the seven men on the dais scoffed and chuckled as people screamed. Each time someone cried in pain, their shoulders shook with laughter.

Like it was funny.

But no one was dumb enough not to bow to the witch first, and Lyla grabbed their hands, chanting under her breath until the wounds healed.

Before I knew it, Lothaire gestured at me to step forward.

We'd made it to the last in line.

It was my turn.

The heavy weight of everyone's eyes burned against me, and my skin crawled at the attention.

Too many threats.

Steel bars rattled as my monster begged to be released, to show itself to the other predators. It wanted to assert that it was bigger and scarier than them.

A red haze filled the edges of my vision as my monster battled for control.

Sweat streaked across my temples.

I bowed deeply to the witch, averting my eyes as was respectful of someone of her station.

You didn't look fate straight in the eyes, not if you wanted to live.

My monster screamed, slamming against my consciousness as it begged to be released. The rage at my helpless situation had driven it into a frenzy.

The steel bars of the cage bent, and my monster snarled louder in my head.

No. I am in control.

So I did the only thing I could do.

I slammed my palm down on the blade as hard as I could.

Cartilage snapped. Warm blood spilled.

A sound didn't escape my lips, and my eyes were bone dry as I skewered myself on the blade.

I'd learned to suffer pain from a young age—learned how to take torture without making a sound, learned how to feel nothing—before I'd learned how to care.

Hot pain flooded my senses with adrenaline and allowed me to focus.

The haze overtaking my vision receded as I shoved my monster back into its cage.

Hand throbbing, I welcomed the distraction. Dug my

nails into the cold bark and concentrated on breathing slowly.

Piece by piece, I recreated my calm facade.

Then, with one last inhale, I ripped my hand off the blade.

Scorching pain screamed across my nerves, but I didn't make a sound.

A twisted part of me welcomed the agony. I recognized the familiar sensation and embraced it like an old friend.

It was the only constant in my life.

But I didn't look down.

Knew the warm blood would trigger my memories and cause me to spiral and allow the darkness to rear up and take control.

I counted to ten.

Rebuilt control.

Control was such a small thing, but I'd somehow completely lost it.

Now the struggle for discipline overtook every facet of my life and strained every breath I took.

Lyla chanted softly and held my hand, her witch's skin impossibly cold against mine. An unnatural chill rolled through my body, like a phantom's kiss, as my skin reknitted itself.

"Aran Egan," I announced to Lothaire before he could ask.

You are royalty. You need to learn how to lead. Just in case.

With a deep fortifying breath, I opened my mouth to seal my fate. "Roy—"

I didn't finish.

"Assassin division!" Lothaire boomed as he stared at the tree. "Welcome, you're now a recruit. Join the other men at the high dais. You'll be working with me directly.

You've been selected for the highest honor in all the realms. In the next few months, you will either seize your future or…"

He trailed off.

I forced my face into a blank mask and donned the expression of a vapid fae princess.

Eyes dead.

Cheeks relaxed.

FUCK ME! I internally screamed.

They were men, and I was a female in disguise; this wasn't supposed to happen.

HOW THE FUCK DID THIS HAPPEN?

I wasn't even a fae.

There was no way I could keep so many secrets, and if Lothaire discovered my deceit, he'd murder me. Violently.

I barely stopped myself from shrieking like a child because my odds of survival had just dropped from 10 percent to 1 percent.

Lothaire's eyes raked up and down my frame, and his lips tilted downward, like he'd inspected me and found me lacking.

I was wrong; it was .005 percent.

Turning my back to my jailer, I trudged slowly to the high table.

Forced myself to stare down the cruel men in the assassin division who took in my smaller stature with expressions of humor and disbelief.

They whispered to one another, shoulders shaking with laughter.

Slumping into a golden chair, I curled my head low and counted the number of lines on the wood table. Pretended everyone wasn't staring at me as I kept my head turned away from the tree.

Didn't need the reminder that the barren tree had erupted into full bloom.

A flower jostled off my shoulder and drifted onto the table.

It was black.

Like my soul.

CHAPTER 4
MEETING FATE

The reckoning: Day 1, hour 2

Two hours later the hall was transformed by the loud hum of conversation.

Apparently, the depressive gloom had all been for the reckoning. Now everyone was upbeat.

Not relatable.

Students greeted one another and embraced like they were excited to learn and begin a new school year as they looked over the class schedules that had appeared at the tables.

For the first time, people seemed almost normal.

Almost was the key word.

Power swirled around students in tangible clouds of danger, and the room vibrated with energy, tension, and violence.

Men and women alike were unnaturally beautiful, with unique eyes, curling horns, and even some tails. I'd never seen so many different species in one room before.

Descendants of gods, water sprites, vampyres, shifters,

and demons were just a few of the creatures I could distinguish from looks alone.

But there was one constant—everyone had darkness in their eyes. It was a room full of predators.

For example, Uclydes had fallen onto the floor and was moaning in pain with a pool of blood surrounding his mutilated hand.

But most students at the commoner table ignored him.

Suddenly, the stunning woman next to him leaned low in her chair and dragged her fingers through the pool of blood rapidly spreading beneath him.

She licked her fingers in ecstasy while her vampyre eyes glowed bright orange.

Uclydes pleaded with her for help, but she ignored him and just kept drinking his blood.

I looked away, equally disgusted by the woman's savagery and the man's weakness.

Blood wasn't as much of a trigger as it had been right after the *deed*, but I still didn't enjoy staring at it. Watching it slowly pour out of a person.

The world spun as my breath caught in my chest. Stomach cramped with nausea.

Instead of spiraling, I turned my attention to Lothaire, who stood still as a statue in the middle of the room.

His eyes flickered like he was constantly scanning for threats.

The black sky and lunar eclipse refracted through the mosaic windows that framed the ceiling.

Black petals slowly drifted from the tree.

"They'll just let anyone in these days," a male voice rasped in a baritone that made the hairs on the back of my neck stand up.

I turned my attention back to the uncomfortable silence at the small table.

The assassins weren't buzzing with small talk like the rest of the room. No, the energy at our table was surly and aggressive.

The fire fae I'd noticed earlier was the owner of the impossibly deep voice.

He spoke again. "The tree must have made a mistake."

His high cheekbones pulled tight as he sneered, and the harsh expression fit with his buzz cut and cruel beauty.

Up close, the dagger tattoo that wrapped around his neck was silver with such intricate detail that the blade appeared to cut his throat as he spoke.

It matched his glimmering silver eyes.

The handsome dark-haired fae who sat next to him sneered, his pale skin pulling tight with anger as he said, "Obviously, Corvus. Even I can fucking see that."

His milky white eyes stared off into the distance. He was blind.

Also, apparently the bronze fire fae was Corvus. He was named after the constellation of a raven, rumored to originate from the Olympus realm and represent the sun god Apollo.

Red flames danced across his short dark hair like a crown.

Corvus fit him perfectly.

The blind fae stared off into the distance as he kept ranting, "That old fucking tree hasn't been accurate in three years. Of course it made a fucking mistake."

Nice, another male asshole. Groundbreaking.

His detailed tattoo of an eye spread across his Adam's apple like a choker and appeared to stare at me.

Did his neck tattoo just wink?

Sanity was slipping away from me.

"Really, Scorpius, do you have to be so crass?" whispered the third fae, who was almost pretty in his masculinity.

White-blond hair fell in soft waves around his shoulders and framed soft features. Large chocolate-brown eyes were decorated with impossibly long lashes. He stared at the blind fae with sadness.

Up close, the flower tattoo on his neck shed petals that fluttered across his collarbone and disappeared under his sweatshirt.

He was about half a foot shorter than the other men and looked smaller compared to them. But he was still covered in lean muscles that would make any warrior jealous.

And now I knew the blind fae was named Scorpius.

A unique, harsh name that fit his aggressive countenance. From how he sneered and frowned, it was clear he was a miserable bastard.

Like his brother Corvus, Scorpius was also named after a constellation: a scorpion that stung the hunter Orion and chased him from the sky.

A dangerous name for a dangerous man.

"Really, Orion, do you have to be such a baby at all times?" Scorpius's voice dripped with disgust.

My gut lurched with shock.

Scorpius and Orion were two constellations that could never be seen at once; Orion set as Scorpius rose.

Their namesakes didn't seem like a coincidence.

Corvus, Scorpius, and Orion. Three of the most renowned and impressive constellations.

Also, three of the most intimidating fae men I'd ever

seen, and I'd been exposed to a *lot* of soldiers thanks to Mother dearest and her torture.

Across the table, Scorpius made a rude gesture to Orion.

Orion responded by rolling his eyes at his blind companion, golden skin glimmering as his lush lips pursed with annoyance. His beauty really was shockingly pretty.

The brothers were works of art.

Scorpius's face scrunched as he taunted him back. "Don't be a baby."

Orion leaned forward so his face was closer to the pale fae's, and his voice was barely a whisper. "It's called having a sense of decorum."

"Some of us prefer to fucking say things as they fucking are. Grow up." Scorpius shook his slicked-back black hair.

Suddenly, Corvus's silver eyes flashed as flames leapt across his deeply tanned skin, and he wrapped his long fingers around Scorpius's chin and shook his head back and forth.

"Yes, we know you're so gritty and damaged. Let's focus on getting through this year's training with no more mishaps," Corvus's baritone voice rumbled.

Scorpius just growled like a feral beast.

Orion leaned closer to both men and whispered, "I don't know; Scorpius's mishaps are kind of fun."

Corvus slung his arm over his brothers' chairs affectionately. "Not you too. One of us has gotta pretend to not be completely unhinged."

They grinned at one another, warmth radiating around them with such intensity it made me sad.

I missed my family.

The brothers continued to bicker, and the female in me took her time inspecting and categorizing them.

Corvus was the terrifying leader, all harsh lines and edges, with a buzz cut, silver eyes, dagger tattoo, and flames.

Corvus was hardened.

Scorpius was cold and mocking, handsome with refined features; short, perfectly slicked-back black hair; pale skin; unseeing white eyes; and a lifelike eye tattoo on his neck.

Scorpius was cruel.

Orion was quiet. Stunning with soft, feminine features, white-blond hair, golden skin, chocolate-brown eyes, and roses tattooed across his neck.

Orion was refined.

None of them looked like any fae I'd ever met.

Unique gold jewelry covered the tops of their pointed ears, and they weren't lean and lithe like most fae; they were corded with rippling muscles and impossibly wide shoulders.

Their beauty was harsh and fierce, like the horrible red flames that crawled down Corvus's shoulders and made my stomach hurt.

"What are you looking at?" Scorpius sneered with such vitriol that his handsome face lost all civility.

It took me a second to realize he was speaking to me.

The brothers looked up.

Glittering silver, milky white, and chocolate brown pierced through me.

Instinctively, I averted my eyes.

"I wasn't looking," I mumbled as my face burned hot, and I stared across the hall, pretending to be interested in the dark petals that decorated the tree.

Scorpius scoffed, white eyes flashing. "Bull. Fucking. Shit. I bet a pretty boy like you hasn't seen a day of hard work in his life. You're going to get destroyed."

I gnawed on my lower lip and fought a smile as I

ignored his blathering about me being privileged. *Sun god help me; he thinks I'm pretty.*

Even though I was disguised as a boy, I wasn't dead, and one of the hottest men I'd ever seen had just called me pretty.

"He wasn't looking," Corvus's deep voice rumbled softly as he paused.

I looked back at him in confusion.

The dagger jumped on his throat, and red flames danced across his shoulders. Corvus smirked. "Because he doesn't want to die painfully."

Scorpius sneered and chuckled in agreement.

Orion narrowed his eyes.

A shudder rolled down my spine as they glared at me like I was dirt beneath their boots.

For a second, my shoulders slumped low, and I curled in on myself, fingers trembling around the pipe that was tucked into the waistband of my pants.

Scorpius's laugh was cruel. "Pathetic. Pretty boy isn't going to last a day."

Shame burned hot through my chest, but the oppressive heat kindled into rage and reminded me just who the fuck I was.

My monster screamed.

I'd faced down pompous elite fae men who made small talk at palace balls about the price of my virginity, joked about the tightness of my cunt, and asked Mother what methods she used to control me.

Their vitriol meant nothing to me.

They had no idea the war crimes I'd committed against my own *mother*; they had no idea my capacity for violence.

I straightened my shoulders and refused to cow. *Someday they'd see.*

For sun god's sake, I had a literal monster inside me, and I didn't even know what species I was.

"WHORE" was marked on my flesh for all of eternity.

They should be afraid of *me*.

Plus, even though I didn't want to rule, I was still the technical fucking queen of the fae realm, and they were fae men.

My subordinates.

Barely fit to lick my feet.

I relaxed the tension from my forehead and let my blue eyes reflect the depth of my indifference.

"I'll look wherever I want to look." The corners of my lips pulled into the tight smile Mother had perfected, the one she'd worn when I writhed on the floor and begged for mercy.

"Oh, really?" Corvus's silver eyes sharpened into steel, and his red flames burned so hot that I could feel the heat across my skin.

My stomach rolled, and it took every ounce of willpower I possessed not to avert my eyes.

I fucking hated flames.

Scorpius leaned forward, and the lifelike eye tattooed on his flesh seemed to stare through me. "How cute. The little pampered pretty boy thinks he wants to fight the big dogs. Positively inspiring."

My fingernails dug into the table. I'd show him pampered.

"Don't," Orion said softly, long, delicate fingers grabbing Scorpius's shoulders, stopping the blind man as he lunged across the table like he was going to hurt me.

"No. I think he should." Corvus smiled with malice, and his teeth were startlingly white against his darkly tanned skin.

Scorpius mocked. "But he wants it so badly."

I rolled my eyes and donned my mask of indifference. "Great point. I really do." My words dripped with sarcasm.

Arms relaxed, face dead of all emotion, I lounged back in my chair like I didn't have a care in the world as I slowly inspected the other men at the table.

Just another pampered motherfucker with a dick.

If I didn't treat the three fae like they scared me, then eventually they'd stop thinking I was weaker than them.

It was all about the long game.

However, inspecting the rest of the table wasn't reassuring.

If I weren't pretending to be blasé, I might have frowned at the black veins that crawled down the cheeks of two of the other men next to me.

Might have wondered why the man beside them had long orange hair like Lothaire and pale skin that looked translucent.

Might have thought it odd that the man in the middle of the table looked completely normal. He was built large, but his features were boyish, and there was nothing unique about him.

At a table full of supernatural freaks, being completely plain was somehow weirder than having an interesting physical characteristic.

But it didn't matter what creatures the men were; their body language made it clear I was not welcome among them.

The three fae weren't the only ones radiating hostility.

Waves of vitriol were directed my way.

Fine with me. The last thing I wanted to do was train to be an assassin. Truthfully, I didn't want to be anything anymore.

Aspired to nothing.

I just wanted to sleep until I felt okay.

That was the funny thing about trauma: it didn't need time to strip you of your personality and plunge you into darkness.

It worked quickly.

Mercilessly.

Didn't care that you'd spent years cultivating your sense of self and acting a certain way and didn't give a flying fuck about who you were or what you wanted out of life.

It ripped you apart and left nothing.

I was jagged shards of what had once been whole.

My nails dragged across the table's veneer as I avoided the death glares Corvus and Scorpius were still sending my way.

Orion was whispering quietly in their ears, and it sounded like he was pleading with his brothers not to cause a scene.

Scorpius sneered something about "pampered," and Corvus swore, "—disgustingly fucking pretty, it's embarrassing."

Why are they so obsessed with me?

Sadie would have loved the drama, and throat punched someone already.

Fuck. I'd take a throat punch for five more seconds with her.

My therapist warned me that I was too dependent on Sadie's friendship. She'd said it wasn't healthy to sleep in my best friend's bed each night and strangle her with my love, because she wouldn't always be there to chase away the nightmares.

Well, look at me now. I was all alone.

My therapist would love this shit and probably make a

note on her clipboard, "Aran is fucked," while bragging to her colleagues that she'd been right.

Before I could sink too deeply into my pity party, Lothaire loomed over the table with his singular eye flashing as he stared down at me.

"We begin now. Follow me."

Lovely. Not even enough time to panic appropriately.

The men stood up immediately like they were eager to please their master. Did they know he was nothing more than my mother's man-whore?

I took my time standing because I'd never been one to kowtow to authority figures, aka I had mommy issues. But it was more fun to just pretend I had a rebellious spirit.

As if the universe was mocking my false bravado, my stomach plummeted yet again.

Because the tallest man at the table, Corvus, towered at about seven feet tall.

He was a monster.

Plus, the rest of the men weren't much shorter than him. Orion was by far the smallest, but he was about six feet four, so that wasn't saying much.

Since I was just shy of six feet tall, I wasn't used to craning my neck to look up at people.

Now my spine ached from the strain of trying to look into the eyes of men I was barely chest height with.

Corvus's buzzed head and chiseled features lorded over everyone else.

What did he eat to get so large?

It wasn't natural.

I swallowed thickly as I pushed my shoulders back and discreetly elevated onto my tiptoes as I followed the men out of the room, into the hall.

Each step away from the great hall seemed like a step away from hope.

Lothaire stalked quickly down the dark halls, and the seven men sauntered behind him.

They should have lumbered, but each man moved with the smooth grace of a warrior and glided silently across the black marble floors.

Killers on the prowl.

One of the men who had black veins trailing down his face walked up beside me.

"You're gonna be dead in an hour," he said casually, like he was trying to make small talk.

I took a drag of my pipe. "One could hope."

Laughter burst from his mouth, and he showcased pointed black teeth as he stared at me. "Are you joking?"

"No." I exhaled calm.

"I respect that." He paused like he was thinking about something intense, and after a long moment, he nodded like he'd made a decision. "My name's Vegar. I'm a demon."

I tripped and barely caught myself from slamming into the wall as it lit with lightning.

What an exhilarating way to go.

Electric.

"Aran, water fae." I gave him a mock salute and tried to act like him being a demon wasn't terrifying as shit.

At this point I didn't want to be alone in an alley with anyone in the assassin program.

Vegar smiled, and his pointy teeth gleamed in the hall's shadows.

Demons were rumored to be evil creatures that fed on the pain and misery of others. Basically, they were the elite fae I'd grown up with.

Vegar reached forward, but instead of shaking my hand, he slammed his meaty palm across my back.

I swallowed down a scream as the wound on my back burned like it had been doused in kerosene.

He smiled as I grimaced back at him. Had he meant to break my spine?

A few hours ago, I would have worried about my monster losing its shit at Vegar's aggressive action, but it had gotten progressively quieter after I'd impaled my hand on the dagger.

A small blessing.

Maybe I need to start stabbing myself to control my monster?

Food for thought.

Abruptly, the other man who had black veins under his eyes pushed to stand between us.

While Vegar was dark-skinned with dark features, this man had blond hair and blue eyes. If it weren't for the black veins crawling down his face, I wouldn't have known they were the same race.

But I knew better.

He was another demon, and he was glaring at me like he wanted me dead.

Get in line.

ASSASSIN DIVISION: THE BREAKING PERIOD

In stormy seas and a lightning hall,
I break their limbs and make them crawl,
For only the shattered can face the gray,
Stare straight at evil and bow to pray.

—Lothaire

CHAPTER 5
WELCOME TO TORTURE

The breaking period: Day 1, hour 3

"Don't talk to him. He's going to be dead in an hour," snarled the new demon at Vegar.

I'd have been worried about yet another threat to my bodily health if I had any health left to worry about.

"No way. You really think so?" I asked with feigned shock.

"It's fine, Zenith." Vegar slapped the other demon on the back (that must have been his thing), then dragged him forward and kissed his lips. "Aran already knows he's going to die."

Wow, power couple alert.

Black veins expanded on Zenith's face until his skin looked like a patchwork of black ink as they made out vigorously.

A lot of tongue was involved.

Did the veins expand because he was horny or because he was angry?

Zenith pulled away from eating Vegar's face to yell at

him, "You already know his name? Did you give him yours, you motherfucking idiot? We've talked about this."

Suddenly, the demon whirled on me with his lips curled back like he was going to rip out my throat with his pointy teeth.

As a competent woman with analytical abilities, I recognized my chance of surviving the next five seconds was less than 10 percent.

Do it. Rip out my throat.

Clearly, I had no control over my intrusive thoughts.

"Wait, is his name not John?" I narrowed my eyes with pretend confusion.

Before Zenith could break my femur and beat me with it, the boyish-looking man who was plain compared to everyone else turned around abruptly.

"Did someone say my name?"

I rolled my eyes and sucked on my pipe. "You would be named John."

Vegar choked on another laugh.

John narrowed his dark eyes with confusion as he looked at the two demons and said, "I don't want any more of last year's shit happening this year. We settled it on the battlefield, and I expect you two to respect that. If I suffer a single nightmare, I will be blowing your shit up. You hear me?"

Zenith rolled his blue eyes, the veins retreating so his olive skin was once again visible, as he said, "I don't break my promises like a human. We settled it."

John smiled, his wavy brown hair bouncing around his ears. "That's really great to hear."

I chose to ignore the comment about a battlefield because ignorance was bliss and reeled over the fact that the dude was a *human*.

How the fuck was a human at Elite Academy, let alone a recruit in the assassin division?

Everyone knew humans were the most fucked-up race as a whole, but individually they were powerless and weak.

"You're a human?"

John nodded. "And what are you? A Smurf?" He gestured to my bright-blue hair.

It was cut short, but my curls were an unruly mass.

"I'm a fae," I huffed, wondering if a Smurf was something terrifying like a demon.

I prided myself on knowing a lot about other races, and my chest pinched with worry. How was it possible a human knew about a race that I didn't?

"I've read about the fae. Sexy, with wings, right?" John flapped his arms like they were wings.

Vegar laughed again, and Zenith tugged him down the hall while muttering something about incompetent humans and pathetic fae.

"No to both. Sadly," I said dryly. "And let me guess: you're a weak human with no moral compass and no abilities?"

John missed the sarcasm in my voice because he fell into step beside me and grinned at me like we were besties. "Sounds about right. But I've actually got some wicked powers."

Of course he had dimples.

I grimaced at his cheery demeanor because happy people always freaked me out.

John smiled like he'd never been through anything difficult in life, which was *not* relatable.

"Oh," I said and shuffled away from him, trying to create distance between us.

I preferred my friends with dry sarcasm and inappropriate humor, not whatever the fuck positive energy was radiating off John.

No one interacted with humans for a reason.

They were soulless.

John followed me across the hall like a puppy. "I'm so glad you were initiated this year. It's been three years since I joined, and it's been brutal being the new guy. Plus, everyone already has their cliques, and it's impossible to break in. We're going to be great friends, I can tell."

My brain stuttered as his words sank in. "Three years? How long has everyone been here?"

John beamed like he was talking about something mundane, not an assassin training camp that only lasted for six months like I'd been hoping.

He answered cheerfully, "The kings have been training the longest."

"Who?"

He gestured to the three fae who were sauntering in the front of the group like they were better than everyone else. "Corvus, Scorpius, and Orion."

I wrinkled my nose with disgust.

John shook his head. "No, seriously, they're really kings, and apparently they're a super big deal. Every woman and man in the academy wants to fuck them. They're legends."

I couldn't explain to John that technically I was the High Queen of the Fae Realm, so they couldn't be kings, so I swallowed my thoughts and watched them.

Every few steps, Corvus brushed his hand across Scorpius's shoulder to orient him, but other than that, you would never know from the way Scorpius navigated that he was blind.

It made sense that they called themselves kings.

They were the worst type of people in all the realms—men who knew they were hot.

"Are you sure they're kings?" I asked skeptically.

"One hundred percent. I've heard Lothaire call them kings. Rumor is they've been tasked to work with Lothaire on an important mission. Apparently the fate of realms depends on it. Super intense stuff that they don't just give to anyone."

I scrunched my nose in confusion. Maybe there was some other fae realm that had its own royalty? It seemed far-fetched, but there wasn't any other obvious answer.

"What's the task?"

John laughed like I was joking. "If I knew, they'd kill me immediately."

"Please." I rolled my eyes.

His expression darkened slightly as he thought about it.

"Wait, you're not joking?"

John shrugged. "No, I'm not. All I can tell you is that I've heard its somehow personal to Lothaire, and rumor is there are gods involved."

My jaw dropped. "Gods?"

What have I gotten myself into?

As we walked down the hall, the stained-glass window of a mother holding a baby shimmered red, and I realized it wasn't from the eclipse like I'd first thought.

The artist had portrayed both as covered in blood.

As I passed, the woman's sad eyes seemed to track me like she was calling me out for my masquerade. Somehow it felt like I'd disappointed her by hiding who I really was.

"You okay?" John narrowed his dark eyes at me, and I shook my head to clear my thoughts.

"So how long have the kings been training?" I asked

hastily so I didn't have to explain why I'd been staring at a portrait of a mother with sadness.

John grimaced, and his answer was not what I was expecting.

"It's weird because they're insanely talented, and Lothaire always talks about how they're the perfect soldiers, but they've been training for ten years. Rumor is Lothaire's searching the realms, looking for someone, and they're waiting here in the meantime. But no one knows why."

Ten years.

My back started to itch unmercifully, and panic tightened my chest.

Ten years was significantly longer than my life expectancy.

John must have seen the terror on my face, because his beaming smile returned, and he punched me on the bicep.

I lost feeling in the limb.

John might be a human with a heinous personality, but he was still a little under seven feet tall and covered in muscles.

I massaged my arm and whimpered.

John smiled and pretended he hadn't just attacked me. "Don't worry. I actually haven't been the new guy this entire time. We've had about four other people qualify in the last three years."

I narrowed my eyes.

He continued cheerfully, "They all died within the first week, so they didn't really count as new guys. You know."

No. I didn't know.

I stopped walking, lips frozen in an *O*. *How was that supposed to make me not worry?*

The demons hadn't been joking.

Neither had Corvus and Scorpius.

They *really* thought I was going to be dead in an hour.

I started counting odd numbers backward from one hundred as I forced myself to walk forward down the hall.

Ninety-seven.

Two horrifying demons looked over their shoulders back at me.

Ninety-five.

Three alleged fae kings (maybe I was being a stuck up queen, but I wasn't convinced they were really kings) swaggered ahead, pure power and malice dripping off them.

We followed Lothaire, a terrifying vampyre of lore, down a long hall that dripped with chandeliers and housed priceless mosaics. Lightning cracked and shimmered.

A human walked beside *me*, the Queen of the Fae.

At this rate, I didn't want to meet the last eerily pale man in the group that I was 99 percent sure from his coloring was a vampyre.

From the way he glared at everyone and walked by himself, he didn't want to meet me either.

Seven terrifying males training to be assassins.

The most powerful people in the *universe*, and I walked beside them.

A female masquerading as a male and a fae, with a monster in my head and a bounty on my heart.

There was no scenario where this ended well for me.

Ninety-three.

Lothaire flung open the heavy iron doors of the fortress.

Still air was replaced by a chilly wind that whipped my hair and frothed the dark ocean into a roar. Lothaire led us down the steep onyx path that was more rocks than steps.

Outside the fortress, the lunar eclipse crushed the stars and shed little warmth.

In another lifetime, Sadie would have said it was time to

panic, or some dumb statement like that, and cracked an inappropriate joke. I would have laughed with her and bemoaned the fact that we were so dead.

No one laughed.

Seven men grunted as they walked.

"Grow up. Is this how a queen acts? I'd kill you just to shut you up, and I wouldn't even take your throne," Jinx's twelve-year-old voice whispered in my mind.

Her scorn comforted me and halted my panic attack.

For some reason, it was impossible to spiral when a child was degrading your character.

After what felt like an eternity of climbing down jagged rocks, Lothaire stopped in front of a small steel structure on the edge of the rocky outcrop at the base of the fortress.

He led us inside.

The dingy shelter was empty except for eight cots that barely cleared the rocky ground. Matching black sweat suits were folded atop each one. Metal walls halted the wind, but the air was cold and biting inside.

That was it.

There were no blankets or pillows. No toiletries or necessities.

Not a single throw pillow or sparkly candle holder to bring life into the space. My feminine chakra trembled with horror.

It was an interior design war crime.

To make matters worse, a shoddy toilet sat behind a corner wall, which immediately presented a problem because my enchantment disguised my features and made them masculine, but it couldn't create what wasn't there.

I didn't have a dick.

Going to the bathroom was going to be a problem, and privacy wasn't the only issue.

Dirt caked every surface, and the lack of cleanliness made my stomach hurt.

My fingers curled with disgust.

I'd always liked pretty things, loved the bright colors and rich materials of finely made clothes and clean bedding.

Nothing about this was pretty.

The rickety structure shook as wind screamed against it, and waves roared as they slammed against the rocks and filled the air with salt.

Six men stared solemnly at Lothaire, muscles expanded, stances wide, and faces hard, like they were mentally preparing themselves.

In contrast, John beamed, cheeks pulled wide and dimples on display.

At least I now knew the stories were true…humans were dumb as fuck.

Lothaire gestured to the space that would be too generous to describe as a hut, then rubbed his hands with excitement. The air literally sparked with power around him.

"Welcome back to the assassins' barracks. You have three minutes to shit and make yourself at home. Then we begin training."

Lothaire snapped his fingers, and suddenly his business suit disappeared off his body.

Two things stunned me.

First, *who can shit on command?*

Second, it wasn't an enchantment that changed his appearance. Instead, the black air shimmered around him and moved like a tangible force as it reclothed him.

A black sweat suit appeared atop his bulging muscles.

War paint slashed across his high cheekbones and high-lighted the whiteness of his scar.

The singular long braid trailing down his back pulled apart. He had long, wavy hair that wasn't dissimilar from my own's texture. However, the hair rewove itself into hundreds of small, intricate braids that plaited themselves into a crown atop his head.

Sparks of power glittered around him.

I'd never seen an enchantment do anything like that— Lothaire was *insanely* powerful. How had we survived the gladiator stadium?

Lothaire had always been imposing, but before, he'd been a beast dressed in a business suit. A man of restrained power.

Now he shed the civility like a mask.

His singular eye glowed like it had been lit by the flames from the rumored hell realm.

The hairs on the back of my neck stood up.

A beast was before me.

Lothaire arched his eyebrow and parted his bloodred lips. Fangs flashed as he said, "I repeat, training begins now. Did I stutter, soldiers?"

"No, sir! Yes, sir!" seven voices chorused back as they clasped their hands behind their backs, parted their legs, and bowed their heads.

His eyes glowed as he stared at me with disgust. "Are you so fucking pampered, soldier, that you think you're better than me?"

Something told me if I answered yes, despite how hard it was to kill me, I wouldn't live to see tomorrow. "No."

"*Then why the fuck aren't you showing me respect?*" Lothaire bellowed with such force the barracks shook.

I bowed my head and tucked it low while mimicking the position of the other men. "Sorry, sir!" I shouted back like they had.

The wind screamed, and the ocean roared.

"You will be, soldier. Mark my words: you will be," Lothaire said, then he turned and stalked out of the barracks.

I believed him.

Suddenly chaos erupted as the men grabbed cots, stretched their muscles, and dropped to the ground, doing push-ups.

This was real.

This was really happening.

Why would someone do push-ups right now? Men were messed up. I could feel a migraine coming on.

I walked over to a cot and avoided doing unnecessary manual labor.

"What's your name?" Scorpius asked. His handsome pale face invaded my personal space as I looked over the clothes on the cot.

"Aran Egan," I replied automatically.

Scorpius's voice dripped with malice as he shoved me to the ground. "Well, Egan, a pretty boy like you isn't sleeping here."

He might be blind, but he had no trouble grabbing me and throwing me onto the rocks with so much force that my bones rattled.

Why are they so obsessed with how pretty I am? It was starting to become weird and not flattering.

How the fuck any girl at the academy was into him was beyond me. It didn't matter if he really was a king; he was a bastard of the worst sort.

Rocks dug into my skin as I scurried back to my feet.

"We warned your pampered ass how this would go," Corvus's deep voice rumbled as he slammed his massive foot through a cot in the far corner.

The cheap material ripped in two, leaving the cot useless.

Corvus's silver eyes flashed. "This is where you sleep. Just because you're used to a life of luxury doesn't mean you're going to get any special treatment around here."

I fucking hated being called pampered.

All I'd known was torture and war, but all the elite fae had told me I was a sniveling princess because I liked parties and nice things.

Everyone saw a pretty face and expensive garments and dismissed me as a simpering fool.

It made me homicidal.

To punctuate his ignorant statement, Corvus stomped again with his enormous foot. He mangled the cot beyond repair. Bold move on his part, because if my foot was that creepily large, I would *not* be drawing attention to it.

Corvus stomped one more time.

He was just another dumb, ignorant, judgmental, toxic male.

I'll show him just how pretty and privileged I can be when I eat his eyeballs from his head with a silver spoon. I growled with disgust.

At my sound of defiance, big-foot Corvus became absolutely feral.

His sharp cheekbones cast harsh shadows across his face, jaw pulled tight with rage, as he stalked toward me.

Seven and a half feet of pure muscle cornered me against the wall, and he looked down his nose at me like an arrogant king at a pauper.

Someday I'd make him lick the ground I walked on.

Corvus's skin was covered in growing red flames, and he fisted the front of my shirt.

"You're a new recruit. You will address us as King, sir, or

Your Highness, and you will do whatever the fuck we tell you to. This is *our* division, and you've given attitude to the wrong fucking people, pretty boy. We cane brats like you until they beg us on their knees."

He paused.

"And then we don't let them come."

His meaning penetrated, and I slapped my palms against his rock-hard chest. "Fuck off. Don't call me that."

The world warped and distorted, and for a split second, I was sixteen again at a ball. An elite fae trailed his eyes slowly down my body and said, "Yes, she's pretty enough to breed. Perhaps I'll buy her for myself."

He leaned forward, gross breath hot on my cheek as my stomach churned.

I'd stumbled away in horror, and Mother had apologized for my "embarrassing lack of decorum." The proper protocol was to thank an elite fae for the honor when he asked to breed you like cattle.

"Don't worry." The creepy man had smiled at Mother and said, "I'll break her in."

Harsh hands shook me back and forth, and the aggressive motion threw me out of the past and back into the present.

Corvus stilled, the harsh planes of his face rippling as he blinked slowly. Violence rolled off the psychotic bastard, and he snarled in my face like *I'd* done something to him. "*Never* touch me."

With one hand holding me off the ground, Corvus slammed me against the metal wall with such ferocity that searing pain stabbed across my wound.

If I weren't so busy swallowing down a scream, I might have found the irony of it all funny.

He let Scorpius and Orion touch him constantly. But now he was losing it? It made little sense.

Corvus had *his* hand tangled in my sweatshirt and was pummeling me, but he lost his shit when I lightly slapped his arm?

Fucking maniac. "Let me down," I growled and purposefully slapped his bicep again.

Corvus's eyes darkened, and he pulled back a flaming fist.

Kicking out desperately, I squinted and prepared for the worst.

Orion suddenly appeared beside Corvus and grabbed his fist. He didn't speak aloud but mouthed, "You said you wouldn't. He's pathetic and not worth your time. He's going to be dead soon anyway. We need to finish it this year. Remember the mission."

Orion's words made my chest twist with pain.

From his actions in the hall, I'd thought the pretty fae man didn't hate me like his two companions.

I'd been delusional.

Corvus snarled at me, "You're dead," then shoved me against the wall one last time before he stalked away.

Scorpius sneered something, but I was too busy trying not to pass out from the pain stabbing along my back.

I gasped for air shakily.

Before I could sink into a panic attack, John was smiling in my face. His twin dimples flashed. "I grabbed the cot next to you."

He gestured to the now-ruined bed and jumped up and down on the one next to it with excitement like we were having a sleepover.

I scowled.

John beamed.

The teenage girls back in the manor would have bullied him mercilessly. I wished Jinx was here to destroy his self-esteem. The upbeat energy was *not* it.

He patted my shoulders and prattled a hundred miles per hour. "Don't worry, the kings are good leaders, and they won't do anything to actually harm you."

I scoffed.

I *was* worried.

Also, apparently humans had the awareness of a rock.

John shrugged as he lay back on his cot, his large body hanging over the sides comically. "Honestly, the kings and the demons, who you already met, Vegar and Zenith, aren't too bad. Of all the men, it's Horace you need to worry about. He's a vampyre and Lothaire's nephew, so he gets away with murder. Literally."

John gestured to Horace, who was creepily pale with long red hair and still doing push-ups on the ground. His eyes glowed bright orange in the dim light, and his face was a cold mask.

I'd been right; he was yet another terrifying bloodsucker.

It also hadn't escaped my notice that Horace had laughed the hardest when Corvus had slammed me against the wall.

Bastard wouldn't be laughing when I stabbed him.

John kept prattling and giving unhelpful advice, blissfully unaware of my deteriorating mental state.

"The key is to not think too deeply about anything. Or to worry about pain, because Lyla will heal you. Just try not to get sucked out to sea or take a dagger through the heart. It's all about fighting through the pain."

John might not have to worry about thinking, but some of us were chronic thinkers.

The more John prattled, the harder it was to breathe.

I'd trained for war in the shifter realm and had fought against spiders larger than trees, yet it felt like I was woefully unprepared for whatever was about to happen.

Like I'd only been in village battles.

And this was a galactic war.

The big leagues.

John kept smiling and talking. Either he was aware I was having an extended panic attack and trying to distract me, or he was dumb. My money was on the latter.

"The whole principle of the assassin division is to put powerful people in awful situations until they break down to their lowest form. I thought it was stupid at first, but it actually works. If you survive, you'll learn to harness your abilities like you've never thought possible. You'll be unstoppable. It's worth it, trust me."

If survival came down to dying or trusting John—I couldn't emphasize enough—I'd gladly end my life.

Lothaire bellowed from somewhere outside the hut, "Let's go, soldiers!"

Everyone burst into action.

I stood frozen.

John grabbed my shoulders and pulled me forward out of the barracks as he yelled over the chaos, "You just have to trust the process!"

The red eclipse tainted the chilly air with an ominous glow as Lothaire pointed to the frothing ocean and smiled.

"Trust the process!" John screamed over the wind as he dragged me forward with the group and down the rocky shore.

We plunged into the freezing waves.

I didn't need to understand battle analytics to comprehend what was happening as John dragged me out to sea.

Salty waves slammed me down against jagged rocks as the noxious scent of pungent sulfur filled my nose.

Frigid water slapped my flesh.

It was obvious: I, Arabella Elis Egan, rightful ruler of the seat of death and wanted monarch of the fae realm, was absolutely fucked.

CHAPTER 6
DROWNING IN HELL

The breaking period: Day 1, hour 12

Cold was worse than death.

How had I ever been afraid of fire? It was warm, cozy, and comfortable.

Ice was agony.

It was torture.

Cruelty.

Death.

A frigid wave crushed atop us and slammed our bodies against the jagged, rocky sea floor. Little pebbles tossed in the churning sea and pelted me like miniature grenades.

They were tiny little rocks and should have just been a nuisance.

After hours at sea, they were my worst enemy.

John's arm interlocked with mine, and his tight grip was the only thing that stopped me from being sucked out into the malignant abyss. He was the only thing stopping the water from drowning my lungs and shocking me into stillness.

The seven of us stood waist-deep in the water with our

arms twined together as yet another freezing wave crashed atop us.

Lothaire screamed expletives at us, his imposing presence shrouded in a red haze as he stood atop the rocky shore and frowned down at us.

Rocks pelted.

My feet slipped over the jagged edges, and the pinch of split skin was followed by a burning sting as salt and pebbles dragged across my wounds.

I dug my fingernails into John's forearm and fought to keep my eyes open.

My heart pounded.

The chill locked my muscles, and my heart slowed as I fought the urge to close my eyes and let the water wash away my problems. It wrapped around me like a heavy blanket and offered to solve everything.

All I had to do was let go.

"Stay awake!" My arm was wrenched in its socket as John shook me vigorously.

His actions made my brain rattle in my head and chased away the invading fog.

"I'm up. I'm up," I said before I hastily sucked in air and held my breath as a wave slammed me backward, then pummeled me down.

"You better be," John mumbled as he wrenched me up out of the breaking sea with so much force that my numb limb screamed with pain.

Salt water burned as I blew it out of my nose, and I answered by digging my short fingernails harder into his arm.

Blood dripped from John's nail-gouged forearm and tracked down my pale hand.

It mingled between us, a symbol of our shared suffering.

When we'd first gotten into the water, Corvus had sneered, "Pampered pretty boy goes on the end."

No one had moved.

"That's you, Egan. Fucking move. Or I'll make you."

It seemed wrong that someone so tall and attractive could be so cruel.

I'd locked arms with John at the end of the line and refused to look back at the flaming fucker.

Corvus had decided who I was. I wasn't going to waste my breath trying to correct him. Even though Orion, the quiet man who stood beside him and stared at me with stunning brown eyes, was way prettier than me. Even when I was a girl.

But Corvus didn't taunt him and call him pretty.

The sea shoved her water down my throat, and the choking pulled me out of my musings. I had bigger problems than handsome fae men.

The ocean was a cruel mistress.

The wind screamed like it was dying as the eight of us heaved and hacked.

For the first time since I'd arrived at the academy, no one postured for dominance.

Nature was the great equalizer.

We struggled to endure.

In the beginning, I'd expected Corvus to stand in the middle of the chain of bodies, where it was safest. But he stood at the other end so he was exposed like I was.

His one arm was locked with Scorpius's, who held on to Orion. Next, Horace was linked with Orion, and the two demons were hooked together, with Vegar next to John.

"You got this," John grunted over the wind.

In ten hours, I'd learned everything I'd thought I knew about the human species was clearly a lie.

How had I ever thought humans were weak?

John's strength was the only thing that held me up and kept me going. He was firm and solid and never once complained.

But the smiley man who bounced on the cot and grinned at me was gone. His dimples were a memory.

John's dark features were tight with concentration, and the boyish planes of his face were hardened into something harsh and menacing.

He was a different creature.

And we suffered. Together.

John never complained about my nails or even glanced at his blood. I'd only known him for a few hours, but I felt like I *knew* him.

His chirpy demeanor and harsh concentration reminded me of Sadie.

In the crashing waves and shrieking wind and the endless fight against an indomitable force, I knew that John was going to be my close friend.

Lothaire screamed, "Aran, stand the fuck up! If you fall down one more time, you're going into the sensory deprivation tank."

"Yes, sir!" I shouted back as I lost my footing once again and choked on salty water.

Lothaire held a black baton in his hand and slammed it across your face if you didn't reply with a "yes, sir" immediately after he spoke to you.

I'd learned the hard way.

In the first five minutes in the ocean, Lothaire had shouted an order at me, and I hadn't responded.

Now my right eye was swollen shut from the force of a baton bludgeoning it.

I never forgot to respond after that.

In the present, Lothaire screamed something, and the veins on his forehead bulged with rage, but I couldn't hear him over the crashing of the waves.

"Yes, sir!" I gurgled back instinctively.

For the first few hours, I'd been furious at Lothaire.

This wasn't training.

This was torture.

After three hours, my teeth had chattered with such ferocity that I'd thought my jaw was going to break and my anger had drained into self-pity.

At six hours, the cuts on my feet and legs had burned unmercifully as salt and stones had ripped the wounds wider.

My sweatpants had been shredded with tears, and the sopping material did nothing to stop the cold.

Everything hurt.

Now, ten hours later, I couldn't feel my limbs, and my thoughts were scattered. I couldn't concentrate on anything.

Did we just get into the ocean? Or have I been here for hours?

Everything was a jumble of pain, pebbles, blood, water, choking, and ramming against unmercifully jagged rocks.

I trembled uncontrollably. We were both standing in the same ocean, but John's skin burned hot compared to my icy skin.

If I had any ability to do anything other than suffer, I might have deduced it was because I was so much smaller than the rest of the men. Half my width a mirage created by my enchanted disguise.

They had hundreds of pounds of muscle on me. More than they even knew.

And the ocean was merciless.

She didn't care that you were exhausted and hurting. Didn't give a fuck what you wanted or how badly it hurt.

The wind screamed endlessly, and the surf crashed across the rocks in an unending parade.

A circle of misery.

An inferno of abuse.

Another wave slammed me down, and my arm wrenched at an impossible angle as John's punishing grip just barely stopped me from disappearing into the savage ocean.

Pebbles slapped my face.

The waves pulled away from us, water draining down to our knees, as it gathered into another wave.

Lips trembling, my teeth chattered so hard that my head hurt.

Lothaire walked back and forth on the dry shore in front of us as he smacked his baton in his hand and shouted, "You will *never* be strong enough. You will *never* have enough control. You will *never* master yourself unless you know true suffering."

A wall of ice plunged me face-first into water. My nose and mouth filled with it, and I struggled in a disoriented panic.

Finally, I inhaled sulfur-stained air as I gagged on salt water.

Lothaire's single eye glowed as his voice mixed with the howling wind. "You will *never* be anything more than a slave to your impulses, if you don't know how to *withstand the pain*."

The waves never stopped coming.

In the red haze of an eternal eclipse, Lothaire's pale skin shimmered eerily. Sparks lit the air around him like his power didn't want to be contained.

Please, sun god. Please end my misery.

I tracked every movement Lothaire made as I waited for

him to yell that our time in the ocean was over and we could get out and get dry.

I was obsessive.

But no matter how closely I tracked him with my eyes and pleaded in my head, he never said the words.

The pain made me light-headed, and I lost the will to hack up water—lost the energy to fight against the crushing surf.

Sleepiness returned.

Lothaire continued to shout, "You will *never* amount to anything if you don't learn how to survive on nothing but sheer willpower!"

I kept drowning.

Lothaire kept talking. "As most of you know, the Black Ocean contains high amounts of sulfuryl chloride, a rare chemical compound that degrades all sentient creatures at a cellular level."

Another wave rammed into me.

That explained the harsh sulfur scent.

Lothaire smiled like he had a secret and said, "This is the only ocean in all the realms that is known to weaken everyone. In other words, the toxic compound nullifies powers."

John leaned forward as an undercurrent slammed against our shins.

Arm ripping out of my socket, nails in his muscles, I leaned forward with him and screamed into the wind. The eight of us fought against the pull.

Lothaire paced. "In the Black Ocean, you are as weak as you will ever be!" His single eye twitched maniacally.

This was worse than a nightmare because even at my lowest, my imagination couldn't conjure up this torment.

Lothaire smiled, and his opal fangs gleamed. "This is the

greatest honor any person in all the realms could hope to experience!"

I would have laughed if my jaw weren't chattering violently from the cold.

"You get to exist in your lowest form. Now you know what it's like to be a rock on the ocean's edge."

He paused dramatically. "You know what it's like to be *nothing*!"

Lothaire's voice mixed with the shrieking wind. "Only those who have known what it is to be *nothing* can ever rise to be *something*!"

Shut the fuck up and let us out! I screamed at him in my mind.

The world spun around me.

If my heart weren't slowing further as my muscles atrophied and bones locked, I might have been inspired.

I wasn't.

Please let us out of this water. Sun god, I'll do anything for you.

I would never again take a warm shower for granted.

As another wave crashed over my head and pulled me under, a cold, wriggling animal slammed against my skin.

I was too cold to be disgusted.

Too tired to care.

I stared at Lothaire, begging him to end the torture.

Any second now, he'd tell us to get out.

It would be over soon; I just needed to hang in a little longer.

Any second.

One. Two. Three.

Time trickled by.

Endless moments expanded exponentially.

Five hundred and one. Five hundred and two.

We kept drowning.

One thousand and forty-two. One thousand and forty-three.

I lived lifetimes in the Black Ocean.

Eventually I stopped counting because it wasn't helping.

Five miserable fucking hours later, Lothaire shouted, "Your special time in the Black Ocean is over. Get out. Now."

Get out?

A couple of hours earlier, I might have found the strength to crawl out of the freezing waves with dignity.

But that was *before.*

Before I'd lost count.

Before I'd lost hope.

Before I'd stopped feeling anything.

Limbs tingling, lungs hacking, I barely registered that the men were walking forward.

They had let go of one another and were climbing up the rocky shore.

They can walk?

They barely shivered as they stalked out of the frothing waves.

They looked like gods of the sea.

Competent.

Strong.

Tremors rocked my frame as I coughed up salt water and fell to my knees. I'd just take a quick nap.

John dragged me out of the ocean. "Stand up, Aran. Be strong." Ocean water dribbled out of his mouth as he glared down at me.

His grip was merciless, and I was grateful.

I tried to nod up at my new friend, but that was too much effort. Teeth chattering and body shaking in uncontrollable spasms, I struggled to crawl as he dragged me out of the surf.

The movement rattled my frigid bones. The negative temperatures in the shifter realm were nothing compared to *this*.

Sopping clothes clung to me, and the icy water trailed over me like shards of glass.

I stopped pretending like I was helping. With one hand wrapped around my arm, John followed the rest of the men and dragged my limp body up onto the jagged, rocky shore.

The once-chilly air was now unnaturally warm, a sharp contrast to the frozen ocean.

But it didn't bring any relief. The warm air made my wet clothes seem colder.

I convulsed as John dragged me, my eyes fluttering as all six hundred of my muscles cramped at the same time.

It was almost funny.

The endless cuts on my feet and legs left a sticky red trail across the black-and-gray rock beach.

"Stand up." John grunted as he shoved me to my shaky feet. The bank of the rock beach sloped upward at an angle too steep for John to drag me up.

"I g-g-g-got it." I vomited seawater all over myself and groaned with disgust. I hated throwing up.

Just climb.

I collapsed on all fours and pulled myself up the rocks.

John sighed down at me as he staggered and slipped on his bloody feet. "I guess that works."

A few yards in front of us, Corvus had each of his arms wrapped around Scorpius's and Orion's waists. He walked with power as he used insane strength to hold up two very large men.

Behind them, the two demons and Horace weaved and stumbled like they were drunk.

I kept crawling.

The thought of a warm shower was the only thing that kept me moving.

We were probably a hundred yards from the barracks, but it might as well have been a hundred miles.

A hundred years.

It's all just made-up measurements anyway. Does anything really exist? How can I be alive in this moment and now the next? The past is gone like it didn't exist. Was I ever even in the water?

I'd reached a new level of suffering; I was having an existential crisis.

If nothing exists, then nothing matters, but if everything exists, then must everything matter?

Bloody hands and knees moved forward. One after the other.

So many realms in the universe. So many planets and galaxies. But where is the universe located? How can so much just exist in the vacuum of space? Space cannot be nothing if there is so much life within it.

But where does it come from?

Where are we?

What are we?

How could life be a good thing if there is so much suffering?

I startled as John tripped and crashed to the rocks beside me. He heaved, and his arms shook as he pushed himself back to his feet and kept stumbling forward.

Hand forward. Knee forward. Hand forward. Knee forward.

If I could cry, I would have.

You will never know the secrets of the universe. You will always be a puppet in a shadowland of pain.

A sharp rock sliced my palm, and I was overwhelmed by the sudden urge to beg someone to carry me to warmth. I wanted someone to save me.

No one ever came.

Sadie was the only person who'd ever truly been there for me. Now she was realms away with no clue where I was or what I was going through.

"Pick up your feet and fucking walk." John's hand tangled in my short hair, and he roughly pulled me upward. "Get up before Lothaire looks back or he'll destroy you."

Vomit dribbled down my chin as my stomach rebelled against my movements. But I pushed myself up onto shaking legs and half shuffled, half fell forward.

John wrapped his arm around my shoulder and stopped me from face-planting.

I wrapped my arm around his waist, his heavy weight collapsed against me, and my organs burned inside me like they were exploding.

For a second, we stood still and heaved.

Our embrace was the only thing that kept us standing.

Slowly we stumbled forward.

The friendly human might have become an angry bastard, but he was the only reason I was surviving.

Without him, I would have been sucked out to sea.

I had no doubt the three kings, two demons, and vampyre would have gladly let me drown. Released my arm and watched me disappear into the waves with smiles on their faces.

It didn't matter that I'd survived hundreds of bullet wounds in the beast realm, war in the shifter realm, and torture in the fae realm.

When you were immortal, it was easy to joke about death.

If the Black Ocean weakened a person's abilities, then I wasn't immortal in the water. A creature would have eventually eaten my body and torn my heart to shreds.

A giant sea creature ruling on the seat of death.

I am the new fae queen, said the killer octopus to the elite fae.

Manic laughter bubbled up my throat.

We tripped, and John groaned, "Don't laugh."

"B-B-But g-g-iant octopus-s-s."

The glare he gave me would have withered a lesser man.

The moon's rays cast John in a spooky haze as we leaned against each other and kept stumbling one step at a time.

I wasn't attracted to John, but I recognized that he was impressive.

It was obvious why he was the last person who'd survived the training program. Why he'd lived when four others had died.

The human was much more than he seemed.

"Almost there," John groaned. The barracks was only five feet away.

I was nauseous with relief.

Warm shower. Warm cot. Warm clothes. Warm. Warm. Warm.

But then the unthinkable happened.

Lothaire didn't stop. He kept walking past the barracks, toward the rock steps that led to the fortress.

He walked away from the broken cot that was waiting for me.

My knees gave out.

"Fucking stand up," John groaned in pain, and I locked my knees together before we both tipped over.

"It's time for class," Lothaire said casually, not bothering to turn around and look at the people he'd just tortured for hours.

There was so much further to go.

I couldn't do it.

John leaned into my face with wide, manic eyes and

gritted teeth. He slapped my cheek with a bloody palm and growled like an animal.

"You will walk with me up to that motherfucking fortress. Or you will die pathetic and weak, just like the others."

"Good. I want to die," I snapped back.

"I guess the kings were right. You really are just another pampered little boy."

I answered instinctively, "I'm not a boy."

"Then be a man," John grunted as he took a shaky step forward.

I moved with him and whispered under my breath, "I'd rather not."

If he heard me, John didn't comment.

As we took painful step after painful step, in my head, I chanted, *Arabella Egan. Princess. Queen. Rightful ruler of the seat of death. Woman.* I refused to forget who I really was.

We made it up the steps to the fortress.

Together.

Neither of us would have made it without the other.

CHAPTER 7

A CLASS OF SIN

The breaking period: Day 1, hour 18

Before, I was depressed.

Now I was catatonically slumped over a desk.

Lothaire had informed us with a sneer that we would attend battle strategies class with the normal students, who weren't being tortured to death.

A humbling reminder that my life sucked worse than others.

It was a fact of life that some people were blessed and not stressed. I hoped all those people got gonorrhea.

Yes, I was wallowing in despair.

All eight of us assassin recruits sat together in the back of the small classroom. About a dozen royals filled the seats in front of us.

While we were barely surviving, the other students seemed to be thriving. All the royal students had changed into tailored purple clothes.

The men wore black pants and dark-purple button-downs, and the women wore fitted purple dresses with black stilettos. They were elegant and polished with perfectly coiffed hair and expertly applied makeup.

We were the only ones suffering in black sweat suits.

One of the few things I'd always enjoyed in life was getting dressed up in fine clothes. Nothing felt better than a tailored fit and combed hair.

In comparison, I looked like a drowned rat.

But I struggled to care about my shitty appearance because it all seemed so superficial and pointless.

The bottoms of my pants were still torn to pieces, and I was caked in dried blood, bare toes curled on the black marble floor.

I was still waiting for someone to give me shoes.

As I raked my hand through my mess of wet curls, another tremor racked my frame.

Teeth gnashed with ferocity, I struggled to keep the enchanted pipe between my lips.

The sun god must not have completely abandoned me because our sweatpants had zip pockets, and my two pipes had survived the ocean.

Bless the god for drugs.

The enchanted haze expanding my lungs and calming my thoughts was the only thing keeping me sane.

I shivered uncontrollably and sank into misery. My thoughts were obsessively fixated on one thing: warmth.

A hot fireplace.

A steamy shower.

Mother lighting me on fire each night.

At this rate, I'd take any of it just so the insufferable convulsing would stop.

The pen in my hand shook across the paper, and my usually perfect cursive handwriting was only partially legible as I wrote as fast as I could. I was barely conscious of what I was putting on the paper.

The assignment was to write an essay about the best way to beat an opponent.

A ridiculous question.

It was so open-ended there was no way to answer it without any context.

But our teacher Ms. Gola had just repeated the ridiculous prompt and told us we had an hour to answer.

At first, I grumbled under my breath as I attempted to answer the impossible.

It didn't help that cold water dripped off my hair, left blotchy marks on my paper, and ruined my barely legible words.

Then I just stopped giving a shit.

And from what I could tell, the rest of the assassins weren't faring any better.

John sat next to me at the two-person desk, and his page was even worse than mine. It was covered in holes. He kept accidentally stabbing the pen through wet spots.

"Pens down," Ms. Gola said abruptly, and she walked around collecting papers.

Just like the royal students, our teacher wore a perfectly tailored dress. She glided around the room on stiletto heels, and her bright-blonde hair hung in artful waves around her red-lipsticked face.

Ms. Gola was stunning.

As she moved down the aisle and took my paper, I stared up at her, slightly entranced by her otherworldly beauty. *How does she get her hair so shiny?*

"Aran Egan, isn't it?" she asked as she took my paper.

I nodded, too tired to do anything else.

Her skin shimmered like she was dipped in golden oil, a

sharp contrast to my own pale complexion that had turned an unattractive shade of blue from the cold.

She was dry and clean.

Not relatable.

Ms. Gola leaned closer, and a delicious musky scent wafted off her.

"I always make a point of getting to know the assassin recruits. You guys are my favorite, after all." She winked a kohl-lined eye at me as she sashayed past, her ridiculously plump backside swaying.

Sun god, how many squats did she do to get thighs and an ass like that? Sadie would be so jealous.

Then I realized Ms. Gola had just sexually winked at me. Her student.

I couldn't tell if I felt violated or flattered. It was close.

Ms. Gola walked past my table and said, "Corvus Malum, Scorpius, Orion, I hope you enjoyed your break." She spoke in a sultry whisper as she leaned unnecessarily close to collect their papers. "Or should I say sirs?"

First, wow, this woman was impressively horny.

Second, apparently Corvus was the only one with a last name.

Malum. I rolled it over in my brain. Mal *is a root word that means evil.*

Yep. He was definitely a Malum.

Corvus Malum raked a tanned hand over his shaved head, and the harsh planes on his handsome face pulled tight as he smirked up at her. "Corvus is not fine. This year, you'll continue to call me sir."

I shivered at the deep rasp of his voice. The low octaves should have been scratchy in their resonance, but somehow they were smooth like honey. Creamy.

Gently, I reared back. Then I violently stabbed my pen into my hand.

"What the fuck?" John whispered as he looked at my now-bleeding palm like I was a freak.

I mimed strangling myself. John just rolled his eyes and shook his head like he was used to sitting next to lunatics in class.

What was I supposed to do? Tell him that I thought Malum's voice was *creamy*?

Even thinking the word again made me homicidal.

I needed to die. Quickly.

Malum's shaved head erupted with flames and distracted me from my rapidly deteriorating mental state.

I leaned across the aisle, trying to get closer to the warmth.

He shifted away from Ms. Gola, and I casually scooted my chair closer to him.

Scorpius and Orion sat beside Malum at the only three-person desk in the room.

The blind fae's voice dripped with scorn as he addressed our teacher, "You will also refer to me as sir."

"Of course, sir," Ms. Gola said breathlessly as she leaned across their table to grab his paper. "I didn't forget."

Why did our teacher sound like she'd just ran up a flight of stairs?

Weak-lunged bitch.

Unlike Malum, Scorpius didn't pull away from Ms. Gola's advances. His pale face was completely still, white teeth flashing as he chewed gum.

As I studied him, I realized something horrible—there were no gods.

Because Scorpius's short black hair had survived seventeen hours in the violent ocean and was still slicked back, looking perfect.

I itched at the curls plastered to the back of my neck.

Ms. Gola leaned forward until her face was so close to Scorpius that their breaths mixed, her generously endowed body draped across the table.

Her face hovered inches from his unseeing eyes.

Like they were about to kiss.

"Creepy!" I shouted into my hand as I pretended to cough. John erupted into laughter beside me. Some royal students snickered, and I couldn't help but feel good about my contribution to the class.

However, Horace was not to be outdone, and he fake-coughed, "Penis." At that, every male in the classroom burst into laughter.

"Not funny," I mouthed to all the idiots who were howling like Horace had said something witty.

Why do men ruin everything?

Ms. Gola flushed beet red and pulled back while patting her hair like she needed a minute to compose herself.

What she needed was to learn how to stop being a pervert.

I'd give her Dr. Palmer's number. My therapist would destroy her creepy sexual confidence in five minutes.

However, it quickly became clear that she would probably need heavy medicating and a light round of torture to get her over her proclivities.

Ms. Gola turned to Orion and scolded him playfully as she took his paper, "I hope you'll actually participate in class this year, sir."

Orion lowered his eyes and slumped lower as pink tinted his golden cheeks. Just like Scorpius, his blonde hair hung in perfect waves around his shoulders, and his red lips were bee-stung like he'd applied moisturizer and not drowned for hours.

I picked a chunk of dead skin off my upper lip and grimaced when a pebble fell onto the desk.

Yep, there had been a *pebble* lodged inside my upper lip.

There went my dream of someday frolicking on a fae beach with a cigar in one hand and a large, enchanted glass of sparkly fae wine in the other while a thousand palace aides trailed behind in full ceremonial garb and told me how pretty and smart I was.

Ocean waves were definitely a new trigger to add to the list.

Another trigger was asshole fae men who looked ridiculously handsome after drowning. With their long legs stretched out casually, they seemed completely comfortable.

My teeth chattered so hard I bit my tongue and banged my knee against my desk.

Was there no mercy left in the world?

The only sign the kings had suffered was that their sweat suits were sopping wet and clung to their muscles like second skins.

"I expect you to speak up more this year," Ms. Gola purred again to Orion. His stunning chocolate-brown eyes lowered to the ground as his face turned bright red.

Beside him, Malum's shoulders straightened, and he threatened, "Orion will speak when he wants to speak."

His deep voice was rough with anger, and every hair on my arms stood up. *It's because you're cold*, I lied to myself.

Scorpius snapped his gum as he placed an arm across the back of Orion's chair.

Where had he gotten the gum?

Scorpius sneered, "Never speak to Orion like that again.

From now on, you will not address him unless he addresses you."

Ms. Gola paled as she nodded at the kings.

"Did I make myself clear?" Scorpius's impossibly sharp jaw clenched.

"Yes, sir," Ms. Gola said as she lowered her head in a bow. "Forgive me, Orion."

She turned away from the kings and hurried to collect the rest of the papers.

Scorpius went to stand up, but Orion put a hand on his shoulder and pushed him back into his seat.

"I told her not to address you." Scorpius's voice shook with rage.

"Let it go," Orion whispered.

Malum cracked his knuckles like he was debating beating the shit out of the teacher he'd just been flirting with and nodded like he'd come to a decision. "Leave it. We'll punish her later."

Scorpius snarled but snapped his jaw as he chewed his gum.

The entire scene was so bizarre it was like something out of a fae drama. The ones Mother had always said were "trashy and stupid" and featured "tacky fae."

Who was going to tell her that torturing people was tacky?

Me, that was who.

When she'd made me miss the series premiere because she was too busy ranting about me being powerless while lighting me on fire.

When Mother had finished barbecuing me with her blue flames that hurt but never left burn marks, I smuggled an enchanted screen under my covers.

Convulsing in the aftershocks of torture—with stiff

limbs and chattering teeth—I'd watched the premiere. When a glitzy fae woman flipped a table and crushed her rival, I laughed until I couldn't breathe.

Back in the present, I turned to John and asked the important question. "Are they fucking the teacher?"

"What do you think?" John's dimples flashed as he waggled his eyebrows. "She's smoking hot. I'd nail that."

Oh, right.

All men were perverts.

At least John's dark personality had thawed and the friendly, dimpled human was back. His dark eyes tracked Ms. Gola across the room like he was imagining her naked.

I gagged. "Wait, actually? How is that allowed?"

Thinking about John and the teacher made me sick. But for some reason, the wound on my back itched as I thought about the kings doing…things to Ms. Gola.

Another shiver racked my frame, and I grabbed my elbows, pressing my arms to my chest, desperate for warmth.

Malum's head flames were clearly pointless because they weren't strong enough to heat us at our table.

I'd have to let him know that he was useless.

John shrugged. "They're literal kings and very *dominant* men. I wouldn't mind being underneath them, if you know what I mean. Plus, the academy is very lenient about extracurricular activities." He winked.

I sucked harder on my pipe.

The kings' relationship was extremely close, and it seemed like that of lovers, not brothers. But fae were legendary for their archaic rules about relationships. Three men together was unheard of.

Then again, they didn't kiss and touch one another like the demons did.

It was confusing.

"You know what I mean?" John wiggled his eyebrows, and I remembered he'd been talking about their dominance in the bedroom.

"That's disgusting. I don't want to think about it," I lied as the wound on my back stung.

John laughed like I was being dumb. "Oh, Aran, you're so sheltered. I can't see you as the dominant one, so I think you'd like what the kings are selling."

"Excuse me? You're wrong." I flexed my bicep.

"You're telling me you'd want to be on top? Riding? Telling someone like Malum what to do?"

My face burned, and I knew my cheeks were bright red. "That's disgusting."

"Because a pretty boy like you is on the bottom. No shame. Even I can appreciate being taken care of sometimes." John winked suggestively.

"I would not be on the bottom!"

I realized my mistake when Malum scoffed loudly, "No, you wouldn't be on the bottom."

Scorpius sneered. "You'd be on your knees underneath us as we used you like a hole."

I choked on air and looked over to find the three kings staring at me. Orion was blushing, Scorpius was frowning, and a vein on Malum's forehead was throbbing like he was suffering an aneurysm.

John laughed like I wasn't being verbally assaulted and cut the tension by saying, "We're all adults here, after all. Plus, it's one of the best perks of the division. Everyone wants to fuck an assassin."

"Can we please stop talking about this?" I begged as I sucked on my pipe like it was a lifeline.

At this rate, smoking was not going to be enough and I'd

need to start snorting the enchantment. I made a mental note to research to find a dealer. There had to be *someone* in this place.

John's dimples flashed, and he playfully punched my arm like he wasn't driving me to aggressive drug use. "Can't you feel the energy in the classroom? You're an assassin now. That's a big fucking deal, my small, pretty fae man."

First, I was not small; I was basically six feet tall with a healthy amount of muscles. I literally had a six-pack, and my biceps and quads were impressive.

"I'm not pretty. I'm powerful."

John laughed like I'd made a joke.

A few students turned around in their chairs and looked at us, and I couldn't help but notice the way some of them winked and licked their lips.

I'd assumed they kept glancing back because we'd been *tortured* and looked like shit. Not because they were into us.

I whispered with outrage, "So you're telling me the three kings have really had *sex* with our teacher? And that they were just talking about it in front of everyone?"

They definitely did *not* have a brotherly relationship.

Malum growled in his deep voice, "If you have something to say, Egan, say it to my face."

I glared over at him and refused to be cowed by his bullying.

"Sorry, *Malum.*" I emphasized his last name like it was dirty. "I was just wondering if you'd fucked the teacher, because you were flirting with her aggressively, and frankly, it was disgusting."

John made a strangled noise beside me.

Scorpius straightened. "Do you want to fucking die, my pampered pretty boy?"

Depends on the day.

"Don't call me pampered or pretty, Scorp." I was not going to address the fact that my stomach cramped when he referred to me as his.

He snapped his gum. "Don't worry, I can set that up for your scrawny ass."

"Hm, I don't believe you." I rolled my eyes. "You all said I wouldn't last an hour, but I'm s-s-still here." My teeth chattered and ruined the moment.

Scorpius opened his mouth, probably to eviscerate me, but he was interrupted by Vegar (the nice demon, not Zenith, who was glaring at me like he wanted to eat my eyeballs).

"Aran isn't wrong. We lost the last four recruits to the Black Ocean."

The inky lines under Vegar's eyes had expanded to cover most of his neck, and he was slumped over, looking miserable, as he turned toward me.

Maybe I was a shitty person, but it was nice to see I wasn't the only one suffering.

Vegar said, "Two died from hypothermia. One let go of Horace's arm and was lost at sea. The other refused to stay in the water, so Lothaire killed him. None of them made it past this first day. So I gotta say, Aran, I'm impressed. I really thought you'd be a hypothermia case."

Vegar showcased razor-sharp teeth. Was he smiling or threatening me?

It was as if one of the megalodon sharks from the fae sea had breached the water and grinned at me.

I grimaced and purred, "Thanks, Vegar. Everyone's been so kind. I couldn't have done it without all the support."

I placed a hand over my heart.

"Aw, no problem, Aran." John put me in a headlock and dragged his knuckles through my curly hair.

Unfortunately, my new friend was too dumb to understand sarcasm.

Maybe it's a human thing?

"Let me go, you maniac." I struggled to escape the ridiculously powerful arm that was holding me hostage and giving me a noogie.

Just what I wanted, to be *manhandled* after drowning.

My quality of life had never been lower.

"Don't get cocky, Egan. It's only been one day, and we have a *lot* of training ahead of us." The leader of the kings leaned back and crossed his arms with a cruel smirk on his face.

"Whatever, Malum." If he was going to only call me by my last name, then I was going to do the same.

Someone needed to humble him.

It would be me.

Scorpius's voice dripped with scorn. "Aw, little Egan's just jealous because no one wants to fuck him."

Mother ensured that.

"WHORE." Written on my skin. Forever.

How right he was. I was a virgin and probably would be for the rest of my immortal life.

But he didn't need to know that.

"Nah, I'd fuck him. Look at him. He's cute and pretty with his blue hair. Like a Smurf." Once again, John wrapped his arm around my neck and dragged his hands through my hair as I growled at him.

He laughed at his joke.

For some reason, the kings' faces all darkened with rage, and they glared at John like they wanted to kill him.

Vegar said slowly, "I'm honestly glad you survived, Aran.

It's nice to have a new guy." He spoke as if he'd thought about it a lot and had just decided he was glad I lived.

Next to him, Zenith's eyes promised me certain death if I tried to take his man.

Surprisingly, it wasn't the kings who laughed at Vegar's statement.

It was Horace.

The pale vampire sat unnaturally still as he laughed.

As I wrestled against John, who was still running his knuckles against my scalp, I was extremely grateful that the two demons were sitting between us and Horace.

Because Horace was muttering, "Aran's going to die painfully."

My gut told me that the student hadn't "accidentally" let go of Horace in the ocean.

The vampyre had shoved him out to sea.

To die.

CHAPTER 8

SUFFERING

The breaking period: Day 2, hour 1

The realm's constant dark sky was disorienting.

It didn't help that the assassin program didn't have schedules like the royal and commoner students'.

From what I overheard the royals saying during class, their school day ended at midnight. Then they had breakfast in the great hall at 8:00 a.m. and class at 9:00 a.m.

They'd been complaining about how late their classes went. Spoiled brats.

Currently, the clock in the classroom said 8:00 a.m.

In the time that the royal students had ended class, gone to sleep, and woken up for breakfast, we hadn't left the fucking classroom.

No food.

No sleep.

No shower.

No warmth.

Until now, I'd thought I knew suffering. I'd thought I understood what it meant to be miserable.

I'd been wrong.

Because no matter how hard my life was, I'd always had two things—sleep and warmth. Even in the shifter realm, we'd had heavy coats that repelled the cold.

In the grand scheme of the realms, those two things seemed small and inconsequential.

Now I knew better. They were everything.

As I shivered in the back of the black stone classroom, my teeth chattered as my eyelids slumped and my head tilted forward.

The other recruits fared slightly better.

The men had stopped seeming like they were cold hours ago, and the only signs they weren't well were their heavy lids and growling stomachs.

In contrast, I shivered violently, bright-blue veins stark against my pale skin.

All this pain for no reason.

After class with Ms. Gola, which was at least salaciously entertaining, Lothaire had walked in and announced he was our teacher. And in the ungodly hours of early morning, class had gone from bad to worse.

Lothaire didn't bother to explain when we were going to get to eat and sleep. If we ever were.

Instead, he'd launched into the driest lecture on battle tactics I'd ever heard.

If he explained one more time how to maximize torturing a captured opponent, I was going to punch myself in the face.

Lothaire spent hours drawing a detailed diagram of how to extract information from a person.

With war paint decorating his face, Lothaire said, "The common misconception that fingernail extraction is the most painful method is just that, a misconception. What is a smaller action that has bigger results?"

He looked around the room, single eye flashing, as he waited for an answer.

I ran through methods in my head: *cut out their tongue, cut off their genitals, disembowelment.*

The list was endless.

But I didn't bother to answer, since I was freezing and pissed the fuck off. Instead, I glared at Lothaire and told him with my eyes how much I wanted to do all those things to him.

"Horace." Lothaire pointed to the surly vampyre, who was raising his hand.

"Sir, I would cut off the tips of their fingers and toes. More blood. More pain. It's more effective." Horace grinned and flashed his fangs.

Lothaire smiled back as he tapped his finger to his mouth like he was considering it.

Just two vampyres having a homicidal moment. Not what anyone wanted or needed.

I slumped lower in my seat and fantasized about crawling into a hot tub and never leaving.

After a long pause, Lothaire said, "That would work, and points for creativity. However, there is another method that is more effective. Anyone know?"

Scorpius raised his hand, and Lothaire pointed to him.

"Sir, I'd make small, shallow incisions all over their body at key places. Then I'd slowly peel off their skin."

I scrunched up my nose as I glared at the pale bastard. Sure, I had my own issues, but I didn't revel in my unwellness.

At least, that was what I was telling myself.

Scorpius smirked over at me as he flexed his biceps and placed his hands behind the back of his head. He thought he was *so* hot.

He was extremely attractive in a pale, sarcastic, rude way.

I rubbed at my eyes and flipped him off with both my middle fingers. When he didn't react, I remembered he was blind and whispered, "fuck you."

Lothaire obliviously nodded. "Excellent. That is correct, Scorpius. The skin is the largest organ on a person's body and is usually very thin. The perfect instrument to exact pain while still leaving your captive alive."

When Lothaire turned back to the board, Scorpius smirked and whispered back, "You wish I'd fuck you, pretty boy."

Was he hot? Yes.

But did I have standards? Probably not.

I wasn't going to tell him that though. Instead, I pursed my lips and said, "I'd rather die. Also, you're obsessed with me."

Scorpius mimed hip thrusting into the air, his powerful thighs bulged with strength, and the lower part of his shirt pulled up, showing off a cut Adonis belt.

On his hip, he flashed a tattoo of a snake eating its own tail.

It was a stunning, intricate piece of artwork but seemed different from the eye tattoo on his neck. Like it had been done by a different artist.

I swallowed through a sudden lump in my throat as my stomach pinched weirdly, and I looked away from him.

Orion shook his head as he looked back and forth between us, and Malum glared at me like he was imagining my head catching on fire.

But two could play at this game.

With painful slowness, I ran my tongue over my lips and

popped the side of my thumb against my cheek in a wanton manner.

Scorpius's pale cheekbones burned pink at the sound and Orion delicately arched an eyebrow at me.

Malum adjusted in his seat. He was probably trying to shift closer so he could strangle me or something.

Lothaire turned around, and we all snapped our attention to the front. Which I immediately regretted because he proceeded to draw an extremely graphic rendition of a person getting all their skin peeled off.

Scorpius was lucky he was blind.

John leaned forward and whispered, "Whatever just happened between you and Scorpius was *hot*." He fanned himself dramatically.

Was everyone in this palace a pervert?

Lothaire spent the next few hours naming all the different species in the realm and their abilities. It was all a review of things I'd learned as a princess in the fae realm.

I spent those hours crossing my eyes and doodling pictures of fire and skulls on my notebook. After drawing an extremely detailed bonfire, I started hallucinating that I could somehow conjure warmth.

Every few minutes, I dragged my chair closer toward Malum's flaming arms.

The harsh planes of his face were taut as he sprawled casually in his chair and watched Lothaire. His eyelids weren't fluttering like everyone else's. In fact, he looked completely awake and unbothered. Like he wasn't sleep-deprived and hungry.

He didn't seem to notice my approach.

Malum snapped his head up, silver eyes glowing like the moon. "Are you fucking kidding me, Egan? Get the fuck away from me. Either get on your knees and suck my dick or go back to your table."

Never mind.

He noticed.

Apparently sexual harassment was a problem at this academy.

I awkwardly scooted my chair away from Malum. The scraping noise uncomfortably loud in the small classroom.

Lothaire turned to glare at me. "Am I boring you, Aran? Please explain what I just described for the class, since you've taken the liberty of dragging your chair across the room."

Gnawing on my lower lip, I narrowed my eyes like I was thinking. I had zero clue what he had been saying.

"Um, yes. S-S-Sir. You were t-t-alking about skinning a body." My teeth chattered.

In the space of a blink, Lothaire flew across the room.

Crack.

My head snapped to the side as Lothaire slammed his black baton across my cheek. Warm blood dribbled down my face.

I straightened my head.

There was a long, tense moment as we stared at each other. I'd never wanted to kill anyone so badly.

The room was dead silent.

Lothaire snarled, "We talked about skinning hours ago, you fucking imbecile. I was explaining that we won't need to learn about your individual abilities until later this year when you have more freedom in combat. For now, you are unimpressive soldiers whose only focus is to train and stay alive."

I nodded and made sure to stare straight ahead at him.

My cheek throbbed.

Lothaire shook his head with disgust. "But since you clearly think you're too good for my lesson plan, please explain to the room what type of creature you are that makes you so much fucking *better than everyone else!*"

I jumped in my seat when Lothaire suddenly started screaming. He paused with his massive chest heaving and slapped his baton across his palm like he was trying to control himself.

If hunger weren't gnawing at my stomach, cold eating my bones, and sleep deprivation stabbing my brain, I might have been nervous.

I was dead inside.

"So what the fuck are you, Aran Egan?" Lothaire growled. "*Answer me!*"

A monster.

A girl.

A queen.

"I'm a w-w-water fae from the fae r-r-realm," I gritted out.

Lothaire arched his brow. "How the fuck is that possible?" His lips curled up with disgust.

"I've never known a water fae to be powerful. The ruling monarch has always been a fire fae, and we haven't had one in the academy for years. So what makes you so special?"

Oh, I bet you know all about the ruling monarch. Since you were sticking your dick inside her for years.

Lothaire was trying to trip me up in front of everyone. He'd voiced suspicions about my heritage back in the beast realm, and this was just a ploy to get answers out of me.

But I'd grown up mingling with vipers in the fae royal court.

Eyes dead.

Face relaxed.

I donned the mask of an unfeeling princess.

"I'm not special. I'm just powerful." I infused my voice with strength and refused to let my teeth chatter as I studied my cuticles like I was bored.

"Explain," Lothaire replied.

"Like all water fae, I manipulate water. But my ability is nuanced, and I have mastered transforming water into ice. My specialty is ice daggers."

The key to selling a lie was getting comfortable in it. I was a master at sinking into the deceit until I didn't know where the truth began and the falsehood ended.

That was how Aran the male beta shifter had been born.

That was how Aran the water fae would survive.

"So your only power is you create ice daggers?" Lothaire asked slowly with disbelief.

I smirked as I crossed my arms. "Yes. They're very... effective daggers."

Malum scoffed, and Scorpius said something under his breath that sounded like another unnecessary musing about my impending death.

Lothaire narrowed his eyes.

You're tired, hungry, and sleep-deprived. He has you at your weakest, and he knows something's up. He's not going to stop prying.

Scorpius muttered something else under his breath.

I whipped my head to the left and went into full bitch princess mode.

"If you have something to say, Scorp, say it to my face. I get that you're obsessed with me, but it's frankly pathetic. What can you even do, Scorpius?"

Classic game theory strategy: deflect and redirect.

Scorpius's nostrils flared as he dragged his hand through his perfectly slicked hair and looked off into the distance with his white eyes.

After a second of heavy breathing, he visibly calmed himself and sneered, "You'd like to know, wouldn't you? But you spoiled brats are all the same. Don't worry, Egan, I know just how to handle pretty boys like you."

Scorpius slowly rolled his hips, and Malum smirked like he was imagining me on my knees.

My lower stomach pinched with a strange sensation.

Scorpius was probably a weak earth fae, and that was why he was so fucking rude all the time. He and Orion definitely depended on Malum's flames for protection.

He was just another mediocre man overcompensating for his shortcomings. And his small penis.

I chuckled darkly. "That's a lot of talk for someone who clearly gets by just riding Malum's coattails."

Scorpius snarled, and he clenched his cut jaw so tightly that it twitched.

"Enough!" Lothaire roared. "Aran, you aren't in any position to make demands of the kings. Their abilities are on a need-to-know basis, and *you* aren't need-to-know. They've also proven themselves, while you have done fuck all."

My head hurt from the effort not to tell him to pull the stick out of his ass.

Double standards much? The kings were fae, and there was nothing secret-worthy about that. Just more garden variety wastes of space with dicks and balls.

I'd never been around people with larger egos than Malum and Scorpius. Which was saying something because I'd lived with Sadie's Alpha mates.

Calling out Scorpius worked, though, because Lothaire stopped asking me questions about my heritage.

After another few hours of Lothaire saying "blah, blah, blah" while I doodled a three-dimensional image of Scorpius getting his head sawed off, I was ready to fall asleep at my desk and just take the beating.

When Lothaire glanced at the clock and said, "You have two hours to sleep in your barracks, then we will meet at the ocean," I thought I had misheard him.

Two hours? I needed two fucking weeks of uninterrupted sleep, a bubble bath massage, a case of enchanted wine, and a few hours in a dark room with my pipe.

Devastation hurt my chest.

I slid lower in my chair.

"Was I clear?" Lothaire's voice dropped threateningly.

"Yes, sir!" we chorused back in synchrony.

Lothaire sauntered out of the classroom and casually said over his shoulder, "Two hours starts now."

Chairs scooted across marble as the men quickly stood up.

I half fell, half rolled out of my chair.

The loud clicking of my teeth chattering in my mouth was distracting and made it hard to whimper appropriately. My limbs seized with cramps as I dragged myself up into something that resembled a standing position.

With a smidgen of dignity left, I limped next to John as we walked toward the barracks.

"So we don't get to eat and sleep?" My voice was small and unfamiliar.

John stretched gingerly. "No, we do, but…" He trailed off as we exited the fortress.

"But what?" The cold rocks burned the cut-up bottoms of my feet, and I hobbled.

John grimaced. "The first few weeks of the school year is what Lothaire likes to call the 'breaking period.' He says we all get weak from time off and we need to get reacclimated to the stakes."

I stumbled over a rock. "So what does that mean?"

John sighed heavily as we entered the barracks. "It means he runs us into the ground for the first few weeks. He keeps us sleep-deprived and hungry so when we start the real fighting, we're prepared."

Sleep-deprived and hungry.

I face-planted dejectedly onto my cot. Too late, I remembered the kings had ripped it to shreds. My nose slammed into the ground, and I groaned in misery.

Turning around on the awkward netting, John pulled off his wet sweatshirt and showed off a lean, muscled torso. His shoulders weren't as wide as a door like the kings', and he was built leaner, but he was still impressively strong.

Then the unthinkable happened.

Admiration turned to horror as John pulled down his sweatpants *and* his boxers in one fell swoop.

I averted my eyes and fought back a gag reflex.

One thing I did *not* need to see was my new friend's dick and balls. That was the final straw.

Unfortunately, when I turned away from John, I looked directly at Malum, who was also standing stark fucking naked. His darkly tanned skin was pulled tight across the most impressive male physique in all the realms.

The weird sensation pinched my lower stomach.

Sharp *V* lines framed what could only be described as an eight-pack of lean, rippling muscles that widened out to his impressive shoulders.

I swallowed a gasp.

His massive fucking dick hung purple and long against his leg. Even with it limp, veins popped across it.

An impossibly deep voice asked, "Like what you see, pretty boy? Keep challenging us and maybe I'll reward you by letting you suck it."

Holy shit.

Malum was definitely into men. I ignored the small mentally ill part of me that was disappointed.

Heat flamed across my cheeks as I realized Malum was watching me ogle his massive flaccid penis.

Fuck, what would a dude say?

I coughed and looked away. "Please. Nothing you have interests me."

Everywhere I looked, large males were standing ass naked as they grabbed the dry sweat suits off the cots and pulled them on. Apparently a shower was out of the question.

Malum chuckled darkly, and I ignored him.

Grabbing my clothes, eyes turned downward, I shuffled behind the flimsy wall that jutted out in front of the toilet.

I ripped off my wet clothes and pulled on the dry ones.

It wasn't as good as a shower, but the shivers calmed as fleece material enveloped my limbs.

I nearly cried with relief.

With my modesty protected, I relaxed my shoulders and emerged from my hiding spot.

You can do this. How hard can it be to pretend to be a dude? You've been doing it for years.

I jumped backward because Horace was standing as still as a statue outside the divider. His eyes were wide and manic. "Why did you hide, Aran?"

The hairs on my neck rose because he said my name like a predator identifying his prey. I didn't want to have Horace's attention.

"Had to piss," I said casually as I walked by him, grateful that Scorpius had forced me to take the cot in the far corner. It was furthest from Horace.

"Please. I'm not surprised that the pampered pretty boy is insecure. He barely has any muscles," Scorpius sneered.

All the gratitude left my body.

"Oh, please," I snapped back tiredly and lifted my shirt to show off my ab muscles. "Keep calling me pretty, Scorp. We all know you just want some of this."

I flinched as I said it. I was starting to channel toxic masculinity a little *too* accurately.

Oh my sun god? A horrible thought struck me. Was I becoming part of the patriarchy? Was I the problem?

Malum tilted his head back and laughed. "Were those supposed to be muscles?" He was still standing starkers, and I couldn't help but admit defeat.

Compared to Sadie, I was a beast of a woman, but compared to these men, I was pathetic and weak. Especially since I was still enchanted to look wider and stronger.

They would die of laughter if they saw my true form.

Fuck them. If I was going to be stuck in this miserable place, I better get jacked as hell.

From my peripheral vision, Scorpius dragged his nails down Malum's abs and asked, "Aw, is pretty boy blushing?"

Maybe they weren't brothers? My stomach twisted into knots, and I patted my cot like I was getting ready for bed.

"Whatever," I mumbled as I gingerly lowered myself onto the broken fabric. I rested my head on the corner piece still attached to the frame, while half my body pressed against rocks.

Pure comfort.

I would have killed for a soft blanket.

Across the barracks, Zenith and Vegar lay down on the same cot. Their combined weight strained the material, and it looked like it was one second away from ripping. But they cuddled close and looked content. Warm.

The three kings pressed their cots together. Malum spread out on the middle cot, and more flames erupted across his arms as he spread them wide.

Orion and Scorpius lay down on either side of him and used his biceps as pillows.

I shivered with jealousy.

Horace smiled big with his wide eyes open as he stared at me.

Nope. Absolutely not.

John scooted his cot closer and blocked my view of Horace. He didn't stop until our arms were touching.

"Body heat, for warmth." John flashed a grin and closed his eyes.

The ground was cold beneath me.

I scooted my cot as close as it would go to John and fully wrapped my arm around his. I stuck my fingers in his armpit and swallowed a moan at the delightful heat. "Body heat," I whispered.

John nodded and didn't move away.

My eyes fluttered shut as my aching body shut down.

A thought pierced through my hazy tiredness. "What did you mean when you said we'd begin 'the real fighting'?" I whispered.

John's mouth moved, and he spoke nonsense.

"What did you say? I misheard you." My ears were deceiving me.

Wind shrieked as it slammed against the flimsy metal walls of the barracks.

John's dark eyes opened, and intensity transformed his human features into something unexpected and deadly.

"War. We train for war," John repeated.

It wasn't cold that made my limbs tingle and my skin crawl.

John smiled and flashed his dimples. "Go to sleep, Aran. We only have two hours. If you use every break you get and are smart about it, you'll survive."

I closed my eyes.

Then hyperventilated until I fell asleep.

CHAPTER 9
"RUN," SAID THE DEVIL

The breaking period: Day 2, hour 5

Two hours of sleep did nothing to refresh me.

Along with my head being heavy with exhaustion and stomach screaming with pain, my vision was blurry and the wound on my back sent jabs of agony down my spine. Sleeping on the ruined cot had exasperated my injury.

The worst part? I wasn't the only one that had woken up.

The steel cage rattled in my mind as my monster screamed and bellowed for blood.

Lothaire had screamed at us to "wake the fuck up," and there was a clattering of pushed-over cots and swear words as we hurried out into the cold wind.

Now I stood still on the rocky edge as the endless ocean churned before me like a frothing beast of malignant hate.

Salt sprayed as waves slammed and white caps exploded with a vengeance.

The lunar eclipse glowed an angry red.

I stood like the other recruits with my head down and

legs parted wide. Arms behind my back. Like an obedient sheep.

Like a soldier.

Lothaire walked back and forth in front of us, and his scar was puckered and ugly as he narrowed his single eye.

Please don't make us go into the ocean, I prayed to the sun god.

Without a warm shower to heat my bones, the tremors still shook through me periodically. I didn't know if I would survive it.

Lothaire nodded as he paced like he had come to a decision. "Your second day of training begins now."

Please no ocean. I dragged my fingernail across the back of my hand and made a small blood offering to the sun god.

It was a fae tradition that was typically done in exchange for a god's intervention.

At the prick of my nail severing flesh, my monster stopped screaming. It quieted like my pain had weakened it. Or maybe it was just a distraction?

"Today, we will be running," Lothaire said casually.

I took in a deep breath of relief.

Since I was a little girl, I'd loved to run through the endless fae flower fields. I'd push myself to run further and faster under the dual hot suns. I ran until my skin was slick with sweat and I couldn't remember why I was miserable in the first place.

Lothaire continued speaking, "You will run on the shore, through the surf, and along the perimeter of this island. As you know, the island is three miles wide."

I didn't know.

My stomach plummeted at the mention of running along the shore where the white caps broke. Cold was inevitable.

Lothaire's eyes glinted with malice, and his gaze lingered on me. "You will run until I tell you to stop running. I will stand here with my watch and clock your mile pace. Anyone who falls behind the pace will spend a night in the tank."

Whatever, I can run. I'll be fine.

"*Am I clear*?!" Lothaire suddenly screamed.

Dr. Palmer would have a field day with him. I'd have to give him her number.

"Yes, sir!" we chorused back.

"Begin."

With that, we were off.

I settled into an easy pace, legs pumping forward, arms relaxed, as I regulated my breathing and jogged beside John.

We quickly settled into a pack.

The kings ran at the front. Malum led the group, and he grabbed Scorpius's elbow every few minutes to guide his path. Orion ran close behind them both.

For such large men, they shouldn't have been able to move with so much agility.

None of the recruits should have.

Behind the kings, Horace glided through the ocean with such graceful precision that the water didn't kick up behind him.

He moved like a ghost, like he was flying with his feet not touching the ground.

On the vampyre's heels, Zenith and Vegar ran side by side, steps synced as their feet pounded against rocks.

The demons weren't agile like the kings or graceful like Horace. They were predators.

Water sprayed in every direction as they slammed their large bodies forward. Inky lines traveled down the backs of their necks, and they ran like they were hunting prey.

Beside me, John fell into an easy rhythm. He also ran on the tips of his bare toes like he was prancing.

His dimples were gone, and his face was a smooth mask of concentration.

Malum glanced back and shouted over the wind, "I'm surprised you can run, Egan!"

I didn't reply.

His silver eyes sharpened. "Let's see what you're really made of." He sped up and we followed his lead.

Malum set a brutal pace.

As a group, we navigated the shore as the chilly water soaked our clothes.

On the far side of the island, our hair whipped into a frenzy as the wind gusted against us.

Heads lowered. We fought against it.

If the front of the island was sloped and dangerous with stairs carved into the rocks leading up to the building's entrance, then the backside of the island was uninhabitable and treacherous.

The land behind the fortress was spiky cliffs; sheer cliff walls cut parallel into the star-studded sky.

Loud cracks sounded. Rocks tumbled hundreds of feet down the walls and shattered into thousands of pieces.

Rocks pelted us.

It was low tide, so there were ten feet of exposed black rock between the water's edge and the sheer face of the cliff.

At high tide, it would be perilous. No separation between the water and the ridge.

We'd be trapped.

Chest pinching with worry, I pounded my legs faster as I cracked my neck back and forth and tried to loosen the tension from my arms.

The key to running well was staying relaxed.

I dropped my shoulders and slowed my breathing as I lost myself in the rhythm of a good run.

After five laps, sweat dotted my brow, and I noticed the stars twinkled oddly in the sky.

They spun in circles.

Like they danced.

I tipped my head back and inhaled the pungent, salt-soaked air.

There was something magical about being in another realm. Something darkly sinister about a churning ocean, ominous moon, and the endless cover of a red night.

A beautiful cruelty.

Calm flowed through me.

Running always mellowed my edges.

The world took on a nightmare-like haze in the best possible way. Nothing had consequence.

It didn't matter if I was a man or a woman. A queen. A monster. They were all just useless labels constructed by society's need to exert control over people.

Everything horrible in life was about order.

But freedom was ragged lungs and losing yourself in a mindless motion. Chaos was freedom.

My monster stopped bellowing. The constant pressure in my chest lifted away.

Endorphins exploded like stars.

My beast was so quiet that it ceased to exist.

All my woes were small.

Because they were.

I was nothing.

Just pounding legs, splashing surf, and burning lungs.

Scorpius whispered something to Malum, and the leader of the kings kept sneaking glances over his shoulder at me.

He narrowed his silver eyes like he was surprised that I was still with them and muttered under his breath.

They were talking about me. They wanted me to fail.

Too bad for them the one thing I'd always been good at was running away.

There was peace in the violence of a long run, and I pitied anyone who'd never felt such bliss.

Comfort in the agony.

At least, that was how I felt for the first ten laps around the three-mile island. Thirty miles flew by in a blur of exertion as my mind wandered far away.

John and I matched pace, and neither of us jockeyed to surpass the other.

The human moved in tandem beside me as he lost himself in his own world. We cut across the coast in companionable silence.

A couple of times, I glanced over to find John's dark eyes studying me like he was trying to figure me out.

I studied him back.

My instincts screamed at me that the human was more than he seemed. My new friend was a duality.

"Just give up if you're getting tired, Egan!" Malum yelled over his shoulder back at me.

Our feet splashed across the surf.

"Suck my dick, Malum!" I yelled back, and John chuckled beside me. It wasn't my finest come back.

"I'm not into pretty boys," Malum called back. "Why would I need you when I have Orion for that?"

I stumbled over a rock with surprise as my stomach pinched. Everyone laughed at his statement, and Orion just smirked. Apparently, the kings were lovers. Good to know.

In the beast realm, the don had said something about shifters going feral. These men might not be shifters, but my gut told me the term already applied to them with the way they talked about sex constantly.

Since I didn't actually possess a dick, I really needed to stop talking about it. But for some reason, I couldn't stop.

The men were infuriating.

Still, a small kernel of respect expanded the longer we trudged around the island. There weren't many people in the realms who could run like we were running.

Hard. Fast. Dirty.

Malum set a brutal pace that demanded nothing but excellence and full concentration.

I tipped my head back, lost myself in the savagery of it all, and pretended I was running on the surface of the blood moon. With the world sparkling around me.

Things changed on the eleventh lap.

Thirty-three miles hit hard.

My arches cramping from pounding against jagged rocks, I became hyperaware of the trail of blood behind me.

The salty air was hard to breathe. My arms tingled from exhaustion as blood was pumped to my organs and away from my limbs.

I'd never run so far.

In the fae realm, the trail around the royal palace was twenty miles total.

In the shifter realm, the longest I'd run was probably about fifteen miles during battle.

Sweat poured down my face and stung my eyes. It reminded me of how Sadie had complained after a few miles. How she'd break down like her body physically couldn't go on any further.

One night, she'd explained that it was like hitting a wall, and I'd laughed at her, thinking she was being dramatic.

Now I understood what she meant.

I was fine.

Then?

I wasn't.

The problem was that the other recruits didn't show any signs of exhaustion. Malum easily held the pace, and the smallest shimmer of sweat on the men's foreheads was the only sign they were exerting themselves.

My breath rattled louder.

No matter how many times I shook out my arms and focused on driving with my glutes, my pace slowed.

We passed Lothaire, and he yelled, "Four-minute, ten-second mile pace. You're slowing down. Unacceptable!"

Malum nodded and started running faster. Everyone adjusted to match pace.

It was the worst timing possible for an increase in speed. I could barely keep up with the prior pace.

Thighs burning, chest heaving, I fought desperately to stay with the group.

But for every step the men took, I took two.

It wore me down.

The tide was creeping higher on the far side of the island, but I was too tired to notice. Too tired to care.

My vision blurred.

John glanced down at me as he continued to run faster and his steps creeped further and further away from me.

The distance grew.

I might have been hallucinating but disappointment flashed on his face as he looked back at my retreating form.

He turned away.

The next time I ran past Lothaire, I was a good ways behind the other recruits, who were still running as a unit.

The vampyre's face was mottled and purple as he screamed down at me, "Aran, *what the fuck*?! Do you think this is a joke? You're running a five-minute mile. Hurry the fuck up and catch up to the group right now or you *will be in the tank*!"

Did Lothaire have a monster in his mind? Because he sure as shit acted like it.

A tank sounded like water, and my tongue was uncomfortably dry and heavy. The salty ocean mocked me.

I tried to increase my speed, but sleep deprivation and hunger had taken their toll. Toe jamming into a rock, I stumbled and barely caught myself from face-planting into the surf.

Lothaire screamed something else, but I was too far away to hear. Or maybe I just didn't want to listen.

The next three miles passed much slower than the last ones as each step grew more painful, the trail of blood increasing behind me.

When I completed mile thirty-nine, I couldn't hear what Lothaire was screaming at me over the buzzing in my ears.

He heaved with anger.

He definitely has a monster inside.

Lothaire didn't let my failure go unpunished. As I ran past the raging vampyre, he flicked his wrist and sent his baton careening in my direction like a boomerang.

CRACK.

Jolting with surprise, I fell over as a burning fire spread across my arm.

I face-planted into the frigid water, and the surf slammed atop me and dragged me forward.

For an endless moment, something close to infinity, I floated face-first in the black sea. The waves dragged me back and forth.

Peaceful.

Calm.

The moment ended with a stab of agony, and I screamed as Lothaire wrenched me out of the ocean by the arm he'd just snapped.

Then Lothaire tangled his hand in my short hair and dragged me out of the ocean like a caught fish.

He screamed in my face.

We were inches apart.

He kind of reminds me of someone? I couldn't put my finger on it, but his features were familiar.

I could barely hear what he said.

"You *will* finish the last lap of this run! You will do it in under a five-minute pace or I will personally throw you into the ocean to drown. Either you're an assassin or you're nothing. *There is no other option!*"

Steel rattled.

This was the same man who crawled willingly into my mother's bed and stood by her as she tortured me. How dare he speak to me like that? He should be bowing at my feet.

My monster bellowed.

It screamed at me to slit his throat.

Lothaire threw me down onto the hard rocks and walked away. He didn't care if I lived or died.

Like I was expendable.

Garbage.

Just a powerless fae princess on fire and writhing on the palace floor.

I stumbled to my feet and set off down the path. Tried to relax my shoulders and drive with my legs, but each jostling of my arm sent agony shooting along my collarbone.

Broken arm clenched across my chest to steady it, I forced myself to run with everything I had.

But I stumbled from the awkwardness, and my legs

barely propelled me forward. There was no way I was making the time.

Resignation washed over me as exhaustion made my head fuzzy.

This was it.

The end.

Mother's consort would win.

My vision turned partially black as my monster bellowed and bent the steel bars of its cage. It ripped itself out of its prison, desperate to take over.

Suddenly, my head was tipped back, and I was laughing with manic abandon.

Body shaking, chest rattling with horrible glee.

Fuck it. I giggled with delirium, and as the salty wind whipped my short hair, I did the unthinkable.

I let my monster free.

Lothaire will not win.

Black fully overtook my vision, and the bloodlust that exploded through my veins burned like lava.

My laughter morphed into a roar.

And I disappeared on the rocky shore of a faraway realm.

For the first time in twenty-four years of suffering, I let my monster control me. My consciousness flicked off like a piece of my soul had disappeared.

Never to be seen again.

A MONSTER OR MAN?

The monster

The breaking period: Day 2, hour 8

"What the fuck is wrong with Egan?" Malum gripped my shoulders painfully and shook me back and forth.

He was a fire fae who hated me. He was just like Mother.

"I'll slit your throat," I promised as I snapped my teeth at him, desperate to sever his artery and bask in his blood.

It would feel so fucking good to kill another cruel fire fae.

They didn't deserve to live.

In my bones, I recognized the history between our species. The feud that lived within us.

I reached back for an ice dagger, but nothing materialized in my hand. Stomach growling. Head fuzzy. It was embarrassing how weak I was.

I screamed in frustration.

He was so close, but I only had my teeth to bring him down. I'd worked with less before.

A flaming hand wrapped around my throat. Malum held

me off the ground with one hand, and for a second, it felt like he was slowly dragging his callused thumb across my enchanted Adam's apple.

It seemed sexual.

Before I could comprehend how I felt about it, Scorpius tangled his fingers in my hair and wrenched my head back at an impossible angle.

My teeth gnashed at the empty air.

They immobilized me.

I fucking *hated* being helpless. Never again.

Kicking and shrieking with frustration, I slammed my fists into Malum's kidneys. Pain streaked up my arm as he grunted at the contact.

I smiled.

I hurt him, and that was all that mattered.

Bands of steel bound my arms to my chest and immobilized me. It took me a second to realize Orion had his biceps wrapped around me.

Warm brown eyes as dark as chocolate were framed with long, sooty lashes. He blinked inches away from me.

He didn't speak, but he didn't need to. He was speaking with his eyes and telling me to calm down. Relaxing energy radiated off him.

For a second, I felt chastised.

Orion leaned back, and Malum replaced him. "Thanks, Orion," he said as flames shot across his head.

Oh yeah, that's why I was fighting.

He wouldn't break me.

I slammed my leg into his knee as hard as I could and grinned with success as I heard something crack.

Deathly cold fingers wrapped around my ankles and halted my kicks. I screamed and flailed, but the hand tightened painfully.

"Aran, how could you kick at me? Is that how you treat all your friends? I'm hurt." John laughed, then flashed a dimpled grin as he easily restrained me.

I shrieked.

He laughed.

Lothaire stood to the side, watching the men hold me in place like he was bored. Mother's fucking consort.

He'd slept with a monster.

I turned and spat as hard as I could, mollified when it hit his face.

Once I severed his head, I'd mount it as a trophy on my wall. With him dead, I'd fully conquer the demons of my past.

Lothaire wiped spit off his cheek and just smirked like he'd won something. "Ah, now this is what I've been looking for. There's so much darkness in his blood I knew he had to be more than a water fae." He laughed. "Such delightful rage; it reminds me of myself when I was a youth."

Sun god, I wanted to rip out his teeth slowly. The bastard didn't know *anything* about who I was, and he never fucking would.

"Sir, do you know what he is?" Malum asked. "Why are his eyes black? Why is he acting like this?"

His fingers were once again wrapped around my neck, and a callused thumb was trailing small circles down my throat in big, sweeping motions.

Lothaire sounded happy when he said, "I have no idea, but I can't wait to find out."

"How did this happen?" John asked.

Lothaire answered, "I broke his arm and threatened to kill him if he didn't match pace. He stumbled and looked pathetic. But then his eyes changed, and his posture shifted.

Before I knew it, he was sprinting at a three-minute pace and overtook the rest of you."

"Shit, I didn't know his arm was broken." Scorpius's voice didn't have its usual sneer, and the arms around my chest loosened.

He thought I was weak and pitied me. They *all* thought I was weak.

Malum's hard face leaned closer to mine as he narrowed his eyes. "Pretty boy didn't punch like his arm was broken. Are you sure?"

"I'm going to rip your flesh off your bones and eat it," I promised him.

Lothaire chuckled darkly. "Oh yeah, I heard it crack."

I *hated* being talked about like I wasn't present, and I promised them, "I'm going to kill you all."

"How original," Scorpius said dryly.

"Just what the fuck are you, Egan?" Malum shouted and tightened his grip on my neck until I was gasping for air.

My lower stomach pinched, and my back burned.

"Fuck, look at him," Scorpius whispered to Orion and Malum, who were still crowding my personal space.

I gnashed at them with my teeth.

Malum's fingernails dug into the sensitive skin on my neck, and shivers trailed down my spine.

"Shit," Malum swore softly. "His pupils are dilated and his breaths shallow."

Suddenly Scorpius's sneering voice was whispering against my ear. His tongue snaked gently against my outer lobe, and I almost cried out at the contact. "Pretty boy is turned on."

Malum's silver eyes were molten steel. "You might be pretty. But the only man we're into is Orion."

The black haze receded from my vision as I processed his words.

I couldn't stop myself from glancing over at the quiet warrior who was watching me with a strange light in his eye. What an interesting dynamic the three of them had.

But what Malum didn't understand was that I agreed with him. So far, if I had to choose a guy to fuck, I'd take Orion hands down.

Orion was at least six and a half feet tall, and his white-blond hair hung to his shoulders in glistening strands. His exquisite lips and high cheekbones were pretty.

However, it was the warm brown eyes that made you want to eat him up.

Too bad he was apparently in a relationship with two of the most toxic men I'd ever met. If only I could spend some alone time with him.

No. What the fuck are you thinking?

They were restraining me.

Literally choking me out and threatening me.

They were stuck-up men who thought they had a reason to rage. But they'd never know what it was like to be viewed as less than a person. A sexual commodity or a trophy for an arm.

My rage bubbled through me until all I felt was the fucking endless parade of indignities and shame that had brought me to this point.

Black overtook my vision.

I laughed like a lunatic and snarled at Malum, "I'd rather die than touch you in that way. You are nothing but dead to me. And I *will* kill you."

He was just like my mother, and killing him would be the greatest thing I ever did.

Malum's voice was a low rumble. "Are you threatening me?"

"Whoa, whoa. Let's all relax here." John maneuvered his body so he was holding my legs in one hand while he clapped Malum on the back with the other. "Aran's just got a little anger inside him. Look at how weak the guy is. Who could blame him?"

"Don't fucking touch me," Malum snarled, and John immediately dropped his hand.

"I'll fucking show all of you how weak I am, you pathetic human," I shrieked and bucked.

"See?" John smiled and laughed like he found my merciless urge to destroy them all *funny*. "It's nothing personal. Aran's just not in his right mind."

Malum nodded slowly, but he didn't release my throat.

"Maybe he's a demon," Vegar said with excitement, and Zenith glowered beside him. "Our eyes also turn black."

"He's not a demon. He doesn't have the veins," Zenith immediately countered like the idea of me being of demon blood was the biggest insult.

They should be bowing before me and wishing I were one of them.

"Let's check his blood." Vegar eagerly gouged his fingernail into the exposed skin of my collarbone before anyone could say anything.

I growled like an animal, but it ended with a whimper. There was nothing worse than people touching me without my permission. I fucking hated it.

John must have noticed because he said, "Don't touch him. He doesn't like it."

No one listened because they all peered closer to stare at my blood.

"Nope, it's red. Not black." Vegar frowned, and Zenith visibly exhaled with relief.

Most species had red blood except for demons and the handful of people who were the children of gods.

"He seems to be calming down, but his eyes are still black. What are we supposed to do with him?" Malum asked as he choked me harder. "Want me to kill him?"

I blacked out from the boiling fury that rushed through me. *How Fucking. Dare. He.*

There was a long pause like Lothaire was considering it, but then the vampyre said, "No. He completed the run, and it might be more wasteful than I first thought if we were to lose him. He might be more than the weakling he seems to be at first glance."

Scorpius scoffed, "That's highly doubtful. He's built more like a boy than a man."

I'd show him I was built like a woman when I suffocated him with my thighs wrapped around his thick skull.

Lothaire ignored him and said, "He owes me a night in the tank anyway. We'll throw him in right now. Something tells me that when he emerges, he'll be back to his old self."

I started to scream but stopped myself. I needed to remain composed if I was going to somehow kill all of them in the next few minutes.

Before I could come up with a plan, I was manhandled into a small metal shelter, which was hidden behind our barracks, and pushed into an empty metal sphere that was barely large enough to lie in.

A lid started to close, but Lothaire popped his head in and said, "Don't take this the wrong way. I look forward to working with you in the future."

Lunging at his throat, I missed because the lid slammed down and trapped me.

I was plunged into darkness.

No noise.

No sight.

Dragging my fingers around the inside, I started to panic when I felt no sensations. Was I paralyzed?

No. The throbbing in my arm every time I moved it let me know I still had mobility.

It must be the tank.

I screamed as loud as I could, but the sound disappeared like I'd never made it. Mouth opened, I bellowed until my throat was sore from the strain.

There was no sound.

The lack of all sensation was horrifying and dizzying.

Sorting through the endless library that was inside my mind, I pulled out a book on advanced technologies. I'd read it when I was a teenager back in the fae realm.

Mentally flipping through the pages, I snarled with annoyance when I came to the chapter on torture devices.

I was in a sensory deprivation tank.

They were enchanted so the user lost all use of their senses and were used to drive prisoners insane.

I was trapped with nothing but a throbbing arm and loud thoughts.

Lying down, eyes open and unseeing, I fantasized about dismembering Lothaire into a thousand small pieces.

After an eternity of mentally eviscerating the vampyre, I switched my attention to Malum's flesh. Then Scorpius's. Finally, I destroyed Orion's beautiful face.

After endless hours of fantasizing, I could feel their blood sticky and wet across my hands.

It caked my chest and chin, and there was disgusting copper on my tongue.

I swallowed, and chunks of gore lodged in my dry throat.

It was my mother's beating heart.

No.
I didn't want this.
Never wanted it to end this way.
I screamed, but no one heard me.
No one saved me.
From myself.
And in the silence…
I broke.

CHAPTER II
A DEVIL'S TOUCH

The breaking period: Day 2, hour 12

I drifted away in silence.

Just me, myself, and my monster.

Bright lights and loud sounds accosted me out of nowhere, and my cells exploded at the sudden onslaught.

After being alone in the darkness for so long, everything throbbed with pain.

Curled into a fetal position, I whimpered, "Turn it off." I missed the cloak of darkness.

"Get the fuck out of the tank," Malum said roughly, and in my hypersensitive state, his deep voice made all the hairs on my body stand up.

Callused hands grabbed my arms and threw me to the ground.

The three kings spoke to one another, and there were no other sounds. I was alone with them.

I bit down on my lip to stop from screaming as my broken arm jarred across the hard rocks.

It usually took me about two days to heal broken bones,

so I must not have been in the tank for that long. It was an eternity.

The hard floor was abrasive against my sensitive skin, and everything was fuzzy as my eyes struggled to adjust to the dim light. A loud buzzing filled my ears.

Malum's terrifyingly handsome face leaned close as silver eyes glared at me. "Just what the fuck are you, Egan?" He spat my last name like it was a curse.

My scalp prickled with pain as Scorpius once again tangled his fingers in my curls and yanked me up by my head.

I stumbled and pushed against him, desperate to orient myself. I was stunned speechless when ice-cold fingers, longer and thinner than Malum's, dragged across my face.

Featherlight fingers trailed down my forehead, across my cheekbones, and along my jaw.

He mapped my face.

Scorpius's breath caught as he touched me like he was surprised by what he found.

For a second, I forgot to breathe.

"Just as ugly as I thought," Scorpius sneered.

He wrenched my head to the side at an impossible angle and asked, "You think you can lie to us and get away with it?"

My head ached, and I groaned with misery, still too disoriented to do anything other than fight weakly.

Chilly fingers pushed my curly hair to the side and traced my exposed ears. Scorpius chuckled, and I shivered.

"Just as I suspected, he doesn't even have fae ears."

"What?" Malum sounded like an animal growling. "You think you can train alongside us and lie to us? You think you're so much better than us?"

My vision adjusted to the light just in time to see Malum's flaming fist arching toward my stomach.

Pain exploded across my sensitive skin.

I bit down on my tongue and forced my muscles to relax so I hung limp in Scorpius's harsh grip.

History had taught me not to fight back or antagonize my abusers.

They would do whatever they wanted to do to my body, but how I responded controlled the narrative of events.

If I struggled against Mother, then I was an ungrateful bitch that needed to be hurt more to instill obedience. But if I was docile and took it quietly, then I was just a nuisance that had learned my lesson.

It was clear what was happening.

The kings wanted me agitated so I'd reveal my secrets. They were taking advantage of the torture tank and trying to interrogate me when I was at my weakest.

They'd misjudged me.

Sure, I might be courting insanity and suffering from at least a dozen undiagnosed mental traumas, but I wasn't dumb.

They'd have to be smarter.

Muscles relaxed, eyes dead, expression blank, I stared up at Orion pleadingly as Malum slammed his fist into my stomach. He was the only one who might care enough to stop them. Probably the only one with a soul.

Pain exploded across my cells like an old friend.

He kept punching me.

I needed a smoke.

Malum's face hardened, sculpted lines tightening with rage as he realized I wasn't going to fight back.

Orion stepped up beside him, and I kept making eye contact while hanging pathetically.

However, the corner of the bastard's lips smirked upward like he knew what I was doing. There was a twinkle in his eye. A literal fucking *twinkle*.

Orion didn't tell them to stop.

Scorpius wrenched my head back further as Malum kept ramming his flaming fist into my stomach, and I did nothing but take it.

From what I could tell, we were in a structure that appeared to be a smaller version of the barracks. Wind pounded against the outside, and water crashed.

We must be in the small shedlike building I'd seen tucked behind the barracks.

Behind Malum, the only thing in the room was a large silver egg. A hollow structure just big enough for a body to fit inside.

Just me and the three kings and a sensory deprivation tank on an island.

It seemed like the beginning of a bad joke.

I was too tired to care.

The kings could do whatever they wanted to my body, but they wouldn't know to eat my heart, and I would never die.

What a fucking fate.

I needed to get drunk.

Mother had always wanted me to be stronger. Now I was taking a beating and barely noticing it.

You couldn't say the woman didn't know how to get results.

A manic chuckle escaped my lips as Malum once again reared his fist back.

He stilled. "What the fuck are you laughing at? Are you going to threaten to eat my flesh again or are you still pretending to not be a psycho? The ruse is fucking up. Just tell us what you are and we won't have to do this."

"Who said I was pretending?" I was genuinely curious why he thought I was acting. I'd been very clear from the beginning that I was cripplingly dependent on drugs and really not well.

"I don't know, Malum, I'm kind of enjoying this," Scorpius sneered as he wrenched my head back further.

He was 100 percent a sadist.

So boring and predictable. Dr. Palmer would tell him to just keep a journal and write positive thoughts.

I'd never really thought about what I wanted in a male partner, but now I realized I wanted them to be completely unhinged. Like, super messed up in the head. I wanted to look at them and think, *I'm normal.*

They would bring me flowers and tell me I was being cute when I killed someone.

And when they razed the world to the ground for me, I'd compliment them on their technique.

Was that too much to ask for?

Orion stepped forward, bit down on his ridiculously plush lower lip, and leaned so close that I could see the dark swirls of his eyes and the intricate details of the flower tattoo that covered his neck.

Warm breath left his lush lips in a soft whoosh and tickled the side of my face.

Are you my fictional man?

"Who are you?" he whispered so softly I could barely hear it. I understood him by reading his lips.

My spirits sank. He wasn't coming to tell me that the universe had sent him to be my dark protector.

Disappointing.

I'd have to keep on the lookout for sexy monsters.

Malum and Scorpius definitely did *not* count. They just pissed me off and didn't treat me with even a smidge of the reverence I would expect from my dream man.

As if to emphasize my point, Scorpius wrenched my head back even further so it felt like my neck was going to break.

The angle aggravated the wound on my back.

"You're going to be a virgin forever," Mother had promised, and her taunt reminded me why I wasn't searching for a man.

I dismissed that thought.

My fictional man wouldn't need to have sex with me to find completion. He'd be so overwhelmed with my beauty he'd come from just looking at me.

Endless moments passed, and I realized they were all waiting for me to answer.

I giggled.

The three fae kings were frothing at the mouth, trying to get me to reveal my secrets. Meanwhile I was detaching from reality and building the perfect man.

Sun god, I loved being a woman.

Forehead relaxed, shoulders lowered, I stared straight into Orion's chocolate eyes and said, "I'm Aran Egan, water fae from the fae realm and cousin of the monarchy."

Orion arched a golden brow like he knew I was lying.

I arched my brow back.

"Liar," Scorpius whispered into my ear, and Malum slammed his fist into my stomach with so much force that hair ripped from my scalp into Scorpius's grip.

I doubled forward and dry-heaved.

"Erotic," I muttered.

Good thing I hadn't eaten in days.

Straightening up slowly, I infused my voice with strength

as I stared blankly at Malum. "I'm exactly who I say I am. I was born with a rare genetic disease that results in disfigured ears. Because of my disorder, I have episodes of uncontrollable rage."

The knife tattooed on his neck rippled. Malum narrowed his eyes like he couldn't decide if I was lying or not. Scorpius's grip in my hair lessened.

Orion scoffed, but no one was paying him attention.

I spoke like Mother did when she read a death sentence to one of her citizens. My voice was unrelenting and firm.

"I've never manifested any ability other than ice daggers, and sometimes the rage overtakes me. That is it. You can beat me till I bleed. Torture me until there's nothing left, but that's the truth. I've just come out of the tank. Do you really think I could lie right now?"

The fingers in my hair lessened further, and Malum took another step back.

"He does seem pampered and pathetic. That would be hard to do," Scorpius mused.

Orion mouthed, "I don't believe you."

My stomach fluttered like he was flirting with me.

I needed to be put down.

Instead of focusing on the gorgeous, quiet man who was quickly gaining my fascination, I plowed ahead. "I'm not lying. I don't know what else you want from me. If I was some unique creature, do you really think I'd barely have survived the ocean? I barely just survived the run!"

Silence stretched as they considered it.

The best lies were closest to the truth, after all, and I believed everything I'd just said.

I yelped with surprise when Scorpius suddenly released me and shoved me to the ground.

"Get up," Malum barked, and I scrambled to my feet,

then became annoyed that I'd obeyed him instinctively. "We'll be watching you, Egan."

With those comforting words, the three kings turned and stomped out of the structure.

Orion gave me a lingering glance over the shoulder but turned away when Malum placed a hand on his lower back and led him out the door.

I suddenly had a burning, irrational urge to steal him away from the two other men. A bubble of happiness grew in my chest as I imagined Malum's face when he realized his man had left him for me.

What the actual fuck is wrong with me?

Gingerly, I turned around and started to come up with a plan. After analyzing the situation from all angles, I did the only thing I could do.

I punched myself in the throat.

Gagging, I let the pain remind me that I was *that* bitch. Which meant I needed to stop having intense dissociations where I created romantic scenarios with the men who were literally beating me up.

Plan accomplished, I felt a lot better.

Oh my sun god. Is this Stockholm syndrome?

If I ever got back to the beast realm, Dr. Palmer was going to need therapy for herself after we unpacked all my new issues.

And to think she'd told me, "You're as ill as a person can be," *before* all these recent developments. I knew she was a quack.

Joke's on her—I was still getting worse.

"What the fuck are you still in there for? Follow us!" Malum shouted and startled me.

That was how, a few minutes later, I found myself sitting in the great hall beside John and the other recruits at the small table on the dais.

A steaming buffet of exotic foods was spread out on the table before us, and everyone helped themselves.

The large hands on the clock said it was 8:00 p.m., and I estimated I'd been in the tank for a few hours.

All the tables were full.

Royals and commoners chatted happily and stuffed their faces. They were all nicely dressed and didn't look sleep-deprived. Unrelatable.

My teeth started to chatter as the cold fortress floors burned against my toes. It didn't help that my clothes were once again crusted with salty water.

I was no longer jealous of the other students' finery.

Similar to the royals, the commoners wore tailored dresses and suits. The only difference was that their clothes were a deep forest green instead of a plum purple.

At least my black outfit matched my mood.

It seemed dumb to wear a dress or a suit to dinner. Like, didn't they have anything better to do?

People were literally being tortured.

I was people.

The time in the tank had left me in a sore mood, and I was jumpy and on edge. Every noise was too loud, and the light was too harsh.

The wet cotton material of my clothes scratched like nails.

I had to clench my hands into fists and repeatedly swallow down screams every time someone moved their chair and it made a harsh sound.

The only blessing was that our small table was silent. We were all exhausted.

I pushed my food back and forth on my plate and

slumped low with misery, flinching anytime a recruit at the small table talked too loudly.

"We lifted boulders the entire time you were in the tank," John said when he caught me staring at the rips in his sweatshirt and bleeding cuts along his biceps.

He flashed his dimples. "So how was the tank? Do you feel like screaming right now?"

I furrowed my brow. How did he know that?

John laughed at my expression. "In the beginning, I spent my fair share of time in the tank. Trust me, I know how it feels. Everything is so overstimulating afterward that your body can't process how to react."

"Yeah, just like that," I mumbled as I took a small bite.

I was ravenously hungry, yet my stomach cramped unpleasantly with each bite of food, and nausea overwhelmed me.

It didn't help that Malum's fist had pummeled me. I lifted my sweatshirt up discreetly and checked out the patchwork of black-and-blue bruises that marred my pale skin.

It looked heinous.

Even without the kings' handiwork, the ocean, the classwork, the long run, the monster issue, and my time in the tank had fucked me up.

It didn't help that a large plate of ribs was sitting right in front of me at the narrow table.

The scent made my stomach gurgle unpleasantly. I tried not to breathe in.

Ever since the "incident" with my mother, I hadn't been able to stomach the scent or taste of meat.

It was all too familiar.

Back in the beast realm, Jinx had told me I was "the first cannibal vegetarian and an embarrassment to the family."

I missed her.

A few seats down, Horace gulped from a massive glass that definitely didn't hold wine. Red dripped down his lips, and he licked it greedily.

I slumped lower in my chair, buried my head in one hand, and moaned softly as I rode out another wave of nausea. Yawning as exhaustion hit me, I cradled my broken arm against my chest.

You'd think the tank would have been an ideal sleeping spot. But something about the lack of stimulation had made my brain think too much to fall asleep.

My monster had been loud.

I just needed a few hours of rest to forget about my pain —forget that I'd released my monster from its cage and let it control me.

The marble table was cool against my forehead as I slumped forward and closed my eyes.

Half delirious, I sank into a dreamlike state.

I was running. I was drowning in the ocean waves. Lothaire was screaming at me and beating me with his baton. The kings were beating me. Mother was lighting me on fire.

All I knew was nightmares.

I jolted awake for a second, then shut my eyes again.

Think happy thoughts.

A handsome, tall dark man rubbed my back gently and told me he would vanquish all my enemies. He promised he'd bring me their heads on pikes for ever daring to upset me.

Then he moaned and trembled as he did nothing but stare down at me. He was coming.

I drifted into a peaceful slumber.

All was well.

CHAPTER 12
TORMENT

The breaking period: Day 2, hour 14

"Egan," Malum snapped loudly.

I jerked awake, banging my head on the table. The harsh motion made my broken arm scream with pain.

"I'll slit your throat," I replied automatically, still partially in a dreamlike state. I always woke up homicidal. It was embarrassing how many times I'd woken up choking the life out of Sadie or one of the girls.

"What the fuck did you just say to me?" Malum leaned across the table in front of me, silver eyes flickering with the shadows of the red flames that leaped across his arms.

Plates were overflowing with food, and the men were still shoving their faces with ridiculous portions.

The hall buzzed with laughter and talk.

From the hands on the clock, I'd only gotten about thirty minutes of sleep. *Fuck.*

I felt sick.

Rubbing my eyes with my nonaching arm, I groaned with despair.

Scorpius sneered beside him and ran his long fingers

through his slicked-back, perfect hair. "Pretty boy clearly has a death wish."

I groaned again but didn't argue, too busy feeling miserable and exhausted.

"It's not personal." John chuckled beside me, but his eyes were tight like he was faking it. "When I woke our Aran up from the two-hour nap, he tried to wrestle me into a choke hold and promised to 'skin me alive.'"

"Sorry about that," I mumbled.

I'd woken up from our two-hour sleep with my fingers around John's throat. At least he'd been warm.

Unlike Sadie, who liked to grapple for dominance (she always lost; let's be real), John had just arched a dark brow and smiled. Then he'd easily slammed me back onto my cot and detangled himself.

He had said nothing afterward, and that worked for me.

This was the shit Dr. Palmer said would come back to bite me. Digging my good hand into my pocket, I took out my smaller pipe and took a long drag.

Instantly, I felt calmer.

Relaxation settled through me.

I was fine.

Horace moved his chair with a squeak, and I screamed at the sudden loud noise.

I wasn't fine.

Malum chewed slowly on a piece of steak and said, "You've got a lot of problems, don't you, pretty boy?"

He had one of his arms draped over Orion's chair, and his thumb was trailing slowly over the flower tattoo on the blond man's throat.

He'd traced that callused thumb in a similar pattern across my neck. My lower stomach pinched, and the wound on my back burned.

Is Orion looking at me?

Pipe between my lips, I inhaled slowly and stared down at the table. There was no scenario where the gorgeous fae with chocolate-brown eyes ended up being mine.

I needed to concentrate on being a toxic dude with a dick.

Grabbing the pitcher of ale at the table, I tipped back and chugged. Sticky beer running down my throat, I slammed the glass down and let out a rumbling burp.

"Fuck yeah." John high-fived me, and I grinned back at him.

Sixty percent bruh. Thirty percent dude. Ten percent fuckboy. Those were Aran's stats, and I was embracing them.

I grimaced as I wiped ale off my lips. The aftertaste was rancid; how did anyone ever choose beer over wine?

Scorpius stared at my lips with disgust as I wiped at the sticky substance.

He said to Malum, "Egan's probably crumbling because he's never had to work hard a day in his life."

I shook my head and sighed as I pushed my food back and forth across my plate. "Bruh. You wouldn't survive a day in my life."

Faster than I could track, Scorpius lunged and slammed my unbroken hand against the table. Plates clattered around us, and the other recruits turned to watch.

"Let me go, you pale fucking weirdo." I yanked my arm back, but his long fingers were a vise around my much smaller wrist.

Scorpius tightened his grip. "First, I'm not your anything. You can call me sir, my lord, or master." His other hand traced slowly across my fingers.

My breath caught.

For a second, it looked like yellow sparks were leaping between our hands.

"Second," Scorpius sneered slowly. "You haven't worked a day in your life, pretty boy. There isn't a single callus on these soft hands."

His rough fingers danced slowly along my palm as milky white eyes looked off in the distance.

The more powerful the species, the harder it was to have scars or calluses. The skin on Scorpius's fingers was broken and scratchy. So were Malum's.

I looked down at my hands with surprise. But it made sense.

Being lit on fire didn't leave marks. And in the shifter realm, we'd done hand-to-hand combat, running, and fighting with enchanted guns.

I'd never had to do anything that tore apart my hands. Not consistently enough to counter my fast healing.

Scorpius kept mindlessly trailing his long fingers across my palms.

Mother's words taunted me. *"You're a spoiled princess who doesn't understand anything about the world. Someday you'll thank me for doing this. Now don't be a brat, and take it."*

Was I spoiled?

My childhood flashed before me: flames, torture, isolation, cruel taunts, beatings, crying, running away, and terror. Nah.

Jinx's voice sneered in my mind, *"Wow, letting your dead mother gaslight you, Aran. That's even more pathetic than usual."*

Lately I'd been thinking about Jinx more and more.

There was something about a twelve-year-old tearing you to shreds that gave you perspective.

I realized Scorpius was no longer restraining me, and we were both staring off as he caressed my hand.

Yanking my hand away, I cradled it to my chest. "Some experiences don't leave calluses. I'm not pampered."

"Enlighten us," Malum demanded, and he made a show of putting his other arm around Scorpius's chair so he was holding both of them. He was staking his claim.

Whatever. My fictional man would destroy you.

I pushed food back and forth with my fork. "Trust me, you don't want to know. I'd have to kill you."

"Why?" Orion whispered so quietly I barely heard it. His full lips were slightly parted as he took a bite of food.

The table was silent as the kings waited for my answer. Even John had turned to give me his full attention, and the demons were leaning closer.

Because I'm the wanted fae princess who became the fae queen by brutally eating her mother's heart. I'm wanted by millions of fae. Also, I'm a girl in disguise and lying to you. I'm not fae at all and have no clue who my father is. Or what I am.

I swallowed thickly and lamely said, "Just kidding."

"No. You will explain," Malum snarled, and fire crackled higher atop his shaved head.

He sat directly in front of me, and the brutal symmetry of his face was slightly overwhelming. Harsh angles framed almond eyes and a thick brow.

The girl in me couldn't help but rate him.

Eight out of ten for looks. Negative one thousand out of ten for personality.

Malum was handsome in a way that was meaner looking than any of Sadie's men. The neck tattoo of a dagger screamed, "I am toxic."

Orion's tongue darted out as he licked the ale off his lips, and I had to force myself not to stare at him with moon eyes.

Fifteen out of ten for looks. Undecided on personality.

Scorpius twirled the steak knife through his long fingers with a deftness that spoke of extreme control and skill. Only an idiot would think he was held back by his blindness. His masterful control of his other senses was terrifying.

Eight out of ten for looks. Negative two thousand out of ten for personality.

Malum was the harsh leader who ruled with brute force, but something told me Scorpius's cruelty and sneering was a front. A disguise that hid an even bigger monster.

I studied the men for so long that my enchanted wound started to ache. It was a good reminder of why it didn't matter how attractive *any* male was.

Dragging my hands over my forehead, I sighed. "Please, I just have anger issues. There's nothing else to say."

The kings and John stared at me in silence as they ate.

After an endless moment—where I was sure Malum was going to throw his chair back and beat me over the head with it until he uncovered my secrets—Scorpius broke the silence by sneering at me.

"You need to eat. You're acting like a pampered fool who's never had to fuel himself to survive."

I couldn't help myself. "And how do you know I'm not eating, Scorp? It's not like you can see my plate."

Scorpius's upper lip curled back. "Because, Egan, I can fucking hear. You've been snoring the entire meal. And when you're not snoring, you're running your mouth. You haven't chewed once. So why don't you shut the fuck up and eat?"

I shoved a piece of lettuce into my mouth and smacked my lips obnoxiously. "I'm eating."

After three minutes of my choking it down pathetically, Malum interrupted my struggle by pushing a heaping plate of food in front of me. He'd been piling stuff onto it since

I'd woken up, and I'd thought he was just going for fourths.

"What is this?" I pushed it away from me with horror. It was covered in meat.

Malum's eyes flashed, and I wondered how long it would take before he lit me on fire. "That's your fucking meal, Egan. All the recruits have to eat at least two full plates if they're going to survive training. We eat irregularly, so when we get to eat, you have to eat a lot."

"I don't eat meat." I pushed my pipe into my mouth and inhaled the calming smoke.

A muscle in Malum's jaw jumped, and Scorpius scoffed.

Orion shook his head, brilliant blonde hair shining in the light.

His hair reminded me of Xerxes's. But where the omega's hair was yellow blond and hanging to his butt, Orion's was white blond and straight to his shoulders.

It was pretty.

I pushed the meat back and forth across my plate and tried not to gag at the scent. I wasn't eating meat.

Never again.

The problem was I'd grossly miscalculated just how unwell the kings were.

"Hold him down," Malum suddenly snarled at Vegar, who was sitting next to me silently.

Before I could blink, the demon wrapped his hands around my shoulders and held me down with freakish strength.

"What the fuck, Vegar?"

Black veins trailed across his cheeks, and the demon just shrugged as he pushed my chest against the table.

That was the only warning I got.

Malum lunged across the table and shoved a forkful of

food into my mouth. I gagged at the sudden intrusion and tried to spit it back at him.

"John, hold his jaw shut," he snarled and glared at my best friend.

John grabbed my face and squeezed so I couldn't do anything but choke down the food. His dark eyes were sad as he whispered, "Sorry, Aran. It's for your own good. If you don't eat, you won't survive training."

I glared at him as I swallowed thickly, and my stomach burned with nausea and betrayal.

"Open his fucking mouth," Malum demanded again, and John's fingers pried my mouth open.

So much for friendship.

The massive hall fell quiet as everyone turned to stare at the assassin table, where the leader of the kings was force-feeding the newest recruit.

If I could cry, I probably would have.

Instead, I death glared at Malum and let him know with my eyes that I was going to rip him to shreds.

If he noticed or cared, it didn't stop him from shoving the fork between my lips.

Scorpius smirked next to him and kept adding food to the overflowing plate. Orion did nothing but watch me.

For the first time, I felt like my monster.

Our interests were aligned.

I gagged and gagged as more food, which included disgusting meat, was shoved down my throat. The men were so massive they easily overpowered me. I was helpless.

The meat tasted like my mother's heart.

Juices dripping down my lips.

Chunks of gore in my throat.

Tangy copper.

Finally, after what felt like an eternity, the plate was

empty, and Malum sat back into his seat with a triumphant expression on his cruel face.

His voice was rough and low. "This is *my* assassin program. If you want to survive, you'll do everything I say when I say it. This isn't a democracy. I'm a fucking king, and I will be treated as such. Do you understand, Egan?"

My legs trembled with rage as I stood up.

I leaned across the table.

Intent on my action.

Long fingers tangled in my short, curly hair and wrenched my head back. Scorpius had also stood up, and once again he pulled my head back at an impossible angle.

What was the fucker's issue with my hair?

Scorpius used his height to hold me immobile. My hips dug uncomfortably into the side of the table as he towered over me.

"Don't you fucking dare throw up on him. I'll take you back to the tank myself."

How did Scorpius know exactly what I was planning to do?

I trembled with anger.

"You don't know who you're messing with, Egan," he sneered dangerously, then flung me backward with so much force that my chair clattered to the ground beside me on the floor.

Broken arm screaming with pain, I dragged myself back into my chair. Chest heaving, I stared down at the table and refused to look at any of the men.

John shuffled uncomfortably beside me, but I didn't look over at him. He'd betrayed me.

They all fucking sucked.

I was going to make them pay. Someday, they'd regret how they treated me.

With my head lowered, the next hour passed in a blur of nausea as I rode out the pain of an overly full stomach and the taste of Mother's heart in my mouth.

I sat with the other recruits in a small classroom as we waited for Lothaire to enter.

Malum had ordered us all to go to the classroom after the horrible meal.

From what I could gather, Lothaire informed Malum about the daily plan, and he was in charge of ensuring we showed up on time.

Malum was our leader.

I'd never felt less like following someone.

Suddenly, the classroom door flung open, and Lothaire stalked into the room with Lyla following gracefully behind him.

The witch's green hair shone like emeralds, and white runes glowed across her dark skin.

Lothaire looked at me. "Every few days, Lyla works with us to ensure you're well enough to perform at your highest."

He narrowed his eyes like he didn't believe our wellness mattered. "Most importantly, she reads the aura of each recruit and lets you know your biggest weakness. What's holding you back from being your best." Lothaire snapped his fingers. "Stand in a line, recruits, and show some fucking respect to her for having to deal with your miserable asses."

"Yes, sir," we chorused back and shuffled quickly into a line.

I made sure I was last because I didn't want to give the kings my back. Who knew what type of shit they'd do when I wasn't looking.

One by one, Lyla inspected the men with her glowing hands.

Apparently, Horace was blood deficient and needed to drink another pint. Lothaire pulled out a bag of blood from beneath the front desk and handed it to him.

Who kept bags of blood in a classroom?

Creeps. That was who.

Vegar and Zenith had hairline fractures in various places, and Lyla held her hands over those spots on their bodies until she was satisfied that they'd healed.

John's body temperature was dangerously low, and Lyla chanted in Latin until his pale cheeks regained their healthy olive flush.

The three kings were completely fine, which made my petty ass seethe with annoyance. Not a single broken bone or latent sexually transmitted disease.

It was official.

There was no god in the realms.

Finally, it was my turn.

For a long moment, Lyla trailed her glowing hands across the air in front of my body, and her emerald eyes bore into me like she could see my black soul.

I shifted back and forth under her piercing gaze.

Lyla's perfectly shaped dark eyebrow lifted slightly, and it was the most outward emotion I'd ever seen her express.

I swallowed thickly.

She kept staring.

For some reason, I knew in my bones that she saw every single one of my secrets.

My stomach dropped. Was this it? Would she out me and sign my death warrant?

Her lips parted. "Severe hypothermia. Arm broken in four places. Cracked femur. Internal organ damage, and…"

I held my breath, certain she was about to say, "He's a she."

"Severe psychological trauma."

A manic giggle bubbled up my throat, and I couldn't swallow it in time. The last one I could have told her for free.

The leg part was a little surprising.

I'd noticed a slight pain when I walked and wondered why my leg hurt. It was probably from one of the many times I'd been shoved to the ground.

Was it the ocean, run, baton, monster, tank, beating, or the public force-feeding? So much to choose from.

The room was uncomfortably silent as the other recruits gaped at me, and even Lothaire narrowed his eyes like he was surprised I wasn't complaining.

What did they want me to do, cry about it?

The white light on Lyla's hands shed warmth as the pentagon runes on her skin glowed brighter.

Her hands lingered on my arm, stomach, and leg for a while.

Searing pain split through me with such ferocity that I barely swallowed my scream.

Lyla chanted louder as her Latin words transformed into another language, one I'd never heard before.

Knees trembling, it took all my willpower not to collapse as she kept giving attention to my wounds.

Finally, she pulled away, and the agony stopped rocking through me.

She'd healed all my wounds, except for the constant dull ache that pulsed through the wound on my back.

Still. It was better than nothing.

Lyla stood in front of me with a blank expression back on her serene face.

"Thank you," I whispered reverently and infused my words with everything I couldn't say.

I knelt before her and bowed my head.

She lightly patted the top of my head like she understood I was thanking her for not outing me, for keeping my secret.

Lothaire's harsh voice broke the moment. "Aran, you will wear thermal compression wear under your clothes at all times, do you understand me?"

"Yes, sir." I nodded and took my seat like the rest of the recruits.

"You will also eat more at every meal until you're no longer pathetic and scrawny."

I gritted my teeth and said, "Yes, sir."

No one had ever called me scrawny in my life, and it was only because the other men were built like tanks.

It wasn't fair.

It also didn't slip my attention that Lothaire had ignored doing anything about my severe mental trauma.

No wonder he'd crawled into bed with Mother.

They both thought physical violence was the only acceptable solution.

Lothaire pointed to the witch. "Lyla will now read your auras, an ancient practice that is more than some of you deserve." He lingered on me when he spoke, and I fought the urge to roll my eyes at him.

He really was annoyingly dramatic. I mean, it was obvious when he'd started demanding the "yes, sirs," but it still surprised me how aggressive he was.

Did he ever just chill?

Have any hobbies besides torture?

I couldn't see it.

"Your fear for Vegar holds you back, and it will do nothing but hurt him," Lyla said to Zenith.

She moved to the next desk and said to Vegar, "You're too dependent on Zenith."

The demons stared back at her with sullen faces.

Lyla turned to Horace and said, "Your lack of empathy will doom you. You will be destroyed by a close friend if you continue to not care about others."

Horace glowered at the witch.

I'd bet all the fae palace riches that Horace was a dead man walking. You didn't fuck around with a witch's prophecy.

And since you could see in his eyes that he didn't give a single fuck about anyone but himself, he was so dead. Good.

The real question was, who would ever befriend such a jerk?

When Lyla got to the kings, she spoke to all three of them and paused for a while.

Then she said, "You're incomplete and will never be what you need to be until you're whole. You will never serve *him* properly if you can't find your missing fourth."

Her green eyes glowed brightly as she spoke.

Scorpius scowled, Malum squeezed his fist, and Orion slumped his shoulders like he was defeated.

John had talked about them having a secret mission for Lothaire. Was that the "him" they were serving?

What type of psychotic man could ever earn Malum's respect and be their fourth? I couldn't see it.

My musings were interrupted when Lyla moved in front of John and said, "You are split in two. You must find balance, or they will tear you apart."

Maybe he's split in two because John is also a girl in disguise?

I swallowed down a chuckle at the ridiculous image of John in heels. Nah, he couldn't pull it off.

John shifted uncomfortably and looked away as his dark eyes glittered with some intense emotion.

I was still mad at him for obeying the kings and holding my face, but something about the way his body tightened with tension made me want to ask him if he was all right.

One second, John was jovial and sweet, and the next, he was radiating danger. That was probably what Lyla was referring to.

Even if I was mad at him, I didn't want to see him torn apart.

I thought back to how we'd slept side by side with our arms entwined for warmth. And he hadn't admonished me for trying to choke him in his sleep.

He was becoming my friend.

John slumped lower in his chair, and I awkwardly patted his back. He looked up at me and flashed a dimple, and I was glad I'd extended the olive branch.

But now it was my turn.

As Lyla stood in front of me, my heart rate went through the roof. I rubbed my clammy hands across my pants.

Please don't out me. Please don't reveal my secrets.

"You will not be who you need to be until you embrace the dragon."

What?

In my peripheral vision, Malum reared back like he'd been hit, then whispered something to Scorpius.

Sun god, talk about confusing.

An awful sensation squeezed my gut. Technically, I knew a dragon. The half warrior Demetre's alpha form was a dragon, but he was the man who'd betrayed me to Mother.

I was going to be sick.

Maybe the dragon is symbolic of something else? It better be.

Malum looked over at me and glared with vehemence like I'd done something yet again to offend him.

I itched my nose with my middle finger.

Lothaire clapped his hands, and I whipped my hand down before he could beat me with his baton.

Malum's silver eyes promised death and pain.

"Thank you, Lyla," Lothaire said as the witch exited the room like she hadn't just eviscerated all of us. "Now we have one more announcement. Our other instructors this year have been away completing a mission for me. However, things are not progressing as expected." His scar pulled tight as he scowled.

Their mission seemed important, and Lothaire was clearly *not* happy about it.

He continued, "As a result of some unanticipated obstacles, they're going to split their time between their mission and training your sorry asses. I'm pleased to introduce three of this academy's most successful assassins. For the last two centuries, they've served me and successfully infiltrated the fae monarchy. They've gathered political support in the region and are experts at espionage."

The door opened.

Three men stalked inside.

The room tilted, and my white-knuckle grip on the desk was the only thing that kept me from falling out of my chair.

"Demetre, Noah, and Shane will be helping me train."

I roughly swallowed down the scream that burned my throat.

What were the odds that just after Lyla told me I needed a dragon, a *literal* dragon shifter walked into the room?

The three reasons I had an enchanted slur carved into my back stood before me.

"We're excited to see what you can do." Demetre's pink eyes flashed as he smirked at us.

Noah and Shane nodded, and their orange mohawks were bright against their dark skin, green eyes gleaming like snakes.

My first true friends.

The men who'd turned into my worst enemies.

The three men who'd dragged me from the fae sex clinic and thrown me at my mother's feet.

The half warriors were my new teachers.

I needed harder drugs.

CHAPTER 13

OLD ENEMIES RETURN

The breaking period: Day 5, hour 1

"Haul!" Demetre yelled as we hoisted the *massive* fucking slab of stone above our heads.

Lyla's prophecy was coming true because if the dragon was Demetre, then I was mentally embracing him. In my head, I punched him in the dick and beat him to death with a stick.

"Haul higher!" Demetre bellowed over the wind.

Mentally, I hit him harder with my stick.

Prophecy fulfilled.

Arms trembling, shoulder blades screaming in agony, I whimpered as seconds dragged into minutes.

We'd been standing outside the barracks, hauling the fucking slab from hell for the last five hours. We'd been generously given a thirty-minute rest beforehand to prepare.

It had not prepared me.

Sleep deprivation made my head pound.

"Lower!" Noah shouted, orange mohawk gleaming red in the shadow of the eclipse.

Sulfur and salt filled my nose.

The wind howled.

"Fucking pathetic." Lothaire slammed his baton against his hand with a loud crack. "It's just a little stone, and you're all trembling like weak bitches. How the fuck do you expect to the be the best when you're weak as fuck?"

Little. Stone. My. Butt.

The granite rock was a foot thick and as long as a small boat. It weighed at least a ton.

The worst part was that since I was a little shorter than everyone (with all our arms raised above my head, the other men pushed the rock out of my reach), I was forced to stand at the very back with the slab tilted downward.

It was crushing me.

Bloody cuts covered my bare feet as the granite crushed me from above.

"Haul!" Shane shouted, and we pushed our arms up so our elbows were locked.

My arms shook.

The sun god had abandoned me in this hellscape of a realm.

Everything hurt.

Even though the wind was chilly and the salty air sharp, sweat dripped down my forehead and stung my eyes.

I blinked aggressively and internally screamed in agony.

If I released the stone, it would crush me with a splat and my arms could finally rest.

But it wouldn't kill me.

So I didn't bother.

"*Aran, stop fucking trembling like a little bitch!*" Lothaire slammed his baton against the wound on my back.

CRACK.

I saw white.

My knees knocking, the only thing that kept me standing

was the promise of vengeance. I'd play the vampyre's game, and then when he least expected it, I'd rip out his throat.

"Yes, sir!" I half yelled, half moaned.

"Boy, you better get that tone out of your voice." Lothaire slammed the baton against my side.

CRACK.

When I inhaled, it was like a thousand knives were stabbed against my side. The bloodsucking fucker had broken ribs.

I shook like a leaf.

"Lower!" Demetre shouted, and my straining forearms wept with relief as I tilted my head to the side and transferred the crushing weight to my shoulder.

"I don't know, Lothaire. Aran's holding up better than some of the men our year," Shane said with a chuckle as he grinned at Lothaire. "Remember Croxy. He gave up an hour in and decapitated himself."

Shane winked at me like he was trying to make me laugh.

It wasn't funny.

Lothaire nodded, and the corners of his mouth turned up like decapitation made him happy.

He reminded me of my monster.

The three half warriors all laughed with Lothaire, like this little horror show was hilarious.

I imagined Croxy's decapitation. Gore splattering in an arc as he collapsed into nothingness.

Lucky bastard.

"Haul!" Shane yelled.

We hoisted the motherfucker above our heads.

Shoulder blades and biceps burning, my fingers cramped and slipped against the smooth stone.

Life couldn't get any worse.

"All right, now we're going to haul the rock while jogging around the perimeter of the island!" Lothaire yelled.

It got worse.

I whimpered, and I wasn't the only one. Explicit words were grunted as the massive men in front of me struggled with the task.

Even the three kings were dripping in sweat, and their expressions were hard as they breathed raggedly.

"*It wasn't a question. Begin*! Lazy fuckers." Lothaire stalked toward us while cracking his baton like he was going to beat us senseless.

We began to move.

Slowly.

Knees aching, they almost buckled under the excessive weight I was balancing above my head, and pain streaked along my thighs.

The three half warriors jogged beside us.

"Lower!"

We lowered our arms.

"Haul!"

Muscles twitching, we heaved upward and navigated the impossible terrain as a unit.

Every few minutes, Shane would say something encouraging and clap his hands like he wanted us to succeed. He'd always been the nicer twin.

In contrast, Demetre and Noah glared at us like we were pathetic.

I didn't give a single fuck.

Just wanted to survive the death march. I puffed in sulfur-stained air and breathed out misery.

The eclipse mocked me.

Minutes bled into hours, and every muscle in my body twitched.

One step forward. Don't stop.

I shut down my thoughts until the only thing rattling through my brain was *one step*.

That was all it was.

One step in front of the other.

That was all I could process, because if I thought about how long we'd been suffering and how far we had to go, I'd collapse.

One step.

After three laps around the island, nine nauseating miles, Scorpius leaned over and whispered something in Malum's ear. The silver-eyed prick turned around and glanced back at me over his shoulder.

I didn't have the energy to sneer.

Sun god, they were obsessed with me. *Get in line.*

I squeezed my eyes shut every few seconds to try to relieve the salty sting. Sweat blinded me.

When Malum turned his head back around, I let loose the breath I hadn't realized I was holding.

His flaming fist slamming into my stomach and the cruel expression on his face as he'd force-fed meat down my throat was going to play starring roles in my future nightmares.

I wished I could let my monster free like I had during the run. It would be too easy to let the mindless rage take over.

But it was dead silent and hadn't let out a single snarl since the time in the tank.

There was no rage left inside me.

Only emptiness.

And pain.

John, who was holding the stone beside Malum, looked over his shoulder to see what the kings were whispering about.

His dark eyes were hard. There was no sign of the nice human. He glanced at the oversize sweatpants that hung loose on my hips.

I was built lean compared to him, and exercising for ungodly hours was not helping my figure.

At least my pants hadn't fallen off, and I had on boxers in case it did happen so no one would know my secret. Even with my being exhausted, panic exploded in my chest at the thought of them finding out I was a girl.

Why was being a man so difficult?

"Haul!"

One. Two. Three.

One step at a time. I focused on the blistering ache in my lungs and the shooting pain in my arms rather than the anxiety crushing my chest.

"Lower!"

Somehow the anxiety was worse than the physical pain.

We completed another lap.

The more we ran, the more my vision blurred. The world twisted in ruby shadows around me as I climbed closer to my limit.

Giving up wasn't going to be a choice.

My body would collapse beneath me.

Each step became shakier.

Sisyphus, an ancient earth fae, had rolled a boulder up a mountain because he'd pissed off the sun god. His punishment was now mine.

If he can do it, so can you.

Like Sisyphus, I kept going.

As if the sun god was rewarding my dedication, the crushing weight on my arms lessened slightly.

"I'll help them out for the last lap," Shane said to

Lothaire as he positioned himself beside me at the back of the group.

Massive biceps straining, Shane smiled at me as he took a considerable weight off my shoulders.

"So you're the new guy? Lothaire said you were from the fae realm, but I don't remember you," Shane asked casually as he fell into step beside me.

He wanted to talk.

I swallowed thickly, unable to make my dry throat work. "Cousin," I huffed. "Of the—" I coughed. "—monarch."

Shane's good-natured expression dissipated like smoke, and his handsome face transformed into hard planes. The blood-orange mohawk was a stark warning against his dark skin—he radiated violence.

Shane dropped his arms, putting the brunt of the stone back onto my struggling arms.

Bones crushing, pain streaked across my spine like the white lightning in the halls.

Don't pass out.

"I hate them." I huffed. "Fae monarchy." Gasp. "Loathe them."

Shane's hateful expression melted away, and he hoisted the rock back up and relieved me of the crushing agony. "Good. Good. We don't tolerate fae monarch sympathizers. They're all scum."

I nodded shakily.

The irony was not lost on me.

I *was* the monarchy.

Hi, Shane, actually it's Arabella. Remember when you used to be my friend and then decided you hated me because I obeyed my mother? Same.

I'd hoped that with my mother dead, the half warriors might have lost their grudge against me.

Maybe they'd seen when I killed her that I hated her as much as them. I hadn't wanted to hurt them. I'd been practically still a child, and my mother had forced me.

It was her they hated, after all.

But that didn't seem to be the case. Apparently they had more of a problem with the entire royal institution.

Not good.

Shane grinned over at me, like we were bonding over our hatred of the monarchy.

I grimaced back.

"Haul!"

We lifted.

We jogged forward, arms straining, with ragged lungs.

"Lower!"

We lowered.

One step at a time.

Shane looked over at me, and his proximity made the hairs on the back of my neck stand up. "I've only known one person with blue hair like yours, but theirs was straight."

My stomach plummeted.

Thank the sun god for mother's enchantment that had given me fae ears and straight hair.

Now my natural hair was a curly, unrecognizable mess. But the shade was still the same unique, vibrant turquoise.

It was unmistakable.

"Runs." I breathed shakily. "In family."

Shane nodded.

I held my breath. Waited for him to point out that the fae rarely procreated. If I was a cousin of the queen, then I would've been known in the realm.

Shane just nodded. "I like the color. It's pretty sick. Reminds me of mine."

His blood-orange mohawk was pin straight and stuck about three inches off the rest of his shaved head.

The color was just as vibrant.

I smiled back, or at least tried to, but I'd lost feeling in my face hours ago.

Thank the sun god he was buying my excuse and not prying further into my shitty cover story. The only good thing was the fae realm was insanely large, so technically there were faraway lands I could have lived in.

We ran past Lothaire, and the vampyre said, "Done. Drop the stone."

There was a sun god.

"Yes, sir!" we said.

The heavy granite fell to the side with a massive bam. Rocks vibrated beneath my feet as the slab cracked into smaller pieces.

I collapsed onto my back and breathed roughly.

My eyes closed as I soared on a cloud of aching agony.

Every muscle and bone creaked within me.

I opened my eyes to see a large palm hovering in the air above me. John stared down at me with his harsh demeanor.

He'd held my face as the kings shoved food down my mouth. I might have forgiven him, but I didn't want to touch him.

John kept his arm extended and stared at me with an unreadable expression. Sweat dripped down his cheeks.

Oh, what the fuck.

I was too tired to care.

Torture did that to a person.

I let him haul me to my feet, and we didn't say anything because we didn't need to.

Besides us, the kings were the only three also standing.

But Malum was holding up Orion, and Scorpius was rubbing his back while whispering something.

It was an intimate scene.

Beside them, Vegar was on his knees, vomiting a thick, clear mucus, and Zenith knelt, holding his hair. Horace had his hands on his knees and was coughing aggressively.

No one was well.

"I see you've met my twin brother," Noah said as he walked over and held out his palm.

I shook it and pretended the shaking motion hadn't made pinpricks of light explode across my vision. There was no muscle left in my arm.

"We're also part fae, and we've been working on a new mission in the fae realm. It's great to see a fae in the assassin program." Noah stared down at me with a blank expression, and he didn't smile like his twin, Shane.

I nodded, unsure of what to say.

Since you were enslaved and fighting in the fae gladiator games for my mother, how was that a mission? Also, aren't the three kings also fae?

Demetre walked over to stand beside Noah, pink eyes hard. "We haven't had a new recruit last more than a few hours in years. Interesting."

I tried not to think about the prophecy as he talked to me.

Shane grinned and clapped me on my back, directly across my enchanted wound.

I bit down on my tongue and swallowed a scream.

The world spun.

It took every ounce of willpower I possessed to not stagger to the side and face-plant into rocks.

Why do men always hit each other on the backs?

It was heinous.

Lothaire smacked his baton against his hands. "All right, you lazy fuckers get a break in the bathhouse because I'm so generous. Follow me."

He was the queen of gaslighting.

Knees knocking together, I was too tired to even care about being clean.

My teeth had been chattering for so long that I'd forgotten what it was like to be warm. Also, I was 99 percent sure this was a trick and Lothaire was about to drown us in cold water.

I didn't get my hopes up.

John joined me, and we silently dragged our aching carcasses up the endless stairs. He grabbed my shoulder a couple of times to steady me when I tripped and almost fell backward.

I returned the favor.

The cliffside was jagged and deadly.

We were weak.

All the bad blood was behind us.

It was hard to hold grudges over inconsequential things like forced feedings when you'd both just hauled a stone for hours. We didn't need to speak to understand that all was forgiven.

Shared trauma did that.

Side by side, we followed Lothaire down the lightning-streaked halls.

The stained-glass mosaic of the bloody woman holding the baby seemed to stare at me with disappointment. Chandeliers threw sparkles across black and gold.

Her eyes were large and sad, as tears streaked down her face. In their shimmery depths, she accused me of abandoning all women.

We're all just surviving, I snarled back in my mind. Who was she to judge me?

I stumbled when Malum placed Orion's arm around Scorpius. He slowed down to walk beside me.

He leaned down and overwhelmed my personal space with his seven-feet-tall size. Silence and aggression swirled between us.

Even though Malum was a sweaty mess, the decadent scents of tobacco and whiskey wafted off him.

I inhaled discreetly.

What did it mean when your tormentor smelled divine?

John moved closer to me as we waited for Malum to speak.

Silver eyes flashed, and his deep voice rumbled, "Stop playing games with our instructors."

For a second, the combination of his rough voice and smoky scent made my toes curl.

I decided my fictional man would have a similar voice and scent. It obviously couldn't be Malum, but he provided a nice template.

"Did you hear me?" Malum snapped, and I realized he was waiting for me to speak.

What were you supposed to say to a deranged lunatic?

"I'm not playing games," I croaked from my dry throat. The act of speaking was too much effort and left me breathless.

Scorpius and Orion slowed down so they joined our little gossip group. Being blind didn't stop the pale bastard from elbowing John out of the way.

He and Malum loomed on either side of me and pinned me between their warm bodies.

The eye tattooed on his neck blinked as it stared at me. *Creepy.*

Scorpius sneered, "Don't fuck around with the instructors. It never ends well."

What?

"At best, they'll stick their dicks in your mouth and call you handsome. At worst, it's a test and they'll slit your throat as you come."

My jaw dropped at their explicit language.

"I'm not into the instructors. At all!" I said with outrage. Why were they so unnecessarily vulgar?

Malum's deep voice dripped with disgust. "Plus, Orion is more attractive than you'll ever be. The half warriors tried to fuck him a few years ago, and they're still pining over him. Don't waste your breath."

I glanced over at the stunning fae who now had pink splotches across his high cheekbones. He was hanging onto Scorpius's arm and walking with a limp.

White-blond hair slicked back with sweat and red lips pouty from gnawing on them.

Orion looked like a cover model.

Ladies always obsessed over Sadie's mate Cobra. He had strong features and precious jewels embedded in his skin. They'd die if they ever saw Orion.

Because the fae man *was* a jewel.

The half warriors have good taste.

"You're just embarrassing yourself." Scorpius's voice dripped with scorn as he slammed his shoulder against me.

I swallowed down vomit, and John's hands against my back kept me upright.

Why did they think I was competing with Orion?

He was 100 percent more attractive than me.

"Got it?" Malum asked with a growl.

"I'm thinking…" I held my fist up and pretended to wind up a child's toy.

My middle finger popped up. "Go fuck yourselves."

Malum exploded into flames, and Scorpius lunged forward, but Orion weakly wrapped his arms around his shoulders and whispered in his ear.

The kings stalked off without another word.

Pussies.

"What was that about?" John asked. "I've never seen the kings so worked up."

I shrugged. I had that effect on people.

In front of us, Malum and Scorpius transferred Orion so the two of them held him up. Malum tenderly ran his fingers through Orion's hair, and Scorpius placed a kiss on his forehead.

They looked back at me with death in their eyes.

Lightning streaked across the walls.

Electricity crackled.

I'd been so concerned with the kings that I didn't realize the half warriors were walking near me. They were the biggest danger to my disguise.

I needed to worry about them, not the kings.

Everywhere I turned, enemies surrounded me.

"Follow me," Lothaire said as he shoved open a black door I'd never seen before. As I walked into the room, I forgot to breathe.

Holy shit.

CHAPTER 14
FLAMES & WATER

The breaking period: Day 5, hour 14

I stared into the promised land of the sun god.

If I had any emotional capacity left, tears would have streamed down my face because it was that beautiful.

Divine. Wonderful. Exquisite.

Eyes bone dry, I stepped into the bathing *palace* and sighed as warm steam curled across my chilled flesh.

Water bubbled and frothed throughout the dimly lit, low-ceilinged space.

Heated waterfalls streamed down all four walls, and in the middle of the room, the largest tub I'd ever seen popped with churning bubbles. In the center, water spilled from a turquoise tile spout into the frothing tub.

I'd never seen anything like it.

Paradise.

The eight of us stood along the narrow tile walkway that led to the tub.

Lothaire glared at us.

His harsh features and cold demeanor were out of place among the lavender-scented bubbles floating in the air.

Bro needed a good smoke in the bath.

The intrusive thoughts told me to push him in. *What can he do? Beat you up?*

Lothaire snapped, "You fuckers get this room for the next six hours. The water is infused with crystals and has been blessed by Lyla to accelerate your healing. I don't care what the fuck you do with your time in here; just be ready to work afterward. Don't get used to it, you lazy fuckers."

What does he mean about doing stuff? It's just a bathing room.

Lothaire glared.

We stared back respectfully.

He arched his eyebrow slowly, and his face darkened as he waited.

We must have all realized what he was waiting for at the same time because we chanted in unison, "Yes, sir!"

I wasn't the only one struggling to keep my eyes open and focus.

Lothaire spat, "Lazy, useless, ugly fuckers," but he didn't bludgeon us to death with his baton.

A win.

He stalked out of the warm room and said something to the half warriors, who waited for him in the hall. The door swung shut behind him.

Water trickled, and bubbles floated.

We were alone.

The eight of us stood in silence. Covered in ocean water, cuts, dirt, and sweat. Our feet left bloody footprints on the marble floors.

Six sun-god-blessed hours.

An eternity.

Trembling, I yanked desperately at my sweatpants, freeing my legs from the freezing material.

The boxers preserved my modesty, and I was too tired to worry.

I went to pull off my sweatshirt, but my shoulders screamed as I tried to raise my arms. My eyes rolled back with pain.

I remembered the scars.

The sweatshirt stayed on.

Teeth clacking loudly, my body shivered from cold and muscle aches.

This is misery.

In my sweatshirt and boxers, I took a tentative step forward, then face-planted into the whirling pool.

Heat enveloped me, and pinpricks of agony exploded across my cold flesh.

It was the opposite of the tank. I was overly stimulated.

I dragged myself to the low bench on the perimeter of the tub and washed my hair with soap that had been left out.

Afterward, I rested on the edge.

Closed my eyes.

Far away, water lapped as seven men threw themselves into the pool.

I drifted away.

In my dreams, I begged the sun god to take me from this heinous place and make the suffering end.

I screamed at him. Shouted as I begged and prostrated myself at his divine feet.

But he did nothing.

I was all alone.

No one saved me because they never did.

And they never would.

I woke up to grunts and moans.

Rubbing at my eyes, I was momentarily disoriented by the hot water that slapped my face.

Neck aching, I groaned and rolled out my shoulders.

Consciousness returned in a slow trickle.

I was pressed against the hard edge of the pool, and for the first time in days, I didn't feel like I was going to die from sleep deprivation.

My skin no longer felt like it was falling off my bones from exhaustion, and my muscles didn't throb in time with my heartbeat.

Warmth bubbled around me.

It was wonderful.

A smile pulled at my lips as I sank contentedly into the heat. Against all odds, I'd regained my will to live.

Loud noises interrupted my blissful state.

Women moaned.

Men breathed harshly.

Flesh slapped.

The smile fell off my face as I took in my surroundings.

What. The. Flying. Fuck.

I covered my mouth with my hand as I tried to process just what in the sun god I'd woken up to.

"Oh, please more, Master. Harder. Yes, yes, please, yes, don't stop."

A familiar burn streaked across my back.

In the far corner of the tub, Zenith and Vegar were wrapped up in each other's arms, kissing.

A few feet away from them, John was sitting on the shallow pool ledge with half his naked body in the water as a man bobbed down and sucked him off under the water.

Ew, I didn't need to see my friend getting head. I needed bleach.

John groaned loudly.

Nope. No. I am not doing this.

I ducked under the water and prayed that I was just having a horrible nightmare.

When I came back up, the room was still full of people having sex.

Suddenly I understood what Lothaire had meant about us doing whatever we wanted.

But this?

All I wanted to do was sleep for hours, smoke, and eat sour candy. We'd literally just been *tortured* for days.

What was wrong with men?

Even Horace was making out with a girl, although his yellow eyes were wide open as he kissed her, which was beyond creepy.

I grimaced and looked away from him, and I immediately regretted it.

Close enough that I could reach out and touch them, the kings were ass naked, fucking two girls.

I choked.

Weren't they in a relationship with Orion?

Malum knelt on the tile floor, massive butt cheeks rippling, as he slammed his dick into a woman on all fours. Even more shockingly, Scorpius stood in front of the same girl and fucked her face.

But he had a steak knife in his hand, and he pressed it against her neck. *Did he take that from the dining hall?*

In the future, I would not be using the silverware.

Blood dripped down her chest.

But they weren't the only ones groaning with ecstasy.

Beside them, Orion's too-pretty face was flung back, and

his wet blond hair was plastered to his flower tattoos on his neck. He was fucking a woman from behind.

The quiet man slammed her against the water-streaked wall with so much force that the marble rattled.

Holy. Fucking. Shit.

He had a divine butt.

The pain across my back increased in intensity.

The fae were notoriously open about sex, at least the *nonelite* fae, who weren't breeding tools. But everything always happened behind the closed doors of the sex clinics. And I never watched the sexual broadcasts that exploited people.

So technically, I'd never seen people having sex before.

Well, I was fucking seeing it now.

Scorpius pressed the knife harder against the delicate skin of the woman's neck, and he smeared her blood across her breasts.

Moving in rhythm, the three fae slammed their cocks into the two women at the same time.

Malum had a belt in his hand, and he slapped it across the woman's bright-red ass.

She moaned around Scorpius's cock and begged, "Please. Please, more, Master."

I jumped when the belt smacked her harder.

Scorpius and Malum were sadists.

I hated to be that dumb bitch virgin, but I couldn't wrap my head around what was happening.

There was. No. fucking. Way. That what they were doing was pleasurable.

This was a hate crime.

Blood dripping, loud grunts, heady moans. The forceful pistoning of hips made the endless muscles ripple across their bodies.

Each king had a detailed tattoo of a serpent eating its own tail on his hip.

They also had words written across their ridiculously wide shoulders.

"Venimus" sprawled across Orion's golden back.

We came.

"Vidimus" covered Scorpius's pale skin.

We saw.

"Vicimus" was tattooed in thick black letters across Malum's flesh.

We conquered.

They had ancient Latin words on their backs, and everyone knew Latin was the language of the gods.

It was spoken to children at a young age.

Everyone knew the rumors.

If a world stopped speaking Latin, then it meant the gods had abandoned the realm. When Latin was dead, people died.

But why did the kings have it tattooed?

Oh no, I was starting to worry about what other people did with their bodies.

I was truly becoming a man.

At least you're not the only one with words on your back. You could pretend "whore" means something in a different language.

A chuckle burst from my throat.

Malum's buzzed head snapped to the side, gray eyes hard as steel as he kept slamming himself into the girl between his legs.

I sank lower into the water.

Never mind, him watching me while he fucked a woman was the *real* hate crime. My cheeks burned, and I knew my face was the color of a tomato.

Malum licked his lips slowly like he was taunting me as

he tipped his buzzed head backward. The endless lines on his abdominals pulled and bunched deliciously.

No. Not delicious. Horrible. Heinous.

I couldn't look away.

Predator stared at prey.

Hint: I was at the top of the food chain.

My breath caught as he slammed the belt harder along her ass. All while maintaining brutal eye contact.

Scorpius dragged the dagger across the swell of her full breasts.

The woman pulled her head off of Scorpius's dick and moaned breathily, "I'm coming. I'm coming."

"I don't care," Scorpius growled as he choked her with one hand and shoved his dick back between her lips.

Malum's belt hit harder. Angry purple welts rose along her ass.

Tears streamed down the woman's face as she shuddered and bucked, the knife pressed against her breast, face turning purple from asphyxiation.

Steel eyes never left mine.

My lower stomach pinching, the burning sensation across my back spiked hotter. Like knives were jammed into my spine.

Malum's thigh muscles bunched and his face scrunched as the woman's eyes rolled back like she was about to pass out.

"You're fucking dead, pretty boy," he mouthed as his hips snapped harder while Scorpius pulled her hair and moaned.

Pain blinded me.

Eyes dead, face relaxed, I revealed nothing.

Cum flooded out as Malum pulled his cock out of the woman's ass. He never looked away from me.

They released her.

The woman collapsed onto the tile, boneless and satiated as her hips continued to buck.

Scorpius came all over her face with a grunt.

What species is she? Everyone knew it was nearly impossible for a female to come from having her ass penetrated. Let alone while having her ass beat and a dagger to the boob.

I was lowkey impressed.

Not my thing—but good for her.

The moaning woman sat up, and she tiredly reached for Malum. Pressing a kiss to his cheek, she grabbed at his tanned shoulders to steady herself.

Malum shoved her violently away, and her skin smacked loudly across the tile.

"Never touch me, slut," Malum growled, his raspy voice brimming with malice.

"But. I didn't mean…what? Master?" the woman stuttered as her brows pulled tight with confusion.

"I don't give a fuck what you meant. Don't touch me."

Her eyebrows rose higher. "I don't care if you're a king and a dom. You don't get to treat me like this." She leaned forward to push at his chest.

All great points.

I silently cheered her on.

But the second her fingers touched his skin, Malum snapped upward. Pure hatred radiated off him, and he transformed into the evil fucker that had shoved food down my throat.

Fire leaped across his arms.

"You fucking cunt. I warned you." His voice was a low rasp. "You have five seconds to leave or I'll light you on fire."

Tears filled her doe eyes as she chose a different angle. "Master?"

Orion stopped fucking the woman against the wall as he watched his leader.

"Five. Four," Malum counted.

Her lip quivered as she looked up at Scorpius. "You're going to let him treat me like this, Master?"

I grimaced.

He was not about to help her.

White eyes staring across the room, Scorpius tipped his handsome face backward and laughed cruelly.

"Corvus is everything to me, and you're nothing. He *told* you not to touch him, and you did it anyway. You're nothing but a hole to fuck. Now listen to him and get your used ass out of here. Also, you suck at giving head."

Malum continued to count, "Three. Two."

Sobbing, the beautiful girl bent to grab her clothes off the floor, but Scorpius kicked them into the water.

"You'll fucking leave naked, and tell everyone that you were punished for touching Corvus. No. One. Touches him. Understood?"

She sobbed harder.

"One," Malum snarled.

"Stop it!" I yelled as I grabbed her wet clothes from the pool. "Don't listen to them. They're just ugly bullies."

She blinked at me.

I handed her the wet clothes. "At least you can cover yourself with these. Seriously, you can find *way* better men to have sex with. Trust me. Like anyone would be better than them."

I winked at her, hating the demoralized hunch of her shoulders.

"I cannot emphasize enough how *anyone* would be better."

Her lips turned up slightly.

Public humiliation was Mother's favorite, and it never got easier. It never stopped hurting.

The shame changed a person.

All I'd ever wanted was for one fae to stand up for me and tell Mother to go fuck herself.

Just one person to show a little empathy.

No one ever did.

"Thanks." She smiled shyly. "I'm Tara."

"Aran." I smiled back.

"I know." Tara was impressively tall for a woman, probably taller than myself, and had curves that I envied.

Where she was all ass and boobs, my female form was built like a barn door.

A slight exaggeration, but I still had more muscles than the average woman.

Where I was lean and strong with small curves, Tara was soft and lush like a dream woman come to life.

She was stunning.

I couldn't help but reassure her. "No worries, and seriously, you're way out of their league. I'm not joking. Don't let it get to you."

I whispered and fanned my hand like I smelled something rancid. "I've heard they have bowel problems."

Tara choked on a watery laugh as she covered herself with the wet clothes.

"See you around, Aran." She smiled as she stomped out of the bathing room with her dignity.

"I can't wait," I called back to her.

I slumped with relief when she disappeared into the safety of the hall.

The kings couldn't hurt her.

"Are you kidding me, Egan?" Malum snarled, and his voice was so deep I could barely make out his words.

Scorpius sneered, "So you wanna play white knight to our sloppy seconds? You think she'd want your scrawny ass? Tara likes to be dominated; that means she needs men. Not prissy little boys."

I silently mimicked his words, knowing he couldn't see me mocking him.

Malum growled. "You think you can disrespect Scorpius like that? A pathetic weakling like yourself *dares* to mock a king."

Actually, I'm a queen.

The two massive kings took steps toward the edge of the pool.

Two against one, not the best odds.

Orion pulled his cock out of the dark-haired woman's ass. Why were none of them fucking their vaginas? I might be a virgin, but that just seemed wrong.

Of course they wouldn't fuck a girl where it would pleasure her.

I tried to look away from the gorgeous man, but his naked muscles gleamed like gold silk. Orion was leaner than the other two kings, and his dick wasn't as thick but was slightly longer.

Stop staring at his penis!

A strange sensation pinched my chest, and I had the irrational urge to tell the girl to step away from the quiet king.

The dark-haired woman stepped closer and whispered something in Orion's ear. His expression slowly fell.

She kept talking, and the longer he didn't respond, the more he looked dejected.

"Why won't you say anything?" she snapped at him.

Orion's face fell at the words. His lush lips parted, but no words came out.

Malum and Scorpius turned their attention away from me as they zeroed in on her.

"Are you okay?" Scorpius asked Orion tenderly as his long fingers gently caressed his bobbing cock. He whispered something in his ear and pressed his body flesh against him.

Orion's chocolate-brown gaze stared sadly up at Scorpius, and the pale man kept stroking his dick as he gently pressed their lips together.

Bee-stung lips met a cruel mouth.

The pinching in my stomach got worse, and I struggled to breathe.

"Why are you ignoring me?" the dark-haired girl sputtered at Orion.

"*Get the fuck out, commoner whore!*" Malum grabbed her by the arm and physically dragged her out of the room. "He doesn't talk to filth like you."

I froze.

Whore.

W-H-O-R-E.

One small word that said so much and yet said nothing at the same time.

Enchanted knives carved my back to pieces.

Malum stalked back into the room with his disturbingly thick cock bobbing between tree trunk legs.

Scorpius ran his thumb across the tip of Orion's dick as he pressed himself against the man with one last sloppy kiss.

He pulled away and kissed the tears that glistened under Orion's wet lashes.

All softness left his expression as he turned slowly and stared me down. Malum walked up beside him.

I had their full attention.

It was two against one.

Malum's cock is the thickest. Scorpius's is shaped the nicest. Orion's is the longest. I mentally slapped myself for the unnecessary observations.

Sadie would have made a bad penis joke.

And in the midst of an extremely serious situation, I giggled. Sun god, I missed Sadie.

Red flames jumped higher across Malum's arms as he glowered at me.

He thinks I'm laughing at their naked bodies.

Might as well.

I laughed harder and pointed at their dicks. "Wow. You guys have a lot of self-confidence walking around naked when you look like that. Embarrassing."

Violence crackled as they bristled.

Malum smirked. "Really? Because it seemed like you were jealous that we were fucking while you were sleeping like a wimp."

"Hey." I scoffed with indignation. "Sleep is *very* important. Not all of us are man whores."

"Stay away from the women we fuck," Scorpius snarled. "What we do with them is our business, not yours."

I snapped back before I could stop myself, "Why did you treat them like that?"

Why did you only fuck them in the ass? hung unspoken between us.

The dagger stretched wantonly across Malum's Adam's apple as he spoke. "Women are weak creatures that need to be taught their place. Otherwise, they don't fucking listen."

My teeth hurt from grinding them.

"We only fuck them in the ass because they're nothing but holes. Our true love's Orion, but during training, we

don't want him to be too sore. As doms, we like it rough."
Scorpius leaned over and gently kissed bee-stung lips.

Long pale fingers wrapped gently around a flower-tattooed neck like they were imagining choking him.

Red blurred my vision. "So you're just misogynistic pigs?"

Flames crawled atop Malum's shaved head like a fucked-up crown. His voice rumbled like honey, but what it spewed was acid. "It's just the truth. Women are weaker than men in every way. They're good for fucking. That's it. No one compares to Orion."

Scorpius chuckled. "Exactly."

Pink stained Orion's golden cheeks as he leaned into Scorpius's hands. His brown eyes were unfocused like he was desperate for the cruel fae to choke him.

Who the fuck did these men think they were?

They needed five minutes alone locked in a room with a pissed-off Jinx and a numb Sadie. That would shut them the fuck up about women being good for nothing.

Scorpius sneered at me, "You got something to say, pretty boy?"

"Yeah, I do," I snarled. "You're all dumber and more pathetic than I fucking thought."

Faster than I could react, Malum lunged down and dragged me out of the pool. He slammed me face-first onto the deck.

Crack.

My nose broke, and blood splattered.

The leader of the kings moved so quickly I struggled to process just what the fuck was going on.

I bucked and kicked, but he dug his knee into my back, and I nearly vomited from the pain that streaked across my wound.

Harsh fingers tangled in my curls and shoved my face into the water.

I screamed out bubbles.

Struggled.

Aimlessly.

More pressure was added to my back as someone else held me down.

Water filled my lungs, and I panicked.

It was too much.

Fuck. Fuck. Fuck.

I didn't stop.

Far away, John yelled, and there was the sound of fists on flesh, then a loud splash. It was suddenly silent.

They must have knocked him out.

Scorpius laughed, an awful, cruel sound, and Malum joined in a chorus of sadism.

They shoved my face down for long minutes until I inhaled water and thought I was going to die from the pain in my chest.

They were like devils from the rumored hell realm.

Just when I thought I was going to pass out, they lifted my head, and I vomited water. I gasped desperately for air.

They shoved me back under.

They drowned me.

Held me under until my monster woke up.

It bellowed against its cage.

I screamed. My lungs burned.

My monster bellowed.

Back.

Agony.

Pain.

Everywhere.

They didn't stop.

They had no mercy.

But in the throes of agony, I rediscovered my will to survive.

They drowned it into my subconscious with every cruel movement.

My new life purpose—I would destroy Malum and Scorpius.

They'd beg for mercy as I tore them to shreds, but I'd laugh at their pain. Just like they did now as they taunted and shoved me under.

Malum whispered against my ear, "You want our sloppy seconds, pretty boy?" His rough voice was that of a monster.

Scorpius sneered, "Not such a pretty boy now. In fact, you're pretty fucking hideous."

Malum said, "If you don't learn your place, it will only get worse for you."

They laughed as I choked and sputtered, lungs burning, water running painfully out my nose.

The bars of my cage rattled as they were forced apart. Ripped wide by the creature inside.

In the warm water of a bathhouse, Aran was tortured while Arabella watched.

He suffered.

She learned.

After a particularly brutal beating, I'd asked my mother why she did it.

She'd responded, "A fae monarch must be ruthless, cruel, cunning, and the coldest of them all." Her voice was sad. "That's why you'll never be one. You're too weak."

At the time, I'd thought it was a good thing that I had none of those traits.

But as I got older, Mother started to make me do more and more heinous things.

That was why I ran.

Why I hid.

I wasn't like her or the kings; I didn't revel in the suffering of others.

"Fuck you," I snarled between coughs and gasps as hot water drained out of my mouth.

They laughed as he shoved me back under. Orion said nothing, but I knew it was his gentle fingers that held down my legs. His touch was like an iron brand.

He was just as horrible as the men who loved him.

My lungs filled with water.

My chest throbbed.

No matter how hard I struggled, they never let up.

But in the overwhelming pain, I found the capacity to loathe others so deeply it scorched my thoughts and rebuilt my will.

Through violence and hate, fate had its way.

I will make them suffer.

The mantra repeated in an endless loop and tethered me to reality.

I'd enjoy their pain with every molecule in my black soul. I screamed out bubbles of rage, and my monster bellowed in agreement.

For the first time, monster, girl, and monarch were completely aligned.

Our interests in synchrony.

I will rend their limbs from their bodies.

I will bathe in their blood.

I will laugh as they writhe.

Malum's taunts rang in my ear. "You're nothing but a spineless coward who doesn't deserve to be an assassin. You're weak and pathetic. You're going to die under my watch, and I don't give a fuck."

Those were the words he said to Aran.

All Arabella heard was *"Women are weak creatures that need to be taught their place. Otherwise, they don't fucking listen."*

My limbs trembled.

I saw black.

Malum wrenched my head back painfully, gray eyes flat and unfeeling. Scorpius smirked beside him, the eye tattooed on his neck staring at me. Orion was a silent shadow.

"Got anything to say now, pretty boy?"

Head pulled back at an impossible angle, my stomach heaved, and I vomited water onto him.

It trickled out my nose and eyes, burned like acid as it drowned my lungs, but I showed him my teeth.

"You've done it now," Scorpius sneered.

A flaming fist reared back, and white exploded across my vision.

Malum punched me in the face.

Copper filled my mouth, and I spat blood at both of them. Red droplets dripped across their hate-filled faces.

Orion mouthed, "Learn your place, Aran." His big brown eyes were wide and sad.

But I didn't fall for it.

He was evil.

Scorpius wrenched my head forward and shoved me back under the water until it turned pink.

Their sadism seemed to last for hours.

And in an infamous academy, under an ominous bloodred eclipse, another fae monarch discovered their capacity to hate.

Because there was one universal truth—leaders were not born.

They were made in unanswered pleas for help, muffled sobs, silent screams, and the crack of knees against hard tile.

Leaders were forged in misery.

Mother was wrong.

I was ruthless. Cruel. Cunning. The coldest of them all.

A queen was born.

L ight-years away, sparks traveled through the gilded fae palace.

Like a shadow come to life, the gold skulls on the seat of death turned ivory black.

A palace aide who was passing the throne room dropped his chalice in shock.

The harsh clang echoed off the marble.

His lips parted.

The seat only turned black for the darkest and most powerful leaders. That meant the fae queen wasn't just alive; her power was unrivaled.

The rumors of the princess being powerless must have been a ploy.

She was much stronger than her mother.

The aide nodded. He'd always sensed something was up with the blue-haired beauty the realm worshiped.

He'd always known there was something wild in her aquamarine eyes.

Now he knew what it was; the black throne was proof of it.

Power.

He ran off to share the news. Parades would be launched at once, and the realm would rejoice.

This was a once-in-a-lifetime occurrence.

He shook his head as he ran. A leader so powerful the seat of death turned black. Who could have imagined?

He was thousands of years old, and the seat had only ever been gold. He'd never thought he'd see it in his lifetime.

The princess was hiding so she could prepare to come back and take her throne. That must be it.

With so much power in her veins, no one would dethrone her.

She'd return soon and lead them.

She was the next great fae monarch, a queen strong enough to rule over some of the cruelest and strongest beings in all the realms.

He leaned back and laughed with abandon as sheer exhilaration coursed through his old bones.

Once again, the sun god had blessed the fae realm.

Tears trickled across his cheeks because her enemies would tremble as she brought them into the glory days.

Arabella Egan was their savior.

The sun god had blessed her like no one else.

"Long live the queen," he sobbed. Then he shouted to the gods, "LONG LIVE THE QUEEN!"

CHAPTER 15
THE CLASS OF SINNERS

The breaking period: Day 6, hour 8

John nudged my shoulder to get my attention.

We were sitting in the back of Ms. Gola's classroom, except this time, it was the morning class with the commoners. At the blackboard, Ms. Gola droned on and on about how to follow directions during battle.

I used a fork I'd stolen from the dining hall to whittle my name into the desk.

After the break period / torture fest in the bathing room, Lothaire had made us run thirty miles around the island.

Ten miserable laps.

Then we'd trudged back into the fortress for class time.

A class where our unnaturally hot teacher's boobs defied gravity as she wrote on the board. Was she jiggling like that on purpose? Probably.

It would have been iconic if she weren't such a creep.

"Are you sure you're okay?" John asked with concern for the fourteenth time in the last five minutes.

"Never better."

"Seriously? Because you don't seem okay."

"Oh, I'm more than okay. I'm fucking fantastic."

"That feels like sarcasm."

"Feels like you should shut up."

"Someone is a little touchy after the bathhouse incident." John held up his hands at my glare. "Which is totally understandable. I just think we should talk about it. You know, for mental health and general group dynamics."

"What is there to discuss?"

"Well, I mean it seemed very traumatic. I tried to stop them, you know, but they knocked me out." John gave me puppy dog eyes and flashed his dimples. "So just tell me about your emotions. Lyla says it's helpful to talk things out."

"John."

"Aran."

I stabbed my fork into the desk. "If I asked you to commit a murder, would you help me?"

"This feels like a trap."

"If I asked you to disembowel someone while I bludgeoned them to death with my knuckles, would you do it?"

"Um. I think it depends on who it is and why we are doing it."

"John. Answer the question. Yes or no."

"Well, I really think there are a lot of factors that—"

"Yes or no. Don't think. Tell me right now what answer pops into your mind."

"Yes. Fine. Fuck. Yes, I'd help you."

I stopped twirling my pipe with my tongue and stared at the friend I'd only known for a couple of days. "Are you serious?"

John slumped forward. "Well you're my friend, right? So yeah, if you wanted me to kill them, I'd do it. That's what friends do." His dark eyes were wide and sincere.

Holy sun god.

He wasn't joking.

Damn. I really liked this human.

I glanced across the room. "There's a 99 percent chance in the future that I'm going to take you up on that offer. That is how I'm feeling."

John followed my line of sight and whispered, "Which one are we taking out?"

"All of them."

John choked on air. "All? Even Orion?"

I nodded because I didn't trust myself to speak. Inhaling enchanted smoke, I focused on the slight burning sensation in my lungs.

If I opened my lips, I'd scream.

"Are we strong enough to take them out?" John asked with disbelief as he sized up the three massive warriors who were built more like statues of gods than flesh-and-blood men.

"We are."

I thought about the surety in my bones when I'd murdered my mother. When I'd stabbed my blades into the two shifters in the beast realm and they disintegrated into dust.

It was unfathomable power.

"Shit. I didn't realize you were built like that," John said as he sized me up with awe. "You know, for a weirdly pretty man, I get the vibe you're a scary motherfucker."

I grunted.

He had no idea.

There were people who did bad things because they had no choice and there were no other options. These were the accidents that they always regretted. The deeds that haunted them.

Then there were people like me.

I'd committed war crimes when there wasn't even a war.

And I'd do it again.

And again.

John nudged my shoulder. "I know you're still mad, which you have every right to be, but just so you know, this isn't like them. Sure, when I was the new guy, Malum let go of me in the dark sea, and I had to swim for hours until I got back to the shoreline."

The fork creaked in my hand.

Just another reason to kill the fae bastard.

I pulled the fork back to throw it across the room and hopefully take out an eyeball, but John grabbed my hand and tried to wrestle it away.

We grunted and fought silently.

"But." John held the fork out of my grasp and whispered aggressively, "Listen to me. They're not acting like themselves. Everyone knows they're devoted to Orion, like crazy, *burn-the world-for-you*, *kill-everyone*, *if-you-touch-him-you-die* devoted."

Great, Orion was living my fantasy.

Life wasn't fucking fair.

But it would be. After I murdered them all and found *my* man. Singular.

Just one handsome-as-sin man who would raze the world for me but still have a sensitive side.

He'd enjoy long days of shopping and trying on clothes, getting ready for parties with me, dancing drunk, and smoking. We'd sleep in and wrestle in bed.

I sighed.

"Um, Aran, are you listening to me?"

"What?" I shook my head to clear the fantasy that was never coming true.

I groaned and buried my hands in my messy blue curls.

John grabbed my arm. "Listen. I'm trying to tell you something important. Orion has a feminine beauty about him, right? Who else do we know that's like that?"

"I don't know?"

I squeezed my eyes shut and thought about it. "A good-looking horse? The rumored god of sex? I don't know what you want me to say. Yeah, I like chocolate. It's fucking tasty."

There was a long moment where John stared down at me like I'd lost my mind.

I had.

But it was rude to stare.

"You are pretty, you idiot!" he yelled but lowered his voice when students turned around. "They call *you* pretty boy. But they're crazy devoted to Orion and have never touched another man because of that. I think they're into you and they don't know what to do. They all see you as a threat to their dynamic."

Enchanted smoke turned to ashes in my mouth. "Bullshit."

There was a whooshing sensation in my stomach.

Realistically. I do want to kiss Orion.

John nodded with excitement like he'd figured something out.

"Malum and Scorpius are probably freaking the fuck out because they're into you and they shouldn't be. They probably feel like they're cheating on Orion, so you're now the enemy. And Orion probably hates you because he thinks you'll take his men."

I gaped at John.

My jaw opened and closed as enchanted smoke streamed from my lips.

"But I want Orion, not them."

John fell back in his chair. "You did not just say that."

Shit.

You are not into massive fae psychopaths. Even if they do have bee-stung lips and warm eyes with long lashes.

Cut it out, bitch!

John put his fist into his mouth and silently screamed.

"This is bad." He vibrated in his seat. "This is really fucking bad. You're dead. My new friend is dead." He rocked back and forth violently. "Why can't I just have one thing at this place? Fuck my life."

I smacked his arm. "Stop it! I'm not going to do anything about it. Seriously, I don't actually want him. I was just saying if I had to choose among the three monsters, I'd choose him."

John rocked harder in his chair, and more people looked over at the commotion.

"John, listen to me." I gritted my teeth and smacked him harder. "I can never be in a relationship. Ever. So don't make a big deal out of this. I'm going to be alone for the rest of my miserable immortal life. Okay?"

John stopped rocking.

"Okay?" I whispered more aggressively.

He stopped panicking, and a weird expression crossed his face.

It was pity.

"No, you won't be alone," John said with vehemence. "I know fae are weird about love, but you can be with whoever you want to be."

John grabbed my shoulders and squeezed. "The rest of the realms don't put labels or constraints on love. If you want five men, Aran, you can have five men. If you want one, you can have one. There are species that don't even bother to label themselves as anything other than sentient creatures. Don't ever limit who you can be because of rules made by dusty prudes."

Warmth blossomed.

I couldn't help but flash a toothy grin. "You're a good person and an even better friend."

"Thanks, mate." John smiled and smacked me across the back with all his strength.

I swallowed a scream.

Through gritted teeth, I clarified, "But that's not what I'm talking about. My issues are much bigger than petty prejudices. I agree the fae are fucking dumb. Trust me, I hate them more than anyone else."

Elite fae asking to breed me.

"WHORE" carved across my back.

Enchanted to burn when I was turned on to ensure I never lost my virginity. I couldn't even imagine how painful it would get if I ever tried anything sexual.

So many problems.

And the biggest one was currently tipping back his chair with an arrogant smirk.

Ms. Gola leaned over Malum's desk and flashed impressive cleavage as she handed back our essays from last week.

How is her dress work appropriate?

But she wasn't the only person fiending over my enemies.

Half the women in the classroom, and a few men, kept sneaking glances at the kings. A familiar commoner student with dark hair turned around and winked aggressively at Orion as she crossed stiletto-clad feet seductively.

It was the same girl the kings had thrown out after she'd had sex with Orion.

"Turn around, Sari," Ms. Gola snapped at the pretty girl.

Really, the teacher was jealous of someone looking at the kings? This was getting ridiculous.

Even if the girl had gotten to feel Orion's lean golden body against her.

My stomach pinched uncomfortably.

No! You're not jealous of Sari. You're a dude. Act like one.

I pretended to adjust my sweatpants like I had a penis, but it didn't relieve my discomfort.

Sari ignored Ms. Gola and kept making moon eyes at all the kings. Not just Orion.

Apparently her brain cells had stopped working.

They'd thrown her out of the room like a dog.

And if she knew what they'd said about women, she wouldn't be smiling at them.

A sudden chill racked through me, and I ignored the kings.

I sucked in smoke.

My clothes were soaked with sweat, the handiwork of the brutal mile pace we'd kept during the morning run, and it had dried on my skin.

I itched aggressively at my blue curls and wished they would stop clinging to my face.

Once again, I was cold and miserable.

John twirled the fork he'd confiscated from me between his fingers. I resumed scratching my name into the desk with my fingernail. While passing out papers, Ms. Gola demonstrated how to dodge a sword by aggressively hip thrusting into the air.

Okay.

She thrust with all her might.

She has to be doing it on purpose.

A headache throbbed behind my eyes.

Sari turned around for the sixteenth time and winked at Malum suggestively.

I gagged.

Malum's words echoed like a bullet.

"We only fuck them in the ass because they're nothing but holes."

Holes.

H-O-L-E-S.

That was my new least favorite word. It replaced whore at the top of the list.

I'd show him what a woman was good for when I used my mouth *hole* to bite off his face.

Jinx's voice drawled in my mind, *"Try to keep your cannibalistic tendencies at bay, Aran. It's not becoming."*

I slammed my forehead against the top of my desk.

Horace turned around in the seat in front of me and stared at me with his creepy yellow eyes.

He didn't blink.

"What do you want?" I groaned with half my face still smushed against the table.

Horace showed off twin fangs. "Is little Johnny boy annoying you? He has a tendency not to stay the fuck out of other people's business."

Little Johnny was probably 250 pounds of muscle.

John rolled his eyes. "Oh, please, Horace. You weren't just fucking that girl; you were draining her dry. If I hadn't stopped you, she'd be a corpse."

Wonderful.

While I was being submerged, Horace had tried to kill the girl he was fucking.

What a nice place.

Not.

CHAPTER 16
DANCING WITH THE DEVIL

The breaking period: Day 6, hour 9

Horace's yellow eyes glowed brightly.

"It's my business what I do with my food and not yours, human." He spat out "human" like it was a curse word.

John's dimples disappeared as his face hardened. "But it is my job when it's a dead body. I'd be careful what you say next, vampyre. Or did you forget just who I am?"

Horace scowled, and John glared back.

Men were stupid.

Instead of talking shit behind each other's backs like normal people, they talked shit *to* the person they were insulting. Then they had the audacity to get butt hurt when the person got pissed.

It was like when they were growing up, they were so busy trying to be all macho and strong that they never learned how to gossip effectively.

A critical life skill.

They wouldn't survive a single day with teenage girls.

They'd be torn to shreds.

Eviscerated.

I missed Sadie and the girls.

Horace whispered, and his voice was a creepy rasp. "No, human. It seems like you've forgotten just what *I* can do."

They were literally talking gibberish.

I banged my head harder against the table.

I can't live like this.

The dark expression that had overtaken John's face melted away, and he laughed as I banged my head.

My new friend 100 percent suffered from a personality disorder. It reminded me of a story in the banned books section in the fae palace—something about a nice Dr. Jekyll and a mean Mr. Hyde.

"What are you doing, Aran?" John asked with concern.

"Trying to lobotomize myself."

"Are you sure you should be acting like a lunatic in front of your crush?" He pointedly looked across the room.

"I'm going to kill you." I shoved at him. "I told you it's not like that."

John slapped my hand.

I slapped him back.

He slapped harder.

I slapped faster.

Yes—at the ripe age of twenty-four—I engaged in a slap fight with a grown man. Not my proudest moment.

"A little poke and tickle, I see," Ms. Gola purred suggestively as her shadow fell across our shared desk.

Massive perky tits, ten times bigger than my embarrassingly small cup size, stared me straight in the face. They leaned closer like they wanted to smother me.

A decadent vanilla scent wafted off Ms. Gola's cleavage.

I had to forcibly stop myself from asking her what the name of her perfume was. Because it smelled great.

Wait, why is the cleavage still coming closer? I winced and leaned back in my chair as far as I could.

She leaned closer.

I was 98 percent certain I was being sexually harassed.

"I can't live like this," I said to no one in particular.

It was official: I would never recover from Elite Academy.

Ms. Gola placed a paper on my desk and beamed down at me as she curled a lock of her shiny blonde hair around her finger. "Amazing work, Aran. I only know of one other student who can make such an insightful analysis."

She traced her red nail over the 100 percent on my paper like she was caressing a lover.

Help?

If Ms. Gola noticed I was turning purple and gagging, she didn't show it. She just kept smiling and twirling her hair as she leaned into my personal space.

Does she have a knot?

Someone give the woman a brush.

Ms. Gola purred, "For the rest of the assignments, I want you and Corvus to work together. You each have a rare gift, and I think it would be best if you strategized and learned from each other. I'm afraid you're both too advanced for the rest of the class."

Corvus?

The enchanted drugs did nothing to calm me. "No. I won't work with Malum."

He thinks I'm nothing but a hole.

Across the aisle, Malum leaned back with his hands behind his head and taunted, "Aw, pretty boy's afraid of me. How pathetic."

In my head, a monster screamed.

Pipe cracking between my teeth, I didn't bother to respond.

"Can't wait to get started, partner." He chuckled, and the raspy, harsh sound matched his whiskey-and-tobacco scent.

No.

He smells like the patriarchy.

Could the universe leave me alone for *five minutes*?

I turned to my enemy and exploded. "Why do you want to work together so badly? I thought you wanted to torture me because you hated me. Too pampered and pretty or some bullshit like that. So make up your fucking mind!"

If he refused to work with me, Ms. Gola would listen to him.

Why wasn't he putting a stop to it?

Horace made a harsh, breathy noise that I thought was a laugh, and John covered his mouth.

Scorpius mocked in a baby voice, "Aw, is the pampered pretty boy scared?"

I couldn't decide who I hated more. "I wasn't talking to you. But you probably don't know the difference because your head is so far up Malum's conceited flaming ass. How does it feel to be a lackey?"

Scorpius growled, and Malum exploded in flames.

Bigoted jerks.

But the corner of Orion's lip turned up in a smile, and a weird strumming sensation rang through my chest.

Probably heartburn.

The commoner students shifted in their chairs.

Ms. Gola clapped her hands as she walked back to the front of the room, her voice upbeat and chipper like she didn't notice the three of us were about to murder one another.

"Okay, class, for the next two hours, you're going to write an essay on the best weapon to use against an opponent fighting with a triple-blade sword. Corvus and Aran, please work together and hand in one essay."

The class tittered as she said our names.

Sari looked between the two of us and then fluttered her lashes aggressively.

Malum ordered softly, "Scorpius, switch seats with Egan. I need to work with my *partner*."

"Try not to antagonize them," John whispered furiously in my ear. "If you make it clear you're not a threat to their relationship, they'll chill out. They haze everyone at first. You just need to stop riling them up."

Fuck.

That.

"No. Scorp, stay where you are," I ordered. "We're not partners. Malum misspoke."

Red flames shot higher.

Scorpius stood up and stalked over. "I don't take orders from you."

"Well, I'm not moving."

John buried his face in his hands. "Why did I befriend you? Keeping you alive is going to be impossible."

If only he knew how difficult it was for me to die.

I didn't bother to correct him.

"You don't want to do this, Egan," Malum said softly as he fisted the hands that had held me down as my lungs filled with water.

Just. A. Hole.

My monster shrieked inside my head.

"No."

Horace's nostrils flared, and he smiled like he enjoyed the smell of violence. "New guy is growing on me."

Of course. The guy who murders people likes me.

Malum slammed his chair back and stood up. Seven feet of flaming bronze muscles towered.

I rolled my eyes.

He could set me on fire, slam his fist into my stomach, drown me, but I was not going to take it like a little bitch.

After Mother had perished (died violently by my hand), I promised myself I'd never let another person torment me.

Sari fanned herself dramatically as she licked her lips. "It's getting hot in here."

She needs an intervention.

"I'm going to ruin you," Malum whispered as he leaned closer.

"I'm already ruined."

Malum arched his dark brow, and for a split second, his silver eyes glinted with something that didn't look like manic hatred.

Like he had a soul.

A flaming hand shot out, grabbed me by the neck, and threw me to the ground.

Nope.

He was soulless.

An unhinged egomaniac with the body of a dark god.

Scorpius and Malum circled around me like wolves inspecting a carcass for the juiciest bits of meat.

I breathed deeply. There was only one thing left to do.

Instead of launching myself at him, I gave him the Sadie special and flipped him off with both my hands. "Suck my dick."

The class oohed, and Horace broke out into aggressive, breathy laughter. Even Zenith and Vegar cracked smiles. John muttered something about the underworld and regrets.

Malum took a step closer, and I prepared myself for his fist.

He bent at the waist so our faces were close. "Orion's the only man whose dick I'll ever touch. I don't handle trash." He smirked. "I have standards, unlike some people."

The class howled, and someone yelled, "Burn!"

For some ungodly reason, the wound on my back began to ache.

Why was l feeling weird?

Was I constipated?

I tried to act calm and studied my cuticles, which desperately needed a manicure and fresh gloss.

Ew. Why is there so much dirt under my nails? It was giving off sewage rat.

I realized everyone was staring at me, studying my hands with disgust, so I tried to cover them. "It doesn't matter anyway. You're *not* my type."

I glanced over at Orion, who was staring at the three of us with his lips parted and pupils blown. His lashes really were stunning.

He also had nice cuticles.

Did he use oil? He'd look good with black nails. Or a deep emerald green.

I cracked my head against the ground. What the actual fuck was wrong with me?

Every time my best friend flipped people off and told them to suck her dick, it tended to end conversations.

But this situation seemed to be escalating.

I was hyperaware of the two massive fae standing on either side of me.

Faster than I could track, Malum grabbed me behind the neck and shoved me into Scorpius's empty chair.

"Stop touching my neck," I snarled and pulled away.

"No" was all he said.

I considered picking up the chair from beneath me and chucking it at Malum, but Ms. Gola chose that moment to pretend to be a teacher.

"Okay, that's enough. Malum and Scorpius, please take a seat and stop posturing. Aran, please refrain from causing more problems in the future. Even though the assassin program is unique, this is still a classroom setting."

Yep.

The woman who'd dry-humped the air was lecturing me about what was appropriate.

Was there no justice in the realms? No sense of decency?

Malum and Scorpius must have felt similarly, because they both remained standing.

The class looked back and forth between them and Ms. Gola with wide eyes.

Malum spoke slowly, each word dripping with poison. "What did you just say to us?"

Someone whispered, "Oh shit."

Ms. Gola paled.

Flames leaped across bronze shoulders.

Orion sat next to me, and his perfectly clean nails tapped against the desk. He had nice hands. Up close, a tantalizing aroma wafted off him, rich like dark chocolate with a sweet edge.

"Don't look at him." Scorpius grabbed my curls and yanked my head forward. "He's disgusted by you."

Raspberries. That's what he also smells like.

In my peripheral vision, Orion narrowed his eyes at Scorpius like he wanted to disagree.

My heart fluttered.

"I believe I was clear," Ms. Gola said slowly.

Malum made a noise in his throat that was a mix between a scoff and a hiss. A "sciss."

Scorpius's fingers dug harder into the top of my head as he physically kept me from looking over at the stunning fae sitting inches away from me.

In my peripheral vision, chocolate eyes widened. Long lashes rested on light-golden skin. Smooth and silky.

I'd always liked silver more than gold because it complemented my blue features.

But maybe gold would look good on me?

I turned my head to the side to get a better look.

Scorpius's fingers trembled as they pulled my hair, and he whispered, "If you try to look at my man one more time, I will snap your neck." His words dripped with malice.

I kept my head straight.

There was a whooshing as Malum exploded with flames.

It was official.

This was worse than any fae drama.

CHAPTER 17
A VOICE LIKE SIN

The breaking period: Day 6, hour 10

"Corvus and Scorpius, sit down," Ms. Gola snapped, and her blonde hair rose off her shoulders like she'd been shocked with electricity.

What species is she?

"What did you just say to us?" Scorpius's long fingers were still tangled in my curls.

"I said to sit! This is *my* classroom, and I will be obeyed." Ms. Gola stomped her high heel and raised her chin.

Malum crossed his flaming biceps. "You will refer to us as 'Your Highness.' You don't have permission to use our names. I thought we already discussed this."

The torches on the wall flickered, and papers fluttered off desks.

Danger.

Ms. Gola took a step back, eyes wide, like she just realized she'd fucked up.

Since she was the one who demanded I work with the psychopath, I didn't have sympathy for her.

"You think because we fucked you that you can tell us

what to do?" My head yanked to the side as Scorpius trembled with rage. "You are nothing but a whore that should be honored to touch our cocks."

W-H-O-R-E.

That fucking word.

I jerked my hair out of his grasp, and he let me go.

High cheekbones glittered like glass in the shadows.

Scorpius's expression was pure evil.

The class looked back and forth between the two kings and Ms. Gola with fear.

For a second, I could see the difference between the commoner and the royal students.

These people were used to being collateral in other people's games.

In contrast, John twirled his fork like he was bored, and the demons weren't even paying attention. I was pretty sure Horace was taking a nap.

The assassins were used to angry power.

Ms. Gola gulped. "This is not appropriate. If you don't sit down right now, I'll be alerting Lothaire that the assassin recruits require extra punishment. Perhaps another run?"

Chairs squeaked around me. We were all paying attention.

That cunt.

Ms. Gola's expression was ugly as her hair crackled. "Sit. Down. Now. Or I'll make sure Lothaire throws you all into the Black Ocean for hours."

My stomach fell to my knees.

"Can she do that?" I whispered with horror to no one in particular.

Golden fingers brushed gently across my shoulder. Sweet raspberries filled my nose as silky white-blond hair parted.

Orion nodded softly.

"Fuck." I buried my face in my hands.

I was so tired. All I wanted was sleep and warmth. I couldn't do another round in the black sea.

There was nothing left for me to give.

If I had the capacity to cry, tears would have streaked down my face from pure exhaustion.

"Don't worry. Corvus won't let her." A lyrical voice tinkled so softly that it seemed like a trick of my imagination.

Holy sun god.

Orion looked like a god of sex and smelled delicious, but his voice was the whipped cream on top of my favorite dessert.

It was hypnotizing.

"You can speak," I whispered with surprise. So far, he'd only mouthed silently or not spoken at all.

Orion's bee-stung lips pulled up into a breathtaking smile. Golden skin shimmered like dual suns on a fae beach.

Malum and Scorpius were arguing with Ms. Gola, but I couldn't tell you what they were saying if my life depended on it.

Orion winked, and he mouthed, "Sometimes. If you're lucky."

I swooned.

"Say something else. If you want to, that is. No pressure," I whispered and flushed.

Orion leaned closer, and I inhaled his rich scent. He was intoxicating.

I understood why Malum and Scorpius were so protective of the stunning fae. He was *so* out of their league. Sun god, he was out of everyone's league. If he were mine, I'd never let him out of my sight.

A whispered melody stroked my ears. "My name's Orion. I believe we've gotten off on the wrong foot."

Long lashes fluttered, and bee-stung lips were inches away from mine.

I forgot how to breathe.

"I'm Aran. It's nice to meet you," I whispered back just as quietly, afraid to break the enchantment that had wrapped around us.

Orion's lyrical voice was heavy with melancholy. "What happened in the bathhouse was wrong. Please forgive me. It's hard for me to...go against my men."

"I totally understand," I quickly assured him. "Seriously, don't worry about it. I don't hold you responsible for their actions."

I was rewarded with another smile.

Pure bliss.

What the actual fuck are you saying? He held your legs as they drowned you! my rational inner voice pointed out.

But he's so perfect, and he apologized, my dumb bitch side argued back.

"I'm glad we're sitting next to each other. I'd like to get to know you." Orion's voice washed over me like music from the strings of a harp. "Just ignore my men. They mean well."

Do they?

Who was going to tell him that they sucked and he deserved to be my lover for all of eternity?

As if to punctuate my thoughts, Malum stalked forward down the class aisle with Scorpius's arm on his shoulder, the fae man trailing behind him.

Seven feet of rage crowded our teacher until her back was pressed against the board.

"Did you just threaten all the assassins for your own

insolence and inability to show respect to those better than you?" Malum took another step toward her.

Ms. Gola's knuckles turned white as she clenched her chalk.

Scorpius chuckled cruelly. "Don't you remember? The cunt said she was going to snitch to Lothaire."

"Is that true?" Malum leaned close so his face hovered inches above hers.

Ms. Gola straightened her shoulders and glared up. Her voice was steady and strong. "No, I didn't threaten. I said I was going to do it."

The silence was deafening.

If she weren't threatening to have us thrown into the freezing ocean, I would have been impressed by her lady balls.

I wasn't.

Shivering from my dried sweat, I slumped lower in my seat.

Lothaire was going to kill us.

The vampyre might defer to Malum as our leader, but he was top dog. All the "sirs" and frequent beatings made that clear.

Fingers gently rubbed my back.

My stomach clenched, and the wound on by back burned with an unholy pain.

"It will be fine. Don't panic, Aran." Orion's fingers traced a small pattern.

I liked my name on his lips.

But I wanted him to say Arabella. Reverently and softly. As bee-stung lips trailed gently across my boobs.

It was official.

Being a twenty-four-year-old virgin was ruining me.

Why else would I be lusting over the freakishly gorgeous fae who'd stood silent as his lovers tortured me?

Jinx drawled in my mind, *"Because you have the brain capacity of a dead ant."*

I rubbed at my eyes tiredly. "I can't go back into the sea."

Orion's gentle lyrics had a harsh edge. "You won't. I promise you."

Stunning boy and disguised girl sat shoulder to shoulder and watched.

Malum reached his hand toward Ms. Gola—but instead of choking her out and throwing her onto the floor like he did to me—he slowly traced a finger across her lips.

The rough man disappeared into something softer and more cunning, something much more dangerous than the jerk I always encountered.

Ms. Gola trembled.

"Who am I to you?" Malum asked suggestively.

Every woman in the room and a few men sighed.

Ms. Gola shuddered. "A king, Your Highness."

Malum slowly pushed his thumb into her mouth. Smoke sizzled.

She arched into him.

"And did you not demand that Scorpius and I fuck your cunt last year? Did we not comply?"

Ms. Gola's eyes glazed over. "Yes, sir."

All feelings aside, they were stunning together. A masculine god worshipping a gorgeous woman.

Orion shifted beside me, and I wondered how he was taking it. To see the man he loved touching a woman like that?

I'd be pissed.

I nudged him with my elbow to distract him. "I'll bet you he lights her on fire."

Orion held my gaze. "He better."

Flames sparked in the front of the classroom, but in the back of the room, something softer blossomed.

In my peripheral vision, Scorpius joined Malum and trailed pale fingers across Ms. Gola's arm.

She gasped as both of them touched her.

They touched her gross ass while a priceless treasure sat a few feet away.

They were dumber than I'd thought.

I held Orion's gaze. "Men are idiots."

Pop.

Ms. Gola screamed as Scorpius broke her humerus.

A sickening crunch.

She shrieked.

Malum created compound fracture after compound fracture. "If you say a word to Lothaire, we will kill you. No questions asked. You will be dead."

Scorpius laughed like he was enjoying her screams. "This is not a threat."

"It's a promise," Malum finished his sentence.

I stared at Orion's knowing smirk as a sense of betrayal burned my chest. "You knew they would do that."

Leaning back in his chair, Orion didn't bother to say anything more. He just crossed his arms and gloated.

I felt ill.

Logically, I knew the kings were bad guys. Villains. Tormentors. Horrible people like Mother who didn't care about the suffering of others.

But for some reason, it always shocked me.

The endless capacity for violence.

It made me sick.

Cobra, Sadie's mate, had once told me that the most dangerous predators were the pretty ones because your mind tricked you into seeing them as less ugly. It allowed them to be the most hideous of us all.

Now I understood what he'd meant.

I had a sinking suspicion that the breathtaking, quiet man sitting beside me was one of those creatures.

He was so fucking dangerous.

I shuffled my chair to the side and tried to put distance between us at the small table.

Orion smirked and arched his brow like he knew what I was doing. Rich brown eyes taunted me. Told me it wasn't going to work.

He had me in his web.

"Actually, I've decided I'm not going to forgive you," I said haughtily with my chin tipped up.

"Good," he mouthed. Then the bastard winked. Like he was playing with his kill.

I inhaled enchanted smoke like it was my lifeline.

Sun god.

I really needed to find stronger drugs if I was going to survive this place.

"Why are you looking at Orion?" Malum growled from above me. Ms. Gola was still crying at the front of the classroom with her arm at an awful angle, and the two kings had come back to their seats.

"I'm not," I snapped, disgusted with myself.

Scorpius took my old seat next to John, and Malum made a point of repositioning his chair between the two of us so he blocked Orion.

I was glad.

Ms. Gola had tears streaming down her cheeks, but she faced the class like she was determined not to break. "You have two hours and thirty minutes to write your essays on the best weapon to use against an opponent fighting with a triple-blade sword. Begin now."

She didn't say anything about Lothaire, and I prayed the threat had worked.

"Throwing knife. Write it down, partner." Malum snapped his fingers like I was a dog.

It took me a second to process he was speaking to me. "First of all, don't speak to me like that. Second, the best weapon is clearly a throwing ax. A knife can be deflected by a blade, but an ax gives you the range and the power to dodge or even break the triple blade."

Malum laughed. "Good joke."

"Coming from the dude who said *throwing knife* like a ten-year-old boy in a street fight. You write down 'ax.'" I shoved the paper at him.

"I'm not writing; you write. I'm the king."

"I'm the smart one. You write."

"You actually think you're smarter than me? Do you have any idea who I am?"

I rolled my eyes so hard I was worried they would get stuck in the back of my head. "Yeah, you're the dude who just assaulted the teacher. A sexist pig who uses his power to hurt others."

Silver eyes sharpened. "Did I not just get all our asses out of having to take a plunge in the ocean? Since you're sitting here shivering, I'd thought you'd be fucking grateful, Egan."

"Your temper tantrum is the only reason we would have had to swim in the first place, Malum."

He shoved his pen into my hand. "Write down 'throwing knife.'"

I pushed it back into his. "Write down 'I'm a petulant bully on a power trip, and the answer is an ax.'"

"You know, you've got a lot of hubris for a pampered, scrawny boy who doesn't seem to have any discernible abilities except sucking, then losing your mind." He pushed the pen back at me.

"That's because you know nothing about me."

"Then tell me. Just what the fuck are you, if you're not a fae? I will not have secrets in my program."

"I'm a fae." I started writing our essay.

"No, you're not. And don't you dare write down an ax; they're too heavy and move slow enough an opponent can easily dodge them, especially one agile enough to wield a triple blade."

I paused because he actually made a good point. "But we need distance from our opponent's blade."

Malum nodded. "And enough force to disarm him."

We both paused as we pondered the problem.

Our eyes widened at the same time. "A whip."

There was a loud squeak. Sari turned around in her chair in front of us and said seductively, "Kinky."

"Really?" I asked with despair.

The corner of Malum's lips turned up like he was trying not to smile.

Sari smiled at me softly. "I saw how you stood up for Tara in the bathhouse. That was really hot."

I choked on my spit.

"Um, okay…" I trailed off awkwardly, unsure what I was supposed to do.

I wasn't interested in girls, and Sari was looking at me like she was ready to climb over the table and jump my bones.

Why do women have such a thing for assassins?

Living with the recruits was making me question my sexuality because as far as I could tell, men served no purpose in society.

I'd rather have intimate relations with a rock. At least a rock wouldn't insult me.

I started debating whether a metamorphous or igneous rock was cuter, then took a deep breath to stop myself.

Great, I was officially a lunatic.

Sari was still smiling and staring at me, so I ducked my head and focused on writing the essay.

The problem was that no one had ever made a book on "what to do when you're a secret queen disguised as a dude training at a supernatural academy to be an assassin and women come onto you."

"Aw, you're shy. Just like Orion," Sari cooed. "Just how I like 'em."

I grimaced. In my peripheral vision, pink tinted Orion's golden cheekbones. But I refused to find it adorable and endearing.

We both avoided looking at Sari.

Malum grunted. "Turn around and work on your paper. Stop bothering them, and don't talk to us. It's pathetic."

Sari's expression fell, and her shoulders slumped.

"Don't talk to her that way," I said automatically.

Malum arched his eyebrow at me.

Sari looked back and forth between us with wide eyes. "Thanks, Aran." She flashed a quick smile and turned around.

I relaxed into my seat.

She turned back around and winked at me aggressively with a sharp giggle before she righted herself.

I grimaced.

Malum shook his head. "Just ignore her."

I blurted out the question that had been eating me alive. "Why do you think all women are weak?"

"Because they are," Malum responded immediately.

Sometimes I forgot that men had no depth.

I tried a different angle. "Why did you drown me? Why do you hate me?"

Malum cracked his neck, dagger tattoo rippling on his throat. "I was making a point with Tara, and you interrupted me. I'm the leader of this group. I won't be questioned by a scrawny, pretty boy."

I looked away with disgust.

He couldn't even give a good reason for why he'd tortured me. "You're a prick."

The almost friendly expression on Malum's face dissipated like smoke. "I haven't forgotten that you're keeping secrets. I haven't forgotten about your little anger episode. My job here is to break you to keep us all safe, so don't fucking forget it. And I will do whatever I need to do to protect my men."

He reached over and ran his fingers through Orion's silky hair.

My pen jabbed a hole in the paper. "Whatever." At least we were pretending my complete psychiatric meltdown was just a 'little anger episode.'

I snorted.

"Add a comma." Malum pointed to my sentence. "Your grammar sucks."

I poked another hole in the paper and whispered, "Your face sucks."

"Oh, and Egan. I don't hate you."

I didn't look up. Instead, I stuck out my front teeth like I had buckteeth and mocked him.

Was there anything wrong with his teeth? No.

Did I feel better? Yes.

Apparently bullying others was my therapy. I loved that journey for myself.

"I absolutely loathe you, and I'm disgusted that I have to train and fight alongside such a pathetic man."

If I hadn't lived with Jinx, I might have been offended by his cruel words.

Good thing the twelve-year-old had already shredded my self-esteem. Her nickname for me was literally "the cannibal."

I didn't look up as I wrote. "The thing is, Malum, I don't care what you think about me. Because no matter how many times you try to assert yourself, we both know the truth."

He took the bait. "What truth?"

"That I'm better than you."

A red flame jumped off Malum's arm and burned my hand.

My skin sizzled.

We both watched as the small fire turned my pale flesh black. The burning sensation was nothing compared to the pain mother had doled out every night of my fucking life.

I didn't flinch.

"People like you are always the same," I said quietly. Blue fire or red. Queen or king. "You'll always just be a pathetic bully."

Malum glowered at me but didn't say another word for the next few hours.

Neither of us did.

We didn't need to.

The hate between us said it all.

CHAPTER 18
FIGHT LIKE THE DEVIL

The breaking period: Day 12, hour 5

Six days.

Eleven hours.

Five minutes.

Twenty-two seconds.

That was how long ago I'd slept.

In Lothaire's words, "I gave you lazy fucks six hours to rest in the bathhouse. For every hour you rested, that's a day you'll stay awake for. What's with the face, Aran? Did you think becoming one of the most powerful assassins in the realms would be fucking easy?"

"No, sir!" I yelled back, arms behind my back, legs parted, head down like a good soldier.

My monster screamed with defiance.

Someday I'd slit Lothaire's throat, and it would be the best thing I ever did.

Until then, I suffered.

We ran barefoot through the cold surf for hours. Lothaire gave us lessons on weapons, war, and torture. We held the stone above our heads until our fingers broke from the strain. Sat through Ms. Gola's class.

A pattern emerged.

Outside to run. Inside to learn. Outside to hoist stones. Inside for food. Outside to run until we threw up the food. Inside to shiver from dried sweat.

Repeat.

One thing was constant: we didn't sleep.

Now, eyes bleary, muscles heavy after a thirty-mile run, I collapsed beside John onto the black rocks.

The other recruits fell down around us.

We lay choking on salty air as the red eclipse glared down from above.

I didn't flinch when John rolled onto his side and dry-heaved bile. I would have joined him, but I was too tired to throw up.

My limbs tingled.

My stomach ached.

I wanted to die.

John had said that the first weeks of training were called the "breaking period."

Well, I was broken.

I'd never pushed myself so hard physically and mentally. I was a mess.

My monster was uncaged.

Every few hours, my vision went dark with bloodlust and the urge to kill someone nearly brought me to my knees.

So far, digging my fingernails into my skin and counting backward from ten was the only thing that helped me not rip off someone's face in a fit of unexplainable rage.

Things were not well.

As I lay praying for death, Shane's orange mohawk filled my vision.

He leaned down to give me a hand up. "I'm impressed. You're fast, fae man."

The half warrior had given me a nickname. He thought we shared a special bond because we were both fae.

Just one more lie to feel like shit about.

"Thanks," I grunted as I grabbed his hand and let him hoist me up.

It took all my effort to lock my knees and not collapse.

Shane flashed white teeth. "Just wait until you start fighting in the field. Then you'll be missing these good days where all you had to do was train."

Didn't see that happening.

Shane continued trying to be my friend.

I continued wanting him to shut up so I could try to sleep while standing up.

Shane crowded my personal space. "I've never met a powerful water fae. My mother was an earth fae, but as you know, half-breeds only take after one parent, so I only have an alpha tiger form."

Half-breeds were extremely rare, and unlike my friend Sadie, I'd never heard of one that had abilities from both parents.

The more powerful parent's genes always won out.

But Mother was the mad queen, the most powerful fae in all the realm for centuries.

And I wasn't a fae.

Who the fuck could my father be?

Shane was unaware of my tortured thoughts. "So what's it like controlling water?"

I shrugged as an answer and patted John on his head as he moaned and imitated a slug.

Three days ago, after a particularly brutal run, John's

cheerful, talkative demeanor had disappeared. Eyes midnight black, he'd stopped smiling and started glaring.

Dr. Jekyll had become Mr. Hyde.

Now I helped a heaving John to his feet.

He glowered, and neither of us spoke.

We were on the same page—hurting, angry, and in pain. Also, slightly constipated. Sleep deprivation truly was the silent killer.

There was nothing to say.

We suffered.

"So what's it like? Your water powers?" Shane asked again as the other recruits slowly pulled themselves together (the man was a broken record).

"Like I'm a monster," I said harshly, wishing he would just shut up and get out of my personal space so I could suffer in silence.

Shane whistled. "When you have some free time, I'd love to talk more about your experience in the fae realm. Between the two of us, we've been tasked with finding the missing fae queen and killing her."

Holy.

Sun god.

I was the queen he was searching for; they were trying to find and kill me. If only he knew who he was talking to.

The Black Ocean roared as it crashed against rocks.

Sulfur stained the air.

Eyes dead. Face relaxed. "Sure. I'd love to share what I know. Fuck the fae monarchy."

Shane tipped his head back and howled with laughter.

It wasn't funny.

He kept chuckling. "Perfect, fae man. I look forward to picking your brain. Don't worry, I have a feeling we'll get the bitch soon."

A manic bubble of laughter traveled up my throat, and I covered it up by clasping my hand over my mouth.

Wait a second.

Maybe it was exhaustion, maybe it was the monster screaming in my head, or maybe it was delirium. But telling the half warriors who I was didn't seem like such a bad idea.

They didn't want me to rule.

I didn't want to rule.

Maybe we'd be able to come to a mutually beneficial agreement. He treated me like a friend, after all. Maybe he was my way to freedom.

Shane ruffled my curly hair.

I flinched.

And fought the urge to cover my beating heart with my hands and get away from the man who wanted to rip it from my chest.

A silent scream burned my throat.

Ten, nine, eight.

Shane was a nice guy. If he was ever going to help me, I needed to pretend to be nice back.

Even though I stayed silent, John must have sensed my discomfort, because he wrapped his arm around my shoulders and pulled me away from Shane's touch.

I relaxed with gratitude.

John heaved aggressively, and his puke got on me.

Never mind. He was just using me as a crutch.

Still, I'd rather have a sick John touching me than be near Shane. John was a friend.

He said he'd kill *for* me.

Not that he wanted to kill *me*.

The difference mattered, and it was what made John safe.

Lothaire stomped over from the side of a cliff, where he

had probably been laughing maniacally and brainstorming more ways to torture us. "Recruits. Stop being fucking pathetic and stand at attention."

"Yes, sir!"

We fell into line.

The three half warriors stood beside Lothaire. "We have one more exercise before you get a break, and then the true training starts."

I can't.

Usually we went to class after we ran. It was the only reason my body hadn't collapsed beneath me.

Opal fangs flashed as Lothaire smiled. Sparks of power glittered in the air around him.

The wind howled like it was crying for help as it slammed against the looming fortress.

I swayed with exhaustion.

"You've all gotten too used to your schedule. It's making you weak. So we're going to work on close combat training. No weapons. Pair off into partners. You're going to wrestle. First one to tap out loses."

Lothaire was soulless.

I dug my dirty fingernails into my palms to try to wake myself up.

"John, you'll wrestle Scorpius. Vegar, pair with Horace. Zenith, go with Orion. Aran, you're with Malum. Pair the fuck up and begin. You'll wrestle right here on the rocks."

I was too tired to care.

Staggering on aching legs, I barely navigated the jagged terrain without face-planting.

Unlike in the shifter realm, there were no mats to protect us.

Flames licked across Malum's jaw as he sauntered forward. He was so big he should have lumbered.

He floated.

I swallowed thickly.

Scorpius positioned himself in front of John, and he smirked as he looked off into the distance with a relaxed posture. His lack of sight wouldn't hinder him.

From the way John cracked his neck with a grimace, he was aware that the blind fae was deadly.

John raised his eyebrow as he looked back and forth between myself and Malum.

He relayed an unspoken, *You gonna let him toss you around?*

I yawned tiredly and shrugged. *Most likely.*

John shook his head like he was disappointed in me as he turned his full attention back to Scorpius.

I wanted to collapse onto the rocks and fall asleep.

"You got this." Shane gave me a thumbs-up as he walked around and positioned the groups.

I didn't "got" anything.

Even my monster's aggression was muted from exhaustion. I had nothing left.

Lothaire's voice was too loud. "Begin! First person to tap out loses. Trust me, you don't want to lose."

Skin slapped as the men launched themselves at each other.

Malum didn't move a muscle.

Neither did I.

We waited.

Lothaire had said no weapons, but he didn't specify if Malum could use his flames.

No one used their powers in the program, but Malum was the exception. His flames perpetually smoldered across his shoulders.

And from what I'd experienced in Elite Academy, you acted first, then asked for forgiveness after.

Malum could do anything.

He ruled.

There was a 100 percent chance he was going to set me on fire.

A vein on Malum's bronzed forehead popped out as he clenched his jaw tightly and leaned forward like he was about to spring.

I didn't take the bait.

I stood still.

There was no way he would bother to exert himself by charging at me. I blinked lazily and smirked.

Silver steel became molten with hate.

Red flames multiplied.

I knew he was going to do it, because if I had flames, I'd light him up like a fucking torch.

But first I'd toy with him.

You were more likely to break your opponent if you could startle them with the force of your attack.

That was what Malum was doing.

I inspected my dirty nails like I was bored.

Sun god, the grime made my skin crawl. I'd kill for a fresh coat of black gloss with nail extensions. Long and pointy talons.

A girl could dream.

Next to us, Horace chucked Vegar hundreds of feet in the air, and the demon crashed into a boulder with a bang.

John grunted.

Scorpius body-slammed him to the ground. In a blur of movement, John twisted and returned the favor.

Orion and Zenith circled each other, lunging forward, then retreating.

Malum and I stood still.

Lothaire walked around shouting over the wind like he

was giving a fucked-up inspiration speech. "Your true character will not be revealed until you've given everything you think you can give."

In a blur of agility, Orion kicked out Zenith's knees and slammed his fist into his face. Black blood sprayed as the demon fell to the ground.

It sprayed across Orion's golden skin and was a harsh contrast to his blonde locks. He savagely pummeled the demon with his fists.

He had a dark side.

I gawked at him.

It's kinda hot.

When Orion finally climbed off his victim, the demon whimpered but didn't move.

Lothaire walked up casually, then stomped on Zenith's leg.

SNAP.

His femur cracked.

Zenith screamed.

I stifled another yawn.

Lothaire yelled down at him, "When you're comfortable, you're weak! *Pain is the true divider between the strong and the pathetic!*"

Zenith bellowed in agony as he dragged himself up onto one leg and kept fighting.

The ocean roared.

Wind whistled.

Blood sprayed.

I struggled to keep my eyes open.

Malum didn't move, and neither did I. Lothaire weaved between the two of us.

He was tired of waiting.

So was I. So sun-god-damn tired.

Purposefully, I turned my head to ogle Orion. He was covered in black blood, and he looked like an ancient god of war had had a baby with the god of seduction.

It was hard to look away from such perfection.

I turned back to Malum and licked my lips slowly as I glanced over at his man.

His molten silver eyes were flat, and there was nothing but cruelty reflected in their harsh depths.

I braced myself.

Malum's sharp jaw ticked with rage.

I'm going to steal him from you, I said with my eyes. Was I going to? No. But was it fun to watch the fae bastard seethe with jealousy and rage? Hard yes.

His eyes promised suffering.

And he delivered.

With a roar, the world erupted into shades of red and burnt orange.

He set me on fire.

My flesh charred, then sizzled.

For an endless moment, everything went quiet—adrenaline rushed, and all my senses flatlined.

I felt nothing.

In the midst of nothing, I noted my clothes were untouched. He'd set all my exposed skin on fire and had spared my clothes.

Thank fuck. There would have been no way to explain my lack of dick without outing myself.

My relief was short-lived.

Every nerve in my body clicked back into existence as my body acclimated to the blinding pain that was burning the skin on my hands, feet, neck, and face.

My mouth opened with a silent scream.

But I'd done this countless times.

I had a routine.

BREATHE IN—ONE, TWO, THREE, FOUR, FIVE. HOLD. EXHALE. HOLD. FUCKING HOLD.

As my body screamed with agony, I screamed into my brain.

Pain was everywhere.

I focused on my monster. On the endless rage. On the fact that he thought all women were pathetic. Objects that were only good for fucking.

I'd show him.

I screamed inside my mind until my brain became a jumbled mess of deafening noise.

Far away, my legs gave out, and my knees hit rocks.

Kneeling.

FOUR, FIVE.

Internally, I screeched louder. Externally, I was silent.

Far away, I was aware that Lothaire and Malum stared down at me, waiting for me to tap out. To say that I gave up.

Scorching heat.

Air whistled harshly through my parted lips.

But all the noise was inside me.

ONE, TWO, THREE.

My monster's scream added to the paralyzing cacophony.

It was so fucking loud in my head.

Flesh bubbled.

Red flames disappeared as my eyes stopped working. Crashing waves became a dull roar as my ears shut down. There were no smells. No feeling.

The nothing returned.

Just me, myself, and the endless pain of a tortured existence.

FOUR, FIVE. KILL. DEATH. BREATHE IN. ONE. HE

THINKS YOU'RE WEAK. FOUR. KILL HIM. THREE. EXHALE. HOLES. TWO. WHORE. ONE. HOLD. HOLD. MOTHERFUCKING HOLD.

Everything was chaos.

"Yield. Tap out, Aran!" Malum's angry voice bellowed from somewhere far, far, away.

The deep, raspy voice distorted into a high-pitched feminine tinkle.

Red flames became blue.

They covered every inch of me.

Mother stood above me with a serene expression on her perfect face. "Tsk. Tsk. Arabella. You're a queen's daughter. You don't get to be powerless. We'll do this little song and dance every night until you decide to stop being an embarrassment."

The flames tore me apart.

"Please, Mother," I begged with a sob catching in my throat.

I was only eleven years old, but I knew I couldn't do this every night. I wouldn't survive. Mother's flames were different from other fae's. They were electric blue and burned unmercifully, but there was no heat.

Just agony.

"Don't be weak, Arabella. It's embarrassing." Mother shivered with disgust and lounged back in her chair as she inspected her red nails.

"TAP OUT NOW!" Malum's deep voice cut through the mirage. Mother disappeared back into the darkness.

But the pain remained.

"This is too much!" Shane shouted.

Lothaire laughed. "No, this is character building."

"Maybe Egan can't speak?" Scorpius asked, then sneered, "I mean, his face is practically melting off."

"I can," I breathed out harshly, and it felt like I was blowing bubbles into lava. "Speak."

Silence.

Everything hurt worse in the quiet.

FIVE. ONE. THREE. BREATHE IN. WEAK. FOUR. EXHALE.

I concentrated on the screaming symphony.

"I *demand you tap out!*" Malum's booming voice distracted me from my counting.

My monster answered for me. "I'll fucking—" Gasp. "—kill—" Gurgle. "—you."

"TAP OUT NOW!"

I'd show him just how weak I fucking was. I was nothing but a hole, after all.

The shrieking in my brain was too loud to contain, and I screamed at the top of my lungs, "YOU TAP—" Gasp. "—OUT!"

"NO!"

I spat up blood. "YES!"

John growled, "Stop this."

"This is wrong," Shane said.

Lothaire disagreed, "It's character building."

Scorpius chuckled. "It's fucked up, but it is entertaining."

"Aran smells good." Horace sounded gleeful. "I think we should do this more often."

"I don't know…" Vegar trailed off.

I choked, coppery blood coating my mouth as my skin slid downward off my face.

The nothingness was turning into a buzzing sound. Static everywhere.

Unseeing eyes rolled backward into my head, and I collapsed forward onto the rocks.

Everything was so far away.

Even the pain.

Silence.

Stillness prevailed.

The absence of heat.

It took me a long moment to realize I wasn't dead. The flames had stopped.

Relief disappeared.

White agony streaked across my face, neck, hands, and feet, and the world burned in darkness.

"I won," I gurgled out as blood and flesh dripped from my mouth.

Malum swore viciously.

Hands gently grabbed my unhurt shoulders and pulled me up.

John's voice was close. "I could tell from your blue hair and attitude that it would be difficult keeping you alive, but I didn't predict *this*."

I groaned.

"But I'm starting to understand." John's arms went under my shoulders as he supported me.

He avoided the charred skin of my hands and neck.

I coughed weakly, "Brignfkckckem."

"What are you saying?"

"Bring me to Malum," I whistled through teeth.

John held me upright and moved slightly, but the motion caused pain to explode.

I still couldn't see.

My eyelids had melted off my face.

Malum's voice was rougher and grittier than usual as he growled inches from me, "You're fucked up, Aran. You were about to fucking die. What the fuck is wrong with you?"

I wished.

I coughed weakly, and it took every ounce of will I possessed to part cracked, melted lips.

My voice was barely a whisper. "If this is your assassin program, then how come I'm so much better than you?"

The cherry on top—I forced my scorched skin into a mocking smile.

Malum swore.

Excruciating sensations destroyed me, but I held the expression and let my words sink the fuck in.

I was petty like that.

Pursing my lips, I tried to spit on Malum, but it was too much.

I passed out.

CHAPTER 19

REST FOR THE WICKED

The end of the breaking period: Day 14, hour 8

"You've been in a coma for three days." John hovered inches away from me.

Finally, some good news. I shifted and regretted it as my arm fell through the hole in my cot.

"You could have died!" John's brows were pinched with worry, and he didn't move away to give me some space.

I rubbed my hand across my face and was pleased by the feel of smooth, cold skin.

I'd healed completely.

"Say something!"

I sighed heavily. "I'm trying to enjoy my coma and you're ruining my peace." People had no manners these days.

"Seriously?" John whined, "That's all you have to say?"

I rolled my eyes. "Yay. I'm awake. Now I can be tormented by a vampyre who has the hair and temperament of a large horse. How's that?"

John's dark eyes were midnight black as his frown deepened. "You're a real piece of shit, Aran." He flashed two dimples. "I'm gonna fuck you up if you ever do that to me again."

My shoulders relaxed, and I lightly punched his shoulder.

He gently punched me back.

I punched him harder.

He slammed his fist against my bicep, and bones creaked.

"Really?"

"Oh, man up." To punctuate his statement, he punched me in the gut. A full wallop. "If you can take fire, you can take a punch."

My eyes watered. "Not sure that's how it works."

"I make the rules, so I say it is. Don't be a wimp. It's awkward for everyone." John smiled and pushed me over so he could lie next to me on the cot.

We didn't fit.

He shoved me through the hole so I was half-smushed on the rocks.

But I couldn't stop smiling.

There was something about John's intense persona that put me on edge.

Like, when he was all dark and moody, our energies were too similar, but when he was all smiles and dimples, there was hope for us yet.

John's dimples were a balm to my soul.

I couldn't wait for him to meet Sadie.

Out of nowhere, red lights exploded as flames consumed me.

Oh, wonderful. I'm already having flashbacks.

I dug into my sweatshirt pocket and nearly wept with relief when I felt my pipe.

Lifting it to my lips, I closed my eyes.

The enchanted smoke filled my lungs with something blessedly close to indifference.

When I opened my eyes, the fire was gone.

I sighed out a ring of smoke. "So what did I miss?"

"Zenith, Horace, myself, and Malum lost our fights, so we spent an entire night in the Black Ocean. Since then, we've attended some classes and run twice, but it's been pretty chill."

"Sounds like paradise."

Only a masochist would consider running twenty-plus miles at a sub-five-minute mile pace "chill."

The sudden memory of Sadie trying to survive a singular mile had me chuckling.

She'd be so dead by now.

John's voice filled with concern. "Just a heads-up. During our night in the ocean, Malum whispered all the ways he was going to kill you. I've never seen him so mad. No one has ever beaten him before. I'm pretty sure like ever. In his entire life. Plus, he said you were eye-fucking Orion and he was going to have to teach you a lesson."

I laughed.

John shoved at me, and my face cracked against the jagged ground. "I told you not to do anything stupid with Orion, but you just couldn't listen to me."

"He's cute," I said defensively as I twirled my pipe expertly with my tongue. It felt right to have it back between my lips.

John choked. "He's not cute, Aran. He's one of the most powerful beings in all the realms. He's a serial killer."

I shivered with excitement.

Nice. Apparently, I wanted to die.

John was definitely being dramatic, but my heart rate increased at the thought of Orion as such a badass. Hot.

"So where is everyone now?" I expertly changed the subject.

"We've been off for the last three hours. Field training starts soon, and Lothaire's just been waiting for you to wake up. The other guys are letting loose."

I grunted at his unspoken words—all the men were fucking.

"Then why are you here and not letting loose?"

John winked suggestively. "Oh, I already had my fun. Don't worry about me, Aran. Just thought I'd come check up on my little Smurf shish kebab."

"What did you just call me?"

"You resemble a blue gnome's skewered meat." He waved his hand. "You know, since you were crispy."

I laughed. "That's some bullshit my friend Sadie would say."

"Oooh, a lady friend. Is she hot?"

I imagined what Cobra would do to him if he ever tried to come onto Sadie. Her snake shifter mate would probably disembowel John. He'd done it before.

"Don't be a pig."

This damn assassin program was a constant reminder that men were inferior to women in every way.

Like how were they even functioning? I didn't get it.

Not that I was doing much better.

If Sadie were here, she would wrap her arms around my shoulders and sob for me while we cuddled and talked shit about Malum.

It would have healed me.

John lazed beside me on the cot and watched me smoke. The punch to the stomach had been nice (my abs still throbbed), but it wasn't *enough*.

My soul was not healed.

It fucking ached.

John shrugged, and his pointy shoulder shoved me harder into the rocks as he spoke. "Well, maybe I'll get to meet her at friends-and-family week. We have a week for visitors in about a month. They use an enchantment to find those close to us, and it's basically just a massive party to help boost morale."

I'd get to hug Sadie.

A bright kernel of excitement burst through my chest. It was so startling and foreign that it took me a moment to realize what it was.

Happiness.

"Egan finally decided to wake the fuck up." Malum's deep voice filled the small space as the other recruits stomped into the barracks.

Good vibes died a swift death.

Scorpius sneered, "Aw, he's not dead. That's too bad. Now I owe Orion fifty thousand credits."

I rolled my eyes and tried not to feel pleased that Orion had bet a small fortune on my surviving.

It was kind of romantic.

I cracked my forehead against the ground and focused on smoking. At this rate, Dr. Palmer was going to heavily medicate me.

Hopefully max dosage.

"Why are you sharing a cot with John?" Malum suddenly sounded pissed off.

"Just two bros chilling, killing, and spilling the gossip." John took the pipe from my mouth and blew on it. "Oooh, that's the good shit."

I grimaced as I pulled it from his lips and wiped it on my shirt.

He was making us sound *so* lame.

Why had I befriended him?

Horace stood over us, and his yellow eyes glowed. "You don't smell good anymore, Aran."

Sun god, give me strength.

"Sorry, I'll have to set myself on fire again so I can smell good to you, Horace."

The vampyre stilled.

I tensed my muscles, prepared to throw John at him as a sacrifice so he wouldn't hurt me.

John noticed me trying to hide behind him. "Really, Aran? People have no loyalty these days."

He put his arms behind his head, and his elbow slammed into my temple.

"Ow, what the fuck, John?"

John bounced up and down on my cot like he was trying to ruin it more. "You know for a dude that was just all flaming and, frankly, psychotic, you're being very dramatic."

"You just elbowed me!"

Dimples flashed as John wrapped his bicep around my neck and aggressively ruffled my hair. "Come on, be a man and fight."

"You have the personality of a rock." I pinched his forearm until he let me go.

"Thanks!" John kept smiling.

A harsh, breathy rasp burst from Horace, who was still staring down at us like a creep. "You're funny, Aran." He leaned forward and plucked the pipe out of my fingers like John had.

I growled and tensed.

Horace took a long drag from the pipe, his deadly fangs flashing. "I've had better." He dropped it back into my hand, then walked away, pulling his clothes off.

Now I couldn't smoke until I'd cleaned it.

Fuck them.

"Damn, I think Horace likes you. That's really good for your chances of survival." John smiled as he climbed off my mangled cot and pulled down his pants.

Penis!

Ever been violated? Same.

My eyes burned, and I pinched my nose with my fingers.

Once again, against my will, I was surrounded by nude men changing.

"Oh, fae man, you're awake." Shane sauntered into the barracks. Beside him, Noah scowled. Demetre's pink eyes were flat and unreadable.

"Yep," I said awkwardly as I hid my pipe in my pocket.

I didn't know what the drug use policy was.

"Just in time. Lothaire told us to get everyone ready to leave. We're doing a special activity to celebrate the end of the 'breaking period.' It's a tradition."

Demetre walked over and handed me a pile of black clothes that had bright-red markings. And I realized everyone was changing into them.

His pink eyes were hard as rose quartz, but he nodded at me.

For a moment, I was dumbstruck. Whenever I was around the famed half warrior that shifted into a dragon, he glowered with vitriol. Now he seemed almost approachable. More normal.

Like he had been when I was a teen and he'd befriended me. Before he hated me.

"Thanks."

Demetre's lips pulled up in a half smile, and I almost fell off my cot in shock.

I'd never seen him smile.

However, the moment was fleeting. He turned around,

massive muscles rippling, as he stalked out of the barracks with the other warriors.

Weird.

"Ninety seconds until we leave!" Lothaire yelled outside.

The room erupted in a frenzy of movement.

"I gotta piss," I said dramatically as I ran behind the barrier in front of the toilet to change.

With impressive speed, I pulled on the new clothes.

The material was expensive and buttery soft, and the outfit was much tighter than the heavy sweat suit.

It was so tight that I was grateful the enchantment created the illusion of a bulge at my crotch. I wasn't sure how it worked, since it didn't actually give me a penis, but I was grateful for it since the clothes fit like a second skin.

A part of me wanted to compare my bulge to Malum's to see whose was bigger.

I blamed sleep deprivation.

For a long moment, I admired the bright-red stripes that crisscrossed over my biceps, chest, and thighs.

It looked pretty intense, and I loved it.

Once upon a time, I'd loved playing dress-up and wearing nice clothes.

I barely remembered what it was like to care about small things like looking nice. Fashion. Art. Expression. They were all luxuries that I didn't know I'd loved until I lost them.

Crammed behind a shoddy metal wall in front of a toilet, sadness washed over me.

I mourned. For the feminine parts of me that were smothered away. Maybe lost forever. The softer, lighter ones that had no place in an assassin academy filled with warriors.

"Out of my way." Malum shouldered past me and slammed me against the wall.

Before I could blink, he whipped out his cock and started peeing.

Who did that?

Rude.

"Gross." I covered my eyes. His heady whiskey-and-tobacco scent filled the small space.

"What are you whining about now, pretty boy? You afraid to look?"

A weird feeling pinched my lower stomach.

"I'm reporting you," I said as I stumbled away from him as fast as possible into the jumble of men rushing out the door.

Malum laughed and yelled over the clamor, "To who?"

Since we were training to be assassins for the High Court who oversaw realm wide peace, *we* would be the law. A terrifying thought.

Plus, if I complained to Lothaire, he'd probably just beat me with his baton and tell me to "man up." If it wasn't clear, I hated the male species.

"Let's go." John tugged me along.

Before I knew it, we stood in a line at attention while a homicidal vampyre with anger issues lectured us on not being pathetic.

Literally.

Lothaire kept repeating, "You need to start acting stronger and less like weak little bitches."

We stood and took it.

He spoke with disgust as he looked us up and down, "As is tradition, Lyla is going to lead us on a retreat."

I gulped.

It was never a good thing when the witch got involved. Usually, she was on standby to heal us during the worst training exercises.

Plus, there was that one time she'd told me I was selfish.

Was I selfish? Probably.

But you still didn't just tell people things like that to their faces. She could have at least given it in a compliment sandwich.

For example, "Aran, you have great abs. You're a little selfish. But you're also a loyal, great friend."

That was how I would have done it.

Lothaire brandished a glowing, circular device. "We're taking an RJE and going off realm. Lock arms."

Realm jumping enchantment? I knew they were virtually impossible to get, because Mother had always raged that she couldn't get her hands on one.

That was the only warning we got.

Lothaire held a small, glowing white ball in his hands, and when he reached out, the world disappeared in flames.

We ripped through time and space.

My head spun as I stumbled around. Wet leaves crunched beneath my feet, and I was enveloped in warm rain.

Everything was different.

The red sun and black rocks were replaced with gray skies, green foliage, rushing water, and rustling branches.

Trees towered around us.

Lyla stood beside us, which was weird because I swore she hadn't been with us before.

For the first time, the witch wasn't wearing a dress. Instead, she had on tight garments similar to ours, but hers were emerald green.

Hers were prettier.

The white runes on her dark skin glowed impossibly bright as she stared at us with a serene expression.

Green hair floated around her head like it defied gravity. She wasn't touching the ground.

Wait a second.

I wasn't touching the ground.

None of us were.

We all floated inches off the forest floor. My body slowly drifted downward onto twigs. I tensed my thighs and gave a small jump. I floated a few feet higher.

I was flying.

Elation bubbled up my throat, and I giggled uncontrollably.

Whatever realm we'd jumped to had weak gravity.

My limbs were light, and delicious, warm rain pattered gently against my skin like a caress.

I breathed in deep.

Even the air was different.

There was no sulfuric stain. No harsh, pungent aroma that made your eyes water.

It was fresh and crisp with a smoky undertone. Like drinking a refreshing glass of water.

It was intoxicating.

I barely stopped myself from throwing my hands into the air and spinning like a fae ballerina.

The other recruits floated with scowls on their faces and didn't look impressed. Even John twisted back and forth like he was uncomfortable with the lack of gravity.

I swallowed down another giggle as I pushed off higher into the air.

It was *everything*.

Lothaire's angry voice was muted by the peaceful sound of rushing water. "Lyla will lead you through a practice to prepare you for what's to come. I recommend you focus because your sorry asses are going to need all the help you can get."

I gulped with trepidation.

Lyla nodded gracefully, and the runes on her skin glowed brighter.

The patter of rain became a loud rush as the gray sky opened up in a downpour that turned the spaces between the rustling trees dark.

Lyla opened her mouth, and words I'd never heard spilled out like the richest honey.

She chanted.

I inhaled deeply. Clean wood-smoked air cleansed my lungs.

Water streaked across my face.

Rain filled the forest.

Lyla stopped chanting. "Follow my practice. I will lead you through a soul cleansing."

The witch grabbed the bottom of her foot and slowly lifted it above her head. She levitated in the air and spun in a circle.

"Close your eyes."

I obeyed, grabbing my foot and pulling it high.

Her voice mixed with the rain; the rain mixed with the endless emptiness of existence.

I spun slowly. In a forest.

Far away.

"Very good, Aran," Lyla praised, and Malum said something nasty under his breath.

Scorpius grumbled, "Don't tell me Egan can do this shit."

"Holy fuck, Aran," John said.

I gritted my teeth as the men ruined my inner peace. Yet again.

Had they no sense of decency?

Opening my eyes, I was surprised to see that they were all struggling to lift their legs above their waists.

In contrast, mine was hyperextended, foot against my head as I easily held a standing split.

I might have noticed Orion staring at me with an impressed expression, and I might have pulled my foot a little straighter and spun faster.

He stared, transfixed.

I flashed a gloating smirk at Malum, who was looking at me like he wanted to set me on fire. Again.

The half warriors were a little more flexible but not by much.

Shane whistled. "I'm impressed, fae man."

I tried not to grimace at the growing familiarity of the man who wanted to murder me violently.

Lyla led us into another pose, and I closed my eyes and tipped my head back to the sky.

Water washed over me.

It was euphoric. It was everything.

For the first time in a very long time, tension drained from my body, and I lost myself in the stillness of just being alive.

I opened my ears.

The forest whispered the secrets to inner peace.

Lyla hummed silky-smooth words.

The downpour cleansed away phantom flames.

My body contorted to its limits.

I floated in the stillness of a dreamy forest.

In the haze, I fell away from my sense of self.

For the first time in forever.

Everything was okay.

And I was free.

ASSASSIN FIELD TRAINING: WAR

They came in black with marks of red,
And wielded pain with blades of hate,
They slit our throats and cut our knees,
Heartless beasts—the assassin's eight.

—The Ungodly

CHAPTER 20

THE UNGODLY

Field training: Day 15, hour 1
First battle

Flames exploded.

Monsters roared in falling snow.

I gasped, hyperventilating with my hands pressed desperately against a stone wall. I dug my nails into dirt.

Suffocated.

And learned my lesson.

Death was petulant in his brutality, and the rumors that he served the sun god were a lie.

Death served no one but himself.

A weapon cracked against my cheekbone.

I whirled.

My twin daggers skewered through stomach muscle, and my nails buried in organs.

A person convulsed atop me.

We embraced.

Blood gushed in a warm spurt as it slowly drained.

They were still.

And for the first time, I understood that death was not just a part of life.

He was evil.

In a crumbling hut on the side of a mountain, I lost a piece of myself—and as I breathed in snowy air stained with ashes and the shrieks of the dying, I knew I'd never get it back.

For death had arrived.

And once he came, he never left.

———

F *ive hours earlier*
We RJE'd back from the forest. Rich browns and greens were replaced with malignant reds and blacks.

The sulfuric air stung the senses, and the wind shrieked at the frothing ocean. Waves bellowed as they crashed.

All sense of inner peace evaporated as gravity slammed us to the rocks.

I missed floating.

Before any of us could do anything, Lothaire shoved twin daggers into our hands.

He yelled over the wind, "You will wield these blades as you fight the ungodly!"

What?

There was a whooshing sensation in my ears as I struggled to keep my wits about me. But I knew in my bones that everything was about to change.

I gripped the daggers tightly.

Lothaire walked back and forth as he ordered, "About two dozen ungodly have taken over a remote village in an uncivilized realm. You will not be permitted to leave until you have eliminated the threat. Do you understand, soldiers?"

"Yes, sir!" we answered.

Lothaire stared at me. "You will not use *any* powers that you possess. Your *only* weapon is the daggers. If you disobey, you will wish you were never fucking born. Understood?"

"Yes, sir!"

Lothaire's upper lip pulled back with disgust as he looked us over. "We're RJEing to the base of the mountain, then we'll be hiking up to the village. I'll be watching from a distance, but under no circumstances will I interfere."

He paused.

"Link arms, soldiers."

I threaded my arms through John's and Horace's. The eight of us were linked in a chain.

"There is no strategy! The village has already been compromised, and there are enough of you that you should be able to handle them."

Sweat streaked down my side.

The whooshing became a buzzing roar.

Lothaire stopped in front of me and leaned close. He smelled like death. "Not all of us have met the ungodly. This will be an introduction."

Eyes dead, expression blank, I stared back and showed him nothing. Didn't give away that I was freaking the fuck out.

My fingers itched for the enchanted pipe in my pocket.

I craved the release of hard drugs. Anything but reality.

Lothaire took a step back, and sea foam sprayed around him as a wave pummeled the rocks behind him.

"The rest of you have met the ungodly, but not like this. They are growing more advanced, and there are more of them than we've ever faced."

I swallowed thickly.

That didn't sound good.

"The next few hours are going to get messy. But like always, after the battle, we will analyze every second of it and each one of your choices. You will *not* disappoint me! Understood?"

"Yes, sir."

Lothaire lunged forward with the white, ball-shaped RJE in his palm.

Flames exploded.

And once again, we disappeared.

The cold prickled. Snow crunched beneath me as I stumbled into a pine tree. Icy needles clattered.

My feet burned.

We stood barefoot on the side of a snowy mountain.

Lothaire pointed up the side of the jagged mountain, where huts smoked far above us. "The ungodly are up there! Remember, don't be fooled."

Don't be fooled?

I breathed out rapid puffs of frosty air.

"What are you fucking waiting for? Climb!" was Lothaire's parting comment as he disappeared into the forest.

We moved.

Malum led us at the front with Scorpius and Orion trailing close behind. Zenith and Vegar were close on their heels, followed by Horace.

John and I climbed at the rear.

Numb fingers balanced as I dug my toes into icy cracks and pushed upward with my thighs.

Snow weighed down my eyelashes as I kept myself pressed against the rock face to avoid the icy wind that whistled against us.

Thighs burning.

Precise foothold after precise foothold.

I'd learned how to rock climb in the shifter realm when we fought arachnid monsters on the sides of snowy mountains.

What would they have done if I couldn't climb?

My biceps trembled with fear.

Breath in. Hold. Exhale. Hold.

I buried any emotion until I was as unfeeling as the rock I scaled.

Seconds crawled into endless minutes.

"Keep up! We don't have all day."

I tipped my head back to see Malum hanging off the side of the cliff with one hand. He glowered down at me.

He was barely fifteen feet ahead. There was no reason for him to stop and yell at me.

I glared, toes pressed painfully in an icy crack, as I removed one hand from the rocks and flipped him off.

Fuck off.

The bastard mimed shooting me with his fingers, and Orion smirked down at me. Then they kept climbing.

Higher into the sky.

As I peered down, ice and rocks clattered off the rocks and fell around me, and I couldn't see the bottom.

One wrong move and I'd splatter across jagged rocks at the base of the mountain. But I wouldn't die unless someone scooped up my heart matter and consumed it.

When I was a child, a traveling diplomatic wolf shifter from the beast realm had thrown a banned explosive device at Mother.

Before anyone had realized what had happened, she was blown to smithereens. Gore and blood had splattered across the throne.

I'd almost clapped.

But palace guards had slaughtered the wolf shifter, and I'd watched in horror as the pieces of Mother's body slowly coagulated back together and re-formed.

It was a lesson—the power of the fae monarch was not a joke.

Consuming their hearts was the *only* way to kill them. Kill *us*.

There was nothing else to it. No secret weakness that could be exploited.

It didn't offer much comfort as I trembled against the ice-slicked surface. Because I knew I was going to suffer heinous atrocities over and over again.

The memories smothered me.

Bullets ripping through my flesh; an enchanted knife carving up my back; blue flames that burned without heat eating me alive; red flames that were nothing but heat, melting the skin off my face.

So much pain.

The truth fucking sucked. But then again, would it even be the truth if it didn't?

Finally, after a half hour of ascent, I hauled my ass over the edge of the outcrop. No one offered me a hand. And I didn't expect one.

"The ungodly are stronger than ever. Don't be fooled by them," Lothaire's voice echoed.

For a long second, the eight of us stood staring at the smoking village before us. Boulders were piled up in dozens of makeshift huts that had pine branches for roofs.

They were all on fire.

The air reeked of the all-too-familiar scent of burning flesh.

My eyes watered as smoke and icy wind slammed

against us like battering rams. Malum gestured with his hand, and we all crouched and squinted through the smoke.

Goose bumps prickled the back of my neck—the howling wind and crackling flames were the only sounds.

Eerie silence prevailed.

I swallowed thickly as I slowed my breathing and lowered my heart rate. My body shook infinitesimally to the beat of the blood rushing through my veins.

A punishing gust of wind cleared smoke from the village, and a teenage girl dressed in furs stood in front of a hut.

Tears streamed down her face, and she screamed, "Help me!" Blood coated every inch of her skin.

My heart twisted with sympathy, but Malum motioned for us not to move.

None of us did.

She looked helpless and desperate. Her pretty cheeks immediately inspired a visceral reaction—anyone would want to save her. Protect her.

"Please help me! Please! It hurts so bad." Her voice trailed off into gulping sobs.

Who did this to her?

There was a loud roar in my brain, and my monster bellowed.

I closed my eyes.

Forced myself to ignore the emotions welling hot and desperate in my chest and focus on the reality.

Ten, nine, eight.

I focused on the numbers and the cold facts.

The teen was covered in blood…too much blood. Deep gashes covered her arms and legs, but there was also a lime-green substance mixed with the blood.

She shouldn't be standing.

Her wounds were too severe.

But she was.

Suddenly, the teen didn't look so weak and pathetic; she looked fucking terrifying.

Roof branches crackled with fire as the negative temperature scraped against us like needles.

The girl kept crying.

We kept waiting.

Suddenly, my stomach was twisted into hundreds of knots as I realized that I'd only ever fought in battles in the shifter realm.

We'd fought massive spider monsters that had been too large for the forest. Their clunky bodies were easy to hunt. Easy to anticipate. And we'd killed them with enchanted machine guns.

Fighting in the shifter realm had been messy and unorganized. Loud and dramatic.

I'd been surrounded by dozens of soldiers with guns as we faced down a clear enemy.

The battles had been simple.

"Please. Please help me," she kept sobbing and begging.

Five. Four. Three.

Now I crouched on a cliffside beside seven men with sixteen small daggers among us all.

Abruptly, a woman dressed in furs and covered in blood and the same lime-green substance walked out of the hut and stood beside the teen. "Please help us. They're hurting us."

Her voice was filled with emotion, eyes large and glassy, as she stared at us like we were her salvation.

Malum slowly shook his head again, and his grip tightened around his daggers. "On my count of three," he breathed quietly.

"Please, they're killing us!" An injured man hobbled out

and stood beside the woman. He gripped her arm and held the hand of the girl. He looked the same as them and was covered in similar gore.

A family.

In a desolate realm, begging for our help.

Nine. Eight. Seven. Six.

My stomach knotted further, and I closed my eyes one more time.

The gash on the man's forehead was deep enough that you could see his skull. He shouldn't be standing let alone pleading for help.

"One," Malum said under his breath.

"Please." A matching teen walked out and stood beside the girl. They were twins. The sight of them side by side triggered a memory that was just out of my grasp. It felt like it was important, but I didn't know why,

"Please help us."

"We need your help."

"They've hurt us so bad."

Choked sobs.

Malum's lips didn't move. "Two."

Another man walked out and joined the group.

Then another.

Then another.

People streamed out of the huts until there were at least two dozen bloody villagers standing in front of huts begging for our help.

The oldest were gray and hunched over, and the youngest were teens.

They all looked the same—covered in blood mixed with green.

Malum whispered, "Three."

There was a whoosh, and a dagger flew through the air

and landed between the eyes of the man with the gash on his forehead.

I winced.

Scorpius held one blade in his hand.

His white eyes looked off into the distance with his head tilted to the side. He'd used his hearing to hit the man perfectly between the eyebrows.

I expected Malum to charge forward or for there to be a battle cry as we attacked...whatever the ungodly were.

We kept waiting.

Bright-green goo oozed out of the wound.

The villager fell to his knees. "How could you?" he babbled with the hilt protruding from his forehead.

His hand was still gripping the girl's.

She screamed, "Dad!"

The knots in my stomach became boulders that weighed me down.

Intellectually, I understood that everything was not as it seemed because something was wrong with these people. But emotionally, I couldn't distinguish anything.

A girl sobbing over her dying father.

It was heinous.

Nine. Eight. Seven.

However, the man didn't pitch face-first into the rocks like he should have.

For a long time, he wobbled back and forth, then a horrible smile contorted his face, and he said, "You ruined this suit."

His skin wriggled and pulled like something was crawling beneath it.

There was a horrible ripping noise.

The man's mutilated body was torn in half and thrown to the ground like a used coat.

A creature like nothing I'd ever seen before emerged from his flesh—it looked like an insect melded with a man.

It stood tall and naked with light-pink skin covered in patches that resembled an exoskeleton.

The hard carapace-like substance covered its face in a mask.

It had a neck, arms, legs, all covered in exoskeleton patches like armor.

It also had six long, spindly legs protruding from its back with massive pincers on the ends.

Somehow, the towering creature had been *inside* the short man.

The mask moved, and I realized it was a face.

It smiled.

And in that moment, I knew exactly why Lothaire had called it an ungodly.

No god would create such a monstrosity.

I covered my ears as it emitted an awful screeching sound.

Then it charged.

CHAPTER 21
GOD'S DEAD

Field training: Day 15, hour 8
  First battle
I whipped my head back and forth.

Slash. Punch. Kick. Thrust.

My forearm burned from gripping my daggers for hours, and my body whirled helplessly as bodies slammed around me in the the village hut.

On the frozen side of a mountain, I fought with desperation.

My brain noted the pattern of the attack and that we should be fanning out for maximum effect to corral the attacking creatures.

But that wasn't what I did.

Knowing something was different from doing it.

I choked on exhaustion, confusion, and violence as my arms swung desperately in every direction.

My blows were frenzied and panicked.

It had been like this for hours. A harried rush of barely defending myself.

Various weapons had pierced my skin, and if it weren't

for my fucked-up fae queendom, I would have been long dead from blood loss.

My body was covered in wounds.

Blood splattered my flesh, smoke clouded my vision, and icy cold slowed my muscles.

I was in hell.

The ungodly didn't all burst from their hosts and attack us as monsters of flesh and claws.

No.

I would have preferred that.

Instead, they fought as villagers: innocent women, men, and teenagers.

When the first ungodly had charged, Malum had brutally cut through its carapace and removed its head.

The creature was nothing but an oozing green mass of death.

There had been a moment of silence as the villagers stared down at the desecrated body at Malum's feet.

The shock of calm.

Before the storm.

Rushing from every hut, hundreds of villagers had screamed and charged us. Some had weapons. Some wielded nothing but teeth and nails.

And it wasn't until you killed a villager that the ungodly would burst through their flesh in a roar of snapping pincers and rage.

It was like fighting two at once.

Once you'd defeated the villager, the battle really began. It was a psychological trip. Not the good kind.

I could barely get past the first step: kill the villagers.

Now I hesitated yet again as a young woman with dark hair and pale skin threw herself at me. I didn't raise my knives as she snarled and contorted.

With dark hair and sad eyes, she reminded me of an older Jinx.

She slammed her teeth against my bicep and ripped through my flesh. Up close, I could make out the lime-green sheen that covered her eyes.

That should have made all the difference.

I knew that one of those *things* was somehow inside her and making her attack.

But logic wasn't always enough.

I hesitated.

My monster had stopped screaming for blood hours ago. It was confused.

I didn't know how to act or what to feel.

She was living a nightmare she hadn't asked for. Mouth at my collarbone, her teeth somehow shredded my skin down to my bone.

I shook at her weakly.

Watched with a sick fascination as she snarled and bit with the ferocity of a rabid animal.

I grabbed her by the back of her neck and tried to gently extract her.

She didn't deserve this.

She didn't know what she was doing.

Her nails dragged across my face, and the gushing blood tinged the snowy world in a ruby haze.

"Please don't," I whispered. "Don't do this."

Her nose scrunched up as she screamed, "You killed them!" She bit down on my hand and slammed her feet into my stomach.

"Please," I begged. "Please understand."

She screamed louder and bit down on my forearm as I tried to hold her away from me.

Around us, knives whirled, fire leaped, women

screamed; men yelled, the wind howled, villagers died, and monsters emerged from their corpses.

It was hell.

"Please. Please. Please," I chanted as I held her.

Maybe I could tie her up?

She screamed mindlessly.

"Please."

I begged the sun god. Pleaded with whoever was in charge of goodness and civility in the realms.

A rusty sword slammed into my thigh, and I grunted as my right leg exploded with pain.

Yet another fucking wound to add to the collection. The girl flailed, and her teeth dragged against my chin.

An elderly man, weathered and gray, snarled as he pulled back the rusty sword and aimed for my other leg. He looked so old.

So feeble.

Someone's grandfather. Maybe hers?

Maybe I could tie him up too?

He swung the sword forward, but it halted midswing as his entire arm clattered to the ground.

Warm blood spurted onto my face and further decreased my visibility.

"What the fuck are you doing?" John screamed as he viciously severed the elderly man's head from his body.

An ungodly burst from the fallen man's form, and John sliced at the creature until it was reduced to a green pile of gore.

He grabbed my arm with his dirty hands. "What the fuck are you doing? You need to kill them!"

His dark gaze raked up and down my wound-covered flesh and the teenager kicking in my hand.

John's fingers tightened painfully.

"She doesn't know any better," I whispered back, and my voice cracked on the dry air and the vise that constricted my airways. It was clear that the ungodly had made the villagers mindless.

John whirled and snatched a throwing ax from the air.

Wind breezed against my cheeks.

He halted the weapon's trajectory centimeters from my face.

With a roar, he turned and chucked it back at a villager, and there was a sickening squelch as it cleaved the woman's face in two.

"Aran, they are not people! They were dead before we got here, so you need to fight!" he yelled as he whirled and ducked knives slashing furiously, fighting without an ounce of hesitation.

But the problem with having an analytical mind was that I couldn't believe his lie.

His statement wasn't true, because they weren't monsters; they were people who'd been *overtaken* by monsters.

The distinction mattered.

Maybe there is some way to save them? Take the ungodly from them without killing them?

There had to be a way.

If the creature got in, then it could get out.

John lunged across the room to battle with another villager and left me.

"But she doesn't mean it." I shook the biting girl in my hand like I could show him. Change his mind.

Make him *see* that she could be saved.

Suddenly the weight in my hand disappeared.

In a flash of knives, an ungodly ripped from the now-dead body and unfurled to tower about eight feet in the air.

Before it could do anything, its head was sawed off, and the body collapsed.

Malum stood in front of me.

Tattoo painted in red and green, his eyes were silver chips of molten steel. "*Start fucking fighting, or I'll kill you myself!*"

I opened my mouth to argue.

Malum stalked toward me with arms on fire. Bronze muscles rippled with unbridled strength, and his harsh features were taut with hatred.

He pointed his dagger at me like he was actually going to attack.

"You're a fucked-up bastard," I snarled.

He kept his blade directed at me.

My monster awoke with a vengeance, and it screamed in my head, egged on by Malum's stupid face.

Kill him. Bathe in blood.

Malum used his size to crowd me against the wall of the hut until I had to tip my head back to look at him.

The sharp edge of his dagger pressed against my cheek.

"You're pathetic and weak." He looked down at me like he was a king and I was nothing.

I shoved at him, but he didn't budge at all as he tensed his muscles and kept me pinned at his mercy.

"And you're a shitty leader." I spat blood across the brutal planes of his face.

The dagger dug into my cheek as the dying screamed behind him.

He was really going to do it.

"What the fuck is going on?" Scorpius shoved Malum away from me and yelled at him as he ran a hand across his lover's face to feel his expression. "I couldn't hear you, and then I find you in the corner threatening Egan instead of the ungodly? What the fuck are you doing?"

Flames whooshed above as the pine roof burned. Ear-piercing shrieks echoed as the demons slaughtered two ungodly at once.

Malum scoffed at Scorpius. "He deserves to die. We both know he's interested in Orion."

"Now is—" Scorpius turned around and dragged his dagger down a villager's torso from neck to lower belly. He turned back. "Not the time!"

Malum growled out, "Fine." He gave me a once-over, lingering on my numerous gaping wounds. "He's probably not going to survive anyway."

My vision blacked out with rage.

To stop myself from attacking Malum, I stalked past him into the dense fighting in the center of the structure.

Snow mixed with fire.

And I used all my hatred to blindly slam my knives into villagers and then the ungodly.

I hacked.

I killed.

And I kept killing.

I didn't bother to stop the teeth, the weapons, and the pincers that scoured my flesh as I attacked.

The pain was welcome.

As I punished others, I let them punish me.

A weapon banged against the floor, and the sound reminded me of a gunshot.

Fighting in the smoke, I barely registered what was the present and what was the past.

Back in the beast realm, I'd been talking to Walter in the foyer when I heard the first bang.

Then gunfire had ripped through the front door, and I'd thrown myself in front of Walter.

But the bullets had gone through my flesh and into his. He'd died, but I kept living.

It wasn't fair.

So I'd lain on top of his corpse and let the machine guns load into me. Shrapnel tore apart muscle and bones, but it was the only penance I could pay.

Now I attacked in a foreign realm, but once again, I wasn't able to save any of the villagers.

So I let them hurt me.

Paid my price.

I wasn't the good guy or the villain.

The gray of a hopeless existence tied my hands and held me hostage.

John yelled something, but I couldn't hear it.

I launched at an ungodly and sawed through its chest. Its pincers cut through the tendons of my forearm, but I didn't release it and kept cutting.

I grunted.

Across the smoky room, Orion looked up and held my gaze as he snapped an ungodly's neck with his bare hands.

His mesmerizing eyes were wide, and it felt like he was seeing straight into my black soul.

I looked away first.

Malum shouted at John to dodge as he threw his daggers across the room with precision.

Scorpius slid across the floor and sliced off the feet of an ungodly. Then he stood up and fought back to back with Orion.

They moved like a unit.

When one ducked, the other lunged, and both of them

were precise and deadly with their knives. They trusted each other completely.

What was it like to have a partner to fight beside?

No. My fictional lover would never make me fight.

As soon as he saw that I was injured, he'd kill everyone with a snap of his fingers.

His sole life purpose would be to protect me.

As they fought, Orion smiled up at Scorpius like he was the sun. It was love.

Hm. Maybe I would fight beside my fictional man.

Malum snarled an expletive, and I realized he was watching me stare at his men with longing.

He chucked his dagger across the room, but this time, he didn't yell a warning, and I barely ducked in time. The villager behind me collapsed.

The fucking hubris.

Chaos raged around us.

I slowly raised my bloody knife and pointed the blade at Malum.

Let it linger at his chest.

"Pow," I mouthed and mimed firing it like a gun. Imagined the enchanted bullet exploding through his heart.

Ending him.

Just like he had done to me earlier.

"Pow. Pow." I pointed in between his eyes, then on the other side of his chest.

The triangle of death.

I let Malum see the desolation in my eyes—the hatred.

The promise.

He was just a normal fae after all; only the queen was impervious to enchanted bullets. And I was her.

Pure rage darkened his face as he stood unnaturally still and seethed with the battle raging around him.

Then he sauntered forward, driving his shoulder into my side with such force that I slammed to the floor.

He smirked as he knelt to retrieve his weapon.

My monster seethed, but this time, I calmly got to my feet and walked into the battle.

An hour passed in a blur of violence.

And when the last body hit the floor, the eerie silence returned, and there was nothing left to distract me from the screaming.

It hadn't been coming from the villagers, because it had been inside my head the entire time.

It was me.

CHAPTER 22
THE AFTERMATH

Field training: Day 16, hour 1

"*What the fuck were you doing back there, Egan?*" Malum grabbed me by the neck of my shirt and flung me across the barracks.

My enchanted wound burned as I slammed against the metal wall.

Clearly, what I needed after fighting in a traumatic battle was *more* violence.

"Exceptional communication skills. Quite the leader," I coughed out sarcastically, my breath short and painful in my mangled chest as I slumped on the ground.

Wounds peppered every inch of my skin.

It was a miracle my clothes were still on with how many rips they had from knives, swords, pincers, nails, and teeth.

I didn't care.

I was empty inside.

Scorpius stalked forward and stood next to Malum.

At least the kings were predictable. After the awful battle, it was nice to have some structure.

"You *dare* criticize Corvus? *He* did his job! You were a

fucking liability and an embarrassment." Scorpius's pale cheekbones were streaked with gore. The eye tattoo on his neck blinked as he swallowed thickly.

"I didn't know it would be like that…" I trailed off, barely able to hear my voice.

The screaming was still loud.

Malum pushed Scorpius aside and once again slammed me into the metal wall. Blunt force trauma made my head spin, and I saw stars.

Either I was heavily concussed, or I was having a religious experience. I hoped it was the former. Praying seemed like a lot of work.

Malum's voice was the deepest I'd heard it. "It doesn't matter what the fuck it was like, or how the fuck it felt. When we fight, we fight as a unit. You didn't fight, Aran. You gave up. I've never seen such a pathetic display. I could fight better at *ten years old*."

Again he slammed me.

Yay, more stars.

The other recruits stood silent and watched. Even John looked pissed at me.

"They were innocent people," I whispered.

"*No, they were the ungodly!*" Gray eyes splintered like broken glass, and Malum reeked of decay. Gore also covered him.

"But we could have helped them." My voice cracked. "We should have done something."

Scorpius leaned close to Malum and ran his fingers across my face as he felt my expression. Unlike when he gently touched the kings, he dug his fingernails lightly across my skin.

I shivered and my stomach pinched.

"You don't look like a dumbass, pretty boy," Scorpius

snarled. "Yet you think you could have *saved* them?" His nails slowly scraped across my cheekbones and down my jaw.

Malum's grip on my shirt tightened, and he pulled my collar so I struggled to breathe. "All we can do is kill them." He inhaled harshly. "That is our mercy."

I shook my head as I hyperventilated and refused to accept that. "We gave up on them."

We failed them. I failed that young woman.

What was the point of big sisters if they didn't fight to save you? If they didn't save you when you couldn't save yourself? It didn't matter that it actually wasn't Jinx. My twisted psyche could see all the implications.

Karma was real.

The young woman I'd struggled with had been the sister, daughter, and friends of someone else. But no one had saved her.

They never do.

I reared forward and banged my head back as hard as I could into the metal wall. Desolation blinded me.

I hit harder.

Malum asked with annoyance, "What the fuck is wrong with you?" He was probably jealous he wasn't getting to do it.

Again, I bludgeoned myself.

"Stop it!" Malum growled, and his grip tightened.

None of us saved any of the villagers from their fate. Just like no one saved me.

I did it again with more force.

And again.

Again.

John shouted. "Aran, stop it!"

Again.

"*I said to stop hurting yourself, you fool! Pull yourself together!*" Malum yanked me away from the wall so my flailing head met nothing but air.

His hand remained tangled in my shirt.

"You don't understand," I whispered as I clawed at myself with my nails. Scoured my skin.

"He's losing it," Scorpius observed coldly.

Malum used his arms to pin me so I couldn't claw at myself. "Get it together, and be a man. This is war! This is what we do!"

I shook my head in disagreement. "You don't understand."

With me fully restrained against him, Malum took a deep breath and spoke calmly, "Get off your pampered high horse. We all understand because we were there."

I whispered brokenly, "I abandoned them."

Just like my father did to me. Just like my mother did every time she lit me on fire.

"I didn't save them."

I'd failed them all, and I was too intelligent to convince myself anything else had happened on that mountainside.

Pressure built behind my eyes. If I could cry, I'd be sobbing.

No tears fell.

My head hurt.

With my body limp, Malum's punishing grip was the only thing that kept me upright. I was broken.

No one said anything because words couldn't make anything better.

Suddenly, a light touch ghosted across my head.

"You're allowed to grieve." The words were so soft I barely heard them but they tinkled with a lyrical melody.

I looked up, and sad brown eyes hovered close.

Orion's mouth moved, and no sound came out this time, but I could read his lips as if he'd spoken. "Don't hurt yourself over the failures of your past."

I whispered back, "What else am I supposed to do?"

Golden fingers gently tucked a wild curl behind my ear. "Move forward and keep fighting."

"It's too hard," I said, too tired to care that I sounded like the pampered wimp they always accused me of being.

Orion smiled, and it was breathtaking. He mouthed, "I know what it's like to be broken. That's why we're a team."

The dark shadows suddenly didn't seem as suffocating.

"You promise," I whispered to the man I barely knew. He didn't owe me anything.

He twirled one of my curls and mouthed, "I promise."

Warmth spread through my chest as Orion's gentle presence smoothed my jagged edges.

"*Let him down*! What the fuck are you doing?" Demetre burst into the barracks, and his voice vibrated with the roar of a dragon. Shane and Noah trailed.

Suddenly I was hyperaware that I was pressed flush against Malum and he was holding me up as Orion leaned close. Scorpius stood nearby watching and saying nothing.

Why had they let Orion talk to me?

Why hadn't Malum and Scorpius freaked out like usual?

My questions were forgotten as Shane rushed forward and pulled me out of Malum's punishing grasp.

Knees giving out, the only thing that kept me from faceplanting was that I didn't like Shane's hands on me.

I pushed away from the half warrior and found my balance.

"Sun god, Aran, you're covered in wounds." Shane turned to the kings angrily. "He needs to see Lyla, not be injured further by you."

"What he needs is to man up," Malum said.

"You're blinded by your own issues with Aran. A true leader would never act this way," Shane said with disgust.

Malum exploded into flames.

At least some things were consistent.

The kings shifted close together. Malum and Orion frowned down at where Shane's hand was gripping my shoulder.

Shane was touching me—the man who smiled when he'd talked about killing me.

I tasted bile and pulled away.

Shane kept speaking. "He's just a fae with no fighting experience. What did you think would happen? It was his first time in battle. Cut him some slack."

He made me sound pathetic.

It hadn't been my first battle; it was just the first one that felt personal.

The many cuts gushing blood across my body must have been affecting me more than I realized, because I opened my mouth to argue that I wasn't a weak fae and I actually had a good amount of battle experience.

But John spoke before I could. "Let's go, then. To Lyla."

"Fine," Demetre agreed, and everyone shuffled out of the barracks.

John didn't smile—Mr. Hyde was back—but he leaned down and put his arm under my shoulder to support me.

Yet again, we limped together back to the fortress.

As the kings walked past us, Scorpius hung back. "Don't question Malum's leadership ever again. Oh, and Egan..." He paused.

"Yes?"

"Orion might be nice to you, but he's ours. If you overstep, we will demolish you." He didn't sneer like usual, and the calm tone of his voice was slightly terrifying.

His warning wasn't necessary.

If Orion even was attracted to me, it was to Aran, not Arabella.

I couldn't even be intimate with anyone because of the slur on my back.

I'd never even had a chance.

Scorpius didn't wait for a response; he just stalked away and joined his fellow kings. Malum and Scorpius flanked Orion on both sides like bodyguards from hell.

At least Orion was being taken care of like he deserved. His kind, gentle energy should be protected at all costs.

He was never mine to fight for.

I was startled out of my depressed thoughts when halfway up the steps, John said, "Never do that again."

"Not you too." I groaned and poked my friend.

"Me too?"

"I think the kings already made the point very clear. I got it. I fucked up."

John stopped walking. In the red eclipse, he looked nothing like the carefree man with the boyish face and dimples. Hard lines wrapped around him like a cloak. He didn't look human.

He opened and closed his mouth twice.

Finally he said, "It only gets worse."

"What does?"

"The battles. The training. The ungodly. The war. It only gets worse. So much worse."

I dug my trembling fingers into my somehow preserved pocket and pulled out my pipe. Eyes rolling back, I sucked in drugs like they were sanity.

What did someone say to that?

John took the pipe from my hand and put it into his mouth as we continued to limp forward.

He blew out smoke.

Before I lost my courage, I asked, "How have you survived this? How have you done this shit for years?"

John passed the pipe back. "Eventually you forget the time before you suffered, and it feels less like abuse and more like you're normal. Sure, there will always be a voice inside you that knows you're being tortured. But you learn to ignore that voice so you can function."

I inhaled smoke. "And if you don't ignore the voice?"

"You go mad."

"Fuck," I responded eloquently as we limped through the arching entrance doors and were greeted by a flash of lightning. The black-and-gold hall shimmered.

"Don't worry. I have a feeling you'll be just fine."

I scoffed. "Why would you say that?"

"Because you're like me."

"How so?"

"You've already lost your mind."

I looked up at him, confused how that was a good thing.

He answered my silent question, "It means you know how to survive."

As we hobbled past, broken light streamed through the mosaic of the mother. In the shards of shattered glass, there was something new.

A red tear dripped down her cheek.

And I knew.

It was an omen.

CHAPTER 23
A BLEEDING SOUL

Field training: Day 16, hour 10

Lyla healed my dozens of wounds, but the heavy sensation crushing my shoulders remained.

She left the classroom, and Lothaire entered.

The crushing got worse.

Lothaire slapped an enchanted stone onto the large desk in the front of the room. The air shimmered, and a snowy mountainside was projected against the wall.

The stone got closer and closer.

Suddenly we were watching an ungodly charge at us. Malum ordered us to herd the villagers into one of the small huts, and we worked as a team, slashing and backing them up.

The stone had hovered a few feet above our heads, floating unnoticed and capturing every horrible moment.

I'd thought the battle was the worst thing I'd ever experienced.

I'd been wrong.

Viewing it all again from a bird's eye position? That was true torture.

I watched as I pleaded desperately with a teenage girl. Watched as I failed her and an ungodly ripped from her flesh.

Hours of captured footage played, and it seemed to go on forever.

The more it played, the more confused I got.

I'd thought I'd been fighting alone in the corner of the hut, but John had never strayed more than a few feet away from me. Slashing and killing the hoard so only a few villagers got through to me.

But what happened next, I could have never expected.

An ungodly threw John across the room, and the three kings immediately took his place.

The three of them shielded me.

Hours passed, and they kept their position in front of me, making sure the worst of the attack never got to me.

Without the kings blocking, I would have been ripped to shreds.

In the classroom, I glanced over at Malum questioningly, but he refused to make eye contact.

More and more wounds covered me as my movements got slower. A villager slipped through and attacked me from the side.

It was the teenage girl.

And I stopped fighting altogether, holding her out with my arm and pleading with her.

When John pushed through the chaos to yell at me, I shook my head, and it was clear I wasn't listening to him.

He was pulled back into a fight, and Malum kept glancing over at where the girl was gouging me with her teeth.

Flames leaped higher across his skin.

Suddenly, he whirled around and screamed at me to

fight. He pinned me against the wall. His seven-feet stature dwarfed my six-feet height and made me look as small and pathetic as I felt.

But as he pressed me against the stone with his blade, his actions didn't seem as insidious as they had felt in the throes of the carnage.

Malum yelled at me frantically. Like he was panicking with worry.

His shoulders visibly slumped with relief when I yanked away from him and threw myself into the chaos. My daggers obliterated villagers and then ungodly.

For the first time in hours, I was fighting.

What was most surprising was when I had my second standoff with Malum, Scorpius and Orion stopped fighting.

I watched myself point my blade at him and pretend to shoot. The promise of his death written on my face.

The other kings didn't get angry like I expected.

Instead, Orion raised his eyebrows and smirked like he knew a secret as he whispered what was happening in Scorpius' ear. The pale fae shook his head like he was exasperated.

For some reason, a weird sensation settled in my stomach as I watched, and I picked at a scab on my hand.

I refused to look over at the three men sitting only a desk away from me.

When the enchanted stone flicked off and the projection stopped, Lothaire turned around with a manic glint in his eye.

"Soldiers. Stand the fuck up," he ordered softly.

This ought to be good.

Chairs creaked and desks groaned as the eight of us stood at attention.

CRACK. Lothaire slapped the baton against his palm

and asked calmly, "So do you feel good about yourselves after watching that? Do you think it went well?"

No one spoke.

SMASH. Lothaire reared back and struck his baton against the wooden desktop with so much force that it snapped into pieces.

"*Answer me! Do you think you did a fucking good job?*"

The intrusive thoughts told me to answer yes.

"No, sir!" I chorused back with the men and feigned subservience.

Lothaire's head snapped up.

"I expected Aran to be a fucking waste of space, but the rest of you have been training for *years*. You're the most pathetic class of recruits I've ever had." His upper lip pulled back as he sneered, "At this rate, you'll never be assassins."

Yay, I lived up to expectations. Awkward for everyone else.

Abruptly, Lothaire chucked his weapon across the room, and it shattered the stained-glass window.

Shards rained down.

Jagged fragments splattered across the side of my face. Glass sparkled everywhere. Blood dripped off us.

I bit my cheeks to stop from laughing.

There was something about a grown man acting like a homicidal maniac that tickled my funny bone. Like, was he for real?

Was this *really* what we were doing right now?

Lothaire took a deep breath, like seeing us covered in cuts calmed him. "You are lucky I am so forgiving," he said calmly.

I bit my tongue to stop the giggle.

He continued addressing us peacefully, like he hadn't just

broken a desk and a window like a child. "As most of you know, the breaking period is over."

He paused and let his words sink in.

"Now you'll be moving into a room inside the fortress. You will have a shower and sleep schedule and will maintain your physical health."

My teeth clicked as I fought the urge to ask if we were going to get shoes. Bruised bloody toes stared up at me mockingly.

It sounded too good to be true.

I'd slept and showered so little in the past weeks that delirium had set in. A few weeks ago, colors had stopped seeming as bright, and a cold, morose energy had settled around me.

Either a planet in this solar system was in retrograde, or I was suffering from depression. It was probably both.

"However." Lothaire paused.

I knew a catch was coming, but it still didn't stop the plummeting sensation in my gut.

"Before you move into your new dorms, we're going to go outside."

I couldn't breathe.

One. Two. Three.

Counting didn't help.

Lothaire slunk forward leisurely down the aisle.

Each step crunched loudly.

He stopped in front of me, but he didn't look down, just stared forward at the space above my head. "Do you think you deserve comfort, Aran? Do you think you've earned it?"

I swallowed thickly as I picked harder at the scab on my hand and stood at attention. "No, sir."

Lothaire's eye snapped downward. "Do you want to die, Aran?"

Yes.

Malum and Scorpius whipped around in front of me, and Orion shifted like he was uncomfortable. John swore under his breath. Behind Lothaire's back, Horace gave me a thumbs-up.

I grimaced. "Did I say that aloud?"

Malum growled, "Yeah, you fucking did."

Lothaire slammed his fist down on the desk in front of me.

I jumped and giggled, then slapped a hand over my mouth when I realized what I'd done.

The vampyre flung his head back and laughed, the awful, scratchy sound like nails on a chalkboard.

Maybe he also thought it was funny?

"Oh, Aran," Lothaire said between manic chuckles, "you think you're the first broken man to come through this program?"

Abruptly, he stopped laughing and leaned over into my personal space.

For a split second, *déjà vu* made the hair on my arms stand up.

Like the timeline was collapsing.

My gut told me we'd done this before, either in the past or the future.

I couldn't decide which one I preferred.

I needed a smoke.

"You're not the first recruit that's begged me for death," Lothaire said calmly. "You're not the first to seek out pain. Let me guess—you're suffering? Horrible circumstances that none of us can understand?" He spread his arms wide and gestured to the room.

Yes. It took every ounce of control I possessed to not roll my eyes.

Just another man with no fucking clue.

My defiance must have shown on my face, because Lothaire erupted. "I can guarantee you that you've suffered less than *every single fucking man in this room*!"

Suffering—what a funny word.

Flames. Mother's screams. Heart in my mouth. Monster inside me. Words on my flesh.

"You can't imagine what I've done," I whispered.

Lothaire fisted his hands like he wanted to pummel me, but he just pointed across the room at John.

My friend was still in his bad-tempered state.

Lothaire's voice was cruel. "I found John at the bottom of a ravine. Every single bone in his body was broken."

I stared at my friend with horror, but his face was expressionless.

Lothaire smiled meanly. "Isn't it true, John, that at ten years old, your family beat you because they feared what you were? Then they threw your broken body off a cliff? They left you. They prayed you were dead?"

"Yes." John was cold as granite.

Lothaire gestured dramatically. "But even then, death would not take you? Correct?"

"Yes."

Lothaire nodded like he'd made a point. "You see, Aran, you don't even know who the man is that you call a friend. You don't know *anything* about what these other men have gone through. You can't even imagine their suffering."

Lothaire lunged down and wrapped his massive hand around my neck like a vise until all the air left my lungs.

His fingers tightened. "Lyla was right. You're unbelievably selfish."

The violence never ended; it was unrelenting. Unfathomable.

I bit my bottom lip to stop from laughing at his tantrum.

"Right now, *choose!*" Lothaire screamed into my face. "If you want to die, I'll put you out of your misery. Otherwise, you agree to stop being a FUCKING COWARD and fight. That's your only choice. There's no in-between. CHOOSE."

Fingers tightened into an iron noose. "There is no gray. We *are* the black. Either you're an assassin or you're a liability to the realms and I'll exterminate you. So choose."

His fingers kept tightening.

My vision dimmed, but I didn't fight him.

I can't die. You don't get it.

I just wanted someone to understand that I didn't want to end myself because of what had been done to me. It was what *I'd* done.

The lies.

The pain.

The legacy.

The throne of death.

The fucking depression.

I should tell Lothaire to eat my heart. He would do it. The thought was tempting.

My neck creaked.

But then he would know who you are, and he wouldn't do it. Pretending there was an easy solution to my problems was a child's fantasy.

Jinx's sneering face flashed before my eyes.

Who was going to protect that crazy girl? She was too mean for Sadie or even her bear shifter mate, Jax. I recognized the edge in Jinx's eyes.

I understood what it meant to be mean.

Mother had always said I was a bitch.

Well, technically she said, "You're a pathetic, weak,

useless bitch and you will suffer every night until you stop embarrassing me."

The gist was that I was a bad bitch. Obviously.

"I'll fight," I mouthed on empty air. *For her.*

Lothaire dropped me like I burned and walked away, ignoring me as I bent over heaving. He'd gotten what he wanted.

"Outside, recruits. You'll run for sixty miles, and I want you to think about your shitty performance the entire time."

The next few hours dragged on as we ran along the island's edge.

The only sounds were harsh breaths.

Our tattered clothes, glass-sparkling skin that bled, and crushed spirits were the only remnants of the horrors we'd faced.

After the run, which felt more like a death march, Lothaire shoved us into the Black Ocean and shouted, "Now try not to drown, you pathetic fucks!"

He was supportive like that.

After twelve hours in the Black Ocean, John broke the silence.

"What made you choose life?" he asked quietly, his bicep tight around mine as we struggled against the frozen waves.

Salt filled my mouth.

I slammed across the harsh rocks, and my abused feet struggled for purchase. "I didn't choose life." Water burned my sinuses and poured out my nose as I gasped.

There was something so tragic about floating away at sea.

John's grip on my arm was so tight that my bones were probably fractured. It didn't matter anyway; he wasn't letting me go.

John was silent as another wave slammed against our frozen flesh.

The only sign he heard me was the pain that radiated down my arm. He clenched me tighter.

"It's never been a choice for me," I spat out salt water as I tried to explain it to my friend even though I couldn't tell him explicitly. "I just remembered who I was fighting for."

John nodded sharply like he got what I was saying.

Our elbows knocked against each other as we tightened our biceps.

Waves slashed.

"Why did they hurt you?" I asked, my voice trailing off in the shrieking wind.

John looked down at me, salt water dripping off his face. The red haze of the eclipse expanded around him until it swallowed him whole. "Because I'm an abomination."

Salt stung my eyes.

His words were like a fist to the gut, and I nodded. "Me too."

Next to John, Scorpius tilted his head to the side like he was studying us both.

For the first time, the blind king stayed silent.

Another wave dragged us under, and a new sound echoed through my skull. My monster didn't whimper or scream; it sighed with relief.

A random smile curled my lips.

I was understood.

CHAPTER 24
FIGHTING WITH THE DEVIL

Field training: Day 24, hour 4
  Second battle

After our punishment, aka drowning in the sea, we moved into a new room in the fortress.

It was a massive upgrade.

The singular stall with the shoddy wall was replaced with a massive en suite bathroom that had rows of marble shower stalls and a steam room.

The adjacent bedroom had four-poster beds pressed along the wall; a roaring fireplace; thick rugs; tall, stained-glass windows; and twinkling galaxies swirling on the high ceiling.

It was as relaxing as our new schedule, which included three square meals a day in the great hall and six hours of sleep every night.

Class in the morning, an hour for lunch, afternoon nap break, access to warm showers every day.

I didn't miss the broken cot and cold metal walls. The wind no longer screeched, and the endless cold had abated.

It should have been a cushy paradise.

It was a nightmare.

All the comfort in the world couldn't make up for the other days—the hours, minutes, and seconds that lasted a lifetime.

An unspoken haze hung around all of us because at any moment, we were expected to be ready to realm jump and fight the ungodly.

Lothaire informed us that he had a network of spies tracking the creatures across the realms, and as soon as they pinpointed a new location, he would bring us there to fight them.

He didn't explain how the ungodly traveled or their motives.

The question of *where* dominated my every waking thought, and I mulled over the possibility for hours. Where had they come from? How could something so heinous just suddenly start terrorizing people one day?

I had no answer, and pondering felt futile.

So I lived on edge.

Whenever Lothaire entered a room or looked at us, I flinched and waited for him to tell us it was time to fight.

I existed on the precipice of disaster.

Until it happened.

Lothaire walked up to us at lunch and said cryptically, "Meet me outside." Then he stalked away.

Now a stiff wind whipped my cheeks, and the bloated moon mocked me from high above.

I was going to war.

Again.

I picked at the scab on my hand that hadn't healed because of my incessant fidgeting.

Lothaire walked back and forth in front of us with the three half warriors standing silently behind him.

"The ungodly are creatures of chaos, and chaos expands. That is what it does. War is coming, and the High Court needs you to be ready."

Crunch. Crunch. Crunch.

His black boots dragged across rocks as he paced back and forth. Back and forth. Back and forth. My bare toes curled with discomfort, and I swallowed anxiety.

No doubt he kept our feet unprotected as some training technique to increase our pain tolerance. You didn't realize how luxurious shoes were until your feet were covered in cuts.

It was a constant reminder that we were nothing but soldiers being molded into killers. We didn't deserve luxury and comfort because there were no such things in war. Only pain.

This is really happening.

Endless moments stretched as we waited for Lothaire to expand on his statement.

He was silent.

Crunch. Crunch. Crunch.

People radiated energy, and right now, the eight of us were all giving off the same vibes—dread.

My back itched, and my monster was eerily silent. It unnerved me.

Lothaire paced for the millionth time.

I blurted out, "What about the other assassins this school has already trained? Shouldn't *they* be handling this threat?"

It took every ounce of self-control I possessed not to flinch as Lothaire cracked his baton across his hand.

An awful smile pulled his scar tight. "What makes you think they aren't fighting the ungodly?"

I narrowed my eyes. "You just said? I thought that—"

He held up a hand and cut me off. "This is a training exercise. You are facing the weakest ones. You will join the other assassins sooner than you think."

I ignored the latter part of his statement and focused on the important part. "So you're saying there are stronger ungodly out there?"

Opal fangs flashed. "Yes. You're fighting their equivalent of civilians. Meanwhile, members of the High Court are fighting the *real* ungodly. Soldiers that are bred to kill, maim, and destroy. Soldiers you couldn't even begin to fucking handle. Especially not with how fucking pathetic you were last time."

I struggled to inhale.

Lothaire rolled his eye. "Yes, I see you do understand."

We stared at each other for a long moment.

Lothaire slammed his baton across my face, and my jaw cracked.

Blood splattered.

"Don't talk back to me ever again. Understood, soldier?"

"Yes, sir." I spat blood onto the rocks. Eyes blank. Face dead.

Someday, I'm going to snap his femur and stab him with it.

I breathed out a small sigh of relief as Lothaire turned his attention away from me and said, "That's why you're all going to fight as many times as I fucking say necessary, for as long as I say necessary. Until I believe you've learned what I'm trying to teach you. Understood, soldiers?"

"Yes, sir," we chorused.

Once again, Lothaire handed out the twin daggers, and the silver blades glinted red in the shadows of the eclipse.

They reminded me of Malum's eyes.

I breathed deep. *Inhale. Hold. Exhale. Hold.*

Lothaire raised his voice. "You all have a long way to go. Buck up, and man the fuck up! Link arms, soldiers."

He grabbed John's shoulder.

The world exploded with fire as we jumped realms.

Disoriented, I shook my head and tried to process that once again, we were on a snowy mountain. It was similar to the last one but taller with more jagged peaks.

It was the same realm.

The snowfall was heavier, and snow gathered on my lashes while a frigid wind kissed my cheeks.

"Follow me!" Malum yelled as he took charge.

This time, I didn't hesitate to follow him up the steep cliffside. The small handholds and brutal fall didn't seem as menacing.

Not when I knew what awaited us.

Once again, we pulled ourselves onto a rocky outcrop, but this time, the village had more huts and was built into the side of the mountain.

Villagers stumbled out. Men, women, and teens. They were all dressed the same.

It was like reliving a nightmare. Even though I expected their cries and ploys, it still shook me to my core.

But this time, I didn't freeze in shock.

Yet I still hesitated.

The screams, the choking flames, the ripping flesh as creatures emerged from body cavities was overwhelming.

I stabbed with my knives as the chaos threatened to consume me.

I saw myself in their tear-streaked faces. They transformed into Sadie and the girls.

Squeezing my eyes shut, I fought blindly.

Hours passed, and as I grew tired, more blows landed on me. So I opened my eyes and stared at the people I killed.

All of a sudden, two villagers charged me with swords as I was distracted fighting an ungodly. Just when I thought the blades were going to fucking *hurt*, Scorpius appeared out of nowhere and decapitated them. They fell over, swords clattering inches from my body.

"Fucking concentrate." He sneered as he moved smoothly back to Orion's side. He fought like a dancer.

I fought like a wounded animal.

Smoke clouded my vision as bodies flung around me.

Mentally, I knew we should be fighting smarter, and it was obvious that we should have used the fire to corral the villagers and kill them at once. It would shorten the battle considerably, and technically we wouldn't be using our abilities or a weapon.

Physically, I did nothing but slash and stab.

Just because I had the capacity to reason and analyze didn't make a single ounce of difference in the midst of battle.

Maybe that's why generals always watch wars from afar?

In the fray, there was no room for reason.

No logic.

Just death.

The closest I got to rational thought was during the seconds where an ungodly died slowly on my blade. I pondered the art of warfare. Recognized the paralyzing terror coursing through my limbs.

Another villager attacked, and the battle haze returned.

Slashing, ducking, stabbing, kicking, punching, and throwing.

Mouth open with a perpetual gasp, I just kept fighting.

I slit the throat of a villager and didn't see the shovel being flung at me.

Suddenly, rusty metal split the side of my abdomen, and I whimpered at the streaking pain.

I threw my arm blindly and stabbed at him, but somehow, he evaded me, and the shovel reared back.

Fuck. No amount of calming breaths was about to get me through this pain.

The blow never came.

Orion had sliced off the villager's arms and was precisely cutting off all his limbs.

I blinked through the smoke, convinced I was hallucinating.

The stunning fae pursed his bee-stung lips and eviscerated the villager with a quiet savagery I hadn't thought he possessed.

When the villager died, the ungodly only pulled itself halfway out of the skin before Orion decapitated it.

"Are you all right?" Lyrical words spun like honey.

I nodded blankly, still shocked by his ferocity.

"Be careful," he ordered, and it was the loudest I'd ever heard him speak.

"You too," I whispered.

For some reason, the stunning fae wasn't comfortable speaking, and it made me want to be quiet around him. I wanted to let him know that I was okay with the silence.

For some reason, I took a step closer to him. Chocolate eyes burned with intensity as he also moved closer.

"Remember what Scorpius told you," Malum said to me as he smoothly stepped between us.

"I wasn't doing anything." We all ducked as a weapon whistled by.

"Wouldn't want an accident to happen during battle." Scorpius's voice was close to my ear as he stepped up behind me and invaded my space.

Even with the scent of decay all around, the intoxicating scents of bergamot and musk wafted off him.

Surprisingly it was Orion who answered, "Leave Aran alone."

For a long moment, as a battle raged around us, Malum and Scorpius froze with expressions of disbelief.

Scorpius whispered so only I could hear, "Mess with my mate one more time and I won't be so forgiving." He deflected a blow and spun so both he and Malum shielded Orion.

I sighed with exhaustion and turned back to the fight.

The kings lingered near me, and I remembered how they had stayed in proximity, helping to protect me in the last battle.

I purposely cut through bodies until I stood on the far side of the room next to John. My pride stung. I didn't need my enemies protecting me.

The remaining hours of the battle pulled out impossibly long. Time crawled forward.

Sticky and slow like tar.

Seventeen hours later, the eerie silence fell, and déjà vu hit me.

Without the chaos of fighting, it was now apparent that we'd been fighting way more people. Hundreds of mangled bodies covered the floors. Piled atop one another.

Holy fucking sun god, did we just fight an entire city?

I was standing in a puddle of broken flesh, and I stumbled out of the hut like I was drunk.

Outside was worse.

The red-and-green gore splashed across snow in a macabre abstract painting. The same colors painted my skin.

John leaned against me, and we held each other up.

Then Lothaire appeared, and we RJE'd away.

As the world exploded in flames, I realized there was no reason for us to realm jump to the bottom of the mountain, and he was making us scale it as some type of sick warm up.

His sadism knew no bounds.

It was ruining me.

CHAPTER 25
HIS KISS

Field training: Day 25, hour 23

Once again, Lyla healed us.

Yet again, Lothaire screamed about how pathetic we were as we rewatched the battle. This time, he drove his fist into the chalkboard during the projection like he was imagining it was our skulls.

Spicy.

To be fair, I really wasn't in a position to judge anyone else for their mental health.

I'd stopped hiding my pipe and was openly puffing on it as our "teacher" (very generous use of the term) lost his mind.

"How the fuck are you supposed to be assassins if you can't handle fucking civilians? You were unorganized and embarrassing!"

Excellent points.

Lothaire gargled and spat across the room, then he resumed punching his fist into the wall.

Personally, I was loving this little feedback session and was really growing as an assassin.

I jotted down notes into my notebook.

"I KNOW *DOGS* WHO CAN FIGHT BETTER THAN YOU!"

I nodded in agreement and scribbled, *Adopt, don't shop.*

"*My blind grandmother who has weeks to live could have reacted faster than you sorry fucks!*"

Well, she sounded fabulous. I wrote, *Meet Lothaire's grandmother before she dies. Seems urgent.*

"*What do you have to say for yourselves?*"

Silence.

Lothaire seethed with unconstrained rage, and it became clear he was waiting for someone to answer.

I raised my hand.

"*Aran!*" Instead of pointing at me to speak, he picked up a chair and chucked it at my head. "*Please answer!*"

I barely ducked the flying projectile, suddenly feeling like this was a trap. I pursed my lips. "Um. I have nothing to say…because we suck?"

That seemed like a good nonanswer.

Lothaire paused and tapped his finger to his mouth like he was considering it.

He chucked his desk as he shrieked like a maniac.

John yanked me out of the way and saved me from being crucified by a wooden leg.

Damn it, my notebook was ruined. I was going to study my notes later. *Not.*

"Do you know what you're all going to do now?" Lothaire asked with creepy calmness.

This time, no one was dumb enough to answer.

"You're going to hoist boulders until you aren't pathetic. Now move. Fucking move!"

The eight of us shoved against one another as we scrambled to obey (escape) our psychotic teacher.

Then we lifted boulders.

Up.

Down.

Up.

Down.

Picking a rock up, then putting it down was *definitely* making me less pathetic.

Lothaire lifted a boulder above his head and chucked it at Scorpius. It took him out.

John and I laughed.

Lothaire whirled around and threw two at us.

We stopped laughing.

After six hours of lifting, all of us had broken bones. Also, all my knuckles were split wide open, and my arms burned like they were going to fall off.

More physical pain. Titillating.

When Lothaire finally said, "You're done for the night. I don't want to see you until lunch tomorrow," no one moved because we were too afraid it was another test.

"OUT OF MY SIGHT OR I *WILL* KILL YOU ALL!" Sparks of power lit the air around him.

Needless to say, we *sprinted* to the fortress.

Back in the safety of our room, I crawled into one of the closed-off shower stalls and turned it to the hottest setting.

It scalded.

I scrubbed off every ounce of red-and-green gore.

Then I scrubbed at the invisible filth: the echoes of yells, the smoke, and the dying gasps of the people and creatures I'd killed.

I scrubbed until my skin was raw.

Then I scrubbed harder. The brush was stained pink with blood.

I didn't stop.

Then, collapsing onto the cool marble, I spent hours hyperventilating.

Like a zombie, I eventually crawled out of the shower and pulled on clean clothes. I wasn't grateful for the privacy of the marble stall, because I no longer cared.

It all seemed so trivial.

Poor me, a pathetic princess in disguise hiding from her throne. Boo-hoo.

I hated that I'd ever thought it mattered.

Who gave a fuck that I was a girl?

Death clung to me.

It wasn't rational, but I couldn't shake the feeling that death was a man and he now stalked my life.

Like my soul had been marked.

For suffering.

Not at all concerning. Nope. I was definitely not depressed.

Like the composed princess I'd been bred to be, I punched myself in the temple as I tried to dislodge the dark thoughts.

I paused and listened. I was still thinking about how death was haunting me.

How do you know? What even is a thought?

Cue the philosophical breakdown.

I punched my temple one more time to try and kill off the intrusive thoughts.

In our next session, Dr. Palmer would 100 percent be reporting me to the authorities. The thought of the infuriating woman filled me with rage.

"I'll never let you take me," I snarled at the towel hanging on the wall and pretended it was Dr. Palmer.

I showed her who was boss.

The doctor (towel) cowered before me. Instantly I felt better.

After my delightful bath activities—very refreshing—I dragged my aching limbs into my overly plush bed. The emerald cover was a delicious, smooth velvet.

The fireplace roared against the far wall, and the sturdy fortress kept the miserable wind at bay.

I closed my eyes.

Clear as day, the carnage unfolded. I watched every person's face as I tore them apart with my daggers.

Fighting with knives was an intimate affair.

First, the villager's hot breath choked and gurgled as they shuddered, limp. But then pincers grabbed wildly.

The soft comforter transformed into a lead weight, and it crushed me deeper into the too-soft bed. The bed was consuming me.

I missed my broken cot.

I thrashed wildly and, after an extended struggle, freed myself. I sprawled on the ornate rug in front of my bed.

World spinning, I turned my head to the side and stared into the fireplace.

Flames crackled like enchanted gunshots. Then the sounds shifted into garbled words.

Oxygen atoms tore themselves apart in a frenzy. Carbon dioxide gloated.

The flames were so *smug* with their flickering glow. I hated them.

The fire hated me back.

It screamed at me in a foreign language.

I flipped it off. *I don't speak your creepy language, so take that.*

A sick sensation coursed through me as I remembered that Sadie's mate Ascher had once said that flames shouted at him. We'd all thought he was just being dramatic.

I listened to the rough garbles that were too repetitive to be gibberish.

There was a chorus of voices.

Holy fuck.

So I did the only thing I could—I covered my ears and panicked.

Even crushed with anxiety, my mind put together the pieces. It was common knowledge that Ascher had trained from a young age to be an assassin and he'd killed a *lot* of people.

Now I'd killed a lot of people.

"You'll get used to them," John said casually as he walked past me and climbed into his bed.

"Used to what?" I asked.

He pointed to the fire and said tiredly, "The voices of the people you killed." Then he pulled his comforter over his face to fall asleep.

Everything stopped.

Understanding hit me like a blow.

There were no such things as coincidences, just patterns and truths that people were too scared to accept.

The truth of John's words was obvious. The flames were the voices of the people I'd killed.

I banged my knuckles against my temple and wished my brain would just *stop thinking.*

But it didn't stop.

Throughout the realms, there were people that denied the mainstream belief that after death, the sun god brought souls into a golden valley.

These heretics claimed that the valley of the sun god was actually a twisted land of fire, ice, and suffering.

They warned that this world of death overlapped with

the world of the living. If we weren't careful, it would consume us all.

Mother had murdered any fae that spread such lies.

It was obvious.

Why would mother kill them if there was no truth to hide?

As if to punctuate my sick realization, a shadow loomed over me.

Shapes contorted and twisted.

Death was visiting.

Never mind. Malum's face was hard and cold as he took a step over my prone body and stared down at me.

Massive thighs spread, face tensed, he straddled me.

He exerted dominance.

I exerted "needs medical help."

The fire screamed at me louder. Malum's muscles tensed, and I did nothing but lie paralyzed under him.

I'd experienced too much violence and was at my breaking point. And by "point," I meant fully on the *other* side of sanity.

I waited for the blow.

He leaned forward, and I instinctively flinched away, cowering into the carpet.

He stilled like a predator and didn't move closer.

I waited for his anger. His punishment. After spending weeks with him, I knew he was a singular creature of flames and violence. In other words, a dumb bitch.

"Don't punch yourself," he said softly.

"What?"

"Don't hurt yourself."

I whimpered.

"What the fuck?" Malum scowled.

"Ungodly. It's an ungodly!" I yelled to alert the others.

"It's taken over Malum's body and is spouting nonsense. Someone kill it, quick!"

Malum tipped his head back and pinched his nose. "Sun god, fucking save me from idiots."

"What's going on?" John must have fallen asleep, because he sat up and asked tiredly, "Who do I need to kill? I'm ready."

"No one needs to kill anyone!" Malum barked. "I was just making sure Aran was okay."

I pointed at him accusingly. "He told me not to hurt myself. An ungodly has taken over his body."

John's panicked eyes met mine.

"For fuck's sake! I was just being nice," Malum growled.

"Well, don't be," I snapped back. "It's creepy."

"Fine," Malum snarled and lightly kicked me as he walked away.

"Ow, that hurt, you bastard!"

"You asked for it."

"Are you okay, Aran?" Orion asked softly from his bed.

His gentle, lyrical voice washed over me like a warm fae day. He hardly ever spoke, so when he did, it felt like I'd won a prize.

I smiled shyly at him. He looked like a painting of a stunning god as he lounged in his bed.

"For fuck's sake. Fuck you, Aran." Malum kicked his bed and muttered unkind things under his breath.

Scorpius sauntered out of the bathroom and went up to Malum.

Holy sun god.

The towels around his waist highlighted a prominent *V* line that framed a trail of dark hair. His tattoos seemed to glow on his pale skin.

My back burned and stomach pinched as I admired the

layers of abdominal muscles that seemed painted onto his lean frame.

Scorpius wrapped his arms around Malum and pulled him down so they were cuddling on the bed. Then he sneered, "Ignore the small, pathetic weakling."

It took me a moment to realize he was talking about me. From the floor, I flipped him off.

Scorpius returned the gesture.

I glanced over at Orion nervously, but the gentle fae was smiling and didn't seem to mind the fact that his lovers were my archenemies.

"So I'm not killing anyone?" John mumbled as he yawned and started to fall asleep.

"Maybe," I said at the same time Malum shouted, "No!"

Whatever.

I rolled over and resumed my panic attack.

Before I could fully sink into the swing of things, long, sooty lashes blinked curiously down at me. Orion's lush lips hovered close as he lowered his large body onto the floor.

He pointed to my arms and mouthed, "You should cross your arms over your chest."

I stared at him in shock.

White-blond hair shone like spun silk as Orion mouthed, "The ground is centering. Especially when you cross your arms over your chest. It will help your anxiety."

Two warm, callused fingers grabbed my wrists and gently crossed them over my chest.

I jumped at the contact but let him position me.

Everything was a hazy blur.

Dark chocolate and sweet raspberries filled the air around him and burned the space between my nose and my sinuses.

"This always helps me." In the screaming firelight, his almond eyes were a soft, honey brown.

I could get lost in them.

How is he so stunning?

Orion gave me a soft smile and a gentle peck on the cheek, then he climbed off the ground and walked over to the kings.

I went into shock.

Malum growled like an animal as he grabbed Orion and gently pulled him down so he lay between him and Scorpius.

They looked ridiculous and barely fit on the bed.

I was too busy getting absolutely eviscerated by pain because the wound on my back was splicing me with paralyzing waves of agony.

But my heart fluttered.

Warm and light in my chest.

I smiled as the enchanted wound on my back punished me for my infatuation.

I was never going to wash my cheek.

Orion had kissed me.

I could die happy.

CHAPTER 26
DINNER WITH THE DEVIL

Field training: Day 30, hour 8

Turned out I spoke too hastily about feeling good.

Shocking. Didn't see that coming.

The glow from Orion's cheek kiss lasted for about three hours, and then the crippling existential dread returned.

I jumped at every shadow in the fortress because I kept thinking it was death in a cloak stalking me. So that was fun.

"Hey, Aran, wait up." Shane's voice was loud and grating.

John flinched beside me at the sound, and Scorpius muttered something derogatory about an orange mohawk.

I stopped in the middle of the hall, and the other recruits stopped beside me.

We'd just finished morning class with Ms. Gola, and we were all walking to lunch in silence.

Ever since the last battle with the ungodly, the eight of us had settled into a comfortable routine. No one spoke about what had happened.

If someone brought up the ungodly, they were bullied mercilessly until they shut the fuck up.

Zenith was the biggest perpetrator.

The demon kept trying to bring up the battle at meals, which sent half of us into panic attacks and made the other half angry.

Malum had dealt with him by gently waterboarding him for six hours in the shower until he agreed to stop talking.

Even Vegar hadn't interfered, because Zenith deserved it.

Now I turned slowly toward Shane as lightning streaked across the walls and the air crackled with electricity.

My already wild curls tickled my cheeks as they leaped against gravity.

"Do you need something?" I asked Shane, confused why the half warrior had singled me out yet again.

Sun god, he was obsessed with me.

"Nope, just wanted to check up on you, fae man." He flashed a brilliant smile as he ran a hand through his orange mohawk.

My teeth gritted as I took in his relaxed posture. The half warriors had been riding us harder during our runs and had joined with Lothaire giving us critiques over our performances. They knew about our horrible battles with the ungodly, and they condoned it.

I didn't like him.

Be nice. You want him to like you so he doesn't rip out your heart and ascend to your throne.

I forced the scowl off my face and relaxed my shoulders like I was a chill person and not high-strung. "I'm doing fine. Thanks for asking."

"That's really good to hear." Shane leaned forward and ruffled my hair. "Everyone is treating you well? I know it must be hard to be the new guy, especially with the battles."

All of us groaned as he broke the golden rule.

It also took every ounce of control I had not to reel away from his touch. I didn't like people invading my personal space unless it was Sadie, Jinx, John, or Orion.

"Don't worry, everyone's been *super* welcoming." I smirked at Malum as I spoke. He rolled his eyes and made a face, the flames crawling across his shaved head making the action seem less childish and more terrifying.

"That's great to hear. I'm glad you're being treated well," Shane said with enthusiasm.

His ability to detect sarcasm was truly impressive.

Also, I hated to be dramatic, but I'd never been treated worse in my life, and I'd had a *cannibal* phase.

Lightning flashed.

Shane ruffled my hair again.

I debated launching myself at him and gouging out his eyeballs with my fingernails. Then he wouldn't touch me.

As if he sensed my dark thoughts, John put his arm around my shoulder and pulled me away from Shane.

"Aran's doing fabulous and has never been better. He's really just thriving. Big killer, this one," John gushed and had the audacity to *tickle* my side like I was a kid.

I gently stomped my foot on the sensitive part of his bare foot.

John laughed and tickled me harder like I was playing.

Shane narrowed his eyes like he realized he was being fucked with. "Okay, just wanted to make sure. You can come by my office anytime if you need to talk."

Did I look like someone who wanted to talk about my feelings?

I rolled my pipe with my tongue and inhaled smoke. "Do you have any enchanted drugs or alcohol in your office?" I asked hopefully.

Shane laughed like I was hilarious. "Nice joke, fae man."

"If you're lame, just say that," I mumbled under my breath.

"What? I didn't hear you." He leaned closer with his big freaking smile.

Sun god, I hated friendly people.

There was something so *nice* about them that it was freaking creepy. Like where was their self-deprecation and hatred for life? Where was the spice?

He was giving me *nothing*.

Shane kept waiting for me to fill him in, and I shifted on my feet uncomfortably with my mouth zipped shut. I couldn't speak without saying something mean.

"Aran's good. We need to go eat. We're going to be late." Malum stepped up beside me and put his hand on my shoulder like he had permission to touch me.

Tension filled the hall as Shane stared at the hand.

Awkward.

"Yeah, we gotta go." I tried to smile, but the action made me feel sick, and I settled for a deadpan stare.

"Okay, remember I'm down to talk or just hang out whenever you need, fae man," Shane called over his shoulder as he walked away.

When he disappeared out of sight, I turned to Malum. "Touch me again and you'll lose your hand."

His hand lit on fire and scorched the shoulder of my shirt. "Oops," Malum said like a mean girl before he released me.

"Great." I mimed gagging. "Now I have chlamydia."

"That's not how that works."

"Sounds like something someone with chlamydia would say."

"Can we just go fucking eat?" Scorpius sighed as he grabbed the seething king and led us toward food.

Did Malum have a sexual disease? I had no clue.

Did I kneel before my bed and pray to the sun god that Malum was riddled with sexual diseases? Every single night.

No one could say I wasn't pious.

"Well, that was entertaining." John flashed his dimples as he draped his arm across my shoulders. "Shane really acts like he thinks you two are best friends."

Since I was about four inches shorter than the human, I was apparently the perfect height for him to lean all over.

"He can think whatever he wants, but it doesn't make it true," I grumbled.

John smiled, and I could tell from the way he grabbed me tighter that he enjoyed the fact that I didn't want to be friends with Shane.

"The eclipse must be getting to Shane, because it's obvious you're not interested," Horace said as he sauntered up beside us. "It gets to people, you know, the lack of sunlight. Makes them act loco." He spun his finger in a circle next to his temple.

"Why are you talking to us?" I asked the yellow-eyed vampyre with confusion.

"I've decided you're not completely pathetic."

"Thank the sun god. It's a miracle," I said dryly.

Horace humphed. "Then you must have no sense of humor."

Before Horace could say something horrible like an offer to make friendship bracelets, we entered the great hall, and he got distracted by a goblet of blood.

Servers brought out overflowing trays of warm food.

Ever since the *incident*, aka the kings shoving food down my throat and humiliating me, I'd learned my lesson.

I piled my plate full with meat, vegetables, and bread.

Then I took a big forkful of meat and discreetly dumped

it under the table into a small pile.

John knew what I was doing, but he wasn't a snitch, so he didn't say anything.

There was a burst of laughter from the far side of the room as the royal students laughed at something that was most likely not funny.

Our table was dead silent.

A group of commoner students burst out laughing, and I gripped my fork tighter.

I fought the urge to stand up and scream at them to stop having fun and just shut the fuck up so we could all suffer in peace.

They kept laughing like imbeciles.

A migraine started to throb in my temple.

We were only a few feet above the other tables, but we might as well have been living in another realm. There was a growing chasm between us.

While they went to class, studied their abilities, and hung out with each other, we fought monsters on mountainsides and got boulders thrown at us.

Grown men and women who were all extremely powerful and impressive. They seemed like innocent, naive children.

Death hadn't visited them.

The gourmet food tasted like ashes in my mouth.

"Hey," a soft female voice broke our table's carefully cultivated silence, and I jumped at the intrusion.

Tara and Sari awkwardly shuffled as they stood next to me. They had a pile of papers in their hands.

Tara was the blonde I'd stood up for in the bathing room, and Sari was her pretty dark-haired friend who'd gotten with Orion and sat in front of us in our morning class.

They both were staring at me expectantly.

"Hi?" I asked awkwardly.

I shifted to try and block their view of the pile of meat on the ground. *Why is everyone trying to talk to me today?*

Tara chewed on her bottom lip as a red flush crept up her neck. "Sari says that you do really well in battle strategies class, and we need help for our homework assignment."

Sari nodded vigorously. "Will you help us? We have to write twenty pages on why an enchanted gun is one of the deadliest weapons in the realm, and we're both really struggling."

Phantom bullet wounds peppered my flesh.

Walter gasped as he died beneath me.

Bullet after bullet ripped through my skin and tore me to shreds.

Gore everywhere.

Malum scoffed, and Scorpius sneered, "That's so easy. You don't need help."

The red flush crawled up Tara's neck until her face was beet red.

Sari rolled her eyes. "We're asking *Aran* because he's smart and nice. Not you."

Both girls kept their eyes on me and ignored the men staring at them.

Horace whispered something under his breath that sounded a lot like, "I'm going to drain you dry. Then I'll drink your blood."

His meaning was so horrifying that it shook me out of my haze.

Sari put her hands in front of her like she was praying. "Please. Please. Please, Aran. We don't know who else to ask. You're the smartest in the class."

My fingers curled as I stopped myself from beating at my own head and screaming at them to leave me alone.

But I was a beacon of self-control.

I smirked at Malum and said pointedly, "As the *smartest* person in the class, I'd love to help you."

Malum's silver eyes were cold as steel. He chewed his steak aggressively and spat, "In your fucking dreams, Egan."

"Oh my sun god, thank you," Sari squealed and tugged on Tara. "Told you he would say yes." She winked.

I smiled faintly, happy that someone's brain was still producing serotonin.

An hour later, my head hurt from explaining at least fifty reasons for why an enchanted gun was superior to a traditional weapon. My hand ached because at some point, Sari had finagled me into writing out the answers.

This was 100 percent just plagiarism.

Good for her.

"Lunchtime is over," Malum growled out of nowhere and pulled the pen out of my hand so I had to stop writing.

"Hey, wait, I wasn't finished."

Shockingly, it wasn't Malum who replied. Orion softly said, "They need to go."

His lyrical voice was smooth like honey, and both Tara and Sari audibly sighed. They stared at the golden fae like they were entranced.

Orion glared back.

The dark expression on his face was such a dramatic departure from his usual gentle demeanor that it took me aback. He gripped his steak knife like a weapon.

Did every man have anger issues?

Well, I knew what my first act as queen would be— mandatory anger management therapy for all men. No exception.

Oh my sun god. A brilliant idea struck me. *I can banish all men from the fae realm.*

Wow.

Suddenly, ruling on the seat of death didn't seem like such a bad gig. Sure, I'd have to fight off attacks for about a century, but everyone would calm down eventually.

Malum flicked an ember at my face. "Realm to Aran. Make them leave."

I shook out of my daydream and turned to the two women.

"Okay, I think you guys should be good now." I pushed the paper back into Sari's hand and flexed my aching fingers.

"You're the best, Aran." Sari squealed and gave me a big hug.

I awkwardly patted her on the back and resisted the urge to push her away. Abruptly, sticky lips that smelled like bubblegum pressed against my cheek.

Orion's glass shattered.

Sari pulled back with her massive smile, and I looked at her lips enviously.

"Is your lip gloss bubblegum? I like it," I said before my brain could process what I was saying.

There was a clatter of silverware as Malum knocked over his plate with his elbow.

Fuck. That wasn't very manly of me.

I coughed and deepened my voice. "I mean. That's hot."

Sari giggled and grabbed Tara's arm, but the blonde bombshell also leaned forward and kissed my cheek. She pulled away with a soft blush and mumbled, "Thanks, Aran."

"No problem." My face burned at their attention, and I

knew my pale skin was flushed bright red. "I'm happy to help anytime," I said honestly.

It was nice to do schoolwork during the meal instead of stressing out the entire time that Malum was going to see me hiding my food and choke me out in front of everyone.

"Leave now!" Malum barked loudly, and the girls scurried off.

I made to stand, but John looked at me weird. "Where are you going?" he asked.

"Isn't it time to leave?"

John pointed to the massive clock. "No, we still have an hour."

I turned to Malum. "Then why the fuck did you just make them leave? I had more things to write."

"Don't do other people's homework. It's degrading." He rolled his eyes like I was pathetic.

"*You're* degrading."

"You're petulant and embarrassing."

"Coming from the man who can't fart without becoming a flamethrower."

Scorpius choked on ale, and John laughed, but Orion just kept glaring at the chairs where Sari and Tara had sat.

"You wanna test out that theory and see?" Malum snarled and leaned forward.

My jaw dropped. "Did you just threaten to fart on me? Who does that?!"

"He's not worth it," Scorpius sneered as he put his arm around Malum. "We just need to find someone to fuck tonight." His pale cheekbones glittered. "Violently."

Malum sighed and nodded like sex was what he needed and not a lobotomy.

Are they going to use the sex knife?

Wait, better question: Why the fuck did I care?

CHAPTER 27
CARNAL SINS

Field training: Day 30, hour 18

What do you do when you're depressed but everyone around you is having sex? You smoke.

Lying on my too-squishy bed, I sucked my pipe between my lips and closed my eyes. *Inhale drug. Exhale calm.*

The grand hearth threw heat and vitriol. Once again, the flames shrieked at me.

I waved my hand at the fireplace. *Hello to you too.*

Maybe they were complimenting me and it just sounded so aggressive because they were very passionate about how much they loved me.

I was going with that.

I sucked in more enchanted smoke as the squelching and moaning sounds of sex became an unbearable cacophony.

The crack of a belt was rhythmic.

How many times did you need to beat someone on the ass? You couldn't tell me that once didn't get the job done.

Crack. Crack. Crack.

Where did Malum even get a belt?

I wasn't an expert on sex, but Malum and Scorpius's sadism seemed exhausting. There was a 0 percent chance that getting cut up with a knife was more relaxing than kisses.

My cheek burned with the memory of Orion's warm, bee-stung lips, and I fingered it as I flushed.

"Swallow," Scorpius ordered, and there was an awful gagging sound.

I hated to say it, but this was definitely more PTSD-inducing than the ungodly.

When the gaggle of girls had come into the room and the first penis had been whipped out, I should have left.

Or maybe hid in the bathroom?

Ripped out my own heart and quickly ate it before I died? Or would that just make me ascend to the throne?

You should try it. There's a chance you'd just break the realm's enchantment and there would be no monarch.

I fingered my pipe and debated going into a shower stall and attempting it.

Nah, I was too tired. I'd try it later.

The weird truth was a small part of me hoped watching seven men have violent sex while I smoked would make me feel something. Because I hadn't felt much of anything lately.

A terrifying sense of blasé had settled into my bones.

Colors were darker.

My thoughts were more erratic.

So when Malum had announced that since we had the afternoon off and it was a free time to "fuck and get our aggression out," I'd just nodded sagely.

How did they have any aggression left?

Fighting monsters for over twenty hours straight had left me feeling strung-out and dry. Raw.

But they were *still* angry. *Never mind. I wouldn't banish all men; I'd have them committed.*

What I really wanted to do was get my hair and nails done with Sadie. Then go to a luxury clothing store and overpay for shoes and dresses we didn't need. I'd bully Sadie for acting poor when she saw the prices. She'd bully me for having a shopping addiction.

Afterward, we'd get wasted on sparkling fae wine and get matching tattoos. Maybe we'd get inspirational quotes or maybe cute little skulls on our wrists.

I could practically feel that delicious exhaustion from retail therapy.

That was my ideal day.

"Come now!" Malum barked, and there was a high-pitched moan/squeal as the girl obeyed.

I rolled my pipe with my tongue and doodled a heart onto my hands.

Smack. Smack. Smack. Orion grunted loudly as he rammed his cock into a woman.

I grimaced.

I inhaled for ten seconds until my chest burned with smoke, then I blew out with my mouth in an *O*.

Smoke rings rose and disappeared into the galaxy across the ceiling.

Horace made a slurping noise.

I twisted my lips and tried to make my smoke rings into squares.

Holy shit, I did it.

I tried a triangle, and a perfect shape formed.

Wait a second.

I sucked on the enchanted pipe and imagined the smoke forming into a crow as I blew out.

Wings burst from the pipe, and a crow cawed as it

flapped lazily in the air around my head. I eyed the enchanted pipe with awe.

"John, look at this!" I shouted excitedly at my friend.

He sat up in his bed, and the girl riding him squealed but didn't stop bouncing.

I puked a little at the sight of my friend being defiled but was too excited to show him what I'd discovered.

"Watch this." I blew out, and a smoke dragon roared to life. It flew in loops until it slowly dissipated.

"Shit, that's sick. Let me try." John started to push the girl off him, and I squealed.

"No, don't come over here! You can try it later." I covered my eyes.

"Okay, fine," John said and then fell back with a loud groan as the woman resumed bouncing vigorously.

Her moans were unnaturally loud, and as I looked around, I realized the kings had stopped what they were doing and all three were staring at me.

Once again, Malum and Scorpius were on the floor with a girl on her knees between them. Malum took her ass and beat it red with a belt while Scorpius took her face and wielded a steak knife.

Similarly, Orion was standing near them with a girl pressed against the wall.

Acting without thought, I closed my eyes, then blew out a flaming phoenix. I directed it in my mind and sent it flying across the room to Malum.

Smoke slammed against him and dissipated with a puff.

I held my breath.

White teeth flashed bright against bronzed skin as Malum grinned. "That was sick." All three of the kings smiled at me.

A singularity had occurred, and space-time was spinning out of control. There was a rip in the fabric of the universe.

Crack. Malum slammed the belt down as he pistoned his hips into the woman's ass.

Moment over.

I resumed facing the wall, but this time, I blew out different animals as I doodled more fake tattoos on my hand.

It was sacrilegious to get tattoos in fae culture, and Mother had said it was a crime against nature because they were on your body for your entire immortal life.

I grinned as I thought about getting a portrait of a middle finger across my back.

I frowned as I remembered I already had open wounds there.

I grinned as I thought about enhancing them with a tattoo.

"WHORE" could become "Whoreable Life," or "Whores, drugs, and bitches." Instantly I felt better. Now I just needed to find a tattoo artist.

"Shut the fuck up," Malum barked suddenly, and his baritone sent shivers down my spine.

Was it really too much to ask for people to have sex in silence?

"Sorry." A gasp, wet smacking noises. "Your highness."

Imagine having a girl call you "Your Highness" unironically while you're penetrating her with your male lover. I couldn't because it was *weird*.

"Stay still," Malum snapped.

I mumbled about overblown male egos as I tried to pet the smoke crow that had settled onto my shoulder. The crow dissipated under my fingers, and I frowned.

"Stop fucking laughing, Egan, or I'll make you."

I choked on my pipe. Why was he talking to me?

Flipping onto my stomach, twirling my pipe in my fingers, I rested my chin on my fist and rolled my eyes dramatically to let him know that I wasn't scared of him.

"You say something, Malum?" I asked dryly as I blew another crow.

His features hardened into ice as I called him by his last name. No way was I calling him Corvus when he only called me Egan or "pretty boy."

One simply didn't call their mortal enemy by their first name.

It wasn't proper.

Malum's hips pistoned fast, and his thighs slapped loudly. The girl shouted something, but it was muffled by Scorpius's dick.

A pity. I was sure she had something interesting to say.

I blew out another smoke crow, and this one nuzzled my cheek for a second before it dissipated.

Yay, I officially had a pet.

"I told you earlier to shut the fuck up, Egan." Gray eyes flared with creepy intensity as his hips pistoned faster and harder.

"Then why are you talking to me?" I asked dryly.

"I'm not," Malum snapped.

This was why men were inferior to women. Jinx would have eviscerated my self-esteem with a comeback about how I was a pathetic prude that was going to die alone.

Something that really cut to the bone.

Malum's comeback just didn't have that *it* factor. She'd eat him alive.

"Please. Please. Yes, Orion!" the woman pressed against the wall shouted.

"Ew," I mumbled, fully jealous of the woman getting

railed by the gentle fae. His fingers choked her lightly as he pressed her against the wall.

I went back to staring at a different wall.

The woman between Scorpius and Malum screamed, probably with a broken hip and not an orgasm, as I brainstormed names to call my pet crow.

The slurping noises got louder.

I pretended not to notice the fact that the girl on Horace's bed was turning paler by the second and there was a concerning amount of blood pooling beneath her. Someone should probably stop him.

He was latched onto her wrist and sucking like she was a milkshake.

What a nice ambience.

Zenith and Vegar were tangled under the covers on the far bed, and from the sloppy noises, they were making out passionately.

And people said that love was dead?

I glanced back at Horace's bed. Yep, the woman was now seizing.

"Sun god, fucking save me," I muttered.

"Horace. Dude." I crawled to the edge of my four-poster bed and snapped my fingers in his face.

Unfortunately for me, fortunately for the woman, our beds were only inches apart.

The vampyre ripped his fangs out of her artery and glared at me, yellow eyes blazing bright.

"Let the girl go. She won't last much longer." I pointed to the ever-growing pool of red.

Horace didn't look down. "So."

He hunched forward, and I lightly smacked him on the cheek to stop him.

"What the fuck?"

I'd slapped him with all my strength and left a red hand-print on his cheek. "Oopsie."

I tried to look apologetic, but honestly, it had been very cathartic hitting him. "Please, just let her go."

There was a long pause, where I was 99 percent sure Horace was considering launching himself onto my bed and breaking my neck, but then the vampyre sat up.

"Get lost," Horace snapped at the *very* pale red-haired girl on his bed.

She blinked groggily and slurred, "Nah. I wanna stay wit you."

Horace arched his eyebrow at me like he was saying, *Told you so.*

Oh my sun god, these women just couldn't see red flags if they were smacking them in the face.

I leaned my face over the bed until I was staring down at her. She blinked with confusion.

I enunciated slowly. "You're going to *die* if you stay here with this homicidal maniac. You need to leave. Now."

She pouted and wrinkled her nose.

It was slightly endearing. She was pretty in an under-stated way, but it was ruined by the ever-growing crimson puddle underneath her.

"*Move it, woman!*"

"Okaaaay," she groaned as she rolled out of the bed and crawled on her hands and knees to the door.

"Go to Lyla!" I shouted after her, and she nodded as she disappeared into the hall. The good thing was the witch's door was only two away from ours, so she'd make it.

Sun god, it was exhausting being a Good Samaritan.

I climbed back into my bed and resumed blowing crows and thinking of names.

There was a blur in my peripheral vision, and suddenly Horace knelt on top of me.

"Ew." I pushed at his chest.

I did *not* think of him that way, and blood drinkers were a big no for me.

Yes, I was self-aware enough to know that this probably had something to do with the fact that I'd dabbled in the lifestyle. Still was a big fucking no.

Horace growled, and he grabbed my wrists with his cold hands. He pinned me to my bed. "You slapped me and made me lose my food. So now you're going to pay up."

Somewhere deep in my drug-hazed brain, a monster woke up and started to scream.

Tear off his eyelids and shove them down his throat. Then we'll see who he threatens.

Apparently, sleep made my monster creative.

"Take your hands off me," I whispered. "Or you'll regret it."

How. Dare. He. Overpower me on *my* bed.

"What the fuck is going on over there?" Malum's voice broke through the aggression that was fogging my thoughts.

"We're fucking," Horace snapped back and gyrated his hips wantonly.

"What is wrong with you?" I asked seriously.

Horace winked at me and whispered, "Just watch."

The vampyre gyrated again, and I gagged as he moaned, "Oh fuck, pretty boy, you've got such a nice face and a tight body."

I gaped and pushed against him. "Really? Do you have to be such a pervert? I have no idea how you keep getting women."

Horace opened his mouth, probably to yell something else obscene, but there was a blur and a loud crash.

The vampyre had been thrown across the room, and the three kings loomed over him.

"Why the fuck would you let that bloodsucker touch you?" Scorpius barked into the room, and his harsh cheekbones were sharper than I'd ever seen them. He looked like death incarnate.

"What is wrong with you three? I wasn't about to fuck *Horace*. He was joking."

Orion slammed his foot into Horace's side with such force the vampyre's skull cracked against the wall.

Ugh, my knight in shining armor.

I slapped myself.

Horace recovered quickly and was instantly at Orion's throat with his fangs distended. However, that set off Malum and Scorpius.

Flames exploded, and suddenly Horace was restrained by Malum with his arms on fire while Scorpius plowed his fist into his face.

Everyone else watched in shock as the kings went nuts.

When Malum released him, Horace just wiped the blood off his mutilated face and sauntered back to his bed.

"Told you, Aran." He winked a swollen eyelid, then lapped at the crimson puddle on his sheets.

I gagged. "You literally didn't tell me anything."

He looked up from his sheets with red dripping down his chin. "I didn't need to. I think the kings said it all. Am I right, boys?"

"I should have known nobody would actually want to fuck your scrawny ass," Malum snapped with cruelty.

That insult was better.

"Oh, please." I sighed. "I'm irresistible and handsome. I know that for a fact."

Malum glowered.

It was true; I was a sexy man and a gorgeous woman.

Fact of life, I was hot. What did he want me to do, be insecure? I wasn't dumb like that.

Orion mouthed, "Don't touch Horace. Don't touch another man." Then he went back to the naked girl waiting for him at the wall.

Since I couldn't let anyone touch me even if I wanted to, I decided to ignore the blatant hypocrisy.

"Watch yourself, Egan," Scorpius threatened me, and his cock jerked.

Suddenly, my back was burning.

I rolled onto my side and faced the wall.

Eight hours crawled by, and the men fucked the *entire* time. Eight. Hours. Not even joking. Women entered and left the room like they were on rotation.

At one point, all three kings were fucking the same girl, and John and Horace had a woman between them.

Only Vegar and Zenith kept to themselves the entire time.

Apparently, demons were the only species with any class.

And I just faced the wall and sucked on my pipe, but even in the chaos, one thing remained the same.

I still felt next to nothing.

CHAPTER 28
PROPHETS OF DEATH

Aran

Field training: Day 34, hour 23

Days passed in a blur of smoke, classwork, long runs, and depressive thoughts. The only difference was at every lunch and some dinners, Tara and Sari sat beside me and I helped them with their essays.

I also had a smoke crow that was sitting on my shoulder for longer and longer periods of time before it dissipated.

Its name was Horse.

I named it after the four horsemen of the apocalypse, because Horse had an unsettling look in his smoky eyes. Like he wanted to raze the world.

It was a nice distraction from the men, and Lothaire didn't say anything about it.

One thing was for sure: without Horse, I would have lost my mind.

In the past few days, the men had become disturbingly horny. It seemed like every time we had a break, they were inviting women into the room for orgies.

After my first disastrous experience, I'd started leaving and hanging out in the library.

I hadn't even known we had one until Sari complained at dinner that the lighting was too dim for her to get her work done.

As soon as I walked in, I fell in love.

It was dark, moody, gothic, and quiet—the perfect place for a depressive episode.

Sweeping chandeliers hung off of high, arched ceilings. Black marble with gold veins decorated every inch of the floors and walls.

Stained-glass windows in shades of blue and gray depicted scholars brandishing words like weapons.

Cherry tables scattered among towering stacks. Shelves were filled with dusty tombs from every realm in the universe.

The best part was hidden in the back corner: a winding iron staircase that led to a sitting nook.

Curled up on a blue velvet chaise, I spent most of the time enjoying the silence with Horse. Sometimes he flew lazily above my head, and other times, he curled up on my shoulder and slept.

I fingered the cracked spines of old books and flipped through to locate some pictures, but I couldn't find the energy to read.

Picture books were just as enriching.

Sprawled on the chaise, I enjoyed the darkness of the stacks.

It was dead silent.

I loved the ambience.

The sense of peace was all thanks to the librarian. He was a floating specter that everyone called Ghost.

According to Sari, the rumor in the school was that he'd

bargained with death, and as a reward for committing unspeakable atrocities, he was allowed to return to the land of the living.

Even if that was true, it wasn't my place to judge others.

I liked Ghost.

Anytime a student spoke, even the smallest whisper, he flew over and kissed their cheek.

They called it the kiss of doom because the offending student would seize and foam at the mouth. But another student always carried them out to get healed by Lyla, so I never got to see how far the symptoms developed.

Usually it was just students who spoke that got kissed, but I'd seen Ghost do it to a student because they opened a book too loudly.

But that had been a one-time thing, and I think he just did it for the drama. Which I respected.

Now I lay on the chaise with my head upside down as I stared down from my nook and looked through the stacks.

I liked to watch.

Ghost averaged about one kiss per hour because people really didn't know how to shut the fuck up. So it was free entertainment. Sadie *definitely* would have been his victim.

He left me alone for the most part.

My first day in the library, Ghost had floated up beside me and stared down at me.

I'd thought he didn't want me to smoke.

But after thirty awkward minutes of staring at each other in silence, I'd held my pipe up into the air.

Ghost had leaned his head forward and taken a spectral drag, his transparent cheeks hollowing as the smoke swirled around his exposed chest cavity.

He'd blown out a skull and crossbones image.

Ghost was chill like that.

Unfortunately, he was the most unproblematic man I knew at the moment.

The kings had been so weird during their little sexcapade, and I'd started to notice the three of them stared at me. Often.

Orion was the only one that looked at me like he didn't want to rip off my face and wear it. But when I helped Sari and Tara, his scowl rivaled Malum's.

My gut cramped at the implication.

They had definitely figured out I was hiding something, and they were starting to treat me differently.

Maybe they're planning to hand me over to the fae? Maybe they're working with the half warriors and they're going to ambush me any day now?

The possibilities were endless.

Which was why I spent my time with my head upside down in the library as I inhaled the musk of old leatherbound books and cracked pages.

It mixed well with the burned taste of my pipe.

I sighed silently as the grandfather clock on the wall struck 3:00 a.m. Half-naked girls had entered our room at 8:00 p.m., so the orgy was hopefully ending.

It was time to leave the library and face the men.

As I silently moved through the stacks, I paused when I heard someone whispering. Excited to see Ghost do his thing, I hid behind the bookshelf and listened.

A girl's voice whispered, "Can you believe the sacred tree bloomed black for Aran?"

"I know," another female voice whispered back. "I read that it means you've been marked by a god."

The other girl gasped softly. "Really? I heard it means you've been marked to do terrible deeds."

"Same thing either way." The voices rose with excitement. "I still can't believe Aran and the three kings are the only ones in the history of the academy that the petals have turned black for."

Abruptly, the girls were quiet. A strangled, choking noise let me know Ghost had arrived, but I couldn't muster excitement about it like I usually did.

Their words were still hammering around my skull.

Marked by a god.

Terrible deeds.

Just like the three kings.

My stomach plummeted because nothing made sense, and my vision wobbled as I panicked.

On shaky legs, I fled the library.

I wandered down lightning-streaked halls with Horse cawing softly like he felt my pain.

As I walked, I barely noticed that the commoner and royal students cleared a path and bowed their heads.

Some openly gaped in awe, while others ran away like I would slit their throats if they looked at me wrong. I wished.

The entire academy had a weird fetish for the assassin program.

When I was finally back at my room, I leaned my forehead against the door and forced any thoughts about black petals from my mind. The gossip mill at the academy was infamous for making shit up.

"They're wrong," I whispered to Horse as I breathed deeply and shoved the revelations from my mind. I already had enough things to worry about.

I pushed open the door and forced my shoulders back.

The men were all clothed and lounging on their messy beds. The room reeked of sex and copper, definitely from Horace, but since no one was naked, I didn't care.

"Where were you, Egan?" Malum snapped. "Where the fuck do you keep going?"

Horse cawed at him aggressively, and I gave him a kiss on his smoky head. "It's none of your business," I muttered.

I was too tired to spar with the deranged king.

Too tired to think thoughts.

How nice it would be to be a single-celled amoeba floating around the ocean without a care in the world.

I yearned for that lifestyle.

Malum made a harsh noise that sounded suspiciously like a growl. "Actually, it is my—"

The door slammed open, and Lothaire entered.

Hell was knowing you were fucked before it happened.

A tsunami of terror ripped through the room. Spines straightened, and muscles tensed as we hustled into a line.

"Are you ready, soldiers?"

"Yes, sir!"

I missed the library. Missed hanging out with Ghost while he sent students into comas.

"Good. More civilian ungodly have been spotted. This time, they've taken over a primitive town in a desert realm. Prepare your pathetic fucking selves. Because of interference with enchantments, we'll have to RJE to a remote location, and you'll have to hover in."

The flames in the fire screamed at me.

Mentally, I screamed back.

"*Did I fucking stutter?*" Lothaire exploded at us, long braid thumping against the floor as he shook his head.

"No, sir!" we yelled back.

Men were so dramatic.

It was exhausting.

"Knives." Lothaire thrust the dreaded daggers into our hands.

My fingers shook as I sheathed them in the thigh holsters that were built into our pants.

Lothaire lunged forward, and yet fucking again, the world erupted into scorching fire as we jumped realms.

Grit stabbed at my eyes, and it took me a long moment to process the new realm.

Blood-orange sand whipped around a hot wind and pummeled.

I was kneeling on impossibly soft sand.

Visibility was shit.

Sand everywhere.

I couldn't even tell how many suns the realm had, but from the scorching heat, my guess was at least three.

From what I could make out, sand scraped against dunes in every direction and made a low scratching noise that accumulated into a harsh buzz.

Lothaire shouted, but his voice was swallowed by the coarse wind. "Take….the hovers. Ungodly. I'll…watch. GO!"

I heard every other word, but the message was clear as Lothaire pointed to a line of thin machines that glowed with blue enchantment and hovered over the sand.

"*Let's move!*" Malum shouted.

Maybe the sleepless nights were getting to me, or maybe I was dissociating, but everything seemed to move in slow motion.

Time crawled.

Throwing myself onto a curved saddle like the rest of the recruits, I jolted because the handlebars were shockingly cold.

I twisted my hand forward.

There was a loud bang and a jolt, then I shot forward like a bullet across the sand.

As I hung on for my life, sand slammed into my face like it was trying to grind off my skin.

It succeeded.

Warm liquid poured down my neck as I gripped the handlebars and bent forward, thigh muscles burning as I fought to stay on the bike.

Barely conscious.

The bike had gone dark beneath me, the enchantment exploding in a burst of power that flickered out. It was a slingshot across the sand.

The "interference," as Lothaire had called it, was a tornado of a sandstorm that whipped particles with a vengeance. My fingers turned ruby red as blood streaked across my exposed hands.

Blurs of black around me were the only indication that I was with the men.

Fingers slipping across the cold handles, I focused every ounce of concentration on holding on.

With me moving at this speed, there was no one to save me.

Abruptly, the number 300 flashed on the center of the bike. I squinted, and it blinked "MPH" before flicking off.

Holy. Fuck.

I lowered my head and put all my willpower into my finger strength.

Why the fuck didn't Lothaire have us wear masks or gloves? That motherfucker did this on purpose.

Time coalesced into endless seconds of desperation.

Suddenly, the wind knocked out of my chest, and like a ragdoll, I slammed into a wall.

The world went dark.

"Get up, Egan. Get the fuck up now!"

Cruel silver eyes hovered inches from my face, and a bloody monster screamed at me.

"*Get up!*" The monster tried to pull my arms out of my sockets as it threw me around.

Throbbing agony burned my face and hands. My eyelids were slabs of meat as I blinked painfully. Pink tinged my vision.

"*Let's go!*"

Slowly, I realized the monster was Malum, and he was dragging me across a sand dune, six other men stumbling to awareness around us.

The storm raged. It whipped sand into the bloody wounds that covered every inch of our exposed skin.

Malum's face was a mess of gore and limp flesh.

"You look like shit!" I yelled at him. "Very ugly!"

He flipped me off, and it weirdly made me feel better.

"*Get your head out of your ass!*" Jinx yelled in my mind, and I nodded with agreement. She always knew what to say.

I opened my mouth to breathe deeply and choked as a mountain of dust scratched my esophagus.

Bent over, I heaved.

"*Didn't see that coming,*" Jinx drawled sarcastically.

"*Move! Why are you standing there?!*" Malum screamed and shoved me forward.

Internally, I answered, *I'm just talking to my best friend's mate's little sister in my head because she's the meanest person I know and she calms me during awful times like this.*

Externally, I followed.

Malum leaned down and hoisted Orion up by his shoulders, shouting something in the other king's ear.

I gained a little more visibility as I grew accustomed to the burn of my mutilated eyelids.

Plugging my nose, I filtered in the smallest bit of air possible.

I slowly got my bearings, and I joined the other men stalking across the sand.

Maybe this wouldn't be so bad?

From what I could see, which was about three meters in every direction, the world was an abandoned wasteland of orange dunes.

Either our bikes had all failed at the same time or Lothaire had gotten shitty intelligence about the ungodly.

As we trudged forward over the dunes, nothing changed. We were alone in this desolate realm.

Lothaire must have been wrong.

Thank the sun god.

Head lowered, shoulders curved inward, I cursed the fact that I could have been under my covers in bed. Sure, the nightmares kept me awake, but at least I wouldn't be being sandblasted.

This is stupid, there's nobody here.

I relaxed.

Pow. Pow. Pow.

Sand exploded all around as bullets rained.

Chaos descended.

Malum screamed something, but his words were swallowed by the stand storm. Someone's dagger whizzed by my cheek, but in the shit visibility, I couldn't tell if it made contact with anything.

A cloaked body covered in white cloth sprinted a few feet from me with a gun pointed forward.

I was three feet away from the figure, but it didn't see me.

As quickly as it appeared, it was gone, swallowed by the punishing wind.

I opened my mouth to scream and choked on the gritty sand. Sharp pain stabbed my thigh, and a chunk of black-clothed flesh sank underneath the sand.

Something had shot me from the other direction.

I whirled around.

Jinx's voice was sharp. *"Are you just going to stand there and take it like you did in the beast realm? Is that all you are, a slab of meat for target practice?"*

Pow. Pow. Pow. Pow.

More bullets spat up sand around me.

I couldn't see any of the men.

Sharp pain stabbed my upper arm, and I looked down with horror. Some fucker had shot me. Again.

A low growl ripped from my throat.

This time, it was personal.

My monster screamed in my head, and metal bars squealed as they were ripped apart.

It woke the fuck up, and it wanted blood.

CHAPTER 29
A DEVIL ON THE TONGUE

Field training: Day 35, hour 18

My monster screamed, and I joined its chorus. The desert scratched my throat as I bellowed, but I ignored the pain.

Red blurred my vision, and it wasn't from my bloody eyelids.

Unlike the first time I'd let my monster free, this time, I didn't lose consciousness.

I was wide awake.

We were one.

Pulsing rage coursed through my veins.

As I stalked forward through the storm, knives, bullets, and bodies flew around me. I didn't let it distract me.

I ducked a bullet that would have hit my head and followed the faint trail of burned ammonia. The shooter was somewhere in front of me.

He would pay.

My back burned unmercifully, the enchanted letters a reminder of just who I was. I reached back and dragged my nails across it.

A motherfucking whore.

Fist clenched around something cold, I paused my hunt, and I stared down in confusion. *When did I palm my dagger?*

I hadn't.

An iridescent ice dagger had appeared in my hand, and it was the same one I'd used to kill the fuckers who hurt Sadie in the beast realm.

The storm raged around me as I stared down at the glowing crystalline structure.

Streaks of light blue danced inside the crystal.

I'd never had a chance to study it before.

The edges were razor-sharp. But the structure wasn't a simple dagger like I'd first thought.

It was an irregular shape.

One end tapered into a thin stalk, while the other end was curved and wide. I turned it over slowly. While the shape was wide and long, it was as thin as paper.

It glimmered and waved in the wind like it was flexible. It seemed impossible that something could be so solid but at the same time barely weigh anything.

Like water floating in my fingers.

My bicep itched with the urge to chuck it forward and end the shooter, but Lothaire forbade any use of powers.

The awful memory of the isolation tank rolled through me, and my fingers loosened on the weapon.

POP.

Agony exploded in my stomach as a bullet nestled in my gut. It fucking hurt.

I was so fucking done with letting people shoot me.

Moving on instinct, I dropped the crystal weapon and flipped forward.

As my body rotated through the air, three more bullets shot where I'd just been standing.

I palmed our issued daggers and landed on top of the shooter.

And stabbed him through the skull.

As the body deflated, it was ripped apart by an emerging ungodly. Its pincers flailed at me, but I'd been expecting it.

Before it could realize what was happening, I wrapped my limbs around its carapace body and sawed off its head.

Dripping in green-and-red gore, I kicked the dead ungodly, then picked up the machine gun and emptied a clip into the dead body for fun.

Lothaire had said we couldn't kill with another weapon, but it was already dead.

The acrid scent of gunpowder surrounded me.

A grin stretched my cheeks.

"For the first time, I'm not embarrassed to know you." Jinx's voice was proud in my head.

Her approval was like warm sun on frostbitten skin.

I was glad Lothaire said we had to kill with our daggers; it was messier that way.

More personal. More exciting.

With a smile plastered on my face, I stalked through the screaming sands, looking for my next kill.

The hunt was on.

In my wake, limbs were severed, and heads rolled.

I killed the white-clothed creatures, then I annihilated the ungodly.

Hours passed fighting in the blood-orange dust, and for the first time in years, I was *alive*.

My fury was a tangible beat as adrenaline sparked my veins, and I fought in sync with the music that only I could hear.

A pile of mutilated bodies painted a pretty green-and-red picture.

Pulling out the pipe I'd tucked into my holster, I inhaled drugs mixed with sand.

Horse burst from the smoke and screamed in rhythm with my soul.

Pop.

My shoulder throbbed with the familiar pain of a bullet wound.

Whirling around, I stalked toward the fucking coward that had shot me in the back. He was going to look so pretty in my pile.

Lunging forward, I took another bullet to the stomach.

Worth it.

Body bent at an awkward angle, I stabbed my knives into the gut of the larger white-clothed figure. From the bulk beneath me, he was a man.

Then more agony exploded across my back as someone peppered me with bullets from behind.

I growled and inhaled more enchanted smoke.

Horse screamed louder.

Crack.

I broke the man's neck. Whirled around and flung daggers into the eyes of the other fucker with a gun.

An ungodly roared behind me, and pincers slammed me down.

Another ungodly emerged from my second kill and stalked to join its brethren.

Lying on my back, I stared up at the monsters, and I brought the pipe to my lips. Horse kept screaming as he attacked the ungodly with his talons. They batted at it but then stopped when they realized he wasn't corporeal.

Smoke, gore, sand, and wrath combined in an acrid ambience. It was fucking delicious.

Flipping to my feet without using my hands, I grabbed

the ungodly and twisted its limbs until they ripped and popped.

It roared as we traded blows.

I laughed.

The drugs muted my pain, and the bloodlust in my veins made it fun.

Pincers slammed into my face, and my cheekbones cracked as the other ungodly attacked me from behind.

But I tensed my jaw and kept my pipe between my lips.

I grinned at my victory.

Then I launched myself off the shoulders of one ungodly and gouged out the beady eyeballs of the other with my bare nails.

Whoosh.

The ungodly lifted me and threw me to the sand.

My spine cracked.

For an endless moment, the world went silent. Orange dust glittered in the darkness as it hung suspended.

Sparkly.

I'd always liked pretty things. I puffed out smoke, and it danced among the diamonds. Horse flew through them in slow motion.

"Are you seriously losing your mind in the middle of battle? What the fuck is wrong with you? GET UP!" Jinx shouted in my head.

Little girl didn't know how pretty the pain was.

Someday she'd learn.

Suddenly, the world reanimated, and the ungodly weren't distracted like I'd been.

The blind one reached down with its pincers and clamped around my bicep.

I smiled at the muted pain. It didn't even hurt.

Drugs are amazing.

Ripppppp. Squelch.

The ungodly held someone's arm and flung it away into the storm.

Why can't I feel my hand?

Shock flooded my brain, and the reality of what had just happened rushed into me like a reanimated corpse.

It had ripped off my arm.

I opened my mouth and fucking screamed.

My. Arm. Is. Gone.

Horse dive-bombed the ungodly, and the creature actually stumbled backward.

Self-preservation kicked in, and I stumbled to my feet. My legs barely complied, and pain signals sent shock waves down my thighs from my broken back as I hobbled into a run.

Every step sent jolts of white light exploding.

My eyes were wide open, but the world was getting darker on the edges, gravity pulling me deeper into the dunes.

Muscles burning, sweat dripping, I barely registered the clomping sound of the ungodly giving chase.

They were only a few feet behind me.

A few weeks ago, they would have already overtaken me and crushed me to death with their pincers.

But this wasn't then.

This was now.

Lothaire's training was the only reason I stood a chance.

Horse flew in front of me and cawed like he was screeching at me to run faster.

It was the last mile of a sixty-mile run.

The last rep of hoisting a boulder above my head after my arms were numb from exhaustion.

The last minute drowning in the dark sea.

As I put one foot in front of the other, agony throbbed

through my missing shoulder cavity, and blood trailed behind me in a sticky path.

Bullets jostled in my mutilated muscles.

I didn't have a plan. Couldn't think fast enough to do anything other than run for my life.

Prey. The lowest form of life. The highest level of experience.

Adrenaline rocked through me like a live wire of shock, and it kept my eyes wide and my breath fast. It kept me moving forward.

The pounding behind me was closer.

Ungodly were gaining.

I tipped my head back and screamed as I pumped my arm with everything I had, expecting a collision at any moment.

Abruptly, a flaming figure appeared.

The adrenaline cut off.

Any will I'd possessed poofed away. Just like when Lothaire had told us we could stop running, my legs immediately gave out beneath me.

Face-planting into the soft sand, I didn't bother to look over my shoulder.

Because I knew he would handle them.

Ungodly screamed as they were torn to shreds.

It could have been minutes; it could have been hours. With my face buried in the sand, time was meaningless as I bled out.

"*Get the fuck up!*" Malum screamed into my ear.

I nodded but didn't move; that was all I could give.

The world tilted as I was yanked around. Strong hands wrapped under my remaining arm and held me up.

I moaned.

"FUCK! WHAT HAPPENED TO YOUR ARM?!" Malum screamed, dark features contorted.

His face was sculpted, like a chiseled bronze statue. There were small black flames flickering in his silver eyes.

"HOW COULD YOU FUCKING LOSE YOUR ARM? WHAT THE FUCK IS WRONG WITH YOU?" the man bellowed in my face as the air got uncomfortably hot around us.

He smelled intoxicatingly harsh, like whiskey thrown into a bonfire.

"Why are your pupils dilated? *Are you smoking during battle*?" Malum's voice was dark. "What the fuck is wrong with you?"

His flame eyes hovered inches from my face.

I choked on sand as my mouth tried to form words.

"What?" He leaned closer.

"You're handsome," I whispered groggily as the world started to plunge into darkness.

"You will be punished for this. Brutally."

Exhilarating.

Once again, I drowned in darkness.

CHAPTER 30
OMENS

Field training: Day 38, hour 9

I screamed.

Eyes open, mouth wide, forearm on motherfucking fire.

"STOP!" I shrieked and wrenched my arm away from the never-ending agony.

Callused fingers clenched my jaw shut, and my loud cries transformed into muffled pleas.

"Shut the fuck up," Scorpius sneered as his pale features filled my vision.

Bucking and squirming, I was desperate to escape, but straps held me down.

I was trapped.

My vision was so hazy from pain that I could barely put together what I was seeing.

Lyla stood over me with her legs straddling my prone body, and her dark skin shone with the white symbols that glowed brighter than the stars.

Her long green hair floated upward around her head and defied gravity. Eyes bright white, her pupils were rolled back inside her head.

Pink lips open, she chanted in a language that sounded suspiciously like the screams of the fire.

She shouted louder, and the agony intensified.

I screamed harder.

Scorpius's fingers tightened on my mouth as he leaned atop me. Malum stood behind him with a dark expression on his face, steely silver eyes promising there would be hell to pay.

I yanked my head to the side, pulling against Scorpius's tight grip, as I tried desperately to see just what the fuck was causing the excruciating pain.

I blinked, convinced I was imagining it.

Orion stood beside me with his arm sliced open as his blood poured down across my arm.

Two problems.

One, I'd lost my arm in the battle, but now it was whole and throbbing.

Two, it would regenerate on its own, so I didn't need whatever the fuck the kings and Lyla were doing to me.

My muffled screams were overwhelming, so I couldn't verbalize that they needed to get away from me.

I mouthed at him to stop.

Orion glared down at me and mouthed, "No. You will heal."

Blood poured from his arm, and he looked like he wanted to hurt me. Cause me never-ending agony. Torture. Merciless suffering.

I shook my head because he didn't understand.

Orion's face darkened. Just like Malum, where he should have had pupils, there were black flames. But fae didn't have flames for eyes.

I must have been hallucinating.

Lyla shouted louder in the foreign language, and the

syllables resonated with so much force that the bones in my arm cracked and re-formed.

I passed out.

"Wake the fuck up, Aran!" Lothaire bellowed.

"Yes, sir!" I shouted back instinctually as I shot up on my bed, chest heaving. I was in my four-poster bed, and a fire crackled placidly in the fireplace.

I trembled from the force of my nightmares, my clothes were sticky with sweat, and I coughed from the strength of my inhales.

"You've had enough beauty sleep. Get your ass up, we're watching film on the battle."

Wait, was it just a nightmare?

"You have five seconds to get out of bed." Lothaire cracked his baton against his hand, and the sound echoed like a gunshot.

I threw myself out with unsteady legs, trembling as I collapsed on all fours and heaved up bile.

I was shaky and weak, my head spinning a million miles per hour. The ground fell out from beneath me.

"GET OFF THE FLOOR, YOU PATHETIC FUCK-ER!" Lothaire's voice boomed with such intensity the floor trembled.

I obeyed.

Scrambling up onto weak legs, I shook with exhaustion and collided with the wall as I struggled to find gravity.

The world tilted.

Lothaire slammed his baton against his hand in warning.

"I'm up. I'm ready," I said breathlessly as I stumbled toward the door, using the wall for support.

The walls and floor changed places, like I'd finally lost my fucking mind.

Hot panic flooded my senses as I used the wall to stumble into the hall.

I leaned forward to grab another wall, but Lothaire hauled me back as white lightning streaked inches from my face.

Electricity sizzled the ends of my hair.

"Thanks, I reall—"

A baton cracked against my cheek, and my face throbbed.

"Never mind." I massaged my aching jaw as Lothaire half dragged me down the hall.

"What was that?" he asked loudly, violence in his voice.

Since he still held his baton, I gritted my teeth and said, "Nothing, sir. Thank you for your help."

He grunted and shoved me into the room that we always watched the battles in.

All seven of the other recruits turned around to stare at me.

The kings glared at me, and John sighed with relief. Horace gave me a thumbs-up. The demons just looked bored.

Maybe it had been a crazy nightmare? John looked normal.

"You're a piece of work." Lothaire released me and stalked to the front of my room.

In my head, I flipped him off.

In reality, I stumbled into a chair beside John and just managed to stop myself from kissing the floor.

Looking over at the kings, I tried to gauge if they had

flames in their eyes. Or had I just been having intense hallu-cinations in my sleep? It was hard to tell these days.

Speaking of hallucinations, digging my hands into the elastic of my waistband, I almost cried with relief when I felt the smooth material of my pipe.

Maybe everything would be okay?

With trembling fingers, I brought the pipe to my lips and inhaled relaxation. I blew out Horse, and he settled onto my shoulder as he nudged me with the top of his feathered head.

Everything's fine.

The pipe was pulled from my fingers by Malum.

I snatched it back before he could break it.

"You fucking dare?" Scorpius said softly.

"No, how dare *you?*"

Scorpius lunged forward across the desk, and Malum held him back and whispered something aggressively in his ear.

Orion stared at me coldly.

Blood pouring into my arm cavity.

Slowly Orion rolled up his sleeve and showcased hundreds of raw red slashes. His arm was mangled.

I gasped.

It hadn't been a dream; it had been real.

He'd mangled himself healing me when my arm would have regenerated on its own. I swallowed down bile as guilt slammed into me.

Orion mouthed, "You smoked in battle. You lost your arm. For the last forty-six hours, Lyla reknitted your arm. For the last forty-six hours, I stabbed myself and gave her the blood to perform the spell."

Malum raised a hand on Orion to comfort, then whirled on me and screamed, "For the last forty-six hours, Orion fucking *stabbed himself for you!*"

Yep, his pupils were flames.

I shifted in my chair, the metal squeaking uncomfortably loud in the silent room as everyone stared at us, but I couldn't find my voice.

Even Lothaire just watched like he was waiting for my response.

I flexed my fingers.

"I didn't *ask* you to do anything," I whispered with embarrassment and tried to tell him with my eyes that his sacrifice had been unnecessary.

Malum growled like a wild animal, and Scorpius swore violently.

Orion just kept glaring at me.

Gratitude and shame were a toxic combination in my gut, and I choked on it.

I just wanted peace.

You never asked them to do anything for you, and now they're mad at you for things you can't explain.

My vision blurred black as my monster suddenly screamed with unholy rage. Before I could focus on my breathing, ice burned my palms.

I'd somehow accessed my abilities and conjured the oddly shaped blades.

Clutching the razor-sharp daggers in my palms, I glared at the kings and let them see the monster in my eyes.

Lightning cracked outside in the hall.

The eclipse burned the room in red.

Suddenly, the tension ratcheted up in a way I'd never felt before. We weren't just eight students training to be assassins and playing war; we were eight of the most powerful people in all the realms.

Malum stood up with flames covering him like battle

armor. Scorpius's milky eyes started to glow, and the tattoo on his neck blinked. Orion opened his mouth like he was about to scream.

I pointed my blade at them and refused to step back.

Next to me, John stood up, and the darkness expanded around him like it was taking shape. His face hardened, and his dimples disappeared as he stood beside me against the kings.

I tilted my head up, unwilling to let Malum intimidate me with his height as I twirled my daggers between my fingers.

Scorpius leaned forward, and his eyes glowed brighter.

"No, Scorpius!" Orion sang out a single haunting lyric that brought tears to my eyes, and he threw himself in front of the blind fae and slapped his hand over his eyes.

The darkness around John kept expanding, and it looked like it was forming something.

I was unsure what the threats were, as my intuition had never sensed danger so acutely before. Fear almost brought me to my knees, and I gripped my blades tighter.

My monster whimpered, the rage draining out of me as self-preservation kicked in.

The two demons stood up, black veins spreading across their skin until they dripped down their fingers and began to form long blades.

Horace's fangs descended with a click, and his orange eyes were wide and manic. He licked his lips, like he could already taste the blood.

In the front of the room, Lothaire had a similar glint in his eye. But he shook his head like he was waking up out of a dream.

Abruptly, he bellowed, "*Stand down, recruits, or we'll spend a week in the Black Ocean!*"

It took a second for us to process his words, but when we did, it sucked all the energy out of the room.

Everyone paused, and the darkness around John stopped expanding. Malum's flames dimmed, but Orion kept his hand covering Scorpius's eyes.

"*Sit fucking down!*"

We sat.

I dropped my daggers, and they shattered across the marble floor, the pieces disappearing like they'd never existed.

Horace's fangs clicked back inside his mouth as the black veins slowly retreated off the demons.

Orion kept his hand plastered over Scorpius's face.

"I'm glad you're okay. I was really worried," John said with a small smile as we sat back down.

A lump developed in my throat, and I was aware I was being such a *girl* when I asked, "You're still my friend?"

"You couldn't get rid of me, even if you tried." He punched me on my newly healed arm.

I almost passed out from the pain.

After a few deep breaths, I smiled weakly and punched him back. He punched me harder, and I puked in my mouth.

It was official: being a man was horrible.

"You aren't forgiven." Malum leaned across the aisle.

"I don't give a fuck what you think." I rolled my eyes as I turned my attention away from John and toward the maniac that called himself a king.

"Really, after Orion saved your ass, this is how you repay him?"

Shame was a lead weight in my stomach. *His pain was unnecessary.*

"Sorry, Orion, I really am grateful," I said self-consciously as he uncovered Scorpius's eyes and they both sat down.

He narrowed his eyes and gave me a curt nod.

It was better than nothing.

"Everyone shut up and focus!" Lothaire yelled, and we straightened in our seats. "The only reason you're all not outside running right now for your pathetic display of zero fucking control is because you actually didn't fucking suck in this battle."

I blushed at the effusive praise.

Lothaire really knew how to butter a girl up.

He tapped the enchanted stone, and it projected the battle across the smooth wall.

Somehow the stone had recorded through the sand-storm, and we were able to see ourselves clearly.

Holy sun god.

The eight of us were surrounded by at least four hundred ungodly, and we had no idea.

Like usual, the battle was sped up, and I watched in amazement as I fought like a maniac. Pipe between my lips, I performed just as well as the other men.

Horse was a badass swooping in the air around me.

Each of us killed like we were born to fight ungodly.

It was amazing; it was horrible.

I dragged kill after kill and threw the mutilated corpses into a pile.

On the screen, it looked like hell.

At that moment, it had felt fun. Like I was alive.

But watching from afar, my throat burned as I swallowed down vomit because there was nothing exciting about what I'd done.

I was murdering dozens and dozens of creatures.

And I was smiling.

I was a monster.

I understood why I'd stuck the enchanted pipe between my lips. Even in the middle of the carnage, a part of me had recognized that what I was doing was fucked up. I'd needed to calm myself.

The rage had been too much.

When the images stopped, I barely heard when Lothaire praised me for my improvements.

I shuffled through the rest of the day in a blur.

Even when John slung his arm over my shoulder and talked my ear off, the weight on my soul crushed me down.

In battle class, I didn't say anything when Malum sneered at me. After repeated attempts to get a rise, he tried poking me to get my attention.

I ignored him.

He vibrated with rage that I wasn't paying attention to him. Which was weird because if he hated me so much, why did he care?

At dinner, I helped Tara and Sari with their classwork. I didn't miss the way they looked at each other with worry at my lack of reaction. I didn't even blush when Sari launched into an explicit diatribe about how a royal student choked her during sex.

I hoped it made her happy.

When it was finally time for bed, I trudged toward the room with dread.

I debated whether I should shower to wash the invisible filth off my skin or pretend to sleep.

However, when I opened the door, the world tilted on its axis.

"You fucking slut!" a scratchy voice squealed.

My legs gave out beneath me as I was tackled to the floor.

"Did you miss me?" Sadie asked.

I passed out.

CHAPTER 31

FRIENDSHIP IN DARKNESS

Field training: Day 39, hour 23

"Bitch, I know I'm sexy, but you don't need to eat shit." Sadie grinned above me with my head on her lap as she aggressively slapped my cheeks.

"Ow." I rubbed my face but smiled like a goon.

She slapped me harder. "You like it rough, huh?"

"Oh, baby." I flipped us so I was kneeling on top of her with my forearm on her throat. "You couldn't handle me."

Sadie licked her lips, red eyes glowing as she smirked. "You aren't even on my *level* until you've been intimately acquainted with a sex knife for over forty-two hours."

What was with everyone and knives?

And they said *I* was crazy. Please.

Sadie chuckled, a harsh, raspy sound that was music to my ears. "Yeah, just imagine pleasure, then stab. Then pleasure. Then stab, stab. It will *really* do something to you. Kind of changed my life. I won't lie."

We both let her words sink in.

"Sadie, sweetie. I mean this in the kindest way possible. You're a dumb fucking cunt."

Sadie reached up, wrapped her arms around my neck, and latched onto me like a koala bear. "You're such a cutie, Aran. Ugh, I missed your aura of morbid darkness."

"And I missed your craziness."

We wrestled for a little bit. Well, mostly Sadie tried to wrestle; I just easily subdued her with one hand and watched her struggle while my heart filled with warmth.

"You both are embarrassing and have the shared brain capacity of a rock." Jinx stood above us and stared down at us like we were lunatics. Which we were.

"Rocks don't have brains," Sadie added unhelpfully as she tried to claw at my face as I bent her elbow behind her back.

"Exactly." Jinx scoffed.

Sadie had walked right into that one.

"Are you done humping on our fucking floor?" Malum's low voice was somehow even deeper with menace, and it took me a moment to take in my surroundings.

For a second, I'd forgotten I wasn't at the manor, hanging with Sadie while Jinx taunted us.

"Am I hallucinating?" I asked as I pinched my hand. Had I lost my sanity in the desert? "Is my arm even real?"

I flailed my arm around as I broke out in a cold sweat.

It felt real.

For good measure, I poked Sadie, and she was solid and warm beneath me.

"Fuck," I said miserably as my heart plummeted into my stomach. The drugs had messed up my brain so badly that I'd lost all grip on reality.

I clutched my head in my hands and rocked back and forth as I crawled away from the mirage.

Red eyes filled with concern as Sadie followed.

"Looks like Aran's finally lost his fucking mind," Scorpius said from far away.

"Stay away." I whimpered as Sadie came closer.

"I told you he'd break," Scorpius jeered at Malum. "He was never strong enough to be an assassin."

I whimpered.

"Shut the fuck up. Don't talk to him that way," John threatened Scorpius as Orion whispered to his fellow king, "Don't speak to Aran like that."

I startled at his voice, but it wasn't enough to pull me out of my breakdown.

Horace sighed heavily. "Aran, man, chill. You're not tripping." He flashed me a pointy smile and gave me a thumbs-up.

When did Horace become my friend?

I gripped my legs tighter and rocked faster. Terrified to look over at Sadie and Jinx because reuniting with them was the greatest desire I'd ever had. When it was all a lie, I'd break. All over again.

"Oh, please." Scorpius flipped off Horace and chuckled. "Aran's just being dramatic like usual."

Clearly, Scorpius had issues with me. He'd been glaring at me more and more lately, but he hadn't attacked me directly in a while.

Roar.

Suddenly, Sadie was gone.

A massive saber-toothed tiger with shaggy white fur and black markings jumped across the room and slammed against Scorpius.

I blinked.

Sadie shook the seven-feet-tall fae man like a rag doll with her arm-length fangs wrapped around his neck.

Scorpius punched and kicked, but Sadie just plopped

down onto her butt and batted him lazily with her paw like she was playing.

"Great. We *finally* get permission to leave the beast realm, and you immediately act like an uncivilized barbarian." Jinx rubbed her temples and sighed heavily. An action that was at odds with her less-than-five-feet, twelve-year-old appearance.

"And who are *you*?" John snapped at Jinx with uncharacteristic suspicion.

Jinx scoffed. "Your antithesis and the bane of your existence."

"What?" John asked with confusion, and I was too distracted by Sadie tossing Scorpius's writhing body into the air to tell him not to bother trying to understand the little girl.

Across the room, Malum burst into flames.

"Should I have brought catnip?" Jinx rubbed at her temples like she was elderly and not twelve years old as John glared at her with distrust.

Malum moved toward Sadie, and she let out an ear-splitting roar that shook the floor while she kneaded her hand-length claws in and out of Scorpius's back.

Everyone winced.

As my body vibrated with the aftershocks of a predator's warning, it clicked in my brain that this was really happening.

Sadie and Jinx were *really* here.

And from the flames spreading off Malum's skin, across the floor, she was about to be set on fire.

"STOP!" I leaped to my feet.

Running over, I hit Sadie's thick, fluffy skull. "Release the big rat. He's not worth it."

Scorpius yelled something back, probably arguing that

he wasn't a rat, but it was muffled by the paw that was smashed over his face.

"Sadie, please. He's not worth it."

I began to sweat as the room's temperature increased drastically. Malum was an inferno.

The fire crept closer.

"Please!" I pulled at her floppy ears.

Blazing red tiger eyes narrowed as my bestie pushed Scorpius's head further into the floor and placed more of her weight on top of him.

Sun god, cats were difficult.

The gods were *really* testing me whenever they made my best friend into a saber-toothed tiger shifter.

Just like a cat, Sadie had a puking problem and authority issues, refused to run for long periods of time, and acted first, then thought about it later.

Flames burned inches from us, and I couldn't stop a shiver as I remembered the flesh melting off my bones.

"What is going on here?" A familiar menacing voice broke through the chaos, and everyone stopped moving.

Malum's flames retreated to atop his shoulders.

I slumped with relief.

All hell would have broken loose if they'd kept threatening Sadie, because Cobra entered the room.

With jewels shimmering in his skin, Sadie's mate sauntered like the alpha snake shifter he was. A predator.

He moved gracefully like a snake.

Surrounded by the recruits, I couldn't help but notice that he was at least half a foot shorter than Malum.

I'd always thought Cobra exuded power, but now he didn't seem as terrifying. Sure, he was impressive and not to be messed with, but he didn't crackle with intensity like the kings.

"If you don't turn back right now, I'll punish you." Cobra smiled. "Kitten, you don't want to disobey me. Or did you already forget what happened last time?"

Just like that, Sadie stood naked in front of the room with her horrible scars on display.

The only sign that she'd transitioned was a lingering crackling noise of reshaping bones because sound traveled slower than light.

Immediately, Cobra ripped off his shirt and pulled it over her head. On her short frame, it fell to her knees, but Cobra still positioned himself in front of her to protect her modesty.

"Really? We've been over this. You don't get to punish me like you own me," Sadie said with annoyance.

Cobra looked confused. "But I do own you?"

Sadie made a choking noise and tried to push past him, but he wouldn't let her by.

"You're not decent," Cobra growled at her.

Knowing how stubborn the snake bastard was, I whipped off my sweatshirt and pulled it over her head. Mine also completely dwarfed her.

My T-shirt still protected my back.

Cobra nodded toward me. "Thank you, Aran."

I gaped at the pleasantry. Was he going to actually be nice to me?

Cobra smirked. "I see this place has been treating you well."

Since I had dark circles under my eyes and various bruises from training, we both knew I looked like shit. The bastard was mocking me.

"I see you're still a possessive asshole." I smirked back.

"I see your hair is still a horrifying shade of blue."

"Have you gained weight? You look fat."

"Have you lost weight? You look like you've lost a lot of muscle definition."

I gasped at his insult. "You're still a bastard."

Cobra smiled like I'd complimented him.

Sadie rubbed her hands over her face tiredly and sighed. "Well, I guess it's a good thing you're talking to Aran. Although, it would be nice if you could stop *insulting* my friend."

She was referencing the fact that Cobra refused to talk to women because of his trauma. He'd broken his rule for Sadie and, because of our friendship, also spoke to me.

A true blessing.

Not.

I glared at him and let him know with my eyes that I was going to tear him to pieces if he hurt Sadie.

He glared back, green eyes flashing to those of a snake, as he wordlessly told me to try it.

Our silent exchange was broken by Sadie smacking Cobra on the back of the head. "You agreed to escort me to the academy and then leave so I could have alone time with Aran. Why are you still here?"

Cobra scoffed. "You thought I'd actually leave you alone?" He gestured to the room. "With all these men. Please. I don't leave what's *mine*."

Sadie's red eyes started to glow, and her scratchy voice was menacing. "Excuse me."

Cobra glared down at her.

Instead of shifting into a tiger, Sadie started to drag her nails down her forearm. Blood welled.

Cobra's eyes widened as he realized what she was doing. "Don't you dare."

"If you don't leave me with Aran this minute, I'll never wear your collar again. This is a massive betrayal of my trust." Her glowing red eyes filled with tears. "You know what Aran means to me."

Cobra swallowed thickly, and the alpha looked panicked at the sight of his mate's tears. He grabbed her chin. "If I do this, you'll wear my collar at all times."

Sadie scowled up at him, then deflated. "Fine."

Cobra's expression was wicked. "If you get so much as a scratch on yourself, you'll be punished for weeks." He looked up and eyed all the men in the room. "Anyone so much as looks at her wrong and I'll disembowel you."

The recruits bristled, but no one said anything. We all knew Lothaire would lose his mind if we got hurt and couldn't fight the ungodly.

I shuddered at the memory of my time in the tank.

Jinx rolled her eyes. "I'm here. Nothing will happen." She snapped her fingers at Cobra to get his attention.

He nodded to her like she was a fellow soldier and not a *child*.

Cobra leaned down and gave Sadie a punishing kiss, then he whirled and left the room.

"I can look after myself," Sadie snapped at Jinx in the ensuing silence.

"No, you can't." Jinx laughed.

I threw myself at Sadie and wrapped my arms around her. "Why don't we ignore the small, mean, and most likely iron-deficient child and tell me how you're here?! With me. In person."

We hugged each other tighter.

Sadie recovered quickly from Cobra's threats and bounced in my arms. "Lothaire sent us a dumb letter telling us he'd kidnapped you to this dumb, motherfucking ugly, gross place."

Relief filled me that they'd known where I was.

"So of course, I was going to rescue you and bring you away from his soul-sucking vampyre ass. Because you're my best friend."

Classic girl code.

"After lots of research, which was just Cobra threatening and killing everyone, I bought a device on the black market to access the realm. But the High Court arrived and confiscated it as soon as I tried to use it."

I nodded. "I'm just glad you tried."

"I may or may not have started a small diplomatic emergency between the shifter realm and the High Court."

"What?" I said with feigned surprise. It was exactly the type of thing my friend would do.

If I shouldn't be in a position of leadership, then Sadie *really* shouldn't be.

I had the potential to be a dictator. Sadie had the potential to be an overlord that took over the realms and enslaved everyone because she also had blood powers.

It was the red eyes.

"So basically. You know how there's a visitors' weekend ball thing for this fucking dumbass school?"

"Maybe?" A small part of me remembered Sari mentioning it. Or maybe it had been John? So much had happened that a dance didn't seem important.

"Is that why you're here?" I asked with excitement.

We had a long history of crashing dances; it was practically our thing.

"No, I got banned from attending because I accidentally"—she made finger quotes—"declared war on every member of the High Court and started to raise a standing army of shifters to fight them for control of the realms."

My jaw dropped.

Suddenly, I understood why Jinx was sighing and rubbing her temples. "You did not?"

"Oh, I did."

"I don't know if I should be worried or scared."

"What you should have is a lady boner for me because your bestie is a bad bitch."

My stomach twisted as I became hyperaware of our audience.

I tried to chuckle deeply and punched her arm lightly. "You mean male boner. This is all for you, honey." I leaned forward and pulled her tight like I was holding a lover as I whispered in her ear, "Don't blow my cover, you slut."

"Oops, sorry," she breathed quietly. Pulling back, Sadie punched me in the abs. "Looking sexy, my dude. Your abs are amazing."

It took everything I had not to keel over; she'd definitely been working on her punch.

"Subtle," I mouthed.

"So you're not here for the ball?" I tried to change the subject and hoped no one had noticed her slipup.

Sadie shook her head. "No. I got special permission to visit because I might have expressed my displeasure at being banned by refusing to perform my role as the moon goddess's chosen general. But the men wouldn't let me go alone, so Cobra agreed to escort me here, and I bargained with them to have Jinx accompany me for protection. This way, we can have some gir—" She covered mouth. "Alone time without the men hovering."

"What?" I choked on spit, still focusing on the first part. "Moon goddess? General?"

"Remember the ball where I lost this?" Sadie held up her hand and showcased her missing finger.

"Yeah?"

"Well, I have a *lot* to tell you. I wish I'd just spilled the revelations, but according to Dr. Palmer, I was in crippling denial."

"Wait, you still see her?"

"Yeah, and she definitely misses you. She told me last session that she 'misses when you came with the fucked-up blue-haired dude because he balanced you out and kept you from sinking into this weird and extremely concerning despair.'"

"Wow." I held her tighter against me.

Sadie nodded and snuggled closer into me. "Also, apparently I'm one of the special types of people that become homicidal when I'm depressed."

"This is a lot to unpack."

Sadie shrugged. "The moral of the story is that Jinx and I get to spend a weekend with you in return for me appeasing a deity and not starting an inter-realm war."

I turned to Jinx—the pale, dark-haired child was staring at us like we were roadkill.

"You don't need to be here. I can protect her."

She mumbled something about me being dumb and ugly under her breath.

"I agree," Scorpius said from across the room, where his gaping wounds were being tended to by Orion and Malum.

Jinx turned to Scorpius and narrowed her eyes. "You've got a lot to say for a weak fucker that's fully dependent on two grown men."

Horace whistled, and the demons looked up from making out on their bed, like they were excited to see the child fight the assassin.

Scorpius opened and closed his mouth like he was speechless.

"Also, your neck tattoo is lame. Who gets an *eye* on their neck and not in the middle of their forehead?"

Scorpius's nostrils flared, and Orion hid a laugh behind his hand. Once again, Malum erupted in flames.

For the first time in weeks, glee bubbled through me. Jinx and Sadie were really here, and they were putting the men in their place.

I grinned like a loon.

"Are you going to introduce me to your *other* friends, who are definitely not your best friends?" John asked with a dramatic wink.

"Excuse me?" Sadie bristled with rage and looked like she was about to shift again. "*I* am his best friend. Who are you?"

"I'm his *new* best friend."

"No."

"Yes."

"So we both agree," Sadie said slowly, and John nodded.

I looked between them, confused when they had come to any sort of understanding.

John smirked down at her. "We'll battle to the death for Aran's friendship, and whoever wins is his bestie."

I choked. "What is wrong with you people? A person can have two best friends; it happens all the time."

"I don't like him," Jinx said randomly as she scowled at John.

John glared back. "And I don't like you."

Sadie talked like I hadn't spoken. "I agree. Neither can live while the other survives."

Why did I like having friends? Suddenly, I couldn't remember.

Malum interrupted their dispute, "Egan, control your girlfriend and your child."

Three mouths dropped.

Jinx pointed at us aggressively, like us being her parents was the worst fate in all the realms. "You think they sired me. Them? Those idiots? Right there? The ignorant ones that are still hugging?"

Sadie sighed and said sarcastically, "Darling, it's almost your bedtime. Don't be difficult for Mommy."

I hid my laughter with a cough.

"I'm going to stab you both in your sleep."

I made a mental note to stay awake the entire weekend. Because Jinx kept her promises.

CHAPTER 32
JEALOUSY KILLS

Field training: Day 41, hour 9

"I didn't know you had a girlfriend."

"What?" I looked up from my paper and over at Malum, who usually passed the class time ignoring me completely.

He only ever spoke to point out an error in my reasoning.

Now his silver eyes were molten steel, and the weight of his full attention made the hairs on my neck prickle.

I stopped detailing the fifty-six ways to asphyxiate someone and turned to him. "What did you say?"

"You have a girlfriend. That Sadie girl." Malum's voice was a deep baritone that reverberated through my bones and made my stomach do a weird swooping sensation.

Next to him, Orion was openly waiting for my response.

I opened and closed my mouth, confused about what he wanted me to say. Why did he even care in the first place?

Hadn't they seen her mate Cobra stake his claim and say he *possessed* her? Why would they even think I was involved?

Sadie and Jinx were exploring the island while I

attended class, then Lothaire had given me the rest of the day to hang out with them because they were leaving tonight.

So far, class had been unbearably slow.

I kept checking the large grandfather clock on the wall every few seconds, hoping it was time to hang out with my bestie.

I'd even started enjoying Jinx's mockery. It was comforting. Like a refreshing slap to the face when you were feeling disoriented.

Malum grunted, and I tore my eyes from the clock and remembered he had asked me a question. Something about a girlfriend?

Orion mouthed, "I didn't know either."

I wiped cold sweat off my forehead.

"Um," I eloquently supplied as I focused on my paper and wrote how to strangle an opponent with your thighs.

"What?" Sari asked loudly as she turned around in her chair. "Aran doesn't have a girlfriend. Right, Aran?" She looked at me with big, sad eyes.

My face prickled with the heat of an intense flush as I gripped my pen tighter.

Why did I feel like I was betraying Sari and Orion with Sadie? I had literally done zero sexual things with them.

Sun god, I wasn't even into women.

I pulled at my collar. Who had turned up the heat in the room?

"Hand in your papers." Ms. Gola's voice broke through the awkwardness, and I shoved myself out of my chair as fast as I could.

"Is it true?" Sari stood in front of me and clutched her books to her chest like a shield. Her pretty eyes were large and misty like she was about to cry.

Shit. I'd just been helping her with her studies.

We were just friends. Right?

Before I lost the companionship of one of the only girls I got to hang out with at the academy, a cold arm was slung over my shoulder.

Horace said, "Don't worry about Aran. He's busy training and not spending time on relationships."

Sari sighed loudly with relief and hurried to do whatever royal students did with the rest of their days. I'd heard snippets of conversations enough to gather it was classes about decorum and statecraft.

"Thanks," I said to Horace, who still had his cold arm slung over mine.

Up close, the yellow hue of his eyes was creepy as fuck. I fought the urge to pull away from the vampyre in disgust and forced myself to relax.

"Poor, dumb thing didn't even notice I didn't say you didn't have a girlfriend." Horace chuckled as we walked down the hall, and I hid my grimace.

Sari was not dumb.

"Uh, thanks for that."

"No problem, my dude. I've been meaning to tell you, I liked what you did in the sand to those ungodly. That was pretty sick how you tore them to shreds."

Great, a vampyre was complimenting me.

I smiled and pretended his words weren't nailing daggers into my crumbled psyche. Even the presence of my best friend didn't change the fact that something inside me had been irreparably broken.

Like music I couldn't turn off, playing on an endless, melancholy loop through my head.

But it wasn't music.

It was the screams of those I'd killed. The pain in their eyes and the desperation that clung to their skin.

I'd thought I'd known torture, but I'd been sheltered and naive. A true princess.

Real horror was what you did to others, that you had to live with yourself.

The closest word I could think of that fit the experience —haunted.

I was haunted by myself.

And it was anguish.

Horace kept chattering, making some creepy jokes about how we were going to have so much fun together in the next battle.

The worst part was that I wasn't completely disgusted by him. There was a portion of me that preened at his friendship and attention. The cold, mean vampyre liked me and wanted to be my friend.

It was as nice as it was awful.

That was the crux.

Of everything.

"Aran, finally!" Sadie squealed and threw herself at me like we hadn't spent all night snuggled on the bed whispering to each other while Jinx walked around the room and talked to the fire.

Yes, I was 99 percent sure Jinx had been talking to the voices in the flames. But I was 100 percent sure I wasn't going to question Jinx about it because I couldn't handle any more trauma.

If she wanted to act demonic, that was her business. Not mine.

"Jinx has been meeting with Lothaire for the last few hours, and she hasn't come back. I think we might need to rescue her."

Sadie's ruby eyes were wide with worry. "If Jax finds out I left her with him, he's going to go berserk. But she pushed me out of the room and shut the door. There was nothing I could do."

I patted her snow-white hair and chuckled. "If we're rescuing anyone, it's Lothaire."

Horace pulled away from me, his face scrunched with disbelief. "She's a little *girl*. What could she possibly do?" He spat "girl" like it was synonymous with pathetic.

"Imagine the most heinous crime ever committed."

Sadie finished for me, "Then imagine someone breaking from psychological torture."

I mimed an explosion with my hands. "Then combine the two. That's Jinx."

Horace laughed like we were pulling his leg. "Whatever, Aran. See ya later, man. I'll save you a seat at dinner."

"Um, thanks?" There were eight seats, and we all sat in the exact same ones for every meal. Since Malum sat on one side of Horace and Zenith on the other, I wasn't seeing how that was possible.

Suddenly, lightning streaked across the walls and left scorch marks in its wake.

At the same time, Sadie screamed and chucked a spoon at the wall.

We both stared at the mangled silverware.

"Sorry, it scares me every time," Sadie said with a shrug.

"I'm more worried about why you had a spoon from breakfast on you?"

"I needed a weapon against Jinx. It wasn't like I wanted her to come on this visit. She forced me to bring her."

I stared down at my short best friend and wondered for the billionth time how she had survived as long as she had. "So you grabbed a spoon and not a knife?"

"Duh. Better to gouge and scoop with."

"What are you scooping?"

"Brains."

Had everyone in my life lost their minds? Were we all tied up somewhere, strapped to gurneys, pumped with drugs, pretending to be functioning in society?

Now that I looked at Sadie, her small build did make her appear a little sickly.

Shit, we were definitely in a cell together.

"Weren't you gaining muscle?" I pointed to her small arms and couldn't help but take a moment to flex my much bigger and more impressive bicep.

Her ruby eyes filled with tears. "Yeah, I was. Until my best friend was forced to attend a supernatural war academy and train to be an assassin. I've been sick with worry."

I wrapped her into a tight hug and inhaled the subtle whiff of cranberries that always clung to her. "I'm okay."

"You're okay," Sadie whispered back.

"I'm okay," I repeated, like if I said it enough, the lie would come true.

Sadie's voice was small. "Why are our lives like this?"

I inhaled deeply and spoke the truth, "Because we're bad bitches."

"The baddest."

"Never has anyone been badder."

"Okay. Yep." Sadie pulled back and wiped the moisture from her eyes as she led us out of the hall corner. "We're fine, and we're going to find Jinx, and she's going to be fine."

"You know you're my best friend, right?" I said as we walked toward Lothaire's office. "John's great, but you know he's a—" I lowered my voice and whispered, "—man," like it was a venereal disease. Because it was.

"Obviously, soul sister," Sadie waxed poetic. "Our wombs are aligned, and our tits unite us."

"Keep that up and he will be my best friend."

Sadie gasped and said darkly, "I'll enslave you with my blood before I let that happen."

"Spicy," I chuckled, and she grinned back as I pushed open Lothaire's office door. "Jinx, are you still he—"

I went speechless.

Jinx was sitting in the chair in front of Lothaire's desk, chugging a chalice full of wine while the insane vampyre general who literally smacked me around for fun leaned back and smiled at her.

A nice smile.

Lothaire was nice smiling. The man who chucked boulders at us for *fun* looked like he was *happy*.

What the actual flaming fuck?

Had I entered into a different realm?

"Nope. Motherhood is too much. I'm putting her up for adoption." Sadie's scratchy voice was uncomfortably loud in the silent room.

Jinx put the chalice down and looked at us. "You will *never* be my mother."

Yep, her teeth were stained red, and blood was dripping off her chin.

I ignored the very disturbing relationship dynamic happening between the two women who had only a nine-year age gap between them.

Instead, I pointed out the elephant in the room. "And you call me a cannibal? Really, Jinx?"

Jinx ignored my excellent point and instead spoke to Lothaire. "Thank you for letting me tell my story. I hope you understand how sensitive the situation is, and I would appreciate your discretion until Aran is ready."

Lothaire nodded. "Of course, little one."

He smiled again, not his creepy "you're in pain, and I'm loving it" smile but an actual soft expression.

Sadie narrowed her eyes at the twelve-year-old. "What story do you have to tell?"

"And what situation is sensitive? What am I not ready for?" I asked incredulously.

Jinx ignored us. "Please excuse their idiocy. It does not reflect on our family or our values."

"What values?" Sadie and I said in unison with exasperation.

Killing people? Mental illness? Looking sexy?

Jinx bowed her head to Lothaire, and the large vampyre bowed his back. "I understand."

Why is Lothaire bowing to Jinx?

Then, as if the entire situation weren't bizarre enough, Shane's voice shouted, "Lothaire, we have a question about the fae queen! We think we've found an answer about where the bitch is probably in hiding— Oh, hey, Aran."

Shane grabbed me in a weird one-arm man hug and slapped me on the back.

Of course, stabbing pain streaked through my open wound.

Marvelous.

I grunted to cover a scream of pain.

"Hey, Shane." I tried to sound welcoming while pulling away from his overwhelming presence.

Suddenly, Noah and Demetre were filling the small office space.

"Sadie?" Demetre stuttered. "What are you doing here?"

"Just visiting Aran," she said awkwardly as she tried to put some distance between herself and them. Probably remembering how Cobra had told her they'd beaten the shit out of Noah for dancing with her.

"You know Aran?" Shane looked between us with confusion. "How?"

Sadie's golden skin paled as she realized what she'd done.

"I was visiting the castle during the fae games, and the princess introduced us. So we became friends," I said in a rush, my voice shaky to my ear in a way I was sure gave me away.

"You knew that cunt?" Shane turned to me, his handsome features hardening.

The vitriol radiating off him had my knees shaking with weakness. Suddenly, I wanted to be as far away from him as possible.

"Yeah, she's my cousin," I said in the best "duh" tone I could muster.

Demetre's voice cracked through the room like a whip. "Do you know where she went? Where she is?"

I remembered Lyla's prophecy about me needing to embrace the dragon and shuddered at the thought. Demetre terrified me. Every time I looked into his pink eyes, I was reminded of Mother beating me and carving a slur into my flesh.

I took a step back.

"No, no one's heard from her." *How would an elite fae act?* "What do you need with her anyway? She's spoiled and good for nothing. Everyone knows she doesn't even have any powers."

For some reason, Lothaire frowned at that statement.

Shane's anger changed into something more sinister, a smirk on his face. "Oh, the dumb bitch is good for something all right."

"I thought you were upset when you saw her bruised?" Sadie shouted suddenly, her body trembling with rage.

She referred to when the half warriors had seen me covered in bruises from Mother's abuse after they'd turned me in for visiting the sex clinic.

I discreetly pinched her and glared at her.

This was *not* what we needed.

"Mad that she was injured?" Noah scoffed.

"We were mad the traitorous cunt was still alive." Demetre laughed meanly. "It was bad enough we had to deal with her mother, but Arabella is just a weaker, more fucked-up version of her. Two of them were insufferable."

Lothaire glowered at Demetre like he wanted to kill him.

My monster screamed, metal snapped as it ripped apart its cage, and my vision wavered.

Shane shook his head with disgust, too caught up in his thoughts to notice my mounting rage. "She is a spitting replica of the bitch, and she showed her true character to us. Filth."

What is a word?

Filth.

Princess.

Assassin.

Whore.

All just words, yet somehow each one held power over me.

"Yeah, she sucked." I laughed awkwardly and dragged Sadie from the room.

Thankfully, Jinx followed, because I couldn't go back into that room without falling to my knees and slicing their tendons off their bones.

The urge to stab their aortas just right, so they bled out in seconds, made my hands shake.

"I'm so sorry," Sadie said as I dragged her down the halls.

"What for?" I asked.

For once, Jinx followed in silence.

"You know what," Sadie snapped as her chest vibrated with a roar and her red eyes glowed.

"I don't want to talk about it."

"That's fine. We don't need to talk." Sadie suddenly stopped, turned around, and started marching back the way we'd come.

"No!" I tried to sound authoritative as I dragged her away from the half warriors and toward the bedroom I shared with the men.

"Just let me bite them a little. Just a few bites. I'll only maim them semipermanently."

I didn't bother to question her about what she meant.

Five minutes of intense struggle later, we finally got back to the bedroom.

"The little bitch returns," Scorpius snarked as soon as we entered.

The beginning of a migraine throbbed behind my eyes. So much for the nice, peaceful nap I'd been looking forward to.

"That's it," Sadie mumbled. "They're going to show you some respect."

"What?"

"Oh, Aran, yes, I can't wait to fuck you and your big cock. Let's go to the bathroom!"

Sadie pulled me into the bathroom and locked the door.

Help?

CHAPTER 33

TAUNTING FATE

Field training: Day 41, hour 17

"Oh, fuck yeah."

"Oh my sun god, your cock is so big, Aran."

"You like that, you little slut?"

"You're the best fuck I've ever had!" Sadie shouted dramatically.

Smack.

Slap.

Water sprayed as we both threw our fully clothed bodies against the shower wall. We were sopping wet and giggling like lunatics as we pretended to have aggressive shower sex.

Sadie smacked her hand against her thigh loudly and screamed, "Ow, harder, baby!"

Smothering my laughter, I backed up so I could take a running start, then threw myself, limbs spread wide, against the shower wall.

The floor vibrated from the intensity of my body slam.

"Oh, how you punish me so deliciously," Sadie moaned wantonly while she fell onto the floor, silently laughing.

Once again, I backed up and flung myself into the wall.

"So hard!" Sadie put her fist into her mouth to muffle her laughter.

Holding my forearms together under the spray, I slapped my hands back and forth as hard as I could.

"Oh sun god. Aran. What are you doing to me?" Tears streamed down her face as she lay in the fetal position, laughing. "No, really," Sadie whispered up to me. "What was that slappy thing?"

"It's okay, baby. Let Aran blow your mind!" I yelled as I shrugged, not entirely sure *why* Sadie had decided we needed to mimic aggressive lovemaking so all the recruits could hear.

Sun god knew they'd had enough orgies in the last few weeks that nothing I could do would even faze them.

A horrible realization hit me. "Wait, Jinx is out there."

Sadie waved a hand dismissively as she whispered furiously, "She 100 percent knows we're faking it. Plus, I couldn't just let those fae fuckers walk all over you."

I sighed and slid down onto the shower floor beside her, exhausted from the last hour and mildly concussed from when I'd slipped and accidentally kissed the shower floor with my skull.

Sex was hard work.

"Ugh, I love aftercare with you!" I yelled just to make it clear that I was a considerate lover who cared about women, unlike all the men.

"Good call."

We relaxed together in comfortable silence.

The warm spray pummeled both of us, and memories rolled through me.

Last time we'd lain in the shower together, I'd been riddled with bullet wounds and Sadie had just saved the girls from a kidnapping.

Sadie spoke quietly as she sidled closer to me and linked our pinkies together. "When I first saw your roommates, I was like, 'Holy sun god,' and thought you were living any woman's fantasy. Wow, the three fae hunks with the neck tattoos. And the blond one is…wow. Just wow."

Sadie fanned herself with her hand.

"Yeah, but their personalities." I held my thumb down.

Sadie sighed heavily and moved her head so the water hit her face-first. "Yeah, they opened their mouths, and oh boy. They fucking suck. Why are you letting them treat you like crap?"

I closed my eyes and tried to explain it to her. "Trust me, I'm not trying to. But it's a little difficult when we're training twenty-four seven and fighting monsters. Also, I'm just one of the guys, remember? This is probably some weird hazing shit men do to other men."

Sadie didn't look convinced.

"I don't know, it seems super personal. I'd say they were obsessed with you, if they weren't fucking terrifying and giving off enough anger waves to make the don seem tame."

I mimed shooting myself in the head. "Yeah, it's fucked up."

"Do you want me to break you out of this place?" Sadie's expression hardened. "I will do it; just say the words. I really don't mind starting a diplomatic emergency."

For a second, I imagined what it would be like to run away from this nightmare.

But then all I could picture was the dying people. The voices in the flames. What I'd already done.

I shook my head sadly, fingers raised as I played with the scalding spray. "I'm afraid this place has already corrupted me. I couldn't just walk away, even if I wanted to."

Sadie stared at me sadly.

I opened and closed my mouth, struggling to put it into words.

Struggling to explain there was no escape from Elite Academy because it had already poisoned every facet of my life.

The ungodly were still out there, expanding and slaughtering. And for some reason, the tree had chosen me.

I finally said, "I'm afraid it's put me on a path I can't walk away from."

Because for the first time, I could see a purpose for my life that didn't involve being slaughtered for my throne.

Sure, that was still a problem that hadn't gone away. But there was a chance I could go years, decades, centuries before my problem was found out.

They'd appoint an interim monarch, and just maybe they'd give up the search and assume I was lost forever.

I'd just get slaughtered fighting monsters in foreign realms. For some reason, I liked that option more.

"I know exactly what you mean," Sadie whispered. "It's time I told you about what really happened at the ball."

I turned my head toward her.

Our faces hovered inches apart, and the weight of the realms was heavy between us.

For the next hour, I listened with horror as Sadie explained the reason behind Dick's abuse. The voice in her head and the army she was fated to lead.

When she finished, I gaped at her and struggled to process the situation.

"A war that involves gods? I wonder if it's connected to the ungodly?" My intuition was screaming at me that everything was connected. "And you're sure Dick had no idea what the poems were?"

"He had no idea."

I shivered. "Well, it's a man's voice, so it's not the moon goddess. And if it's not the High Court, then who could it be?"

"A devil?" Sadie offered. "I was researching powerful beings that could be contacting us, and they kept coming up."

I racked my extensive knowledge of different species, but I had nothing. "What are they?"

"Remember the poem in the beast realm about the place called hell? Well, I used the Mafia library, and apparently a devil is an extremely powerful creature from the angel and demon realm."

I asked the important question: "The Mafia has a library?"

"Yeah, and it's the biggest thing I've ever seen in my life. Apparently, it was modeled after the library in the Olympus realm."

"Alexandria?" I breathed in awe.

"Yeah, you've heard of it?"

"You haven't?"

Sadie waved her hand. "Yes, I'm uncultured and apparently know nothing and basically flunked out of school. Moving on. So you know how Dick has wings and is apparently an angel?"

I nodded. It had been shocking to see the crystal-blue wings arching high into the air at the ball.

I'd always been amazed by the detailed paintings that showcased naked men and women falling from the sky, wings extended, as they plummeted from the stars.

Seemed less exciting now that I'd seen one in real life.

He hadn't sparkled with an otherworldly glow and, for the most part, had just seemed like a normal man with wings.

Sadie continued her story. "Well, apparently angels and devils are from the same realm."

I pictured an entire realm of people with wings, and amazement washed over me.

"According to ancient books in the library, they're closely related species. Angels are from the cold side of the realm and live in snow, while devils are from the hot side that burns with constant fires."

Sadie paused for dramatic effect.

"The book said they're the strongest species in all the realms, and they were recruited by the sun god himself to be his defenders. Because all angels and devils possess unfathomable rage and have the ability to raze the realms."

Sadie lowered her scratchy voice like she was sharing a grave secret. "But the angels are always painted and talked about because they're basically the sun god's ambassadors who help maintain realm-wide peace. But the devils, they're his secret forces. So cruel and horrible that they fight in the shadows."

Sadie pretended to stab the air with an invisible dagger. 'The text said they were so heinous that the sun god would lose the worship of the realms if people saw his devil soldiers. If they ever knew the horrors they committed in his name"

The hot water splattered around us as we contemplated her words.

Devils and angels.

Realms serving the sun god directly.

Rage and unfathomable power.

I sighed heavily.

Why is everything always so violent and dark?

"So if angels have wings, what do devils have?" I imagined a world of fire, ice, and cruelty.

Sadie sighed. "That's the thing: no one knows. Just something so horrible that the sun god would lose everything if it got out."

"Sounds terrifying."

She smiled with excitement. "It is! Now enough about the fate of the realms and all my drama. Tell me about yourself. What have you been doing at this creepy school?"

"Oh, sweetie, you have no idea."

"Hit me with it."

So I did.

Sadie grimaced when I told her about the stabbing ceremony at the tree.

Her expression fell further when I explained the Black Ocean.

When I recounted the thirty-mile run, her mouth gaped and she looked at me with sheer horror.

"No."

"Yep."

"And how fast were you running?"

"Sub-five-minute pace."

Her golden skin paled, and she shivered with dread. "So what would happen if you didn't get the time?"

"Lothaire beat me with his baton and threatened to kill me."

Sadie gaped at me. "Holy fuck. I would be dead if I were chosen for this place. Like kaput. Not a chance in the moon goddess I'd survive."

"Yeah, I honestly thought of you a lot during the runs. Still do. Thank the sun god it was me who was sent to this place and not you."

Sadie's red eyes were saucers. "And Lothaire drank my blood. He said it tasted powerful, like he was tempted to recruit me."

"And that's not even the worst part."

She gasped dramatically. "How could it get worse?"

"Have you ever seen a monstrous creature rip from a person's flesh, like they were wearing it as a suit?"

"No?"

"Let me tell you about the ungodly."

A half hour later, Sadie was on her hands and knees, asphyxiating. "I think I'm going into shock. Moon goddess, you were just explaining the creatures, and I feel like I'm having a heart attack."

The endless weight on my chest was smothering, and I couldn't help but blurt out, "I hear them in the flames."

"What?"

"I think it's the voices of the villagers I've slaughtered." I swallowed thickly around the lump in my throat and whispered, "Maybe even the ungodly themselves. Just like Ascher described."

"Oh, Aran."

"I can't sleep. I close my eyes, and I see them."

Every. Single. Night.

Sadie slung her arm around my shoulders and pulled me tight so my larger body was cradled on her lap under the hot spray.

I couldn't stop sharing. It was equally horrible and cathartic to unload everything that had been eating me alive.

"My back burns unmercifully all the time, like the wound is festering. But it doesn't itch like it did in the beginning. It's more of a constant ache. I don't know if Mother lied or if the enchantment is fucked up. But it's not just when I'm turned on."

"Turn over."

Sadie gently maneuvered me so I was belly down on the cold tile, and she pulled up my sopping shirt.

She inhaled sharply.

"What is it?" The warm water slammed against the wound and helped alleviate the never-ending sting.

"Fuck." Sadie touched my side gently, and her fingers were trembling.

"What is it?" I repeated with more force.

I'd avoided looking at my back in the mirror because I didn't want a reminder that I was mutilated for all eternity.

"The good news is I think the letters are starting to fade a little. They're not glowing as brightly."

Relief hit me like a punch. *Is Mother's enchantment finally fading?*

Sadie's voice trembled. "Has someone stabbed you in the back? Carved you open?"

"What? No." Relief died a swift death.

Her pruney fingers slowly traced across the skin between my shoulder blades, and I almost crawled out of my skin at how sensitive it was.

"You have two parallel cuts running along your shoulder blades. They're extremely deep and look painful as hell."

"What?"

"They're on either side of your spine."

"Do they glow blue like the letters? Maybe it's some delayed sequence in the enchantment."

"No," Sadie whispered, her voice so quiet I had to strain to hear it over the water. "These gashes are pink and bloody. Like you've recently been sliced open."

"Maybe it's some leftover wound from the last battle with the ungodly?" I suggested, even though I healed most wounds within a day, so that didn't make sense.

"No, these are perfect. Surgical.

"You need to get this looked at by that witch you were talking about. You need to heal this."

"No," I snapped and pulled my shirt down as I sat up. "No one can see my back; you know this."

Sadie's eyes darkened as she glared at me. "You can*not* suffer like this. I will not fucking allow it."

"There is nothing we can do," I snarled back, not sure why we were getting worked up.

"There has to be something."

"There is no solution for me. No fated mates to help lessen the blow. No amount of love and support could save me."

The words tumbled from the darkest corner of my soul, the insecure girl who was jealous of everything her best friend had found.

"I refuse to believe that." Sadie's eyes glowed bright red in the darkness of the shower, an imitation of the eclipse outside.

"I've already accepted my fate." I straightened my shoulders and tried to radiate competence for my best friend.

Tried to show her I was strong enough to handle the shit hand I'd been dealt in life.

"Well, I refuse to accept it for you. Mark my words: someday you are going to be a powerful queen, with mates who worship you, and you'll be so fucking happy you won't even know what do with yourself."

I laughed at the imagery.

When I thought of my future, I pictured gruesome battles, crippling PTSD, loneliness, and drowning in my own mind.

"If I have your love and support for the rest of my life, that's enough," I said honestly.

Because it was true.

Women like Sadie were so full of life and special that they couldn't help but pull men into their orbit. She'd been through so much, yet she still managed to be so sweet and full of life.

I'd told her once that her soul was white, and I meant it.

I'd been extremely high, and for a second, I swore I could see into her very essence.

It was bright and pure.

I didn't need to see souls to know mine was not. If Sadie was lightness in the face of suffering, then I was darkness surrounded by pain.

There was no man that could complete me.

Because I was already complete.

Completely *fucked up*.

Abruptly, Sadie launched herself into my arms and burst into shuddering sobs.

I held her as she cried for both of us, grateful that one of us could still feel.

By the time we emerged from the bathroom, we were soaked to the bone and emotionally drained. I carried Sadie, who always got sleepy after she cried.

"Really, Egan?" Malum snapped as soon as I walked into the bedroom.

I ignored the mercurial king and put Sadie on the floor in front of my bed while I helped towel her off.

The revelation that my back was splitting in two from random wounds was more important than whatever taunts the men had for me.

"We're trying to fucking sleep. Could you maybe not fuck your slut so loudly?" Scorpius snapped.

I growled but ignored him as I toweled Sadie's long white hair. She giggled at being called a slut, and I rolled my eyes.

She was so predictable.

I was still confused why any of the men even cared. *Hypocrites.*

After Sadie was dry, I helped tuck her into my bed and then focused on drying myself off.

From the bed across from mine, John's eyes were dark flames, and he was glaring at Sadie like he wanted to kill her.

In fact, the kings were all openly sneering at my best friend, who was cuddled into my bed and murmuring bull- shit about being sore tomorrow.

"So you're not a virgin who's into men?" Malum snapped.

"Excuse me?" I looked over at him with confusion, convinced I must be having hearing failure. *What is he talking about?*

John snapped, "We thought that's why you never joined the orgies."

"Um." I gnawed on my lips as I tried to figure out what a dude would say in this situation.

Sadie giggled loudly. "Oh, Aran fucks all right. Big dick energy."

I was going to murder her.

If possible, the tension in the room ratcheted up until it felt like lightning was crackling in the air.

Horace laughed at Sadie's comment, and the demons looked back and forth like we were free entertainment.

I put on my best toxic male impression and drawled, "Obviously not," as I pointed to Sadie.

Malum's steel eyes hardened like he was trying to cut Sadie with his gaze. John made a joke about me having a micropenis.

Please. We both knew I was hung.

I grabbed a clean sweat suit and changed in the bathroom, then climbed into bed and snuggled Sadie close to me while giving her a big kiss on her forehead.

How *dare* they assume I was a virgin that was into men.

Was I a virgin? Yes.

Was I into men? Yes.

But it still didn't give them any right to *assume* things about me. Nosy fuckers.

Sadie was a warm weight against me, and for the first time in forever, I immediately started to fall asleep.

My eyes popped open. "Jinx. Where did she go?"

"I'm a horrible mother," Sadie murmured like she was worried but then started to snore aggressively.

Glad *one* of us was responsible. Kind of.

"I'm over here, dumbass." Jinx was lying upside down in the wingback chair next to the flames.

I relaxed with relief.

"Wait." I narrowed my eyes through the dark. "Are you tattooing yourself? Where did you get that?"

Jinx dipped a needle into ink and continued to stab it into her forearm. "Yep. Scorpius gave it to me."

"You're only twelve. Stop it!"

"Oh, shut up," Jinx and all the men chorused in unison.

"I recommend a neck tat," Scorpius said in a civil tone like he was actually encouraging a *twelve*-year-old to tattoo her neck. Who did that?

"Actually, I just turned thirteen," Jinx snapped like that made everything better.

"Um, I still don't think—"

"*Shut up, Egan!*" Malum bellowed.

I huffed and turned over in my bed. Jax better not blame me if Jinx gave herself a neck tattoo, because I'd tried my hardest.

Then I proceeded to pass the fuck out and get the best sleep I'd had in weeks.

I woke up with my arm wrapped around Sadie's throat. I'd been choking her out in my sleep. Sadie woke up with a smile.

It was just like old times.

CHAPTER 34
EMBRACING DEATH

Field training: Day 48, hour 7

"The ungodly have taken over the castle and decimated the entire town."

Rain poured around us.

We stood on a gabled bridge that arched dramatically toward the ivy-covered palatial structure. A castle. With its arched windows and breathtaking spirals, it was like walking into the pages of a storybook.

But the dark-gray clouds, cold rain, and monsters inside made it a dark fairy tale.

I cracked my neck back and forth. Inhaled deeply and exhaled the tension that had returned as soon as Jinx and Sadie left a week ago.

Fuck, I missed them.

Jinx's sarcastic voice countered in my head, *"How exhilarating. You have attachment issues. Groundbreaking. Now concentrate."*

I rubbed at my temples.

Among the dark thoughts, monster, and now Jinx's voice, my head was getting crowded.

My overactive imagination was officially going to be the death of me.

"At this rate, that's not what's going to kill you," Jinx replied with a chuckle.

A lump stuck in my throat as I breathed erratically.

If the moon goddess was the voice in Sadie's head, is it possible…

No! I pinched my hand and let the pain center me. The odds of both of us having voices in our heads were basically zero.

Sadie was chosen by the gods.

I was just crazy. Which I was cool with.

Instead of panicking like a wimp, I concentrated on Lothaire, who was handing out daggers and giving instructions.

"I want to see fucking improvement. Last battle, you all performed well individually, so now I want to see strategy. Teamwork."

Lothaire looked at us with something that resembled pride.

Ew. He was making it weird.

Lothaire's expression darkened like he'd read my mind. "If you fail to improve, we will spend seventy-two hours in the Black Ocean."

There he was.

"GO!" Lothaire bellowed and pointed to the castle that was allegedly overrun with ungodly.

Hopefully he had the wrong address.

We jogged in formation up the arched bridge to the grand castle entrance. Unfortunately, the doors were thrown wide open, so there was nothing to slow our entrance.

"Stop." Malum held up his hand, and we stopped.

Two dozen elegantly dressed people sat at long dining tables. Only a handful. This was nothing.

Fireplaces roared at the four corners of the room. If I hadn't known better, I'd have thought we'd interrupted a royal feast.

An elegant soiree.

Women were draped in decadent shawls that sparkled in ruby shades, with crepe veils that covered their faces. Men wore similar clothes, except their shawls were thicker and covered their necks, their veils only covering their eyes.

Rain slammed against the castle walls.

Thunder rumbled, and the pitch was deeper than during any storm I'd heard before. It was deep and rolling like a cornered animal howling.

At the tables, the skin that was exposed beneath the gorgeous clothes was shockingly pale. Through the veils, flashes of yellow glinted.

Wait, there's no food at the table.

An irritating scent lingered in the air, and it reminded me of brass.

No, not brass.

My subconscious brain put the pieces together before I fully processed what we'd walked into.

Copper.

Scorpius flexed his arm, shoulder tensed as he prepared to throw the first dagger like he always did when the ungodly were feigning domestic bliss.

I grabbed his forearm and whispered, "No."

Startled, he narrowed his eyes at me and scowled down like he was debating stabbing me instead.

I breathed out as quietly as I could. "Vampyres."

Pale eyes widened as he cocked his head and listened to the silence. Malum shifted toward Horace and raised his eyebrows in a silent question.

Horace breathed in deeply, nostrils flaring wide, and his yellow eyes began to glow.

He nodded slowly.

Malum's posture straightened, and for a second, it seemed like his muscles expanded.

Prebattle jitters transformed into something more sinister as we all processed the danger.

Eight of us against two dozen vampyres.

All we could use were daggers.

Even if they weren't soldiers, we were extremely outnumbered. If we charged forward like usual, they'd beat us with their speed and numbers.

Vampyres were disturbingly fast and possessed unmatched strength.

None of us so much as blinked as we tried to process just what the fuck we were going to do.

A woman tilted her head to the side as she stared at us. She pushed her chair back slowly, and the loud scraping sound was akin to a battle cry.

My heart raced with such intensity that it hurt my chest.

We need a plan. Think, Aran. Fucking think.

Static.

Now my head was dead silent.

My hands spasmed around my daggers as I held my breath from fear.

Another vampyre stood up and slowly pushed back their heavy chair. One by one, they all stood.

We watched.

"Each of us must take down two-to-three vampyres," Malum whispered.

That wasn't a plan; that was farting into the wind and praying for results.

We need a plan. Think, Aran!

As more vampyres stood, the monster in my head whimpered. I didn't know if it was because it was scared or excited.

Jinx's spoke, and I nearly shot out of my skin at her booming voice, *"Let your monster out, but keep control."*

The made-up voices in my subconscious were becoming a *little* too sentient.

"I can't," I whispered out loud.

The first time I'd let my monster out, I'd lost consciousness.

The second time, I'd kept consciousness but had lost all self-control and had gotten my fucking arm ripped off.

"DO IT, YOU CANNIBAL!" Jinx ordered.

I'm not a fucking cannibal. Agitation coursed through me, hot and bright, and my vision wavered at the edges as her words spurned me to act rashly.

I freed my monster.

As I licked my lips, the tang of copper in the air was delicious, and I vibrated on the balls of my feet with excitement.

I was going to kill them all.

Slaughter them with my bare hands.

Bathe in their gore.

Wait… Something irked at me like there was something I had to do.

I smiled as I stared at my future kills and planned just how I was going to snap their necks. Dancing back and forth, I buzzed with excitement.

Malum narrowed his eyes as he glared down at me.

Motherfucker thought he was in charge. What a fucking joke. I was going to show him how to lead.

Lead. That's it. I need a plan.

Plan to snap their bones. That's the plan.

No. Need something more.

I bounced back and forth faster. The tension was about to snap. I could practically taste how *fun* it was going to be.

Concentrate.

Four fireplaces. Twenty-six vampyres, which meant twenty-six ungodly. Fifty-two total. Eight of us. Sixteen daggers.

One massive foyer.

Five doors.

If they spread us out, we were 100 percent dead.

Backing up slowly, I inched away from the other recruits, back toward the metal box next to the door.

"Get back here, Egan," Malum whispered harshly.

"What are you doing?" John mouthed as he turned to me with wide eyes.

I punched backward, and everyone in the room jumped as the massive metal door slammed down with a crash.

"Five of us guard the doors. Three of us break the tables," I whispered with urgency as the vampyres started to inch toward us.

They weren't completely mindless, but they also weren't completely present. Their yellow eyes had a green tint. The ungodly were inside them.

"Why would we break the tables?" Malum whisper-shouted like I was an idiot.

"Fire."

Recognition sparked in his silver eyes.

John whispered back, "What are you talking ab—"

Malum held up his hand and cut him off. "He's right. Orion, Scorpius, and I will break the tables. The rest of you grab a door. No one leaves."

Everyone nodded, but Scorpius snarled quietly, "If

everything burns, then how the fuck are we supposed to avoid the fire?"

I shrugged. "Don't be a pussy?"

Yep. He loved that.

"I've got this door," John whispered as he backed up in front of the massive entranceway.

"GO!" Malum bellowed, and his voice cracked through the room like a whip. Everything erupted.

I threw my head back and laughed as I sprinted toward the door at the far side of the room.

A vampyre slammed a chalice against my head.

Slipping in the spilled blood, I slammed both my daggers into his eyeballs and fell to the ground atop him.

Rip.

An ungodly threw me backward, and I just managed to pull my daggers from the vampyre's corpse. It stalked toward me with clacking pincers.

Come to momma. I sprinted at the creature, launched myself at its neck, and used all my strength to saw through its neck and decapitate it.

Vampyres screamed, the ungodly bellowed, and tables splintered.

It was beautiful. Like art.

Pumping my arms and legs, I sprinted toward the door, chucking the severed ungodly's head at a vampyre like it was a weapon.

Running as fast as I could, I wasn't able to stop my momentum, and I slammed into the metal door.

A few feet away, Horace was already posted in front of the other exit and fighting two vampyres.

"Let's fucking go!" He grinned at me as he sliced them to shreds, his dagger moving impossibly fast.

"Fuck yeah!" I smiled back as a vampyre launched itself at me.

That was the last thing we spoke.

For hours.

Backs against our doors, we fought the vampyres and ungodly that tried to escape from them. Only problem was the stronger vampyres didn't die easily.

Six hours into the battle, most of the tables had been smashed to smithereens and were piled up in the center of the room in a bonfire.

The room was unbearably hot.

I would have been amazed that the three kings had managed to smash wood *while* fighting off the ungodly, but I was too focused on protecting my door.

The blaze pushed all the vampyres to the outskirts of the room, and they charged at us, mostly because they had nowhere else to go.

Now that the blaze was set, the three kings had joined John guarding the main entrance, where the most vampyres were trying to escape from.

I'd been dancing with a particularly fast vampyre for the last hour, and frustration made me want to scream.

Red-and-orange flames leaped in a wall behind him.

He slammed a foot into my stomach, and before I could recover, I was tossed away from my door. *NO!*

Quicker than I could follow, Horace sprinted over and slammed the door shut with the vampyre halfway through.

He banged the metal door back and forth until the vampyre's head popped like a grape.

"SWITCH!" Horace shouted.

I was a few feet from his door, and I threw myself at it. I got there before a vampyre could realize it was unguarded.

Thick smoke made it hard to see.

My lungs burned.

"Nice work. I like your use of the door!" I yelled and gave Horace a thumbs-up, then coughed as smoke filled my lungs.

"Thanks, man! Nice jab!" Horace complimented as I disemboweled an ungodly with one yank of my knife.

He yelled, "Try this!" Then he launched himself off the door and used the height to stab through the top of a vampyre's head.

"How about this?" Springboarding myself off the door, instead of jumping downward, I dove over the top of an ungodly and sliced its head off from the back using both my daggers.

The head rolled beside me.

"Fucking sick, I like the way you move!" Horace grinned, eyes bulging out of his head like a maniac as he was surrounded by multiple vampyres.

"Whoever kills the most, wins!" I shouted back. "I'm at seven."

"I'm at six! It's on, Aran. You're going down!"

Four hours later, I had twelve kills, and Horace had thirteen.

I was covered in sweat, hair stuck to my forehead and nape. My lips tasted like salt and blood, and my vision was nearly nonexistent as smoke irritated my eyes.

"NOOOOO!" I fell to my knees with horror as I realized what had just happened.

The room was silent, and no one charged at us.

"Fuck yeah!" Horace punched the air, then licked at the blood coating his hands. "I WON!"

"Stupid fucking ungodly." I kicked at a dead body.

I should have won the challenge. I'm stronger than Horace. It was mine to win.

"Loser," Horace mocked as he held his finger and thumb up in an *L* shape on his forehead.

I launched my sweaty body at him but slipped in the gore and ended up throwing us both to the ground.

"You suck, Aran." He pushed guts into my face, and I growled as I threw blood back at him.

"What the fuck are you two doing? Are you serious right now? How fucking old are you?" Malum roared.

He stood in front of the flames, with his own shooting off his shaved head like a dark creature from a forbidden realm.

"Get up," he ordered through gritted teeth.

Horace shoved more gore in my face, so I grappled with him until I had him in a choke hold.

Abruptly, there was pressure on my nape. Malum had pulled me off Horace by my neck.

"Dude, chill. We were just playing." Horace wiped green-and-red sludge off himself.

Malum's silver eyes were molten steel as he pulled my face closer to his. "I gave you an order, Egan, and you disobeyed me."

I rolled my eyes and kicked at his solar plexus. "Put me fucking down."

"Kick me again, and I'll throw you into the fire."

I kicked him.

The bastard didn't pick Horace up by his neck and shake him around.

Flames leaped higher off his head until Malum smoldered.

I totally called him on his dare.

"Put Aran down!" John shouted across the room.

I fell to the ground as Malum complied.

Horace walked up and threw his arm around my shoulder. "Great fighting with you."

"Same." I smiled up at him as Zenith opened the main door and we all headed out into the rain.

Lothaire was standing on the bridge, waiting for us.

"I was wrong about you. You're not weak like I first thought," Horace said thoughtfully.

"I know."

Horace grinned down at me, and I couldn't help but smile back.

Just like that, I made my second friend at Elite Academy.

CHAPTER 35
BLOOD ON THE TONGUE

Field training: Day 48, hour 7

Music swelled, and the floorboards vibrated from the force of pounding feet and the beat of the enchanted song.

Head falling off the end of my bed, feet perched up against the wall, I hung upside down as the room bustled with chaos.

My pipe dangled from my lips, and teal smoke curled around me like a lover's caress. Literally, the tendrils were wrapping around me in a hug because I told them to.

Horse was perched on my shoulder and pecked at my hair like he was grooming me. Or maybe he was looking for seeds?

I wasn't 100 percent caught up on bird behavior.

Inhale smoke. Hold. Exhale slowly. Hold. Repeat.

Swirling my pipe in the air, I was a conductor in one of the great fae orchestras.

With my eyes crossed, everything was a blur or dancing shapes and muted colors. Red haze blanketed the world like I was living in a fucked-up memory.

A violent paradise.

John's long legs blocked my view of the room.

Inhale. You're in control. Exhale.

"Are you okay?" John's voice had a hard edge to it, and if I squinted just right, I could make out the shadows that glittered around him. He was still pissed that Sadie was my best friend and not him.

"No." I blew out a large, satisfying cloud of smoke and watched the blue disappear like John's darkness had swallowed it whole.

At this point, it would be easier to list all the reasons I was fine.

My recent descent into madness had come out of the blue and was completely unexpected.

Just kidding.

I'd been free-falling off a cliff for weeks, but I thought I'd finally found the bottom.

After the battle against the vampyre ungodly, I'd been fine.

Then. I wasn't.

It didn't hit me when the rain had soaked me to the bone as we RJE'd back to the academy.

It didn't hit me when we sat in the dark classroom and watched the battle for hours as Lothaire critiqued us.

It didn't hit me when we went directly to class and discussed the best way to torture our opponents. My hand didn't falter as I wrote our essay. I'd barely noticed Malum glowering beside me.

Walking down the halls beside John and Horace, I hadn't blinked as lightning streaked around us and the air sizzled.

"Wait up!" Sari had called as she caught up with us. "Aran, can you help me with the torture essay? I didn't finish it in class, so I have to do it for homework. Can we go over it at dinner?"

"Sure." I'd nodded.

Her pretty eyes wide, Sari's face had fallen as she took in the bruises and cuts on my exposed skin and the dried gore the rain hadn't washed away.

"Are you okay?" she'd said quietly, brow furrowed with worry.

And just like that—it hit me.

My shoulders had slumped as the weight of *everything* crushed me into the ground. Now that my monster had gone to sleep, there was nothing holding me up anymore.

There was a pit in my chest where my heart should have been.

Hand shaking, ears ringing, I'd swallowed down my ragged breath and calmly told Sari, "No."

I didn't remember walking back to the room. Didn't remember John placing his arm under mine to support me. Didn't remember Horace speaking words of encouragement.

John dug my backup pipe out from underneath my mattress and pushed it between my lips. "Breathe it in. Slowly. You can do it, Aran."

I whimpered and covered my ears with my hands.

The fireplace shrieked.

Children screamed.

Ungodly trembled as they died.

"What the fuck is wrong with Egan?" Malum snarled. "He was fine in class. What did you do to him?"

Orion's golden face filled my vision, and his warm fingers traced over my cheek gently. His chocolate eyes were unfocused as he bit his lower lip like he was concentrating.

His touch was so tender that it made me pause, and I looked up at him with confusion.

Slap.

I yanked my head away from his fingers as he reached forward again after slapping me.

"He's fine," Orion mouthed.

What the fuck? Isn't he supposed to be the kind, gentle one?

I responded automatically, "No, I'm not."

"It's just the battle lust draining away. It was like this for all of us in the beginning. Leave him alone," Zenith said from across the room.

These days, the demons rarely spoke, so the room fell into a stunned silence.

In the quiet, the screams in my head became a roar.

Voices shouted.

Shrieked.

Scoured the inside of my mind.

"Just breathe," Orion mouthed with concern, his words not matching the fact that he'd just slapped me.

I grunted and scrambled away, but he followed me across the room. "Please," I mouthed to no one in particular. I didn't even know what I was asking for.

Orion raked his hands through his white-blond hair, but he stopped moving closer.

Horace sighed heavily. "I need a fucking drink."

"He needs to shower," John said as he grabbed my shoulder and dragged me into the bathroom before Orion could slap me again.

Running water. Cold tile beneath my feet. John's boyish features were tight with tension. The screams wouldn't stop.

"Strip," John ordered.

I stared up at him blankly as I sucked on my pipe. There was definitely darkness glittering around him.

Long fingers tugged off my gore-crusted shirt.

He reached for my waistband.

"What the fuck?" I bellowed as I yanked away from him and stumbled under the cold spray.

The icy water distracted me from my own thoughts and pulled me back to reality.

"I was helping you." John's features hardened, and he fisted his knuckles like he was battling rage.

"Thanks," I said as I pulled the curtain closed and shut him out. Mr. Hyde had been in a fucking mood for a while.

His voice was quiet but filled with menace. "Fuck you, Aran."

"Fuck you, John," I quipped back and held my hand over the curtain to flip him off.

He growled like an animal and snarled, "See if I ever help your sorry ass ever again."

"Good," I snapped, silently begging him to leave the bathroom so I could pull off my disgusting pants and take a proper shower.

"Good."

The door slammed shut and signaled his exit.

I wasn't worried about our friendship. When he was in one of his moods, he was always a miserable bastard. But then the lightness came back, and it was like it had never happened.

I barely tugged off the disgusting garments and turned the shower to the coldest setting before I collapsed onto my hands and knees.

Back in agony.

Ears burdened with phantom shouts.

My thoughts were killing me.

How can a person live like this? How could anyone survive?

So many pain signals were overwhelming me that my stomach cramped, and I vomited bile onto the tile floor.

But I kept my pipe clenched between my teeth. The last lifeline I had to any sort of normalcy.

Horse stood on the top edge of the stall and looked down at me with concern.

The tile floor reminded me of Sadie, and crushing sadness washed over me. I just wanted to hold my best friend and cry.

Instead, I was gagging on all fours.

I stayed under the chilled spray, limbs locked in paralysis, unable to do anything other than *feel*.

Hours later, I crawled out.

With blue lips, chattering teeth, and shaking hands, I toweled off and pulled on the clean clothes I always kept in the bathroom.

When I walked into the room, music was playing from an enchanted stone, and the men were dancing around while drinking from crystal liquor bottles.

"Feel better, man?" Horace asked and threw his arm over my shoulder. He pushed a bottle against my lips and tipped it back before I could protest.

The foreign liquid tasted like salt and death.

"Demon brew," Horace explained as he tipped it back so I was forced to swallow more. "Lothaire got us the good stuff."

"Why?" I asked as I wiped the offending substance off my lips.

Horace tsked like he was disappointed. "Don't tell me you forgot? It's the visitors' ball this weekend. So we get to dance all night and get fucked up."

I pulled the pretty bottle out of his hands and chugged it.

"You should slow down," John said as he appeared to materialize from nowhere.

I finished half the bottle with a loud burp. "When's Dr. Jekyll coming back? I miss him. He was nice."

If John was mad at me for shoving him away in the shower now, he was furious. He *was* violence incarnate.

"Never if you act so ungrateful."

"Well, that sucks," I said honestly as I took another swig.

He flipped me off and resumed partying.

The demon brew tasted like pain and suffering but was flooding me with a heady warmth.

Everything spun, and my limbs were weightless.

Horace and I lounged back and watched as the three kings danced together in the corner.

Well, Orion was dancing.

Malum stood still as a statue and drank the demon brew, while Scorpius leaned against the wall and laughed at something Orion was whispering to him.

I took a long drag of my pipe and positioned myself so I was upside down on my bed. My favorite position.

I tried to take another big sip and choked aggressively.

Horace laughed as I sputtered all over myself, and he took another drink from his crystal bottle.

"I didn't know you could drink anything other than blood," I said conversationally as I waved my pipe around in a pretty pattern.

Why was I so good at small talk?

Sun god, I was amazing.

I chose not to question where the random burst of self-confidence came from. I loved that for me.

"Demon brew is the exception. That's why Lothaire got it for us. Uncle didn't want me to feel left out." Horace grunted as he drank.

The room spun delightfully.

"You've got a fucked-up family."

"You have no idea. How about you? Any nice momma and papa coming to visit for visitors' weekend?"

I let my head fall lower until I was half-dangling off the bed and the room shifted, and it felt like I was walking on the ceiling.

"Let's just say, if my mother's ghost made an appearance, I'd be more afraid of it than an ungodly."

Horace's voice darkened until it had a razor's edge. "Women suck."

I paused with my pipe dangling from my fingers in front of my lips, and I whispered, "Not all women."

"All fucking women. No exceptions." Horace's words were slightly lisped, like his fangs had descended.

I shivered.

Suddenly, the world didn't spin with euphoria. It tilted and shuddered, darkness overwhelming everything and sucking me dry.

Pulling me under.

Heart rate increasing, I gasped desperately and clawed at my throat. There wasn't enough air in this blasted fucking realm.

I was drowning.

Long legs blocked my view of the room. "You've been smoking nonstop for hours." Malum's voice was barely discernible over the thumping music.

"Amazing observation skills." I arched my brow patronizingly and continued to lie upside down as I pretended I wasn't asphyxiating on nothing but my thoughts.

"Fuck you."

"Fuck you."

Like I said, I was a master at small talk.

"Let's finish getting ready!" Horace shouted suddenly and pulled us both off the bed.

A few minutes later, I found myself lining Orion's stunning eyes with kohl. All the men were putting on makeup, but they were impressed with my steady hand, so I was now applying it for everyone.

"How are you doing?" I whispered to the fae who'd seemed more stressed than usual.

Music thumped loudly.

He mouthed, "Not well."

"Why?"

"Because you have a girlfriend."

I chuckled and responded without thinking. "No, I don't. That was a joke."

Abruptly, chocolate eyes smoldered. I burned alive.

CHAPTER 36
THE DEVIL RAVES

Field training: Day 48, hour 17

"Boom," I sang and mimed throwing a grenade into the air as the lyrics crooned about cigarettes and explosives.

You might as well glamorize violence.

It's all about the aesthetic, I chuckled to myself dreamily.

Because if it wasn't a vibe, then it was just torture. So I rocked my shoulders back and forth and closed my black-lined eyes.

I pretended:

War was easy, killing was fun, the voices in my head screamed encouragements, assassins were chill, Aran was a man, and Arabella had never existed.

Sari passed the bottle of demon brew back to me, and I took a swig as I shook my hips against hers in rhythm to the music.

We rocked together.

The beat coursing through me, my head flung back, my electric-blue hair glowed under the blue lights and reflected in the windows.

Pipe hanging from my lips, I lost myself in the darkness.

The windows of the great hall were covered in enchanted mirrors, and black light cast the arched ceiling in shadows. A sparkling dance floor surrounded the white tree that had tinsel and candles hanging from its branches.

It was pretty.

I tipped my throat back and guzzled the demon brew.

So fucking pretty.

At the high dais where we took our meals, a DJ booth was set up, and Lyla played a mix of ethereal and modern music.

Her runes glowed bright. Green hair hanging low, eyes wide, she was completely still as she channeled her power into song.

Witches were rumored to possess a sixth sense that allowed them to experience music differently.

It wasn't a rumor.

The sounds pounding through the room had every student, assassin, royal, and commoner gyrating in a frenzied mass. A few family members, but mostly lovers, had visited for family weekend, and everyone was on the dance floor.

The room reeked of sweat and sex.

Demon brew, pills, and enchanted pipes were passed through the room like candy. Kisses were exchanged, dresses drawn aside, and zippers unzipped.

There was one constant throughout the realms—the greater the power, the better the party.

Something about strength, intelligence, and energy inspired people to get fucked up.

If you were at the top, then you saw the playing field. You understood the corruption. The desolation and bullshit.

The irony of it all.

And no one was more powerful than the people in this

room. We were a mass of greedy bodies unapologetically taking their pleasure.

When sweaty fingers passed me a glowing green cigarette, I greedily stuck it into the side of my mouth and sucked deep.

Two pipes hanging between my lips, demon brew coalescing through my veins, the voices had quieted down to a manageable level.

I was just a normal girl dancing.

Sari pulled her friend Tara closer, and the three of us ground to the music.

I grabbed their hips with each hand and pulled them against me as we rocked back and forth.

Their hair glimmered in stunning curls, and their skin glowed with an otherworldly shimmer. Rosewater wafted off Sari, and warm vanilla surrounded Tara.

Their unnaturally pretty eyes were vibrant in the dark, and their heritage was written when they licked their lips.

The ends of their tongues slightly forked.

They were demons but not just any kind. They were the most loved and coveted creatures in all the realms.

Two succubi.

Commoner and royal men had been pawing all over them as they struggled to free themselves from the unwanted advances. So I'd come in and grabbed them.

Now there was a wide berth around us.

No one messed with the assassin recruits.

It also might have been the stains that covered my pale skin under the black light; I was covered in blood.

No amount of cold showers could change the reality— death clung to me.

Don't think about it.

I grabbed the crystal bottle from Sari, tipped it between

the two pipes at the corners of my mouth, and concentrated on the music.

"Baby, lightning is our fuse,
Cigarettes and smoke,
Nothing left to lose,
Arsenic on tongues,
Suffering's our muse."

Lyla was my musical hero.

Maybe it was the runes that appeared to be carved into her skin, or maybe it was the distant look in her eyes. But my gut told me the witch fucking got it.

She understood the pain.

Tara tipped her head back and licked her forked tongue slowly along my jaw. Vanilla drowned my senses, and my skin came alive.

My back burned unmercifully.

I laughed at the pain.

"What do you say, Aran?" Sari turned around so she was facing me, her black minidress leaving her exquisite tanned skin exposed as she rode my thigh.

I exhaled a cloud of blue-green smoke and traced my fingers over her sparkle-covered cheeks.

Everything would be way fucking easier if I was into women. They weren't the problem. *Most times; RIP Mother.*

But I wasn't.

"I'm not the one for either of you," I said honestly.

I wasn't meant for anyone but myself. Just showing up every day and fighting was too much for me.

Still, my heart plummeted as I waited for their response. They were my only female friends at this fucking place, and their cheery chatter made meals tolerable.

"You're one of the good guys, Aran," Sari said as she

patted my cheek, and Tara nodded. Then we resumed dancing like nothing had happened.

Lightness flooded through me.

Thank you, sun god.

I tipped my head back into the darkness and resumed trying to lose myself, desperate for the silence of a buzz.

Warm hands clasped around my upper arm, and suddenly I was pulled away from Sari and Tara.

Blue lights danced, and the music crooned.

Orion's face hovered a few inches above mine. His breath mingled with mine. Decadent musk wafted off him.

Before I could ask what he was doing, the quiet king turned me around and dug his fingers into my hips. His front pressed against my back.

I forgot how to breathe.

My back burned.

Orion dug his fingers into my hip bones, and he pressed his hard erection against my butt. Then he swayed to the music.

I relaxed back into his arms.

Fingers trailed upward across my chest and grabbed my jaw firmly. Warm breath tickled my cheeks as the fae leaned forward and just breathed against me.

We rocked.

The cocktail of drugs in my system allowed me to ignore the excruciating pain radiating from my wound.

Lyrics repeated as they pounded through the enchanted speaker, and I mouthed them as I squeezed my eyes shut.

Orion gripped me like he was holding on for dear life.

His lyrical voice was decadent as he whispered against my ear, "I'm going to ruin you, pretty boy."

I shivered with anticipation.

He spoke like he was obsessed. Just like me.

Something pricked my awareness, and I opened my eyes to find there was an open space in front of us on the dance floor.

Malum and Scorpius stood still as statues. Silver eyes stared like they were unable to look away. Scorpius has his head tilted toward us like he was listening to each of our raspy breaths.

I trembled in Orion's arms, expecting him to see his men and shove me away.

Warmth trailed across my cheek.

Teeth nipped at the sensitive skin between my neck and collarbone. Then cold air was blown. A tongue lapped gently.

My knees buckled.

Orion's arms were the only things keeping me upright.

His breath was hot as he whispered, "I want to dominate you until you forget what it's like to not be mine."

I whimpered.

"There's something about you that drives me crazy." The lyrical words were like an intoxicating fae wine. "How are you so gorgeous?"

His voice was the most potent drug in all the realms.

I was an addict.

Suddenly, fingers tangled in my curls, yanked my head back at a harsh angle, and plucked the pipes out of my mouth.

Bee-stung lips slammed against mine and ravaged.

Plundered.

Consumed me whole.

The kiss tasted like whiskey, salt, chocolate, and smoke.

It tasted like freedom.

I groaned with pleasure, and Orion swallowed the sound into his mouth as his tongue brought me to my knees.

"Break for me," he ordered as he kissed.

I'd mastered rolling a pipe against my tongue at just the right angle to get the sweetest high, and I devoured him back with skill.

He moaned. "This mouth."

Unimaginable pain throbbed from the enchanted slur, and it reminded me of the lightning in the halls.

My nerves sizzled.

I didn't care.

Death himself couldn't pull me away from this kiss.

Suddenly, when I didn't think it could get any more intense, Orion wrapped his fingers around my throat and tightened.

His lyrical voice was honey in my ears. "I've talked to the men, and I've let them know that I'm claiming you. You're going to be my little toy."

There was nothing to say to that.

Yep. One hundred percent. I would be his toy.

Gladly.

Whatever he wanted so he'd keep kissing me like this.

Our bodies rocked against each other in the darkness, and we lost ourselves. The music wrapped around us, and I swore it matched the intensity of our kiss. The beat of his heart against my back.

The next time I opened my eyes, Malum and Scorpius were still standing in the same place.

Intensity radiated off them. They wanted to ruin us.

I looked around and sighed at the endless pleasure, streaked with violent pain, that Orion was bestowing on my senses.

As I took in the partygoers gyrating, something seemed off.

It took me a moment.

Then I realized I couldn't see the girls anywhere, and the girls had said they were going to dance together all night.

It took all my strength to pull away from Orion's divine embrace.

I searched the room. "Did you see where Sari and Tara went?" I shouted over the music.

Orion's eyes widened as he mouthed, "They left the hall with Horace."

The weight in my stomach intensified, and I struggled to breathe.

I didn't pause to think.

I ran.

CHAPTER 37
MEETING YOUR DESTINY

Field training: Day 49, hour 1

There were moments in life you chose to let define you.

Then there were disasters you had no choice over.

They shattered you. Cut you. Killed you. Rendered you speechless and brought you to your knees.

I thought I'd experienced disasters. After all, how could one break when they were already broken?

My hubris had led me to believe I was untouchably damaged.

It was the catalyst for my downfall.

Arms pumping, lungs heaving, world spinning and writhing in shadows from the cocktail of drugs in my blood, I ran.

Lightning cracked, and the air tasted like desperation. Maybe that was my imagination? Or maybe that was just reality.

I'd checked the entire hall and found no sign of Tara, Sari, or Horace. I had no idea where they could be.

No. You know where they are.

That was the problem with having an analytical brain;

your subconscious put the pieces together before you consciously could accept what was happening.

I ran before I'd decided to run.

It felt like a slow eternity, the halls bustling with happy partygoers and families embracing, as I raced toward the room.

"Horace?" I shouted with desperate lungs.

They'd only been gone for a few minutes. I was probably being dramatic. The drugs were making me overreact.

That was what I told myself.

Flinging myself through the door, I stumbled into the warm firelit room where I spent my nights.

No. No. No.

The world spun faster, reality collapsing around me in a kaleidoscope of desperation.

I stumbled to my knees and patted Tara's cheeks.

She was ice-cold.

Lying on the rug, half-naked, with her pretty dress ripped to pieces, eyes wide open, soft lips parted, she was covered in blood. Strips of skin were hanging off her savaged neck.

The fire screamed.

Minutes ago I'd been laughing and dancing with her as we shared a bottle.

But somehow.

She was dead.

That was the unfortunate thing about training to be an assassin. You knew exactly when the fight had left a body, when they'd passed the point of no return and there was nothing left inside.

Tara's sightless eyes stared up at me. *Why didn't you save me?* they reflected.

Everything collapsed.

The ceiling was the floor, and the only sound was an endless ringing. The air was molasses.

Time didn't exist as I crawled toward the four-poster bed.

Tears sparkled in Sari's eyes and slipped down her cheeks. Her head was turned, arm hanging over the side of the bed as Horace knelt atop her and sucked viciously on her neck.

"Horace, stop!" I half yelled, half whispered as I scrambled up drunkenly and slammed my fist against his back.

He kept drinking.

Maybe it was the demon brew?

Maybe he just didn't give a fuck?

But he didn't stop.

Sari cried harder as her blood pooled beneath her on the emerald bedding, her eyes never leaving Tara's empty ones.

"Stop!" I screamed as I pulled at Horace, slapping him and pummeling him with my fists.

Horace ripped his bloody lips off her neck and mumbled, "Go away, Aran. I'm hungry. I'll dance with you later." Sari's lips parted with a choking sob. She was too weak to do anything other than lie there and take it.

He thinks I want to dance with him?

The world spun faster.

My voice sounded like it belonged to someone else. "She's dying, and you killed Tara. I need to take her to Lyla." I tugged at his hardened shoulders as I tried to dislodge him.

Horace grunted and laughed. "She tastes fucking delicious, and I lost too much blood in the last battle. I need this." His voice tightened with anger, and he easily shoved back at me with his vampyre strength. "Go back to the dance, Aran."

I sprawled on the floor.

Horace leaned forward and attached his teeth to Sari's bloody neck.

My chest hurt from the rapid pounding in my chest, vision blurring as I struggled to breathe.

Inhale. Exhale.

It didn't work. I couldn't breathe.

Horace was my friend. He was the man who'd thrown his arms around me after battle. We'd fought as a unit. Long runs, hours in the sea, endless fights against the ungodly. Horace was always there.

Horace was my friend.

But so were Tara and Sari.

The voices in the fire screeched louder.

My teeth chattered as terror raced through me. It was an icy chill that was colder than any blizzard.

Sari made a heartbreaking mewling sound.

Hands trembling, I brought my knuckles to my teeth and bit down to try to calm the endless shaking.

I hyperventilated because I knew what I had to do.

My monster whimpered.

Mother used to love an ancient fae poem with the line, *The realms don't end with a bang but a whimper.*

Suddenly, I understood how right it was.

I'd thought the hardest thing I'd ever have to do was rip my mother's heart from her sternum and consume it.

But when I'd done it, my monster had filled me with unfathomable rage that made the act easy.

Because it was what I'd *wanted* to do.

Now my monster hid inside its cage and bleated sadly. Softly, like gentle snowfall, it curled into a ball and trembled.

Because my monster wasn't a monster.

I'd categorized it as an *other* after Sadie had told me about the cold voice in her head.

It was special to hear a voice that was not your own.

After all, the blame couldn't be *yours* if there was an *it* inside you that controlled you.

We were just two best friends hearing voices and bonding over our unwellness. A friendship so warm and comforting that I could never have dreamed it up.

But Sadie's voice was that of a goddess, and mine was a lie. Because the best lies are always closest to the truth.

And my monster was a *monster*, but it was also always mine.

My monster.

The screaming inside my skull was myself. The horrible part of me that dreamed of death and destruction. A reality I could never run from.

My monster was my rage.

It was just anger. Compartmentalization. Dissociation. From myself.

And now I wasn't angry. I was drunk off Orion's kiss, and there wasn't any strength coursing through my veins.

No rage would overwhelm me so viciously that it could shield me from what I needed to do. What I didn't want to do.

But I was going to do it anyway.

Because it was easy to kill your mother when you hated her with every cell in your abused body.

It was difficult to kill ungodly who had done nothing to you.

It was hard to kill nameless people.

But it felt impossible to kill a friend.

"P-P-P-please s-s-stop!" I yelled at Horace, teeth chattering viciously as I trembled with horror.

He didn't stop.

Sari's skin continued to lose its healthy glow. Her tears fell slowly as she stared at Tara's corpse like she wanted her friend to be the last thing she remembered.

She didn't even bother to fight, to plead, or to look hopeful.

After all, she was just a student, and Horace was a recruit in the fabled assassin program. She was just another warm body. A woman.

Sari knew Horace was becoming one of my closer friends.

I walked up to Horace and laid my arms across his broad shoulders. Up close, the sound of his lips sucking was reminiscent of retching.

For a second, I imagined I could see a black flame flickering in his chest. A damned soul.

"P-P-Please s-s-stop," I whispered to the man I'd fought beside for hours. The one who had grinned easily and defended me when John and Malum lost their shit.

The awful sounds continued.

He didn't stop.

I closed my eyes.

Ice froze my limbs until my fingertips burned.

And a single tear trailed down my cheek as the hardest thing I'd ever done was easily accomplished.

It was too easy.

It felt *right*.

The gurgling noise intensified.

I pulled Horace back until he lay against my chest as I embraced him. Hugged him tight to me as he turned his handsome face toward mine, yellow eyes glowing.

"Why?" Horace asked with a furrow between his brows.

Because he didn't deserve to live.

I whispered back, "Because she's my friend."

The razor-sharp blade jutted out from his chest cavity, blood spilling from his punctured heart as Sari lay beneath him weakly.

Slowly Sari turned her head and stared at me like she'd never seen me before.

"Why?" Horace asked again, unable to comprehend my reasoning. Betrayal and horror were painted all over his face as he trembled beneath my justice.

You killed Tara.

On frozen lips, I said, "Because no one ever saved me."

Memories of Mother's heatless flames flashed through my mind like a symphony of horrors. Writhing and pleading with the guards. Sneaking glances at my tutors, maids, the half warriors, desperate for someone to step in and save me.

"Why?" He asked a final time.

I breathed out frost, and it danced across Horace's colorless skin. "Because dead men can't kill women."

With that final truth, I pulled the electric-blue ice dagger out of his back and once again slammed it through bone and muscle.

I hated killing with knives because it was so personal.

But this was intimate. Heinous. *Soul-crushing.*

My teeth chattered, my arms cradling Horace as he slumped lower with a confused expression.

Vampyres were powerful and extremely hard to kill. And unlike when I'd stabbed the two shifters in the beast realm, Horace didn't shatter into a million pieces and dissolve like dust.

He didn't crumple in on himself like Mother.

He just lay against me, helpless to do anything but die.

The oddly shaped crystal dagger plunging in and out of

his chest was something neither of us understood.

Finally, when Horace had taken his last ragged breath, I stumbled off the bed and gently laid him down beside Tara.

The voices in the flames screamed at me.

The trembling intensified.

But I knew in my bones, he deserved it. And I'd do it again.

"Sh-Sh-Shut u-up." I whirled toward the fireplace with the dagger clenched between my fingers, and the movement sent twin spikes of pain burning down my spine.

The flames fell silent.

The red-and-yellow blaze extinguished to burning embers, like the flames were cowering before me.

You should cower.

I showed them my teeth.

In the silence, I whimpered. My chilled fingers twitched, and the dagger dropped to the floor and shattered into nothing.

The pain in my back tripled, and I screamed silently.

Stumbling, floor and ceiling swapping places, I bent over Sari and gathered her up into my arms.

She was tall with an impressively defined musculature, and I grunted as I staggered under her weight.

I pressed my hand over her bloody neck to staunch the flow, and she whimpered.

But before I could leave the room, another person entered.

I froze.

It was over.

Dark eyes watched me wearily, then widened when they saw the bed. "What did you do to Horace? What the fuck, Aran! Why?"

John ran to the vampyre's side and looked him up and

down, then looked back at my bloodstained arms.

"I n-n-eed to s-s-ave her." I nodded my chin toward Sari in my arms and silently pleaded with him to understand.

My teeth were chattering too aggressively for me to explain, and there wasn't time.

The moment stretched.

Finally, John's shoulders slumped, and he shook his head. "Fine, Aran, get her help and do what you need to do. I'll stay here and deal with his body."

I was still frozen with shock.

John shook his head. "Go! I told you you're my best friend. I'll deal with the body. Hurry!"

Drunk on demon brew, high on enchanted smoke, and shaking from the adrenaline of murdering my friend, I stumbled down the hall with Sari in my arms.

Staggering under the weight of my deeds, I slammed into the wall and barely pushed myself off in time.

Lightning streaked, and my teeth hurt from the proximity to the voltage.

Sari whimpered.

I didn't know how I reached the hall's door. Didn't remember falling in front of Lyla. Pushing Sari's limp body at her as I collapsed on the dance floor.

I didn't remember the witch kneeling. Runes glowing. Healing magic reknitting Sari's savaged throat.

But I would remember the music.

As I lay on the sticky dance floor, colors and shadows flashing, lyrics vibrated through me.

"Life doesn't end in a bang,
It dissolves in whimpers,
All the weak shall hang,
As the sun god simpers."

Maybe it was a coincidence; maybe Lyla pulled the

lyrics from the realm as she healed a dying girl.

Maybe it was all just one endless, horrible, cosmic joke.

A never-ending irony.

The dance floor bounced beneath me, dried alcohol clinging to my hair, as I breathed in discarded cigarettes and sweat.

Everyone ignored me.

Time continued its slovenly march forward.

Lifting my bloody hands to the ceiling, I smiled to myself. Flexed my fingertips as the realm spun beneath me and everything was a blur of pretty colors.

My cheeks hurt as chaotic chuckles burst from my frozen lips. Tears dripped like glaciers across my skin.

I waved my shaking hands slowly.

In the crush of bodies, an enchanted cigarette fell, and my hand cramped as I picked it up.

Fingers trembling violently, I brought the shaking stick between my lips.

I inhaled smoke and relaxed as the realm trembled. The drug worked quickly.

Shadows came alive, and little balls of smoke flickered where the people danced above.

It was beautiful.

The cigarette bobbed as a sob wrenched from my chest, and the tears poured faster.

Orion had kissed Aran, not Arabella.

It was all a lie.

And I was the liar.

My hands spasmed as I held them up. I no longer needed the black light to see the blood. I didn't need anything to show me what I knew was already there.

The truth was glaring.

No one ever saved you for a reason.

I could have fought to incapacitate Horace. I could have found a way to wrench him off Sari without killing him.

But I didn't want to, so I hadn't.

I'd murdered him.

"You take after your mother in looks and temperament," my tutor had said as he beat me with his belt because I'd stabbed him in the eye with a pen. He had shoved me off my chair and spat at me for getting an answer wrong.

I was eight.

"You're just like her," a fae maid had gasped with horror because I'd slapped her. She'd touched me without permission after one of Mother's beatings. I'd broken her nose.

I was eleven.

"You're worse than she is. You're a cruel bitch that deserves to die," Shane had shouted at me across the gladiator sands. Under my mother's flames, I'd revealed the half warriors were helping me learn to fight. She'd told me to whip them as punishment, and I had. For hours.

I was fourteen.

Mother was known by many names: the mad queen, the executioner, the monster of the fae.

And I was just like her.

Mad. An executioner. A monster.

I inhaled smoke and exhaled a watery sob as I spasmed on a dirty dance floor under a never-ending eclipse.

My monster whimpered.

I cried harder because I was still dissociating.

There is no monster.

I was the monster.

I was her.

There was no more hiding from it—I was the next mad queen of the fae.

And I'd already ascended.

CHAPTER 38

BLOOD IS THINNER THAN WATER

Field training: Day 50, hour 1

In the moment of reckoning, I thought I would be dramatic. Yelling. Screaming. Shouting as I fought vehemently for myself.

But the world wasn't made of shades of red. It was all gray.

And I knew what I'd done.

Quiet was the guilt, and heavy was the soul. Or something poetic and dramatic like that.

Horace's blood caked my arms from knuckle to elbow. I stared silently as Lothaire threw a desk across the room and broke a chair.

"You murdered my nephew!" he bellowed as a chair was thrown through the stained-glass windows. Rainbow shards sprinkled around us like broken raindrops.

"Let him explain!" John yelled as he struggled against the chains Lothaire had wrapped around him.

Lyla had told Lothaire I was covered in blood, lying on the dance floor (should have seen that coming), and then he'd found John trying to get rid of Horace's body.

It wasn't hard to put the pieces together.

"Why would you do this?" Malum radiated death, his upper lip curled as he stared down at me with disgust.

I brought the enchanted cigarette to my lips and took a long draw as I donned a mask of indifference.

The slight tremor in my fingertips was my only tell.

Lothaire kicked another chair into the wall, and bricks cracked. The vampyre leader had dragged me by my short hair from the dance, into his classroom.

The kings, John, and the demons had followed.

Orion stared at me with wide eyes like he'd never seen me before. Probably because he hadn't.

The air cackled with malice as seven men stared at me with distrust.

The cocktail of drugs coursing through my veins kept me standing; it softened the rough edges of my panic.

The room spinning under my feet, my vision hazy, I took another long drag of my cigarette. I rubbed at my eyes tiredly, and sticky copper clung to my lids.

Fuck, I'd just coated my face in Horace's blood.

Marking myself with the blood of my kill. How grotesque.

Inhale.

Pain lanced across my back, and I shuddered from the sudden jolt of agony.

His long braid flying, Lothaire turned toward me and advanced across the room like a beast stalking its kill. "How could you?"

I shrugged, knowing it would send him over the edge.

That was the problem with being able to analyze situations: I knew there was no scenario where I walked away from this.

Lothaire had vengeance to dole out.

I had hatred for myself.

It was clear where this was going.

"You INSOLENT, SPOILED BRAT!" Lothaire flung me across the room like I was a chair.

How nice it is to fly. The inappropriate thought made my lips twitch with a smile.

The wall shook behind me as my bones cracked and shattered.

I slumped to the floor, tangled in broken chairs and glass, and put the cigarette between my lips. I'd managed to hold on to it. A win.

Broken shards bit my skin as I lay still.

In all the stories of the realms, people always fought to their dying breath. They raged and screamed against one another as they went kicking and screaming into the valley of the sun god.

Suddenly, it all seemed like a massive lie. A conspiracy to keep us flailing like dying spiders in test tubes.

I was tired.

So fucking tired.

It wasn't that I wanted to die, because I didn't want *anything*; instead, it was the complete absence of motivation.

Is it so wrong to just not care?

Everyone in the realms was always fighting for something: realm pride, honor, queens, and the gods.

But there was no greatness in suffering. The drugs just made it easier to accept my truth.

Lothaire stalked forward, grabbed me by the arm, and flung me across the room to the other side.

Nice. Maybe he'd put me through the window next.

Lothaire raged.

John yelled something.

The kings scowled.

Two demons watched warily.

And I just existed, a blip in space, less than a millisecond in the grand scheme of time.

Lothaire stopped throwing me and slammed his knuckles into my stomach.

Doubling over, I barely held the stick between my fingers as I gagged from the unimaginable power in Lothaire's fist.

On my hands and knees, covered in glass cuts, I bowed before my guilt.

When Lothaire realized I wasn't going to fight back, he grabbed me by the neck and held me off the ground. My feet dangled.

"YOU WILL EXPLAIN YOURSELF!"

His singular eye flickered.

"He killed Tara. He was killing Sari." My voice was too quiet in the silent room.

Lothaire's expression was murderous. "So what? He was a recruit. He was your fellow soldier, and they were worthless. Yet you KILLED HIM?" His warm spit sprayed across my face. "It was not your punishment to dole out."

Judge, jury, and executioner. Just like your mother.

"I know."

Lothaire's hand tightened around my spine like he was debating cracking it. "Yet you still did it? You murdered him."

"I did."

His single eye narrowed, and suddenly he dropped me to the ground.

Backing away, he looked over at John. "You did this together. This was a plan to exterminate him. This was premeditated."

"No, that's not it!" I yelled desperately.

Lothaire shook his head like he'd come to a decision.

"You're not powerful enough on your own to do this. And I know John has resented Horace's attitude from the beginning."

I staggered toward him with my hands raised. "No, that's not it. You need to liste—"

Lothaire cut me off. "I missed the signs. You both will be exterminated."

"What are you talking about?" I snarled, a small scream of anger ringing through my mind. "Listen to me, John was not in on it! He just stumbled into the room after I did it!"

Lothaire looked at the two of us. "You will all be sent into the Black Ocean. For eternity." Power expanded around him, and his fangs descended.

John hunched defeatedly like he was resigned to his fate.

Why were men so fucking irrational?

He can't understand your motivation, so he made the only analytical leap he can make.

The shaking in my fingers became an avalanche as I pushed the stick between my lips and inhaled.

"No," I said as tremors rocked through me.

Glittering black expanded around John.

Violence was in the air.

"NO!" I screamed as I picked up a broken leg of the chair and slammed it to the ground to get his attention.

Lothaire slowly turned around.

"It was all me! I can prove why I did it!"

His singular eye rolled, jagged scar pulling tighter as he scowled at me with disbelief.

"What reason could *you* possibly have? What power could a fae possess to defeat *my* nephew? Don't lie to me."

There was only one thing to do.

I reached down to my finger and pulled off the invisible ring that was enchanted to disguise me as a boy.

Dropped it to the floor.

Tingles prickled like they always did when I transformed.

In the thousands of broken glass shards, electric-blue hair hung down to my waist, eyelashes lengthened, and features softened. The illusion of broad shoulders narrowed to a lithe feminine figure.

My clothes hung loose off my frame.

Cigarette hanging from my pouty lips, I rolled my eyes at the shocked faces in the room.

I imitated Scorpius and sneered at Lothaire, "I killed him because he kills women."

My voice was lyrical and light.

It was horrible.

Lothaire took a step backward like I'd punched him in the chest. His mouth dropped open.

"Who the fuck are you?" Malum's eyes were wide, and he staggered back like he'd been struck.

Orion's mouth was open in an *O*, and he fell to his knees.

When Scorpius whispered in his ear, Malum spat, "Aran is a fucking girl. He's been a girl in disguise this entire time."

Unseeing milky-white eyes widened, and Scorpius turned around and punched the wall. Over and over. He slammed his knuckles into the bricks.

Flames spread around Malum.

At that moment, the door burst open, and the half warriors rushed into the room. "You called for us, Lothaire?" Demetre asked.

Their entrance was proof that life could *always* get worse.

"Welcome to the party," I drawled sarcastically.

Before I could flinch, Shane had thrown himself across

the room and slammed me against the wall with his forearm against my throat.

Orion yelled, "Don't touch her!"

Chaos erupted.

Malum moved quicker than I could blink, and his flaming hand wrapped around Shane's throat.

Demetre pressed a sword into his side. Scorpius held a shard of glass against his thigh.

Noah was reaching for Scorpius, but Orion had his arm around him.

The kings and half warriors were a tangled web behind me and Shane.

Even though John was chained, he stared at me with his nostrils flared. The darkness glittered and expanded around him.

Lothaire and the demons stood speechless beside him.

"If it isn't the treacherous fucking cunt I've been searching for," Shane spat as he glared down at me. His eyes widened as he took in my clothes, then he looked around the room.

His green eyes sparked as he put it together.

Aran was Arabella.

"Aw, I thought we were friends?" I pouted dramatically and arched my brow just like Mother always had.

Shane shook with rage, but a smile pulled up the corner of his lips. "Oh, Princess, your days are over."

I smiled back. "Actually, it's Queen. Shouldn't you be bowing?"

He snarled and pressed me harder into the wall. "I'll bow to your funeral pyre after I consume your heart and burn your carcass in the streets."

"Oooh, erotic." I licked my lips while my insides churned at my certain fate. At least the pain would be over.

"ENOUGH!" Lothaire bellowed. "Everyone step the fuck away from one another right now or I will flatten this entire academy."

From the sparks shooting off Lothaire, I believed him.

Slowly, the kings and half warriors stepped back from one another.

Shane didn't release me as his forearm pressed me harder into the wall. I focused on the pretty colors refracted by the broken stained glass instead of the growing urge to cough and choke.

I refused to show him weakness.

"We will bring her to the fae realm and complete the mission," Shane said with a smile.

Abruptly, the three half warriors fell to the floor.

I was released.

Lothaire's arm was outstretched toward them. "No, you will not."

The fucker had snapped his fingers, and they'd fallen unconscious. *How could he do that?*

"What?" I stared up at the vampyre who had ordered the half warriors to find the princess so she could be dealt with.

Why would he stop them?

"That was never the plan," Lothaire said slowly as he stepped forward.

What the fuck was going on?

The vampyre stared down at me sadly and said nothing. Time stretched between us. Memories of him talking with Jinx without me flashed through my mind.

What had they been talking about?

Now he was staring at me with a soft expression like he…cared?

In the space between us, the silent pieces fell together.

Lothaire had knelt to my mother in the sands and looked at her sadly.

For years, I'd watched him stalk beside her through the castle halls. Sometimes I'd imagine he was looking after me with something close to longing on his face.

He was loyal to her.

But he'd bowed to me after I'd murdered her. Stared at me with a strange expression on his face.

Lothaire had frowned when the half warriors and I had insulted Arabella.

It was the way he'd arched his brow like I did.

How I'd thought I recognized something in his face. Something familiar.

How a vampyre's bite was supposed to hurt, but it hadn't when he bit me in the manor.

The fact that vampyres could procreate with fae; it was just taboo.

Now Lothaire spoke slowly, "I promised your mother I'd leave your rearing to her."

No.

I pressed myself against the wall, like if I pushed backward hard enough, I'd lose my corporeal form and escape his proximity.

"But the High Court wants you on the throne, so I needed to find you. The half warriors were always just pawns to bring you to me."

Glass crunched under my cut feet as I scooted sideways across the wall, toward the door.

Lothaire walked with me.

"I would never allow them to take you. I just needed them to bring you to me," Lothaire said softly, his expression darkening. "But now they are a threat to you. They want to hurt you."

Death was written in the tension vibrating through his body. "I know they were the reason she beat you."

What is going on? Mother had *always* beaten me, but she'd never let the bruises show until that fateful day in the gladiator sands.

Lothaire snapped his fingers. "They signed their death warrants that day."

Sparks shot from his hand.

Demetre's, Shane's, and Noah's necks snapped to the side.

"It was always a matter of time," he said dismissively.

Holy sun god.

They were dead.

I inched along the wall, desperate to escape. "But on the sands, you didn't kill me. You didn't kill Sadie with a snap."

Even as I spoke the words, I knew the answer.

I shuddered.

Lothaire rolled his eye like I was being dramatic. "Thousands of years old and I couldn't kill some untrained beasts. Please. I knew they mattered to you."

"B-B-But you fought?"

"I put on a show."

"You let me kill my mother? But you were her consort. H-H-Her lover."

"I did, and I was."

"W-W-Why?"

"You know why."

"But I'm not a vampyre."

"Vampyre traits don't pass to half-breeds."

"You can't be." I inched closer to the door and turned to run through it, but he moved impossibly fast and blocked my path.

"Arabella, I am your father." Lothaire smiled down at me sadly.

I couldn't breathe. "You beat me."

Suddenly, Lothaire trembled like he was falling apart. His eye widened like he realized just *who* he was pleading with.

Aran. The person he'd beaten and thrown objects at.

The child he'd tortured.

Lothaire stumbled, then slammed his head into the wall as hard as he could. He left a gaping hole.

Well, now I knew where I got my anger and hitting my head from.

"I DIDN'T KNOW!" he screamed to no one in particular. "I didn't know," he whispered.

"But you still did it," I said coldly.

"I did." Tears streamed out of his singular eye, and he slumped against the wall. A devastated shell of a man.

His face was sorrowful as he said, "I can't change the past. I can only move forward with you."

"No, we won't be doing anything together."

"We will."

"I won't."

"You have no choice." His voice was a broken crack. "I have to make that right."

I shook my head. "Just leave me alone."

"I can't. Thousands are searching for you throughout the realms. Unless you want to be taken to the fae realm and slaughtered for your throne, you have to listen to me."

"I'd rather die."

"I can't allow it, not after what I've—" He trailed off.

"What, don't feel so big and mighty anymore now that you're not throwing a boulder at your *child*? Weird."

"Please." Lothaire's voice cracked, like he was only a man and not a monster.

I scoffed at his ignorance. "So what's your plan? Kidnap me? Newsflash, there's nowhere in the realm I can hide."

Lothaire's jaw jumped, and he bunched his hands into fists. "There is no *place* you can hide, but there are *people* you can hide behind."

I took a shaky step back and brought my cigarette to my lips.

Before I could inhale, a harsh hand slapped the stick to the ground. "My child will not smoke."

It was a testament to how unwell I was that this was the statement that finally filled me with rage.

He thought he could just tell me what to do after he was going to *kill* me?

Oh fuck.

My voice was barely a whisper. "Were you really related to Horace?"

Lothaire's face pinched with grief. "Yes, you foolish child. He was your cousin."

"I still would have done it," I gasped out as I struggled to swallow the bile down my throat.

Would you have? I hoped so.

"We will deal with that later. Right now, we need to hide you so you can't be found until you are ready to take your throne." He spoke softly like he was talking to a wild animal.

"Fucking never," I spat.

"Language!" Lothaire scolded as he fluctuated between distraught and rageful.

Slightly relatable.

Lothaire continued like the world wasn't falling to shambles around me. "In the black market realm, there are enchanted tattoos that bind people together. They cannot die unless the other is killed. It is a dark enchantment that is more powerful than the fae succession magic."

I took another step away as the implications tasted like ash on my tongue. "No."

"Even eating your heart won't kill you, if the other tattooed person is alive."

"No." I became hyperaware of the kings standing in the room. The men who were watching what was unfolding with sick fascination.

Lothaire kept speaking, like he'd spent hours thinking about this. Planning for this.

"Family members can't bind with each other. But that is why I've chosen three of the strongest men in all the realms for this task. Trained them for it. They agreed to serve the High Court and have accepted the mark."

John had said the kings had a secret task that bonded them together.

My eyes flashed down to Malum's waist, where I knew his shirt covered the tattoo on his hip bone.

The one the kings all shared.

A snake in an infinity symbol, eating its tail.

Suddenly, I remembered where I'd seen it. An ancient book in the fae libraries about masters and slaves.

So caught up in the horrible revelations, I didn't notice the men walking closer to Lothaire.

He grabbed my wrist, and we realm jumped.

CHAPTER 39
THE DEVILS ARE HERE

Field training: Day 50, hour 4

"No, let me fucking go!" I screamed and bucked against Lothaire's hands that slammed me into a chair.

"Language!" Lothaire scolded as he locked silver cuffs around my wrists and legs and chained me to the chair.

"Language? Are you motherfucking shit balls serious? You're correcting my language as you're *kidnapping me, you crazy motherfucker*?"

Lothaire's voice was somehow both dejected and powerful. "You will *not* disrespect me with such language!"

Whipping my head around, I tried not to look at the psychopath that was apparently my dad, and I took in my surroundings.

I was strapped to a leather chair in a dark room that had all types of artwork covering the walls.

The kings stood silently behind Lothaire and said nothing as they stared at me with expressions of horror.

Remember when you said I was just a hole? Yeah, I didn't forget.

It wasn't hard to put together what was happening.

Lothaire had taken the four of us to a new realm and

strapped me into a chair. Art covered the walls, and he'd just talked about dark tattoos that bound people.

The kings stood like statues.

"Really? You're going to bind me to these fuckers who don't like me and treat me like shit? I'd rather risk the fae than being bound to them!" I begged Lothaire and let the desperation show in my eyes.

Lothaire sighed heavily and dragged his hands across his face like he was tired. "I'd hoped you would meet on better terms and would become acquainted."

"Malum's fucking nuts. He lit me on fire!" I yanked at the shackles desperately.

"Language!" Lothaire snapped.

None of the kings spoke.

Suddenly, Lothaire was sparking with power, and he turned to the men.

"*Nothing* changes from the plan. You took a vow to protect her with your lives, and you will fulfill it or I will rip out your spines and feed them to you."

I shuddered.

Not because I was horrified by the imagery but because I'd imagined doing something similar to Lothaire time and time again.

I definitely got my rage from him.

I was going to be sick.

"Yes, sir!" the kings chorused as they bowed their heads and fell to their knees.

Before I could point out that everyone had lost their ever-loving minds, a small man walked into the room. He was shorter and thinner than Jinx.

Every inch of his skin was covered in tattoos, but every piece was different.

They weren't artistic like Ascher's tattoos. There was nothing pretty about this man.

Images of black holes, dying animals, and swear words covered his skinny frame in thick black ink.

It was impossible to tell what his skin color was. He walked closer and grabbed a tattoo gun.

"Holy fuck," I gasped.

Even the whites of his eyes were tattooed.

Lothaire snapped, "Language!"

I flipped him off even though my fingers were in my cuffs.

The artist held the tattoo gun out and asked in a feminine voice, "Where do you want the tattoo?"

Was it a woman with a pixie cut? In their androgynous clothing, it was impossible to tell.

"Nowhere." I struggled harder, bucking against my cuffs as I prayed to the sun god to save me.

"Not an option," Lothaire snapped back immediately.

"Fine, give me an eye tattoo like yours," I ordered the artist.

It was horrifying to look at and frankly disgusting.

I wanted one.

"No!" Malum shouted, and the men nodded in agreement.

I glared at the fucker who tormented me and now was going to be tied to me for life.

"Fine." I nodded. "Both eyes."

"She will have it on her hip like the rest of us." Malum's gray eyes were cold as ice, and the edge in his voice told me everything I needed to know.

"*I refuse! He's a sexist pig!*" I yanked desperately as I bucked with all my might.

"Get control of yourself," Lothaire ordered as he

pointed his finger at the artist. "Put it on her hip or you will be punished."

There was a long moment where the small person stared up at the vampyre like they were going to defy him. But they slowly nodded and pulled down the corner of my now-very-loose sweatpants.

When the gun touched my skin, I expected the prick of a needle.

Instead, the world collapsed.

Electric-blue sparks pulsed through me, and an other-worldly scream ripped from my throat as I tilted my head back and bellowed.

It was the worst pain I'd ever experienced. Nothing could compare.

Pressure filled my lungs as power strummed through me like I'd been struck by lightning.

I barely noticed the three men falling to their knees and clutching their heads as they screamed.

Sparks leaped among us.

We were the lightning.

And it was agony.

It could have been hours or minutes. Seconds or a life-time. But when the tattoo gun dropped away from my flesh, the world was vibrant with shades of colors I'd never seen before.

My limbs vibrated with power.

In slow motion, I looked down at my trembling hip.

A silver snake in an infinity symbol, eating its own tail… wrapped in four gold chains.

It was a master-slave tattoo.

And I was the slave.

I looked up at the man who claimed to have sired me

and let him see the full weight of disgust in my voice. "I will never forgive you."

Lothaire looked old and tired. The lines around his eyes and mouth were deep as he stared back at me. "I know."

Blue sparks still leaped off my skin to the three men kneeling on the floor.

And I asked the final question that no amount of reasoning could make any sense of. "How can binding me to three fae save me?"

It wasn't Lothaire who answered.

"You think we're pathetic fae?" Scorpius said with outrage like I'd accused him of being a human.

Orion shook his head, and Malum glowered at me like he was imagining all the ways he could murder me.

"You have fae ears." I bristled at the implication that I was dumb.

"No," Orion mouthed, and energy cracked around them.

Suddenly, the gold metal that decorated their ears glowed bright and drifted upward through the air.

They had rounded ears.

Then the metal split into a dozen pointed shards that glittered and circled atop their heads.

"We have crowns," Malum growled. "Because we're the three kings."

All three men rose to their full height and loomed over me.

Scorpius said, "The three Devil Kings of the ancient House of Malum."

"Devils," I mouthed.

Sadie's story about angels and devils serving the sun god with unfathomable power washed over me.

Malum's voice was a deep growl. "You should be very

afraid right now, because the House of Malum's crest is a dragon for a reason."

Holy.

Sun god.

Lyla's prophecy, "*You will not be who you need to be until you embrace the dragon,*" wasn't referencing Demetre like I'd assumed.

It had been the three kings all along.

Three devils.

"And now…" Malum smiled with his crown floating above his head. "You're our slave."

EPILOGUE

Lothaire

Twenty-five years ago

"No," I snapped, then counted to ten and breathed deeply.

Throughout the centuries, I'd discovered counting was the only thing that worked to calm my anger.

Otherwise, it overwhelmed. Controlled. Consumed.

"You promised fidelity to the High Court, or was that a ruse?" Dick asked with his insufferable calmness as he sat behind his ostentatious glass desk.

"Obviously not. I'd think six centuries of running an academy of brats and training *your* assassins is proof of that." I rubbed my hands over my tired eyes to stop myself from lunging across the space and strangling the life out of him.

How dare he question my loyalty after everything I've sacrificed?

Dick grunted dismissively. "You weed them out and prep them. At the High Court, *we* actually train them."

The angel had his nose perpetually stuck in the air. He

thought he was so much better than everyone else because he served the sun god directly.

I debated the consequences of ripping out his throat with my teeth.

Silence stretched.

I didn't bother to respond to the pompous git. I'd served for centuries, proven myself time and time again, but it was never enough for them.

My past failures always loomed larger than my accomplishments.

Yet again, war was coming.

Yet again, the High Court didn't need soldiers; it needed sacrifices. Pawns. Spies.

Yet again, I was expected to oblate myself to the cause.

It was exhausting.

Dick sighed heavily, like *he* was the one being asked yet again to do the unthinkable. "You're not the only one who has to sacrifice themself for this war."

"What the fuck does that mean?" I spat with annoyance. "Are you being asked to go into the vicious fae realm and become consort to a psychotic bitch? A bitch that is known widely as the mad queen?"

I snorted as I thought about it. "Really spreading peace throughout the realms. Good job appointing her. You both have the same temperament."

Dick slammed his fist down on his glass desk, and it cracked.

His pale skin flushed mottled red like it always did when he got angry. "Oh yes, the fae realm, which has been more known for starting wars and genocides, is in such worse hands now that it's aligned with the High Court and has been at peace for the first time in centuries. Please tell me more about how I failed when a massive war is coming and for the first time, the fae realm is on *our* side."

I laughed at his hubris. "You think you can control the mad fae queen? Just because she's joined some peace treaties doesn't mean she'll side with you in war. You're a fool."

Dick leaned back in his chair with a smirk.

I didn't like it, and my suspicion flared. "What have you done?"

"What is necessary for peace."

"Drop the fucking cryptic bullshit and spell it out, or are you just too cowardly to admit you've fucked up?"

The red flush trailed brighter down Dick's neck. "The mad queen will not be on the throne when war comes. That is where your mission comes in."

"I don't understand." I dug my fangs into my gums and welcomed the sharp jab of pain. Everything about the High Court was a mindfuck. "How does me being her consort put someone else on the throne?"

Dick reached under his desk and pulled out a glowing tube, and he swirled the sparkly liquid back and forth slowly.

"This is a fertility potion for the mad queen."

The urge to flip the desk and skewer Dick with a table leg was uncontrollable. "You fucking bastard."

Dick nodded calmly, like he wasn't asking something so heinous it was mind-blowing.

"She was given options and only agreed to accept *you* as her paramour. She will take the steps to ensure procreation. All she knows is that she must bear a child."

His eyes sharpened as he settled the full weight of his stare on me.

The implications of what he wasn't saying hit me: Dick was willing to sacrifice the woman he knew for a better wartime leader.

In the process, he was willing to have me raped.

Horror grew. "So you've gotten tired of using people, and now you're in the business of creating them." I swallowed bile. "The perfect pawn."

He didn't even blink. "The moon goddess is creating champions for the war. The sun god is not willing to leave peace in her hands. He needs monarchs on his side."

"So you're playing surrogate for gods? How noble."

"I'm playing at survival." Dick's face grew colder, and his countenance stiffened like it always did when he was extremely enraged.

He was a block of unfeeling ice. "You'll breed the queen, and then you'll have no contact with the offspring. They must experience the full brunt of her mothering."

I slammed my hand on my thighs. "I will not leave my powerless child at the mercy of that bitch, and I will not have my offspring be a conceited, vapid fae."

Dick swirled the fertility potion and stared through it like it had all the answers. "This will ensure your child has their mother's powers. We both know how impressive they are."

"They're still just a child. I will not do this."

Dick continued like I hadn't spoken, "It's not a linear plan. The child will be taken from the fae realm when they are sixteen and taught how to survive away from their mother."

"I don't give a fuck what you think you're going to—"

Dick cut me off. "They will be brought back to her when they've grown up and made ties to others. When they're strong enough to see how unfit she is to rule."

I shook my head.

"You'll be the catalyst that pushes them over the edge. You'll threaten those ties. And when the time comes, with the right prodding, your child will destroy the mad queen and ascend to the throne."

I slammed my fist into my temple in frustration. "You can't fucking know that's how it will play out! There are millions of factors you're not accounting for. How do you even know the child will have the capacity to commit such an atrocity?"

Dick smirked. "Because they will be yours."

I lunged across the table and wrapped my hands around his thick fucking throat.

He arched his brow at me condescendingly like I wasn't seconds from snapping his neck and said, "But mostly because they will be hers. The queen's sense of justice has warped to madness over the years, but any child of hers will know the sun god's righteousness. They'll be pure."

I tightened my hands because his words didn't make any sense. Fae never had a sense of justice. They were as removed from the sun god's goodness as vampyres.

Dick should have cowered as I choked him, but he was the only person who refused to be afraid of me.

He was an imbecile.

Said idiot stared unblinking into my eyes. "The child will do what must be done for peace just as I do. They'll see the correct paths forward even if they don't want to. They'll do what must be done because they are *his* soldier."

"No child of mine will be a pawn," I growled into his face and let him see the promise of my fury. My wrath.

"No." Dick shook his head. "They won't be."

"But you just said—"

"After they ascend, your child can lead the fae realm however they see fit. As long as they side with the High Court in the war, we will ask nothing else of them. That is all the sun god wants."

I removed my fingers from his neck and took a step back.

Let his words wash over me.

"The fae ascension is brutal. Who's to say they won't be slaughtered immediately for the throne?"

Dick sat unnaturally still. "They will have their mother's power and the sun god's favor."

"We both know that's not enough," I spat with disgust.

"Then you will think of something. You have years to come up with a solution." Dick shuffled papers on his desk like ruining my life was boring him.

"No." I shook my head and dug my fangs harder into my gums. "I refuse to let you torture my child like you've tortured me."

Dick looked up, and his eyes were empty and cold like they always were.

I hated angels. They pretended to be more righteous than everyone else, but they did the most fucked-up shit in the name of peace.

The Angel Federation claimed the sun god had granted them all insane analytical abilities so they could serve his will.

They played the long game masterfully.

They used people.

Ruined them.

Then smiled at corpses and said it was for the greater good.

If I hadn't seen the atrocities that Dick's scheming had prevented, I would have believed he was the villain. There were still much worse monsters out there.

He was an embodiment of the motto the High Court ingrained into their advanced assassins: *You need to be dark to stop the darkness.*

They weren't wrong.

A flush spread across Dick's neck as he said quietly, "This is not up for debate. Or have you forgotten the city you slaughtered? That the sun god has seen your black soul and marked you for an eternity of suffering?"

My fingernails dug into my palms.

Memories of wading through a river of blood pounded against my temple. Hammered into my consciousness.

The rage overwhelmed me.

The bloodlust guided me.

I let my powers free.

Bodies everywhere.

Hundreds of thousands of bodies.

I couldn't walk by a fireplace without hearing their screams as they died by fangs. The shame was my constant companion.

Ten. Nine. Eight.

I breathed slowly and counted on the numbers instead of the memories.

"You agreed to a lifetime of service to save your soul." Dick slammed the hammer into the nail. "Dead men don't have choices."

I swallowed harshly and spoke my biggest fear, "What if my child has my rage?"

The unspoken question hung thick between us: *What if they're a monster just like me?*

Dick's lips tightened into a line. "Their mother's heritage will counter your disposition."

"And if it doesn't?" I snapped, tired of the constant games and the promises the High Court couldn't keep. "She's called the *mad* queen for a reason."

"Then after they ascend, you can teach your child how to control the rage. You can give them what you never had."

He spoke calmly like everything made perfect sense and wasn't a convoluted mess.

Sun god, I loathed him.

My knuckles cracked as I fisted my hands. "If I do this, my child will never be enrolled in Elite Academy. They will never be forced to be your pawn like I have."

Dick didn't so much as blink at my demands.

I kept going. "They will *never* train to be an assassin at the High Court. They'll be their own person and can make their own choices."

My words rang in the space between us.

Silence expanded as I waited.

Dick nodded slowly. "After they ascend to the throne and agree to side with the High Court during the war, we will remove all influence over your child." The corner of his mouth lifted in the smallest smile.

My rage returned.

I didn't like the look in Dick's eyes; it was like the angel knew something I didn't.

"Promise me on your angel wings," I demanded.

Dick stared at me for a long moment, then his crystal wings glowed like they were lit from within.

His voice was strong and powerful as he said, "I promise that the High Court will not personally interfere with your child after they ascend the throne. *We* will not be the ones that force them to attend Elite Academy. *We* will not force them to serve."

I swallowed thickly. Something about the way he emphasized "we" made my hair stand up. Like I was missing something.

Dick shuffled his papers. "Is that acceptable to you? Or are you going to keep throwing a tantrum?"

My fangs dug deeper into my gums. "Fuck you."

"Yes, yes. You're forced to impregnate the gorgeous fae queen and have an extremely powerful offspring who will ascend to the throne, poor you." Dick rolled his eyes as he wrote on a piece of paper.

His eyes would look nice with the writing instrument sticking out of them.

"Sign here."

I stared down at the dotted line and the words above it, which read, *Lothaire Vord agrees to this mission.*

"I don't agree."

"Sign the paper."

There was no choice to be made, and we both knew it.

My hand cramped as I signed, and the angel across from me let out a long exhale like he'd been holding his breath.

"Your service is not unnoticed, Lothaire," Dick said quietly. "And you're not as alone as you think."

I rolled my eyes at his infinite hubris. "Please, what have you ever had to sacrifice?"

"While you're in the fae realm, I'll be in the shifter realm." His voice was low, but there was an edge to it I hadn't heard. "The tides of war demand new leaders, and the moon goddess is going to create a champion."

"It's not your offspring that will be sacrificed." I shook with the urge to kill the fucker.

"No," Dick said softly. "But it will be my job to prepare a child."

I scoffed. "I'm sure you'll win them over with your cheery disposition and emphatic nature. Father of the year for sure."

Dick's pen creaked in his hand. "I will do what I must for the peace of the realms. Whatever is required. I will do."

"Oh, everyone knows that," I snarled. "Pretty soon you won't be able to differentiate between the evil you fight and your own actions. You won't be able to stomach the sight of yourself in the mirror."

I spoke from experience.

Dick didn't blink when he said, "I already can't."

His self-righteousness knew no bounds.

I would have respected him more if he reveled in the fucked-up shit he did instead of acting like he hated it while doing it repeatedly for centuries.

There was nothing to say to him.

I left.

A few weeks later, I RJE'd to the sun-kissed lands of the Fae realm. Prostrated myself before the mad queen's glittering throne—the seat of death—and promised myself to her.

Seduced her with my power. My body. Impregnated her.

The consequences came swiftly; per the High Court's request, my daughter wouldn't know her father.

The mission was a success, but for some reason, it felt like a failure of the worst kind.

A calamity.

Like in all great tragedies, I persisted and bore the pain.

I left to serve at Elite Academy for most of the year, and when I had any time off, I stalked the palace halls and watched Arabella Elis Egan from afar.

My precious daughter.

A mischievous little child who was too smart for her own good. She had a wildness in her turquoise eyes that I recognized in my own—unrestrained anger.

She was perfect.

Time and time again, I stopped myself from going to her. Holding her. Playing with her. Introducing myself as her father. Apologizing for the High Court, the plot, and her role even though she was too young to understand anything.

But every time, I stopped myself because I'd signed on the dotted line. The mission demanded I let her mother raise her, and not interfere.

At least she was unharmed.

Until that fateful day when earth fae made the ground shake beneath the castle and tried to seize the throne.

I RJE'd from Elite Academy to find half the castle on fire and the other half littered with dead fae bodies.

Sprinting down halls, I nearly collapsed with relief when I found my three-year-old daughter cowering on the ground, hiding behind palace guards.

She turned her head, and her little cherub face was covered in blood and tears.

Arabella was harmed.

Someone had gouged out her eye.

Unholy rage blinded me, and I slaughtered every fae who stood between me and my daughter. All the palace guards and all the intruders.

Every.

Last.

One.

I knelt in front of her with blood-soaked arms, but the little princess didn't cower and scream at the strange monster before her.

Arabella threw her little arms around my neck.

I hugged her tight.

Drawing back, I stared into her missing cavity with sadness because she couldn't grow back her eye from nothing.

Her little fingers tightened around my long braid. Tiny nails digging into the unrestrained curls that I always plaited to keep off my face.

She smiled at me sweetly, and I knew at that moment that I wouldn't allow this.

Her body could regenerate her turquoise gaze if she had a mold to work with.

I dug my fingers around my eye and didn't allow myself to think.

Instead, I pulled.

Wrenched out my eye.

Skull screaming in pain and my vision reduced, I gently pushed my too-large eye into the bleeding cavity of her face and RJE'd to the High Court's healers.

Hours later, after hundreds of enchantments, Arabella's eye looked good as new.

Relief overwhelmed me.

Since his life's purpose was to ruin my peace, Dick stormed into the room and slammed me against the wall with one of his glowing daggers.

"Fae saw the princess lose her eye. People will wonder why she now has one and the prince consort doesn't. They'll put it together."

"I'll come up with an excuse." I was too relieved from Arabella's recovery to care about Dick's perpetual aneurysms.

"Yes, you will."

Suddenly, a crystal blade slashed across my still throbbing face.

Pain exploded.

I didn't flinch.

Refused to look away from the angel who was obsessed with ruining me.

He was strong, but I would always be stronger. Scarier. More fearsome. More respected.

I smirked at him.

Pain didn't affect me.

Dick's cheeks flushed brighter at my defiance. "The healers will give her a memory enchantment to make sure she has no recollection of these events. The High Court has slaughtered every last person in the palace. No one will remember."

"How noble of you." My upper lips pulled back as I scoffed at him. "If everyone's dead, then why would you need to scar my face?"

There was a long pause.

"Insurance, just in case we missed someone. Your excuse is that you lost your eye fighting a monster, and that's how you got the scar."

I let the blood drip off my face, onto him, and said, "It's the truth, after all. A monster did give it to me."

He didn't have the decency to disagree.

Ripping myself from his grasp, I RJE'd my daughter away from the High Court and returned her whole.

But I was broken.

As she got older, Arabella's pale skin glowed with health, and her long teal hair was the envy of the elite fae. Two gorgeous blue eyes completed the picture.

I taught at Elite Academy.

My fae daughter lived a good life.

And time marched on.

But when she was sixteen, I learned she'd run away from the fae realm, and I started to worry.

I knew Dick had said he would take her from the realm, but why would she go? She was a princess. Happy. Gorgeous. Loved.

Without Arabella, visiting the fae palace was like going to a prison.

There was no one to distract me from the mad queen. I

visited her bed. Dealt with her constant mood swings. Listened to her rantings and vile thoughts. Her long nails caressed me as she whispered sonnets about my dangerous looks.

I'd always preferred men.

But it was my penance, and I served it just like I always had.

When I was informed Arabella had finally returned, I didn't need an excuse to visit, because the mad queen demanded my presence.

She told me of a plan to test the powers of the competitors and said she got the idea from a distant relative.

The queen didn't know that I knew she was in the High Court's pocket and there was only one person who had any sort of power over her.

It was Dick's plan.

So I walked onto the gladiator sands, ready to play my part.

Until I saw her.

My daughter was covered in bruises.

Horrible black-and-blue welts mottled her fair skin, and from the way the mad queen smirked next to her, she'd done it.

All rational thoughts fled my mind.

I kept my mask in place and gave the grand speeches about testing for power that the queen had had me rehearse beforehand.

But I was far, far away.

No amount of counting, of calm breathing, could stop the overwhelming rage that shook my vision, and I was barely conscious of the shifters dying in my hands.

Barely aware that Dick was standing like a smug fucking bastard next to the queen.

The show would go on, but I wouldn't be following Dick's script anymore. Once the competitors were dead I'd slaughter her mother.

My soul didn't matter.

An eternity of suffering didn't matter.

What was a monster good for if he couldn't protect his daughter from harm? Nothing.

I would avenge this wrong.

At least, that was the plan.

I never got the chance to execute it because the useless shifter girl I'd been killing turned out to be much more than I'd realized. But she wasn't the one who brought me to my knees.

It was my daughter: Arabella.

She ripped out her mother's heart, ate it, and ascended to the fae throne.

Once again—she was perfect.

Dick smiled with victory as a million fae fell to their knees.

Pride swelled in my chest. Arabella didn't need anyone to save her, because she had her father's rage.

It was beautiful.

Then the stadium erupted in chaos as everyone realized the implications of what had just occurred. I ran down the gladiator halls, searching for her, but Dick blocked the way and RJE'd us away.

If it were any less powerful of a man, I'd have succeeded in killing him, but Dick was a fucking angel, and he evaded my vengeance.

And my daughter went missing.

My rage intensified as I continued to search for my child.

Now that Arabella had ascended, she was wanted, but she had yet to come into her full powers.

She was painfully vulnerable.

It tormented my every waking thought.

But I hadn't taught the most powerful in all the realms at Elite Academy for centuries because I was weak. I hadn't survived the sun god's wrath because I gave up.

After years of research, I finally found ancient texts on tying life forces together so both parties were stronger.

It was an extremely powerful enchantment, and I was surprised I hadn't heard about it before. The ability to prolong lives would have been highly sought after.

I reckoned it was hidden for that reason.

Otherwise, everyone would do it.

The other problem was the books never said how to actually create the bond.

I brought it up to Dick. The fucker was one of the only people with access to the High Court's historical archives, and he gave me the name of a tattoo artist who could perform it.

It would counter the fae ascension, and my daughter would not die unless all the men tied to her were slaughtered.

That was what I was promised.

I asked about side effects, and Dick said, "The archives speak of nothing else."

My hair stood on end, and I didn't like the gleam in his eyes, but I never found anything else as promising in my research.

It was my best bet to save my daughter.

A plan took shape.

Three of my students, the Devil Kings, were extremely

powerful, but they couldn't master their powerful abilities and serve unless they found their fourth mate.

So we made a deal.

In exchange for allowing them to train at the academy while I used my vast spy network to search for their missing mate, they agreed to protect my daughter.

After all, if their life forces were tied together, they'd all be stronger for it.

My daughter would be safe.

The Devil Kings would be whole.

Everyone won.

After they were bonded, they'd all separate and go back to living their own lives with more protection than before. I'd never let them near her. I wasn't about to allow my precious daughter to be in the presence of the Devil Kings.

The men I trained at the academy were hardened ones who had no business being around innocent girls like my daughter.

I just needed a way to find Arabella so I could complete the plan.

Opportunity presented itself when the half warriors confided in me that they were the reason my daughter was brutalized by the mad queen.

And Dick said I had no self-control?

I didn't kill them.

The angel wasn't the only one who could play the long game. No. The half warriors would help me find my daughter, and *then* they would die.

No one harmed her and lived.

So I taught the recruits at Elite Academy like I always did. Trained them for the war that was looming closer and closer every day.

The rage and fear for my daughter consumed my every thought, and I was even more brutal than usual. Crueler.

But only the strong survived, so I made them strong.

Training with me was nothing compared to what the High Court would force them to do once they became anointed assassins.

My ruthlessness was my mercy.

Living within the haze that was fear for my child, I missed the signs.

Didn't put it together when the little girl with darkness in her eyes told me she was Aran's guardian and that they were tied. I didn't see Aran's familiar coloring and put together the obvious.

Until the enchantment fell away.

Aran was Arabella.

My little girl.

The smiling child I'd given an eye to so she could see.

In that moment, something good I hadn't known was left inside me cracked and broke. The waves of shame became a tidal wave of despair.

And I understood.

The oath Dick had given twenty-five years ago put my teeth on edge because he'd emphasized "we."

As in it would still happen, just by someone else's hands.

Dick had known that my child would attend Elite Academy, but it wasn't because of the High Court.

It was all because of me.

I would kidnap her. *I* would torment her. *I* would enslave her to the cause. *I* would make her into everything I hated about myself.

It should have been obvious when Dick said the sun god wanted someone else on the throne. When he'd said the moon goddess was creating a champion.

The entire affair reeked of the sun god's manipulation; he also wanted a champion, and he'd ensured I'd trained her.

Yet again, I was nothing but a pawn.

Yet again, I was the villain.

My sacrifices were not enough.

They took my child.

And so it began.
"I will take my father's place in battle."
—*The Ballad of Mulan*

To be continued….

About the Author

Jasmine Mas loves writing about Alphaholes and kick ass girls that bring them to their knees.

She attended Georgetown University and the University of Miami School of Law. She is a lawyer who loves hanging out with her readers, drinking matcha lattes, and trying to convince her husband that ancient aliens exist.

Sign up for updates and bonus content on the Cruel Shifterverse straight to your inbox at

blog.jasminemasbooks.com

Hang out with her on Social Media
TikTok: @jasminemasbooks
Facebook: @JasmineMasBooks
Instagram: @jasminemasbooks

THANK YOU

Special thank you to all my beta and ARC readers! Also, thank you to Lyss Em, you are an amazing editor.

Also, thank you SO MUCH to everyone who decided to give the Cruel Shifterverse series a chance. ❤

Finally, thank you to my mother, who prefers happy cowboy romance books, but has spent hours doing the final proofread of each book with me. I love you even though you still don't understand how to use Word.

Made in United States
Troutdale, OR
07/11/2024

21163637R00311